# THE HERETIC PRINCE

# THE HERETIC PRINCE

THEO J MALLOY

Farisia Publishing

# Contents


*Dedication*       viii
*Map*       ix

PROLOGUE

1   Mychal       4

2   Samira       15

3   Edris       24

4   Mychal       35

5   Edris       46

6   Samira       60

7   Mychal       72

8   Edris       86

9   Samira       97

10   Mychal       106

11   Edris       114

12   Samira       125

13   Mychal       137

14 Samira … 150

15 Mychal … 165

16 Mychal … 179

17 Samira … 193

18 Edris … 204

19 Samira … 217

20 Edris … 232

21 Samira … 244

22 Mychal … 260

23 Edris … 273

24 Samira … 289

25 Mychal … 307

26 Mychal … 319


EPILOGUE

APPENDIX I. ROYAL HOUSEHOLDS OF THE CONTINENT, 500 AL

APPENDIX II. HOLY BOOK OF THE DUALITY

APPENDIX III.


*Acknowledgments* … 349

*Sneak Preview: The Renegade King, Book 2 of The Heretic Prince Series* … 351

About the Author                                                                371

*For Oliver,
queer and trans kids everywhere,
and Kelly*

# Map

Disputed
Astoria
Bay
Norport
Knife of
the North
New
Astoria
Norport
Falls
Carroll's
Pass
EIROSIA
THORNCLIFFE
The Holy
Mountains
Provinceham
Caspar's
Dale
Illon's
Fast
Fen
Durre
Eastport
Greenfield
THE HORN
OF MORRA
Watershed
Ford
Astora
Post
The
Mages'
Canyon
Cor
Altol
THE
LORDLESS
ISLES
Hollisport
Fen
Faris
Red
Ford
South
Pool
The Golden
Forests
Queenshearth
Haven
—Mychal
Halwood
Brookbridge
THE
HARTLANDS
Fen Eiros
N
W    E
S
Surpoint
The
Great
Forges
50mi

# Prologue

Another assault shook the foundations of the caverns, and Loran was no closer to breaking through the rocks than before. He had never had this much trouble with earth-moving, ever, and it occurred to him that there could be mages aboveground sending inhibition curses down below. Traitors. He took his hands off the boulders for the first time in what felt like hours, though it was probably more like minutes, and retreated to where the others were shielding themselves from falling debris.

"Any word?" he asked his steward, Willard, as he wiped the sweat from his brow.

"I wish there wasn't, sir," he said. "Lord Wright just sent a messenger through the tunnel." Glancing back at the worried faces of the families nearby, Willard led him out of their earshot into the mouth of the tunnel, where the few highborns left in their party were sheltering. "The queen and Prince Mychal were executed this morning. A rider from Queenshearth arrived just before the Army."

Loran felt a knot in his gut that had been building for hours twist his stomach and he took a deep, shaking breath to keep from getting sick. "He's going to open the gates." He felt the hope that had been cautiously growing these past weeks, knowing a third of the Triad was still free, evaporate in seconds.

"Lord Wright's sister is dead," one of the men in the tunnel said—another mage, a merchant named Kir. "He knows it's hopeless now.

The King is only a king by name if they can slaughter his family with impunity. And we're next."

Darya, a woman from his mother's court, stood up and in a somber, subdued voice said, "Then sailing is our only option. We should go before they think to close off the harbor." And silently, Loran heard her private message to him, floating in amongst his own thoughts: "*You need to survive this, Loran. Let it go.*"

"The lady is right," Kir said. "We have to go. It won't be long before someone searches the tunnels."

Loran's frustration started to rise again and in a flat, threatening voice, he said, "I'm not leaving without getting through that wall."

"You're going to have to," Kir replied, matching his aggression and making the others stir nervously. "Your pride may very well ruin us. Your power wasn't enough. The sword will remain where it was forged."

"It belongs to my *people*," Loran exclaimed. "Not the Priesthood."

"These people here are *your people* too!" he said, almost spitting the last words. "I lived through hunts like this before you could walk. If we don't leave now they'll go to the mountains— or worse. We need to move."

His face burning, Loran looked to the ground and nodded once. Without another word, the mage left the tunnel and began ushering the families through the passage on the other side of the cavern, out to the shores of the bay and the ocean beyond.

"Sir?" Willard said.

"I'm coming, Willard, go on ahead," Loran said, staring at the blockage of rocks obstructing the cavern he so desperately needed to reach. Darya approached him and placed a hand upon his shoulder.

"The sword is lost to written knowledge. The Priests won't look for it."

"You don't know that," he said quietly. He had been so close, that was the worst of it. The last hope of the Triad— but maybe that had been the queen.

"Loran," Darya said, finally breaking his reverie. "Let's go." With a final glance behind him, he turned and followed her through the last open passage out of the Forge.

# I

# Mychal

Mychal had been told not to speak unless spoken to during his training days, but he wouldn't have dared in front of the Holy Officers anyway. Those men, armed with Surpoint steel and supposed divine will, were such larger-than-life figures to him that there was never any question he would only do his duty and listen intently to their war councils. It made no matter that he hated them and wanted to watch them all die horrible deaths. Their damned sun god couldn't help them if they were being burned alive, and the goddess never answered to men. But Mychal was skinny and small, and still couldn't swing a grown man's sword at 17. The killing would have to be a job for the Daemons.

The hatred wasn't mutual, fortunately for him. Despite his size and near-complete lack of skill, he'd been made a steward by James Reinhold, a knight of the Horn and captain of the vanguard cavalry, within three months of enlistment. Today, more than a year later, he was serving as cupbearer at the fifth war council meeting in three days, listening to the discussion grow more heated in light of the message received this morning. All of Astor Post was afire with the news: the fight, for the first time, was coming to them.

"We should send for more men," one of the officers, Sir Edward Duane, said as Mychal replenished his wine.

"I don't think that would solve our problem," Sir James replied. "We outnumber them already. It's their fire that's the real cause for concern."

"Mages, then."

"What mages? Most of them are long gone, and the ones who aren't won't fight for us," Sir James argued. "You all saw to that." It was deadly quiet around the table, and Mychal turned to hide his smile. Sir James could take greater liberties than he could, and listening to them helped Mychal stay sane. "We need to leave Astor Post. Assemble further west and gather the full strength of our armies."

Another officer scoffed and asked, "Where exactly would we do that? The Horn doesn't have the land to support 20,000 men. Every inch of it's settled."

"The Hartlands then. We'll go to the Forests," Duane suggested. Mychal furrowed his brow; he hoped no one would take that suggestion seriously, for all of their sakes.

"Reinhold's steward seems to disagree," the man at the head of the table said, and Mychal froze. Jonn Thorne, Lord Marshal of the Holy Army, was watching him now, and he forced himself to gather enough courage to look him in the eyes. "Don't you?"

"...My lord?" Mychal managed to say, still unsure of what he wanted from him.

"Why shouldn't we go to the Golden Forests, lad?" Lord Thorne asked him, and despite his intimidating stature, he sounded genuinely interested.

Mychal almost felt like the answer was so obvious that they must all be playing some kind of joke, but he had no choice, so he said, "I just don't think waiting for fire mages in a forest is a good idea, my lord."

Lord Thorne paused for a moment and then laughed. It didn't sound malicious, and Mychal began to breathe a little more. "I was hoping one of you would make that point. It seems a steward beat you all to it. The boy's right. If the Golden Forests burn, the Triad will never recover, not to mention we'd all be dead as well." He scoffed at his officers and asked, "What's your name, lad?"

"Owyn, sir. Mychal Owyn." The officers went quiet, and his nerves returned. Lord Thorne's face darkened somewhat.

"An unfortunate namesake," he said quietly. "You must come from the Hartlands, then?"

"Yes, my lord. Queenshearth," Mychal said. Understanding the strange quiet, he added quickly, "But the prince was only a baby when I was born. Lots of boys my age in the Hartlands are named Mychal."

Lord Thorne nodded. "Of course. You don't carry the blame for his heresy. May you bring more honor to the name than he did."

"I'll try, my lord," he said quietly, trying to mask his brewing anger. A seven-year-old 'heretic', sentenced to die by men of the gods, and still even an echo of his name hushes a room. He tried to find some trace of guilt in Lord Thorne's eyes, but nothing in his expression changed. He couldn't believe it. Mychal had been there that day, close to ten years ago now. What kind of man can walk away from killing a child and speak of it without flinching?

The council had moved on, and with a kind nod from Sir James, Mychal went back to his serving duties. "Owyn is right," Thorne said. "The Hartlands are no place for us. The terrain isn't suitable for a battle with fire, and I despise the thought of their army marching down through the Horn to meet us there." Sir James nodded assent, and Mychal could tell he was recoiling too at the thought of Daemon raids down the coast of his homeland. "And besides, the kingdom is about to destabilize. We had another rider yesterday. King Eronn's condition has only worsened."

"Mother Morra have mercy," the Hartlander captain muttered, as Mychal tried his best not to show any sign of emotion. "Has the letting not helped at all?"

"The best doctors in the kingdom and no change for the better," Thorne said. "They say the curse is in his blood, and they can't let enough of it without killing him. He grows weaker by the day. He'll be gone before High Summer."

The ringing in Mychal's ears wouldn't stop as Duane added, "And with the princess missing, there's no hope of your cousin marrying into that crown?"

"No, there's another daughter but she's much too young. Edris won't take the Hartlands. They'll have to send for Eronn's son," Thorne said. "He's only eleven this spring. Studying with the Stewards."

"With a regency in place, it should increase our influence there, yes?" Duane asked.

"Possibly," Thorne said, sounding weary. But then his face changed and when he spoke again, he sounded resolved. "We won't run from the Daemons. I'll write to my uncle for more men, but Thorncliffe must defend its borders as well. Besides, if those beasts invade the Triad, the Godhead will bear down on them and the whole continent will be at war. We have half again as many men as Eirosia, let them try to come through the mouth of the Canyon. We'll be waiting for them there. May Morra bless our efforts."

"And Astor sharpen our swords," the officers intoned, and the council adjourned. Mychal turned to leave but before he could, he felt a hand on his shoulder.

"You did well," Sir James told him. "Lord Thorne likes you."

"Thank you, sir," he said, trying to sound respectful despite his intense desire to run.

"I'm sorry you had to hear about your king like that," he said. "He won't suffer much longer."

"Yes, sir," Mychal managed to say.

The knight looked him in the eye, not unkindly, and said, "Alright, you're dismissed. My chambers are ready?"

"Yes, sir."

"I'll see you in the morning for drills, then," Sir James said, and Mychal nodded and left, allowing Sir Edward and two more officers through the door first.

As soon as he was out of sight of the hall, he ran into an alley between the rows of soldiers' tents and sat on the ground, head between his knees, willing his stomach to settle. He'd had no idea the king was even sick. It had been so long since he'd left Queenshearth, the ancient walled city under the shadow of Hartshold Keep. His life now was unrecognizable from what it had been back then, but even so, he couldn't stop his mind from racing.

Before much time had passed, Mychal stood up and forced himself to keep moving. His feelings couldn't be important to him now. Lord Thorne had said they would call the king's son back from Fen Faris. Deronn was just a child, and he'd be nothing more than the Priesthood's puppet. King Eronn had done nothing when they'd taken his wife and son and occupied the Hartlands, and the people scorned him for it, called him the Sleeping King. But a scared child would be even worse. So he kept walking until he reached the first tent for the Fourth Company and pulled back the canvas covering the entrance.

Thankfully, he found what he'd expected to find. Most of the soldiers spent their nights in town if they weren't patrolling, and it was just past supper, so there were only two in the tent: Graham Riley and Luke Payne, the only two in all of the Astor Post encampment that Mychal had begun to trust. Graham got up from the mat they were sitting on together first, and easily helped Luke up; the latter was taller but Graham must have weighed twice what Luke did, and most of it muscle. "Finally! How was the council?" he asked.

"Long," Mychal said. "We're going to make a stand at the Canyon, like we'd thought. Thorne put his foot down about a retreat."

"Good," he said, grinning. "I'd like to cut through some Daemons. It's about time."

"Never mind about that," Luke said. "Are we going out or not?"

"I'm up for Lady May's if you're game," Mychal said, forcing a mischievous smile, and the other boys thankfully matched his enthusiasm.

"We know you're up for it, mate, when aren't you?" Graham laughed. They wove through rows upon rows of soldiers' tents, past the Fourth Company and through the council hall's grounds until they reached the outskirts of the city proper. Only a short walk from there, the familiar old brick house, with lights blazing through the night and music spilling out onto the street, sat perched on the top of the gentle slope of the hill. The foothills of the Holy Mountains set everything in Astor Post off-kilter, and Lady May's was no different: the house leaned into the hillside as if drunk, and despite how many times he'd been inside Mychal was always a little nervous when he ventured upstairs. He figured some mage had to have put an enchantment on the foundation, long ago when that kind of thing was allowed without a Holy decree.

Graham opened the door with gusto, and the muted music they'd heard on the way in was suddenly clear and cheerful, coming from a man playing on a fiddle in the corner of the dance floor. The warm candles glowing in each of the windows and from the bronze oil lamp fixture above them lit the whole party in yellow-orange light and shadow. They weren't the only soldiers there that night. Plenty of sun-and-moon crests could be seen bobbing about the room, among townsmen of all kinds. Girls, too, with lavish dresses, styled like princesses from any part of the world the patrons desired. They were all smiling in the same painted-on manner, and Mychal felt that in a strange way, he knew the feeling.

"Boys!" someone called from a table near the door behind them. Mychal turned and saw Lady May, the oldest woman in the room at close to 50, in a dark red patterned dress that matched the rouge on her cheeks. She was standing up from a table of girls not yet dancing and brought a tray with a flagon and cups with her as she hurried over to them. "We haven't seen you in a right long time!"

"It's been a busy week, milady," Graham said. "What's for drinking?"

"Hollisport wine, the very best in the Triad," she said proudly. "Just got a hogshead of it today, gift from a very wealthy gentleman. Have a little, go on." She set down the tray on a nearby table and poured each of them a generous cup, which they all downed eagerly. "Well, Graham Riley, what's kept you so busy?"

"For me it's been drills," Graham told her between gulps of wine. "They're running the foot soldiers round like never before. We're about to march out, I suppose. Ask Mychal and Luke about that, though, they're the ones by the knights' sides."

Lady May rounded on the two of them, looking much more stern. "Now don't you tell me I'll be losing half my business when the Army leaves town."

"I wish I could, my lady. But I doubt the entire force will leave, we have to keep Astor Post running somehow," Luke said.

"Well," she muttered, "anyway. Anyone fancy a dancing partner?"

Mychal looked around the room and asked, "Is Senna working tonight?"

"Loverboy," Luke snickered, and Lady May chuckled along with him.

"She'll be along. Have another drink, lad, I'll send her over when she's free." He thanked her and paid the silver, trying not to let his face show his discomfort as he did. Luke swept one of the other girls onto the floor as Mychal took his cup over to sit on the windowsill near the fiddle player. Someone had begun to sing along, and as he listened he recognized it, a love song from the Hartlands, one he hadn't heard in years. He drank more to try to stop the hairs on his arms standing on end, but it didn't really help. He was still shaken from the council meeting as it was, but *that* the wine did help with.

"The lady said you asked for me, sir?" He looked up from his cup and saw Senna, tiny and black-haired in a green linen dress that just touched her knees. She was smiling warmly at him, and offered her hand. "Let's go upstairs, Mychal, we both know you can't dance." He kissed her hand before taking it and standing, almost looking tall next to her. She took his arm as they both climbed the narrow staircase at the back of the room.

Senna led him down the dimly lit upstairs hallway, and he nervously glanced out a window at the hills below as she went further into the improbably-balanced second floor. "Mychal," she called softly, and he drew his attention back inside to find her gone. He easily followed her voice, though: he'd been here countless times before.

Senna's room was hardly bigger than a hall-closet, just a bed, a candle, and a washbasin, and when he closed the door behind him, he had essentially no choice but to sit on the bed with her. With the click of the latch, the girl visibly relaxed and asked, "So what have you heard this week?"

"There are Daemons moving out toward the Mages' Canyon," he told her. As he talked, she fished parchment and ink from under her bed and quickly began taking notes. Mychal wasn't entirely sure who exactly Senna worked for, but it felt good to give the officers' secrets to them. The small revenge for the Priesthood's cruelty back home was, sometimes at least, almost enough. "The Army is going to try to stop their passage with as many men as it takes." He relayed the smaller notes of the less eventful councils that week, and then took a breath before adding, "And today they told us that the king is dying."

Senna was visibly startled. "Daniel Hollis is *dying?*"

"Oh, sorry, no," Mychal said, feeling a little stupid. They were in the Horn, and he should have known King Daniel would be the king that came to mind. "Eronn, Eronn Halwood. They say it's a blood curse."

"They would," she said, rolling her eyes. "Bloody fanatics. It's probably a cancer. It can happen in blood." She saw Mychal's face then and frowned. "Sorry. That's awful. And his son's what, twelve?"

"Eleven," he said quietly. "He's got an older sister—or two, I suppose..."

"Yeah, but really just Jullia. Lyha's been gone for more than a year now," Senna said.

"Right," Mychal said. He hesitated before asking, "Do you think, if she went back, it would make any difference? If they could find her?"

Senna shook her head. "No, they'd just send her to Thorncliffe, she was supposed to marry that awful prince ages ago, remember? Never mind that if there's a son, he'll always get the crown first. And honestly, I'm sorry, I know she's your princess, but if Lyha's not dead by now she's probably somewhere the likes of this place. Or worse."

"Yeah," Mychal said, casting his eyes down. "Well, do you have people in Queenshearth? Who could help the prince, I mean?"

"Thinking about going home?" she asked, smiling. "You're from the crownlands, aren't you? You've got the look." She was right, he knew, although he wished it wasn't true. He could blend in more easily here in the Horn if it wasn't; Mychal had the dark thick hair, dark eyes, prominent nose and olive skin of the most stereotypical Hartlander. He looked very much like his family back home, another enduring problem. "You'd be useful if you could get a job in the castle. It's been harder to send people who aren't local there, since the occupation they don't really trust outsiders—well, you know."

"I can't ever go back to Queenshearth," he said quickly, feeling his heartbeat pick up. She frowned, clearly puzzled, but didn't say anything more.

"Okay. Well, no, we don't really have anyone there right now. We had to move more people into Hollisport for the princess's Declaration."

Mychal looked up, surprised. "That's this spring?"

"Yeah. The Godhead himself is coming, to see his future bride. Samira must be *so* honored," Senna said, rolling her eyes. Mychal tried not to lose himself in memory again as she went on. "It's just as well you're staying. You're invaluable here. The people I report to think I've struck gold, meeting you."

"Well... haven't you?" he asked, slipping back into a small smile.

"Oh, yeah, I've been swept off my feet, never met anyone like you," she said, smirking, and kicking off her shoes, she gently pressed him back against the back wall as she climbed over to sit facing him on his lap. "Let me guess, you'll come back and marry me after the war?"

"That's what my friends think," he said. "Luke says I must be in love with you."

"That's funny," Senna laughed. "Well, it's just as well. Otherwise they might ask why you always pick the same girl." She pushed his hair off of his forehead and brought her hand down to the back of his neck. "Just kissing again?"

"Only if you want," he said, shrugging.

She smiled again, but it seemed more real this time. "You're sweet, Mychal." She brought her lips down to his, and he drew her close to him. He would never go any further than this, though; as if to remind him why, the binding holding down his chest constricted his air as he moved, making him wince. Senna was a good friend, but he had no idea how she'd react if she knew that he and the missing princess were one and the same.

His thoughts drifted away from Lady May's. In his mind, he was far west of there, with Samira Hollis alone in her keep, and south, where his father lay dying with poisoned blood in his veins.

# 2

# Samira

The King's Cathedral stood high above the streets of Hollisport, overlooking the water from its 150-foot spire, but great heights had never had much of an effect on Samira. The Skytower was at least 100 feet taller than any other building in the city, in the entire Triad actually, and she had lived there her whole life, except for three years in the Academy at Fen Faris. But even though the height didn't faze her, she still felt uneasy as she passed through the large double doors. The doors inside remained closed as she entered the antechamber, and when the outer ones slammed shut behind her she jumped. She and her parents slipped off their shoes, a matter of course in holy places like this.

They were alone in the chamber with Andrian, the High Priest of Hollisport, who looked especially auspicious today, the usual sky blue robes adorned with golden stoles and a belt and empty scabbard. All the Priests did that when they weren't preaching. She asked why once and they told her they carried their faith as an invisible weapon. She couldn't see why anyone would wear something so cumbersome for such a stupid reason, but she'd kept her mouth shut then.

"Brother," Samira's father said, clasping hands with Andrian and smiling. "Thank you for inviting us." She tried not to roll her eyes. Priests and kings were all 'brother' to each other, it was the law now. Apparently it was because they were equal in the eyes of the gods. Samira saw it for what it really was– just another way to take away her family's power.

"Of course, brother," he said. "Your daughter is a woman today. She should have the opportunity to thank the gods." Only then did the priest finally meet her eyes. "Welcome, Princess. Are you ready?"

Samira gathered herself and nodded. "I'm ready, Your Holiness." The words fell from her lips and left an unpleasant taste in her mouth, but Andrian accepted it easily. She felt his eyes lingering on her for a little too long after she spoke, and held his gaze with as much confidence as she could. She didn't know  if he was measuring her up as a threat, or just a creep, but either way she didn't want him to think she was intimidated. After a moment, he turned around and opened the doors in front of them.

"We love you," Samira's mother whispered behind her. "We'll see you after the ceremony." She clasped her hand and squeezed it, and Samira felt the weight of something slip into her palm as the queen backed away. With Andrian's back turned, she managed to sneak a glance at the whiteflower petal before she slipped it into her gown. She smiled. Risky, bringing a symbol from her mother's house into the Cathedral. Exactly what she needed today.

When she passed through the double doors, hundreds of nobles and common guests alike fell silent and stood in the tiered circles of stone seats above and around her. The musicians in the highest rows started to play a slow instrumental hymn on their lutes and strings, and Samira tried to focus on that instead of all the expectant faces as she followed the High Priest to the center of the hall. Just before she reached the altar, she glanced down and noticed the inscription dedicating the Cathedral by King Haddon, her eight- or nine-times great-grandfather. It occurred to Samira that Haddon was probably the last of her family to actually be as devout as they were all pretending to be. The 300-year-old engraving felt eroded and cold under her bare feet as she passed.

She came to a stop in front of the great altar, a huge construction of circular stone at least ten feet across and carved with intricate spiraling designs of the Duality's sun and moon sigil. Andrian walked around it to the other side and raised his voice to the gallery. As he spoke, Samira saw her mother and father slipping into the front row, next to her younger brother Mason, returned from Fen Faris for the month. "Children of Morra, your anointed Princess Samira Hollis has come forth today on the morning of her sixteenth birthday to pay tribute to the gods."

"We welcome her," the crowd intoned. These kinds of things were routine, but you wouldn't know it from the way Andrian carried himself as he proudly recited his lines. At his signal, one of Samira's handmaidens in the seats brought down the vase of holy water from their keep's temple and handed it to her with hands much less steady than usual. Samira tried to smile at her, even though she understood the fear better than anyone probably thought, but the little girl was already scurrying away.

With a nod from the Priest, she began to pour, walking carefully around the outer edge of the altar. She was short enough that she had to struggle slightly to hold the vase over the top. With every breath, she willed the water to come out of the vase normally, and thankfully, it did.

None of it gathered around her wrists like it did when she couldn't wish it away, and she was, for the moment, safe. There was no telling what they would do if they ever discovered that she was a mage.

As the water spread through the design and flowed towards the center, Andrian read from the holy Book's first chapters.

*"Morra and Astor wandered together, alone, but soon grew lonely and sad at the barren world before them. And so Mother Morra draped the train of her blue gown about the Earth. These trains became the rivers and oceans, which obeyed the rise and set of her Moon. And Astor's Sun grew until it could warm and bring life to all of his wife's creations. So the first life in the world swam in the rivers, and they were called Den Morra, the Children of the Mother."*

Andrian closed the gilded copy of the Book and the servant holding it ran out of the center almost as quickly as her handmaiden had. Water, Samira thought mournfully. Boys got to pour hot glass, and when it was pried out of the altar later they hung the webbed designs in their halls. But it was just as well– she wouldn't have a hall to hang it in anyway. Just her husband's temple.

"Sister," the Priest said, turning to meet her eyes, "may the Mother bless you in the coming weeks as you prepare to meet His Holiness and confirm your anointed betrothal."

"May the Mother and Father make me worthy of the Godhead's hand," she said, stubbornly clutching the whiteflower petal inside the fold of her sleeve as she bowed to him across the altar. He nodded to her, and she was dismissed to sit with her family for the remainder of the regular monthly hour of worship.

Later that night, after they had exchanged dragged-out pleasantries to the Priest and all the notable guests at the service and returned to their keep in the Skytower, Samira listened intently to her father and brother talking about the world beyond Hollisport over supper. "I'm glad you're learning from Anya," the king was saying between mouthfuls of veal. "I studied geography under her when I was with the Stewards."

"Of course, she's an expert," Mason said, all big eyes and enthusiastic, squeaking declarations. The breaking voice was new. He'd been gone so long she'd forgotten he was growing. "All my teachers are brilliant. I'd like to stay another year after the festivals are over."

"Possibly," the king said. "I might have to find you a squiring position soon."

"Oh," Mason said, "right. In the Holy Army?" The tension in the room had come suddenly and unmistakably, and her father coughed.

"I don't see why it would have to be. My personal armies have plenty of knights." Plenty was something of an overstatement and they all knew it, but if Mason thought it he said nothing. "Has any news reached you all before us out here? From Astor Post, perhaps?"

Samira knew he was asking because the Holy men in Hollisport, loyal to the Faith, didn't let on much about the Army's movements. They knew where the Hollises stood, deep down, and giving away the Priesthood's secrets wasn't appealing to them, but he had heard just enough for them all to be concerned about the Daemons coming out of Eirosia. But Mason didn't know much more.

"They don't really trust the Stewards either, Dad," he said quietly. "Sorry. I know they're sending a full guard for Sami's Declaration Day."

The king drew himself up in his seat and said, "I told them that wouldn't be necessary." His words came out strained and unnaturally even, and Samira knew his pride was wounded.

"It might be more for the Godhead than her," Mason said quickly. "Everywhere he goes, holy soldiers follow. He came through Fen Faris last year and you could hardly walk within a mile of him without being stopped and searched."

"Right," their father said. The rest of the family meal was largely quiet, until she stood after finishing her plate and he said, "Sami, wait a moment. Your mother and I have something for you."

"We thought it might be a nice thing to have, once you go to

Thorncliffe," her mother said with a smile that seemed slightly off. She brought out from under the table a thin black handkerchief, with a small, delicate design of a blooming whiteflower in the center. Samira looked at her mother in surprise. "The Dillon white-flower," she confirmed, nodding once at her daughter as she handed over the token. "Eirosia's most beautiful symbol, it grows even in freezing chills. My father King Sander's favor, given to my mother at a tournament before their courtship began." Samira thought that her mother was on the brink of tears already, and hardened herself to be able to get through the rest of the exchange without breaking down too. For very different reasons, she was also about to explode, but that wasn't really something she could say.

"It's beautiful," she said quietly, examining the handkerchief with a gentle touch. It looked frayed, like it would tear at any sudden movement. "Thank you, Mom." Everyone looked grim now, and Samira remembered again the nightmares she'd had as a child when she'd heard the stories about the Daemons sieging the Eirosian King Silas, Sander's son her uncle, and he and his mage husband and their baby son lying dead on the castle grounds in the morning. The moment the humans lost their battle for the eastern part of the con-tinent and Daemons wiped out the vast majority of the royal house and people her mother came from. The Priesthood was very close now to finishing the job. She could almost hear them justifying it with heresy like they'd done every time a new group of refugees was rounded up. It wasn't happening as often as it used to, but that was mostly because there weren't many left to find.

It was easy to forget sometimes, that she was Eirosian. Her mother had the black hair and blue eyes typical of the Dillons, but Samira had her father's famous Hollis fire-red curls, just like Mason, and Farisian dark brown eyes. She never met her Uncle Silas, and had never set foot in Eirosia, a now-dead kingdom that most likely would never see human visitors again. At least, that's what the

Priests said-- and they were the quickest to call her fully Farisian of anyone, of course; an Eirosian Godwife would never be what they wanted.

"Of course," she said. "I just want you to remember where you come from, when you're— when you're married."

*When you're married to the Godhead,* Samira finished internally. It was depressing, seeing her parents helpless. They were the King and Queen of the entire Horn of Morra, and the Priesthood could take their only daughter with no consequences— with their *cooperation,* even.

"Anyway," her father said, standing suddenly, "it's late. Marida?" Her mother nodded and quickly followed him from the room, stopping to kiss both of her children on their foreheads as she went.

A servant held the door until Samira and Mason walked out of the dining hall, and as soon as they were climbing the tall spiral stairs together, her brother said, "Well, you're better at hiding it than my friend Kara. She's training with the mages now in the secret College because she couldn't make it through one day of woodworking without imbuing everything by accident."

"Shh!" she protested, looking around for servants lurking in the shadows, but Mason just rolled his eyes.

"Sami, I'm not stupid, I made sure we were alone," he said. "Come to my room." She followed him up the stairs to the bedrooms of the keep, higher and higher into the sky, until they reached Mason's chambers, still full of wooden swords and old hangings of fairytales from when he'd left two years ago. He rifled through the trunk he'd brought with him until he pulled out a letter that looked like it had been through several different weather conditions at once. The seal with the Halwood sword and fire, however, remained intact.

"You didn't read it?" Samira asked, shocked.

"Of course I read it. Deronn resealed it," Mason said, smirking.

"It was good thinking, though, telling Jullia to send it to us. Some-one would notice a letter from her to you coming here."

"I know," Samira said, getting impatient. "Well? Can she help me?"

"Just... read it for yourself," he said. She sighed and ripped through the seal.


*Dear Samira,*

*I'm sorry to have to tell you this but I don't know anyone who could do magic like that here or in the Horn. There weren't many mages to begin with in the Hartlands and I've never traveled outside of the kingdom. I can't believe you're a mage! I thought it ran in families, but I suppose I was wrong.*

*Lyha might have been able to help you, but I really don't know where she is. I think you're right, she must have run away. She hated the Priesthood and hated the idea of getting married, and she just couldn't have been kidnapped on her Declaration Day, there were too many guards everywhere. I know you thought she might have told someone about your problem before she left, but I don't even think she knew. She burned the letter you gave me with-out reading it. I'm not sure what happened between you two but I don't think she was very happy at the end.*

*I was going to come to your Declaration but my father's very sick. I'm sorry. I hope you can find a way to hide your magic from Him. I'll send word if I find anyone.*
*Jullia*


"Brilliant," she muttered, and after a moment's hesitation, she threw the letter into Mason's freshly stoked hearth. "I'm practically hanged already."

"I think you should talk to Uncle Lyam," Mason suggested. "He used to serve with mages in Dad's army, maybe—"

"They're all gone, Mason. Anyone who anyone knew about is gone," she snapped. It was quiet for a moment before she said, "I'm sorry. I'm just scared."

"I know," he said. "I'd be scared if I were you even if I was normal." After a pause, he said, "Well— not that you're— you know what I mean."

"I know."

"Maybe the Godhead's not that bad," Mason said, though his voice cracked violently on 'maybe' and it didn't inspire much confidence. "I mean, he was a baby when they picked him. This wasn't his idea."

"Maybe," Samira said. "But if they find out I'm a mage, they'll kill me anyway, so it won't matter." Disheartened by the letter, she turned to go, saying, "Goodnight, Mason."

"Wait," he said. "I just wanted to ask— what happened with you and Lyha? Jullia said she burned your last letter to her. I mean... you were friends, right? What happened?"

Samira frowned. *Not now.* "I don't want to talk about it," she told him, "okay?"

"Okay," her brother said, but he looked disappointed. "Goodnight."

"Goodnight." She left his chambers and hurried up to her own, trying not to think about where Lyha could be, freezing in the winter wind somewhere in the Mountains or the Golden Forests and cursing herself for running away. It was hard in those moments for Samira to convince herself that it wasn't her fault.

# 3

# Edris

The sun was beginning to set over the tops of the mountains; Edris could tell it would be dark in earnest soon. And nothing, not even a hunting party, had approached the perimeter the entire afternoon. The men had long since lapsed into small groups of conversation behind him, and he and Captain Landiss were riding together with boredom plain on both of their faces. Edris glanced back at the city gates some miles behind and below them and thought longingly about the many fires burning back in Caspar's Dale. It was still cold in Thorncliffe this time of year, always was until close to High Summer, and his father's keep provided one of the only sources of consistent warmth he knew of. Winter was waning, and he was grateful, but he sometimes envied the other kingdoms' ease in keeping the Chill away.

It seemed as if he and Landiss were of one mind; once they reached the next curve in their winding path, the young knight brought his horse to a halt and said, "I can't see the point in going any higher, Your Highness. What do you think of waiting for the night guard back at the watchtower?"

"Oh, thank the Father," Edris sighed. "My fingers are going numb."

Landiss acknowledged him with a nod. "It's a cold spring." Addressing the whole party of twelve, he spoke up and called out, "Back to the Eye!" The guard tower, about a mile from the mouth of the vale, still couldn't compare to his own bed, but the promise of fire and food gave Edris a last bout of energy. Riding at the back now, he watched the knights and squires in front of him as they wound their way back down the edge of the lands outside Caspar's Dale.

"I heard that we're hosting His Holiness next month," Landiss said, casually, though Edris could hear a curious tinge to his voice.

"That's true," he said, trying to match his casual air. "He's stopping here on his way to Hollisport, for the princess's Declaration."

"Right. I forgot about that, are they getting married there?" Landiss asked.

"I don't remember, I don't think so. She's only sixteen," Edris said, frowning. "And he's how old? Twenty-two, three?"

"He's the Godhead. She'd be lucky if they did," the captain said, blinking at him in disbelief. Almost immediately, he appeared to remember who Edris was and said quickly, "I'm sorry, Your Highness. I didn't mean to question your faith."

"Don't worry, Taylor, I didn't think you were," he said, waving off the nervous knight. As he heard Landiss quietly sigh in relief, he watched the trees he had noticed swaying out of time with the wind. "Do you see that?"

"What?" Landiss asked. Edris didn't respond, and instead started to hurry his horse along a little faster. The captain followed suit, and asked after a moment, "Has your father given any thought to who *you* might marry, Your Highness? I know your engagement was... interrupted."

Edris was finally distracted from the rustling and turned to face the other man. "Taylor, I'm glad for your company. But I don't want to talk about Lyha Halwood."

Captain Landiss bowed his head. "Of course. I'm sorry, Prince Edris." Edris nodded and had barely turned back to face the road when the line of trees suddenly broke and several armed and armored men burst onto the path in front of the guards. All of the Valleyguard men pulled their reins, but it was almost unnecessary with how spooked their horses were.

Edris's own stallion reared back as well, and he pulled his reins back, leaning down to pat the horse's mane. "It's all right, Blizzard," he said as soothingly as he could, as startled as he was himself, and when they were both calm enough, he rode through the party up to the men, who had held up their hands and backed away from them to a safe distance from the kicking hooves. Landiss cut him off before he could speak and drew his sword, forcing Edris back some ways and thoroughly irritating him too.

"Who are you?" the captain demanded. "Where do you come from? You wear no coat of arms."

"We mean you no harm, sir, there's no call for hostility," one of the six men replied, sounding a little affronted. He stepped forward and undid his belt, letting the sword slide to the dirt still sheathed. He then reached up and removed his helm to reveal a pale face with dark hair and bright blue eyes. Some of the Valleyguard grumbled suspicion at the man's complexion, and Edris predicted what he said next: "We're men of Eirosia." Landiss's men drew their swords immediately, and the Eirosian flinched. Edris kept his right hand on the pommel of his own sword, but hesitated to draw.

"You're not welcome here," Landiss told him, more malice in his voice than Edris had heard in all the years he'd known him. "This is King Bastian's land. Heretics and Daemons belong in *your* country."

"Please, sir, I have no quarrel with your gods, and Daemons are our common enemy," he said. "We know this is King Bastian's land. I need to speak with him."

"You won't pass the gates of this city," Landiss promised. "What is your message?"

"I have instructions to speak only to the king," the man said. His stone resolve in the face of Landiss's sword impressed the prince, and he found that the men were too distracted to keep him back.

"You're speaking to his son," Edris called out, and rode around Landiss quickly, ignoring the captain's protests. "I'm the crown prince of Thorncliffe. Tell me what you would tell my father." The leader of the Eirosians stared at him intensely, uncertain, but the dozen swords at his throat ultimately proved convincing enough.

"My name is Alexander Neill. I'm a knight and messenger from the court of King Silas Dillon. He calls for aid."

Edris blinked and exchanged an incredulous look with Landiss. "King Silas is dead. Thirteen years this winter."

"No, Your Highness. Imprisoned, in his own castle. And his men enslaved," Neill said. "I beg you to take us to your father so we can negotiate on his behalf."

"We don't negotiate with heretics," Landiss said. "We'll take you to the Eye of Astor." Edris had not recovered from the news about the Eirosian king quite as quickly, and it took another moment before he gave his assent to the captain to seize the men. The ride back to the tower, with half the party now carrying hostages, was significantly slower and more somber than before, and no one said a word until the Spire of the Eye loomed over the foothills.

By the time the horses rode in through the hastily lowered gate, the sun had finally dipped behind the lowest mountaintop, and the firelight glowing from the valley nearby made Edris ache for a hearth and a warm drink. Instead, knowing Neill and his men had bought him even longer outside the city gates, he begrudgingly dismounted his horse and handed the reins to the stable girl. Landiss dismissed the other riders, and with him leading the remaining party, Edris fell back and watched the Eirosians as they all marched through the courtyard and up the winding steps of the watchtower.

Edris started to feel excited in spite of himself as he walked with the men up to the top of the Eye's spire. He had been inside the tower hundreds of times, but only to the mess and soldier's commons in the courtyard. He'd never brought a prisoner in before, and he knew where they were taken, but hadn't ever seen it: the offices of the Guard of the Dale himself, from which very few prisoners ever returned. The Guard, a high priest named Brother Spencer, was a lofty figure in his father's court, and he had always scared Edris somewhat. That was fine; his father scared him, too. He was still in awe of this man and the iron gate he'd managed to keep shut against ungodly things outside of Thorncliffe's borders for as long as Edris could remember. He'd always wondered how he did it.

When they reached the top of the stairs and were facing the heavy double doors of the offices, Landiss turned around and said, "Wait here," his tone threatening enough even without the hand on the hilt of his sword. Producing a key, he turned the lock on the door and opened it just enough to slip inside alone.

As soon as he was gone, Neill turned to face Edris, and his men parted so they were in clear view of one another. "Your Highness," he said calmly, bracing his arms across his chest. "I don't expect to survive this."

Edris was startled. "What do you mean? You'll be deported, most likely."

He chuckled, his eyes remaining grim. "I won't survive that either." He glanced back at the doors and said, "Regardless, please bring my plea to the king."

The prince barely resisted flinching at the thought of that conversation and said, "My father is a deeply pious man, sir. He has no love for Eirosia."

"Then remind him our kingdoms were founded by brothers, once," Neill pleaded. "Tell him there's piety in mercy as well as justice." Edris was taken aback by the brazen way this man was lecturing about religion, as someone from the land of the god of death, no less. But before he could respond, the doors swung open and Landiss, with two young Priest apprentices, marched the men inside. Edris followed, half in shock, and was struck with the height of the ceiling inside the Spire. He'd imagined they were inside the spire itself, but there seemed to be more grand, lofty spaces in the offices than even some of the rooms in the keep. He took a deep breath, trying to calm his nerves— nerves, that was unlike him. What had shaken him so much about this knight?

He guessed it was finally putting a face to the enemy. He had heard about the horrible deeds of the Eirosians, and their gruesome ends reckoned by the Father and Mother, ever since he was a child. He'd only been eight when King Silas died—at least, when they'd thought he had. But he had never actually met an Eirosian— there were none at Fen Faris anymore, they'd told him they'd all been sent back to their kingdom at the start of the invasions, and school was the only time Edris had traveled for any length of time outside of Thorncliffe.

The Queen of the Horn was Eirosian-born, a Dillon in fact, something his father never failed to sneer at, but Edris had never met her either. He'd been to the Hartlands, of course- once. But a Declaration festival was hardly a likely place to meet someone like them. And now there they were, standing in front of him, and other than the paleness of their faces they hardly seemed different from the Casparians of Thorncliffe.

He'd been convinced that the corruption inside would show on their faces; his father always said you could tell a truly evil man because it would eat him from the inside. But Neill didn't look corroded, not a bit. He looked every bit the righteous man, with the strong sturdy frame and stalwart air of an honorable knight. Even more so, he thought privately, when he remained peaceful and stoic as they stripped him of his armor and forced him to the ground in front of gaunt and gaudy Brother Spencer. Neill stayed calm and steadily met the priest's withering gaze. "Name," Spencer commanded, in his thin, high voice, as the other Eirosians were forced to their knees behind their leader.

"Sir Alexander Neill of the Royal Guard of House Dillon. Formerly King's Councillor."

"Do you understand why you've been brought before me today?"

"I beg your pardon, my lord, but I do not," Neill said.

Without warning, Spencer nodded at one of the apprentices, and he stepped up to Neill and hit him, hard, across his back, a lash Edris had only ever seen as punishment for a tried and sentenced offense. He fell forward, caught himself on his hands, and after a moment straightened himself again, his expression hardened this time. The priest said, "I'm not a lord. I am addressed as 'Your Holiness' or 'Father Spencer'. Understood?"

"Of course. Your Holiness," Neill said quietly. He didn't seem cowed by the display; on the contrary, the quiet reply seemed deadlier than any of the floggings Edris predicted in the knight's future. "To answer your question, I don't know why we were brought here, *Your Holiness*."

"You may be aware of the Royal Decree of 486 After the Year of Landing, that bars any of your countrymen from passing into King Bastian's lands."

"Apologies, Your Holiness, but it was my understanding that Triad border decrees were exempt in cases of *diplomatic* parties," Neill said, his voice coming out tight and strained through gritted teeth.

"Eirosia is *not* a kingdom of the Triad. Our laws do not protect your *diplomatic party*," Father Spencer practically spat. "If your king is indeed alive, why has he never sent emissaries before now?"

Neill was starting to grow earnestly angry, and a great feeling of foreboding was brewing inside of Edris at the sight of the young knight's fiery eyes. "Do you have any idea," he asked slowly, "the kind of pain we have suffered these last dozen years at the mercy of the Daemons?"

"I think you'll find that we do," Spencer threatened.

It didn't quell Neill's rage. "I've endured things none of you will ever be able to imagine. I hadn't seen sunlight until we set out in the last month. We escaped, and it was a *miracle* we did. We would have come sooner if we could have!"

"The last month of 499? A season has nearly passed since then. It would have been intolerably cold in Eirosia, and besides, it takes half that time to walk from Illon's Fast to Caspar's Dale," one of the apprentices smirked. "They're liars as well as heretics."

"Your Holiness, if you could find in my speech since I've arrived one single heresy—" Neill exclaimed, but his outburst was only rewarded with another hit.

Edris was standing behind the prisoners, straight-backed and, hopefully, motionless. It was taking all of his strength not to flinch. He knew that deep down he wanted the truth from these men, and he knew Brother Spencer was the best way to get that, but he hadn't known his methods were so harsh. Even that set the berating voice off in his head: *Don't be so soft. You should have known true holy work would be difficult to watch.* Even so, he was having a hard time seeing this interrogation as holy.

The Eirosian men had been loudly protesting Neill's treatment, and one even rushed at the apprentice with the strap. He was quickly halted by Landiss's sword at his neck and fell backwards in fright. "Quiet," Spencer barked at them, but when they didn't respond, he approached Neill, who was breathing heavily and staring at the ground. "Tell your men to go quietly to the cells. That you'll be killed if they make any trouble."

Neill swallowed with some difficulty, and in a suddenly weary, hoarse voice, said, "You heard him. Go." They didn't look happy, but one by one the other men allowed themselves to be led through a back door by the other apprentice. When they had gone, Brother Spencer nodded and began to show a ghost of a smile. "Your men respect you. You'll keep them safe while you are here, understood?" Neill nodded, now staring at the priest balefully and, satisfied, Spencer stepped back.

"My apprentice is right. It takes no more than seven, possibly eight weeks to make that walk as young men. Something about what you've said is a lie. We'll discover what it is. You and I all have a long night together, Sir Alexander." The apprentices pulled him up under his arms to his feet and marched him through the same door. Neill managed to look back at Edris, the plea in his eyes clear as day, before he was gone.

"Well, Prince Edris," Brother Spencer said, and his manner of speech was light and pleasant suddenly, like night and day, "you've proven yourself a talented patrolman."

"They revealed themselves to us, sir, we did no tracking," Edris admitted, and Spencer grunted.

"Well, all the same," he said, shrugging as he nonchalantly wiped Neill's blood off the leather strap, folded it, and placed it in a chest against the wall. "Welcome to the Spire of the Eye. I believe this is your first time here."

"Yes, Your Holiness," he managed. "I didn't imagine it to be so..."

Spencer turned around again, raising his eyebrows slightly. "The work of the Father's Justice is not pleasant. But we are his stewards in this land until we are worthy of his return."

"I know that," Edris said quickly, "but... I don't think they were lying." He had no idea where this courage was coming from. And when Spencer's eyes reacted to his words, he wished it had never shown itself in the first place.

"What makes you say that?" he asked. His voice still sounded casual, but it was menacing to Edris's ears all the same.

"Well… if they'd been tortured for years, they wouldn't be moving as fast as ordinary men," he said. "And I don't know why they would risk the Holy Army and the Valleyguard attacking them to come here if they didn't have good reason."

Spencer sighed. "Their king very well may be alive. That does not mean they were here peacefully. My prince, you have a great ability to see good in people. I disagree with your father, I think this is a holy quality." That stung, and he tried not to show it in the face of the priest's kind smile. "But these heretics don't deserve it. Their fallen kingdom brought their death god's Daemons on themselves." Edris nodded and the old priest clapped a hand on his shoulder, a gesture much more familiar than he had ever shown him. "Let me handle the prisoners from now on. You should go up to the castle. The Warrens came to court today, and I believe their daughter Nora is eager to see you."

Edris felt himself stiffen at the name and said, as casually as he could, "Oh. Alright."

Brother Spencer's face became more serious then and he drew closer to him, so even Landiss ten paces away could hardly hear, saying, "Your engagement was not a marriage. You're released from it now, and you would do well to find a more fitting bride soon. Lady Nora is a righteous young woman. Princess Lyha was— well, we imagined her father would have raised her better than her wretched brother. It seems we were wrong."

Criticism of Lyha always left a bad taste in Edris's mouth, ever since that summer night in the gardens of Queenshearth, and he instinctively began to shrink away. Spencer stepped with him, keeping them in close proximity. "Your father is a holy man. But the Evangelist King will not live forever, and his kingdom won't be worthy of Astor until after his time. You could deliver our people out of this horrible life. You'll need your own queen to secure your place as the king you were meant to be. And a king without a queen is seldom a holy thing." He looked back at the door to the cells, and Edris took his meaning.

He stepped back more firmly this time, genuinely offended now, and said, "Silas's... *way* has nothing to do with me."

Spencer nodded. "I know, Your Highness. That's what I told the Godhead." Edris's blood nearly froze. "But an engagement before he arrives will be more convincing."

Edris swallowed and cleared his throat, suddenly feeling somewhat faint. "I'll go see Lady Nora."

The priest smiled and said, "Good. I'll see you at Council in the morning." He retreated to his rolls of parchment on the table along the back wall, and Landiss started to follow the prince's hurrying steps. "Oh, and Edris? Best not to involve your father in this just yet."

"Yes," Edris said quietly, and shut the door to the Spire, flooding with relief the farther down the steps he got. He could finally warm himself with a hearth and a hot supper, but knowing who he'd left behind and who was waiting for him, it seemed much less comforting now.

# 4

Mychal

"You see the holdfast off over there? That's where we're going," Sir James said, pointing up to a small sentry post on the shore of the bay ahead. "It's left over from the Farisian Civil War, when the Hartlanders took the bay. The Army's never used it, but we're scouting new outer layers of defense."

"What are we doing when we get there?" Mychal asked, urging his much more petite horse, a courser from home named Gale, to keep up with Sir James's quite impressive and strong destrier.

"You and Luke will clean it up, get it ready for the men. Sir Callum and I will look over the terrain and draw the report for the war council tomorrow." Sir Callum Roth, the knight Luke squired under and a cavalryman of the Holy forces, nodded his assent from Sir James's other side. Sir Callum was a clean-cut, heavyset man, with a nose and expression that always seemed to be looking down, just like the Hornish nobility he'd come from. His height of at least three inches over six feet reinforced the effect.

"Why are we expanding now, sir?" Luke asked as he fell back to ride next to Mychal, and the knights went quiet. "Sorry, did I...?"

"No, it's alright," Sir Callum said, exchanging a glance with Sir James. "Your steward, James. He wasn't in council last night. Do you trust him with this?"

"Of course I do," he said, and Mychal felt a small swell of pride, despite how much he always tried not to care. He kept reminding himself to hate the officers, but he couldn't help seeking Sir James's approval.

"A rider arrived from Caspar's Dale this morning," Sir Callum said. Mychal tried not to flinch when he heard the name. He had never been there, but he'd imagined the fortified valley city often, looming over lone travelers on the dangerous road, with the dark court of the Evangelist King executing 'heretics' daily. "Brother Spencer of the Guard captured six Eirosian soldiers last week claiming to be a diplomatic party from King Silas."

"I thought King Silas died after the Siege," Luke said, frowning.

"He did," Sir Callum said patiently. "But whatever their real reason for coming was, something's changing in Eirosia. We have to be ready for anything. We weren't expecting Daemons until High Summer, but perhaps we were wrong." Mychal only felt the slightest bit guilty about James's faith in him when his first thought was how soon he could get to Lady May's again to tell Senna. These new, far-flung Army outposts could prove easier targets for the budding forces of... whoever it was she was sending his messages to.

When they reached the holdfast, about twenty minutes later, the knights rode on up to the shores of the bay and spoke in low voices over a map of the area. Luke and Mychal dismounted their horses and ventured inside. The entrance hall wasn't as dust-filled and abandoned as he had expected. In fact, there were bootprints of mud on the stone in front of them, far too recent to be from the Civil War more than three centuries ago. He and Luke glanced at each other and drew their swords as they crept forward toward the stairwell at the back of the tower.

They both climbed slowly up to the first floor, and Mychal burst through the door, half expecting a party of Daemons or some other horrible thing from beyond the mountains. But all he found was a well-kept sentry post, bare of all supplies but clean and ready for the Holy Guard. There was charred wood in the hearth, more evidence of recent occupation, but he and Luke were alone. His friend exhaled slowly and said, "Mother Morra, I thought we'd walked in on an Eirosian camp."

"Me too," Mychal said quietly, sheathing his sword. "Who do you think's been here?"

Luke shrugged. "Who knows? Deserters, maybe, or lowborns running from tribute..." He immediately looked embarrassed and said, "Um, sorry."

Mychal often forgot he was supposed to be common, and hadn't even registered it as offensive until he'd said something, but mumbled, "Don't worry about it," anyway. "We should go tell them."

When they'd relayed to the knights what they'd found, Sir James looked troubled, but Sir Callum was unperturbed. "Excellent. Whoever it was did your work for you, boys."

"We'll mention it at council," Sir James said, and Callum nodded.

"Of course, but we should be glad the tower's fit for our guards already." The older knight addressed Luke then and said, "Rest and eat something. We'll return in an hour."

"You too, Mychal," James said. "If you have time you should try to practice with your sword." He managed to stop himself from groaning out loud. He was completely outmatched by Luke, and he knew it'd only be embarrassing, but he resigned himself to it as he ate his portion of the bread and cheese they'd brought for lunch. Luke ate faster, and was getting more and more impatient for him to get up and draw.

Eventually, he burst out, "Come on, Mychal, are you slow or just craven?" and, rolling his eyes, Mychal got to his feet and followed him back to the green in front of the holdfast. He liked Luke well enough, but he also knew his friend very much liked being the best at things. Never mind that he was the one who got to train with a master-at-arms from age six; he was convinced that besting Mychal at sparring showed some natural talent of his at war.

The knights were finished with their report and turned to watch, which only made Mychal want to run away even more. Sighing, he steeled himself and drew his sword. "Be careful, I'm only wearing leather," he said.

"I'll go easy on you," Luke promised, grinning, and Mychal reluctantly raised his sword. Luke made the first cut through the air, and Mychal almost instinctively pushed his sword out to block it. The other boy swung it away easily and stopped his blade inches from Mychal's throat. This was going to be a long afternoon.

"Honestly, Mychal, put up a fight," Luke said, grinning ear to ear.

"Your sword's half again as heavy as mine," he protested, stepping back into his stance.

"That's got nothing to do with it," Sir James called out from his seat on the rocks of the bay. "Your stance is wrong and you're holding the pommel. Step through after you swing the blade."

Luke swung again; Mychal stepped correctly this time and kept Luke's blade locked in the bind between them for about a second before the other boy brought the hilt up to their shoulders and stepped through. Mychal tried to hold his defense, but his sword slid down off of Luke's, and he once again had a blade at his neck.

"Now you're aiming for his sword, not for him. It gives him more room to counter your attack."

Again; dead. Again; dead. This went on for quite a while, until finally Mychal started gaining ground. Sometimes he would actually make it four or five hits before Luke would expose some misstep, and eventually Sir James said, "You'd be evenly matched with any common boy your age, I think." Mychal finally started to smile.

"He's a fast learner," he heard Sir Callum saying as he and Luke kept sparring. "He's not your squire?"

"He's a steward," Sir James said. "I'd take him on, though. I was waiting for Prince Mason but he's going back to Fen Faris after the festivals."

"You would, sir?" Mychal asked, staggering out of Luke's range and breathing heavily.

"Well, yes," Sir James said, smiling, "if that's what you want. And if your father won't miss you at... what does your father do?"

"He's— a tailor, sir," Mychal said quietly, hoping he remembered correctly and that was what he'd told Luke before. "And I don't think he's ever missed me."

"You're common-born?" Sir Callum asked, with an aloof kind of approval. "I would never have guessed. There's a noble countenance to your face, young man."

"Um, thank you, sir," he said, shifting his eyes away from Luke's so he wouldn't laugh.

"What will happen to Master Owyn's tailor shop when his son's a knight?" Sir James asked.

"I think it'll be better for it, honestly, sir," he said. He didn't like lying, but it had to be done, and it seemed like he was alright at it thus far. "I was never very good."

"That's rubbish, I've seen him fix his clothes," Luke interjected.

"You alter your clothes?" Sir James asked, amused.

"He has to, they're all too big when he gets them," he laughed.

"Come on, Luke," Mychal mumbled, rolling his eyes, and Sir James clapped a hand on his shoulder.

"Well, we'll talk about it when we get back to Astor Post. Let's make a final check of the tower and we'll head back." Mychal was elated in spite of himself, and he was completely taken in by the idea of becoming a knight, even if it was for the Holy Army. Riding in full plated armor with the Vanguard, winning gold in the melee at a king's tournament— he tried not to get discouraged when he stooped forward to pick up his pack and his sword slid out of his sheath, clattering to the ground. Thankfully, no one had seen it.

When he finally came out of his daydreams, he realized that the others had already gone up into the holdfast, and he hurried up the path to the great door. Before he reached it, though, he heard peals of laughter and saw rustling leaves in the woods to his other side. He frowned. "Are we making a perimeter?" he called out, and suddenly all the laughter stopped. After several long seconds of painful silence, three strange men came rushing out of the trees.

Mychal barely had time to draw his sword before the first man, the only one with a real blade, bore down upon him, hacking and slashing wildly. Through the adrenaline, he noticed that whoever this was, he had no idea how to properly fight, and Mychal managed to block each strike of his blade with jarring clashes of steel that rang out sharply in the quiet clearing.

Eventually, the man stumbled, and Mychal saw that he was stepping into each thrust, the way Sir James had just warned him not to do. He took the opportunity to respond just the way Luke had, knocking his blade away, and although he didn't manage to aim for the man's neck, a good deal above his reach, he did land a powerful blow to his right shoulder.

The man wasn't wearing armor. With a choked cry, he dropped his sword and wrenched himself away from the blade, which Mychal had unsuccessfully tried to free from his arm himself. The resistance he felt told him he'd probably hit bone. The man dropped to his knees, clutching the wound, and the other two men, until now slowly advancing in stunned silence, advanced on Mychal.

The one to his left, holding something like a dagger or maybe a shortsword, slashed at his right arm, which he narrowly avoided. He didn't know what was different fighting against a shortsword or a longsword, but he just kept instinctively swinging, hoping this man was untrained like the first. As he managed to knock the man off his feet with the hilt, he heard the swinging of the great wooden door of the holdfast and turned to look at the others hurrying outside. He was only distracted for a moment, but it was all the man on the ground needed to plunge the dagger into his thigh.

He was too stunned to even cry out, and heard someone, too distant to really clearly hear, shouting, "Mychal!" before a sudden pain exploded in the back of his head and his vision went black.

* * *

Mychal was dreaming.

He was in the great hall of the keep at home, suddenly, with Deronn and Jullia and Father all there in front of him. His father was furious. He was also, absurdly, dressed like a tailor.

The tailor-King Eronn was throwing bolts of fabric at him now, shouting in a warped, echoed version of his voice, "A tailor? You've made me a tailor?"

"I'm sorry, Father," he said, feeling the same nervousness coming back into his voice from all his confrontations upon disappointing the man.

"My daughter will not be a tailor," he bellowed, and Jullia laughed.

"You were never best at sewing, I was."

"I was never meant to do it," he told her desperately, then with an effort turned back to the king. "I'm sorry," he repeated.

"You're not my Lyha," his father said, shaking his head in disgust. Mychal could feel his eyes filling with tears.

"I– I know. I'm sorry. I'm *Mychal*."

"You're Mychal?" his father asked, then pointed past him toward the back of the hall. "Tell that to him."

Mychal whirled around and stifled a scream. Standing there with glassy dead eyes was his twin, the first Mychal, next to their mother, the front of their clothes both soaked with blood and holding their heads in their hands.

*  *  *

He heard voices before he opened his eyes. They sounded far away, like he was trying to swim up through deep, dark water back into consciousness. The voices were muffled as he floated in this liminal space between sleeping and waking. He recognized Luke's voice, and Sir James, and there was another voice there too— Sir Callum? No, it was too low to be his voice...

"He'll be alright for traveling, sir, so long as he's got a mount or a wagon." Mychal's muddled brain was confused by that. What travel, and why wouldn't he be alright on foot? What had happened again? He remembered using his sword...

Oh. His eyes flew open with the shock of what had happened at the holdfast, and he began to panic when he realized where he'd been stabbed. He steeled himself before looking down and the panic quickly subsided when he saw he was, for the most part, still dressed. They'd removed his leather jerkin and cut off his left trouser's leg up to the wound, but he otherwise appeared untouched, and the wound itself seemed under control.

"It's alright, Mychal. You're in the doctor's quarters," Sir James said. He met the knight's eyes with some effort and nodded.

"You'll be alright," the third man said, presumably the doctor, a balding, aging man in Stewards' wine red robes. "We cleaned and stitched your wound. I'll want you to stay here for at least two nights, but you're young, you'll heal quick."

"Thank you, Doctor," Sir James said in Mychal's stead; he was glad of it, too. His mouth felt dry and his tongue heavy, though with exhaustion or anxiety he couldn't be sure. Turning to face him then,

Sir James added, "You fought well, quick and without fear. I'm sorry we couldn't be there sooner."

"I'm just glad to be alive, sir," he managed to croak out. "Were they Daemons?"

"No," Luke chuckled, "just some marauders from the Lordless Isles. The first had already bled out, and we had to kill the one who stabbed you, but we took one alive. They're questioning him now."

"Oh," Mychal said, a little disappointed but not surprised. They hadn't seemed to be very good fighters, but he'd still hoped he would be able to say he'd killed a Daemon by himself. He had killed a man, though. He'd never done that before. He swallowed uncomfortably at the thought.

"In any case," Sir James said, "you were brave today, and Sir Callum's right, you do learn fast. The fact that you're alive right now is as good proof as any. So what do you say to me taking you on as my squire?"

Mychal's heart fluttered in excitement and he struggled to prop himself somewhat upright in the unstable cot. "Really, sir?"

"Well, once you can walk," the knight said, smiling kindly. "And of course you'll need to accompany me whenever I leave camp, so you'll be joining the guard traveling to Princess Samira's Declaration festival."

*Shit.* He tried not to let his smile waver. "Right. I can ride Gale, can't I?"

"Of course. And if you're not up to it, you can ride in the wagon. The important thing is for you to be there. You'll have to get used to these kinds of things before you're a knight."

Mychal nodded. Sir James placed a hand on his good leg and nodded back. "I'll see you when you're well enough to come up to the hall." He left then, and Luke's grin grew wider.

"The son of a tailor squiring for a Holy Officer," his friend laughed. "If I'd known all we had to do to climb up in the world was get stuck with a dagger, I'd have charged at the marauders myself. I could be a king by now."

"Right, and how many times would you have to be stabbed for that to happen, Luke?" Mychal asked, smirking.

"A lot fewer than you, Owyn, watch yourself," he warned, before they both laughed even more. Mychal had to hide his blush. *He had no idea.* "Really, though, I'm happy for you. You're sure your father won't mind?"

"Trust me, Luke, he wouldn't want to see me," Mychal said, thinking of his dream again with a shudder. "I won't ever go home again."

"Well, then, after the war you can come back to Brookbridge with me and swear your sword to my brother," he said. "We can both fight for King Eronn." He frowned. "I suppose it'll be Deronn by then, though. Morra keep him."

Mychal nodded slowly. He'd done his best not to think about his family lately, but now after the dream he couldn't stop. "I'd like that, Luke. I'm tired now, though. Could you tell Graham I'm alright?"

"Of course, mate. I'll let you rest," he said. "See you in a couple of days."

"See you then," he nodded, and Luke left the tent the same way Sir James had.

Mychal leaned back into the pillow behind his head, and as he watched the old Steward doctor carry water across the tent, he couldn't hold back his morbid curiosity any longer. "Doctor, can I ask, did you happen to see—"

"I'll stop you there, lad," the man said gruffly, without even looking up. "I mind my business. Your letter from your girl or flask of Hartwine or whatever you've got in your pockets is still there."

Mychal breathed normally for the first time and he thanked him as the doctor waddled out toward the well at the end of the row. While he was gone, Mychal felt around his pockets anyway and thankfully found the familiar shape of the Halwood sword-and-fire chain he'd had since he was young, still wrapped in the old fragment of cloth he'd hidden it in, almost two years ago now. As he traced the outline of the aged steel metalwork, he wondered if Samira would get a chain like it at her Declaration.

*Suppose I'll find out*, he thought bitterly as he closed his eyes again and leaned back down onto the cot. He didn't have a choice but to go, even though one mistake at that festival would mean this had all been for nothing. He wanted to ask Senna for help from her friends, but he couldn't see a way to get to her with his leg in this condition. He'd have to survive the next few weeks on his own.

# 5

Edris

The third month of the year was nearly as cold as the second, though Edris started to notice less snow on his daily patrols. Sir Alexander and the other Eirosian men remained in the Eye of Astor, as far as he knew, and he didn't dare ask Brother Spencer what had become of them. He hadn't seen much of his father lately– in the past two weeks the Council had started meeting more often and closed him out of their talks. He had nearly convinced himself that was why he hadn't brought up King Silas's plea to the king yet. Nearly.

It was slow days like these when he resented being considered too important to be fighting in the Holy Army. His cousin Jonn was Lord Marshal, and nearly all of his friends from childhood were serving as well. He wanted to fight. The Daemons were a real threat to everything he knew, and the invaders from Eirosia were hardly any better. Sir Alexander didn't seem so bad, he supposed, but Edris had heard too many stories about the awful crimes committed by his people to let that lessen his resolve.

And as much as he loved the hills and valleys and stone cliff-side towers of Caspar's Dale, it could be incredibly boring after enough time spent inside the walls. When he wasn't patrolling with the Valleyguard, he was studying Steward texts he'd brought from Fen Faris or practicing with his sword. He knew the knowledge and training had to prove useful, eventually, someday.

"What are you reading?" Nora asked, and when he looked up he saw Lord Warren's youngest daughter, his new fiancée, peering over his shoulder with her earnest, curious gaze. He'd almost forgotten she was there.

"It's a... treatise on honorable rules of holy combat. Steward Fredrick Denastor, in the second century."

"Denastor, that's your mother's family, isn't it?" she asked.

"Yes," he said, trying not to take a dismissive tone as he turned his page. The two of them had been sitting in one of the gardens on the rooftops of the Keep, with a view of the Grand Road below them, in hopes of seeing the Priesthood delegation set to arrive that afternoon.

"It must be incredible to be able to trace both your family lines back so far," she said. Everything about Nora was willowy and pale, and her voice carried the same feeling, ethereally light and, he felt, off-putting. "My grandfather founded our house, you know. We're the first lords of Provinceham Manor."

"That's a great achievement," Edris said, putting his book away. He could tell he wasn't going to get to read any more for some time. The girl kept talking, and he did try to listen at first, but the view was a little distracting, especially since over the tops of the city walls he could see the tip of the Eye's spire. He couldn't stop himself from thinking about what must have been happening to Sir Alexander inside.

"And my aunt Malya married Lord Charles," Nora was saying

when his attention came back to her. "So we have the same cousin, you know, the Lord Marshal."

"Right," he said, nodding probably a little too quickly. "Have you ever been to Norport?"

"We went to the Northern Falls when I was little; that's not in the city but it is their land. They were so beautiful. But that was ten years ago, and the canal's so heavily guarded now I doubt it's very nice anymore."

Edris was about to agree when a metallic flash shining in the sun caught his eye on the path just inside the city gate. He stood up and peered over the edge of the balcony, and down on the ground he could see a large party of attendants with a single sky-blue palanquin at the center. They were making their way slowly up the road toward the keep, and if he squinted at the banners the men in front were carrying, he could just make out the blue and gold sun-and-moon sigil of the Godhead. "They're here, we should go." Nora's eyes widened and she followed him as he rushed back inside and down the several flights of stairs to his father's great hall.

King Bastian's hall was long and narrow, to give those making the walk from the keep's outer doors to the base of the throne the feeling that the walls were slowly closing in on them. The effect would be utterly suffocating if not for the high ceilings lined with long windows of tempered glass, bathing the king and his court in sunlight. The throne itself was a tall, narrow stone seat, matching the rest of the room, with the Thorne family sigil of a great brown mountain-bear carved into the back above the king's head.

The long benches on either side of the room were populated with some two or three dozen courtiers and councilors, and Edris and Nora slipped in largely unnoticed, taking seats as close to the back door they'd come through as possible. The king was hearing a petition, from what appeared to be a young squire of the Holy Army. The Godhead's crest imprinted on the breastplate of his armor shone in the sunlight as he gazed up at the king, eyes filled with trepidation. Edris knew the feeling.

"We can't spare men from the southern guard," the king said. "But there are Valleyguard battalions in the western lands we can send to Astor Post. Tell your Lord Marshal he should have 1,000 or so more soldiers by the end of this month."

The squire's face betrayed the disappointment he clearly felt, but he said nothing, and bowed. "Thank you, Your Majesty." With a nod from the king, the boy turned and made the long walk back to the castle doors.

When the squire was gone, Edris's father sunk back into a less regal posture in the stiff, over-large throne and exhaled sharply. "What next?"

"Father," Edris said loudly, standing from his seat, and the court's attention turned to him, startled out of the quiet stupor they'd all been drawn into by the slow business of the kingdom. "The Godhead's party came through the gates just now. They should be here any moment."

The excitement that rushed through the courtiers did not seem to affect the king much, though he did sit back up straight in his throne. "Very good then. And is Landiss here? He needs to send letters to his fellow captains in the west. The Holy Army needs men at the Mages' Canyon," he said, closing his eyes in the way of a tired old man. He was only 50 this year, but battles long since past had aged him, and Edris saw a stout and war-weathered survivor when he looked at his father.

"They took a wider perimeter today," Edris said. "To prepare for tonight. He won't be back until just before the feast."

The king's face twisted into something more akin to annoyance than boredom. "And why aren't you with them?"

Edris felt himself get hot under his father's questioning eyes and said, "... His Holiness is arriving today."

"And? I'm not dead yet, you don't need to be here to receive him," he barked. The quiet noises of surprise and disapproval from courtiers throughout the hall only added to Edris's embarrassment. "You'll learn more defending our kingdom from Daemons and heretics than you will in here with me. You're young and strong, don't be a coward and sit in your hall before you have no choice."

Shame churning his stomach and clenching his throat, Edris was saved from having to respond by the doors being thrown open and the steward announcing, "His Holiness the Godhead Riyan Duane of the Priesthood of the Duality, and his Holy Attendants, the High Priests of New Astoria and the Holy Guard." The palanquin Edris had seen and the horses had been left behind outside, and the men carrying the banners remained at the back of the hall, while the others processed toward the court. Six Priests, with blue robes and golden stoles and empty sheaths for their forgotten swords, walked proudly forward, and a dozen soldiers followed, wearing the same colors but with very real swords on their belts.

In between the two lines of three Priests, a tall, gaunt young man approached the throne. He looked no one in the eye, and moved as if he were floating across the floor rather than walking. Edris was almost of a height with him, and they both had the same short blond curls and blue-green eyes he had always shared with his mythical ancestor Caspar, though neither of them measured up to the large muscular figure of the hero in the tapestries.

The Godhead didn't wear robes, but a gilded doublet of blue velvet and dark trousers, with a golden cloak held at his shoulders by sun-and-moon clasps. Riyan Duane came further forward than his attendants, finally pausing a mere six feet or so away from the king, and inclined his head in an odd sort of acknowledgement. Edris doubted the Godhead had ever bowed to anyone, not even the feared Evangelist King.

The king in question cleared his throat, stiff-backed and self-important. "I, King Bastian the Second of the Thornes of Caspar's Dale, welcome you to our city, Your Holiness. I hope our hospitality will prove equal to your needs."

"Thank you, Your Majesty," he said, and his voice sounded clear but aloof, like there was hardly a person behind the words. "You have a beautiful city."

"By the Mother and Father's grace," the king said. He turned to Edris and extended a hand to indicate him, saying, "My son and heir, Prince Edris Thorne." The Godhead's cool eyes turned toward him and Edris weaved around the benches to the center of the room as gracefully as he could. He couldn't help but stumble a bit; this was the conduit of the Mother and Father themselves, standing right in front of him. So what if Edris was a prince?

Edris bowed low when he reached him and said, "Welcome, Your Holiness."

He saw curiosity flash across Duane's face as he replied, "Thank you. I've heard much about you from my Brothers." Edris's eyes caught Brother Spencer's from across the room, and with a hint of a smirk from the old priest, he was suddenly struck with anxious haste and motioned for Nora to come forward. She grasped his hand when she reached him and Edris could feel she was trembling.

"This is Lady Nora Warren of Provinceham." She curtsied deeply and avoided meeting the Godhead's eyes until he smiled slowly.

"Of course. I've been told the two of you will marry soon. Congratulations." Nora blushed and managed a fleeting glance at Duane's eyes. Edris, who was nervous too but still more interested than intimidated, looked longer and saw a kind of cloudy quality in them. He wondered what was causing it.

The king, clearly displeased with being ignored, interjected loudly, "You must be tired from your journey. We have rooms prepared for you and your attendants, and a feast will be held in your honor at sundown."

Duane turned back to King Bastian, seeming a little surprised he had spoken. "Yes. Thank you, Your Majesty." He nodded to the king once more, then to Edris and Nora, before leading his party from the hall. When they'd gone, the king stood up from his seat, and it was clear that court was finished for the day. Edris expected his father to come down and scold him about something or other, but he had gone through the back door up to the keep before anyone else rose from their seats. That was fine with him.

After giving the king a while to go ahead of him, Edris started back up the stairs himself, and Nora followed. "That was amazing— I mean, he was every bit as... *different* as I thought he'd be," she said breathlessly. "Wasn't he?" Edris nodded, and kept climbing the stairs back to his balcony. Nora came with him. "I mean, I've seen him before, from a distance in a parade back at home, but this was different."

"Right," he said. "Listen, Nora, I'm going to read for a while longer and then I need to get ready for the feast."

The girl was not dissuaded. "Of course. I thought we might do that together. We'll have to enter together, after all."

"I'd really just like to be alone right now," he snapped, nearly cutting her off, and she looked back at him, hurt. "I'm sorry. There's just... a lot going on these days."

"No, of course, I know that," she said suddenly, moving closer to him and grasping his hand. Edris's eyes widened and he glanced down the claustrophobic dimly-lit stairwell for approaching court- iers but found none. "The Godhead came here for a reason, Edris. He could have stayed with anyone else, but he came *here*. I bet that means he believes you could be the Last King." He squirmed even more— prophecies had always made him uneasy, and he thought that was a bit of a leap.

Nora was blushing by the time he looked back at her, and she said, "I know I'm not a princess or anything, but I think I could help you. I want you to be able to talk to me because you can't do this by yourself. If you'll have me, that is," she added, looking down at the ground again.

Edris felt something between pity and compassion come over him and he said, "I don't care that you're not... thank you, Nora. Let's go up to the keep together."

The girl looked relieved, more than he would expect, and he started to wonder what the stakes for her were in their relationship. What was there for her if she failed to become queen? Thoughts like that, about everyone else's problems, had been creeping into Edris's mind more and more lately, and he wasn't thrilled. It was making every decision harder, and every emotion more complicated. He figured that was part of being a future king; all of his decisions had consequences for people he really had nothing to do with. If this was what coming into his crown would be like, he wasn't sure he wanted it at all.

By the time the sun had set, he was leading Nora down to the great hall once again, this time around through the entrance hall. He was clothed in heavy blues and deep browns of the Thorne house, with a small silver bear pinned to his chest. Nora was wearing a dress of the same blue, with a pendant bearing the Warren house owl around her neck, and when the doors were thrown open and their names announced, she managed to smile at him for the shortest of moments before processing in down the several tables full of Caspar's Dale nobles and Holy Guard soldiers alike.

Edris left Nora at the second-highest table with her father, and noticed as he made his way to the High Table that his seat had been placed on Riyan's left hand side, with the king on his right. Edris nodded to his father, looking pensively at his lap, before bowing low in front of the Godhead and taking his seat.

"Your Holiness," Edris said, and Riyan smiled.

"Prince Edris."

The feast began almost immediately after he sat, the last party to arrive ranking high enough to delay serving. Duane ate the meat and cheese put in front of him much more hungrily than Edris would have expected from someone of his frame, and said after a while, "You have better food in the Dale than the Temple."

"Thank you, Your Holiness," Edris said, although he wasn't sure he had ever had anything to do with the cooking there. Hunting he'd done a few times, but his father liked to be alone when he killed things.

"Please," he said, laughing, and for the first time the prince saw a human man around his age breaking through. "We're both men of the Father. Call me Riyan and I'll call you Edris."

"You honor me," Edris said, unsure of what else he could say.

"Honestly, though. This is fantastic. But I suppose it might just be that at the Temple I don't have the urge to eat as much."

"Oh," Edris said, nodding slowly, still confused. Riyan seemed to notice and smiled.

"The Godwine suppresses the appetite. That's why you don't see many fat priests." And that's when the thinness and the cloudy eyes started to make sense. Godwine was talked about at Fen Faris, a little, but it was mostly a secret of the Priesthood. Edris knew there was some kind of leaf or fungus ground up and mixed into the drink, that they were told gave the priests visions of the Duality, Astor and Morra themselves.

"I see," Edris said, nodding, "and I guess you would drink a lot of it."

"At least once a week, when I'm home," Riyan said, nodding. "It's how I open up to the Father. But it doesn't leave the temple, so when I travel I fall out of touch a little bit. It brings me closer to worldly things. So... food tastes better."

"Well, there's the blessing in it, I guess," Edris said, trying to sound light, but as he looked at the cloudy film over Riyan's eyes, he wondered how young he'd been when he'd had his first taste of Godwine. The priests didn't take it until their fifth year of training, and by then almost none of them were younger than 20. That had to make some kind of difference.

The feast dragged on, like these things often did, at least to Edris. Riyan talked about *everything*. Most of it was religious theory, which Edris actually felt qualified to talk about, but when the subject turned to politics he felt himself falling behind out of an ignorance that frustrated him. His father, the undeniable source of this ignorance, engaged with the Godhead and seemed to look apologetically at his son every so often, as if he wasn't the one who'd culled the keep's library of anything that would make Edris 'soft' like cultural studies.

"I heard that you are keeping Eirosian soldiers in your watchtower," Riyan said as they were serving dessert, and Edris sat up a little straighter.

"That's true," he said, before his father could respond, and the young man's eyes swiveled back to him with interest. "I was on the patrol that day."

"Really?" he asked. "What did you make of them?"

"They were... unflinching, Your Holiness," Edris said. Riyan's expression twitched and he amended, "Uh, Riyan. They insisted their story was all there was to say."

"Well, it isn't," the Godhead said, looking somewhat sad. "King Silas is dead. I've seen it, I see the morning after the Siege often." In the wine-dreams, Edris was sure, and despite the awe he felt in the presence of such a man, he couldn't convince himself to put stock in a vision, no matter whose it was.

King Bastian didn't share the hesitation. "That is disappointing, Your Holiness. If there were noblemen left in Eirosia, they might be converted, and could save their kingdom. But we thought long ago they were slaughtered, and it seems we were right."

"These men could be the last remaining highborns of their country, though," Riyan said. "It could be useful to send them to my Army at Astor Post with your reserve forces, Your Majesty. They might be able to bring some of their people to the Father."

Edris felt his heartbeat pick up and a feeling of dread at the idea take hold, though he had no clue why. "A noble thought, Your Holiness," the king said. Edris could hear the dismissal in his father's voice, however polite he seemed. "But they are not easily persuaded. Perhaps if you spoke to them."

"I don't speak with heretics," Riyan said sharply. "I'm sorry, but my Council says it is blasphemy for them to see me. But my Lord Marshal your nephew may be able to make use of them."

"It will be done, Your Holiness," the king said. Riyan looked back over at Edris, who had just finished the sliver of white cake that had been placed in front of him as he listened to the deals made over his head. The sweet taste of the rare pure sugar hadn't sat as well with him once it was certain Neill and his men would be going to the border. He understood his dread now. All his windows into the world outside of the Dale were leaving him at once.

"So are you going to marry Lady Nora after all?" Riyan asked, making his evening somehow even worse. "Brother Spencer told me you would, but I know you're not officially bound."

"It's a very new arrangement," Edris said. "That's the only reason why. We haven't been to a monthly worship yet since I asked her. But yes."

"Congratulations," Riyan said. "I'll be married soon, too."

"Yes, I know," Edris said, "Princess Samira."

"That's been planned for years," the Godhead said, "but it will be nice to confirm it at this festival. Declarations are beautiful ceremonies, I think. I didn't have one, but you know, I'm different, my family doesn't have much of a say in my affairs. Anyway, I love the prayers and the handbinding— it's such a better ceremony when there's an arrangement to anoint. But you remember Princess Lyha's, I'm sure."

Edris tried not to flush as he said, as casually as possible, "Yes. Of course. It was very beautiful."

"I'm very sorry for your loss, Edris," Riyan said, and leaned into him somewhat, his cloudy eyes gripping the prince's attention. "The Halwoods are cursed, there's no doubt about that."

"Yes," he said, uncomfortable now.

"The brother and mother touched by Eiros, then her disappearance, and now King Eronn is dying."

"I know," Edris said quietly, "I heard. An awful way to die."

"Hopefully Prince Deronn will be luckier. I'll most likely go to see him when his father finally goes to Cor Hara. I'll need to do the coronation, of course."

"Right," Edris said.

"In any case, it's good you're moving on. We sent out searches for her in the beginning, but it's been so long now, I doubt anyone will ever find her. It's horrible, but most girls who disappear..." Riyan trailed off before he frowned and added, "It's so strange that no one saw *anything*. Even you. You were with her just before, weren't you?"

"Yes," Edris said, trying not to visibly shudder at the muted intensity of the Godhead's gaze. "She went out to the chapel to pray to the Mother after our binding. They do devotionals at midnight in the Hartlands, so it was dark and I asked to go with her but she wanted to be alone. She never came back."

"Awful," Riyan said quietly. He was unblinking, and Edris's stomach sank. He hadn't believed him, that much was obvious. "Well. We all have obligations. And you'll need a queen. I hope you and Lady Nora will have a happy partnership."

"Thank you," Edris said, and suddenly he felt horribly sick. "If you'll excuse me," he said, and hurried out of the hall without waiting for an answer.

He made it to the toilets without being sick, but found he wasn't really nauseous once he was there. Just horrified, and maybe a little disgusted. He just lied to the Godhead. He didn't have to, he could have finally admitted what he'd done. Riyan was right, she'd never be found, but that didn't mean it didn't matter. Why had he lied for her? Why had he *been* lying for her, all this time?

To save his own skin, he told himself, with a familiar tint of self-hatred that brought him back to his rational mind. He couldn't very well confess what had happened that night *now*, to the Godhead of all people, and leave Nora stranded, among many other even less pleasant consequences. He'd have to live with it now.

That train of thought led from one guilt to another as he walked outside to feel the cool air whistling through the valley, and before he knew it his feet were taking him down the main road toward the patrol gate and through to the courtyard of the Eye of Astor. Just as he'd guessed, the entire Valleyguard was at the feast, and when he reached the Spire and eased the door open, he discovered to his relief that so were Spencer's apprentices. He wasn't sure if he was allowed to be here, but he'd rather not find out that way.

He felt his stomach twisting in knots again as he passed through the back door to the cells beyond, and calmed his nerves as best he could. There were at least a dozen barred doors in the narrow hallway, circling around the spire's outer and inner wall, and Edris walked down the small path carved in the middle past many empty cells until he saw the glint of armor through the bars.

The Eirosians, all six of them, were in the one room, still wearing the armor they'd come there in weeks ago. Neill sat against the wall opposite the cage bars, his armor stripped away, and his tunic was frayed at the edges and stained with blood dried brown. Edris knelt to be even with his gaze, and the knight opened tired, heavy eyes when he did.

"Your Highness," he said, and coughed several times as he sat up straighter against the cell wall.

"Don't get up," Edris urged him. The knight paused, and looked him over in the silence that followed. He broke first, glancing down at the ground. "I came to tell you that you'll be going to Astor Post with a guard of Thorncliffe men."

"Where's that?" one of the other men, clearly in better shape than his captain, asked.

"The Horn of Morra. Right on the Eirosian border."

"Down by the Canyon," another man said, and whispers broke out, anxious and quick.

"Yes. They want you to speak to Jonn Thorne, the Lord Marshal."

"Why is the Guard going down?" Neill asked.

"They're preparing for a battle," Edris said. He couldn't keep the jealousy out of his voice and Neill noticed. The ghost of a smile appeared on the knight's pale face.

"They're going to lose. Don't be so sorry you're here in your walled city, Your Highness. When you're face to face with the Daemons, honor and glory won't really seem worth it anymore."

Edris felt his face burning, and before he could really think it through, he could feel he'd made a decision. He wasn't going to let Neill think he was a coward. And maybe fighting Daemons would stop him from feeling so uneasy about the Spire of the Eye, or Nora, or even Lyha Halwood. "I'm going with you."

Neill raised his eyebrows, and Edris saw to his great satisfaction that there was a kind of grudging respect starting to grow behind his eyes, however disapproving he looked. "I see. Well, then. I suppose you'll see for yourself."

# 6

## Samira

When the first noble party announced themselves on the bridge leading over the Den Morra River into Hollisport, Samira panicked. But it wasn't the Godhead, just her aunt and uncle coming from their seat in the Riverland. She saw the black-and-green banners of the brand new House Bennett just before Roma came onto her balcony to tell her they were there. When she went down to the courtyard with her brother to wait for them, she couldn't hear much cheering from along the road, and that would have been as good a clue as any. Aunt Sanya might have been the king's sister, but her husband was only a knight, and a newly created noble house didn't get much respect from the Hornish until the third or fourth generation.

The doors to the courtyard flew open soon enough, and the couple and their attendants rode proudly through the gates. Aunt Sanya, still graceful and beautiful at two years past 50, dismounted her horse first and was rushing toward the two of them before her guards had even come to a stop. "Mason! Mother Morra, you've grown so much!" She enveloped her nephew in a hug and he disappeared among her long sleeves and skirts. Sanya was tall, especially for a woman, nearing six foot with her riding boots on, and Samira had always scoffed at people's insistence that she was just like her. She was a good seven or eight inches shorter, to start, and Samira had never dreamed to believe she had the poise of her father's famously charming older sister.

With a wide smile, Sanya released the younger Hollis and strode over to Samira, clasping her hands in hers. "And you, Sami, I can't believe you're sixteen. It makes me feel older than I've ever been comfortable with."

"Sorry, Aunt Sanya," she laughed, and they hugged briefly. Peeking under her aunt's arm, she could see that Uncle Lyam was handing his horse off to a stableboy behind them and making his way toward his wife.

"We're so glad to be here, Sami," he said when the women had ended the hug, and instead of going for one himself he took his wife's hand and smiled politely at his niece. Samira's mood dampened as she understood why; grown men didn't touch grown women who weren't their own blood. Her days of hugging her uncle were over. The thought was a little depressing, so she turned around quickly to lead them forward into the keep.

"Let's go find my dad, he's been waiting to see you," she said. Mason and their aunt and uncle walked with her through the entrance hall, up seven flights of stairs overlooking the open room before the door to the inner keep. The Skytower had twenty-five stories of space to fill, and cavernous chambers in the most conspicuous spaces played a large part in that. Aunt Sanya had grown up here, but it was obvious to Samira that Uncle Lyam was not thrilled with the height.

The reception hall was the first room reached through the door on the seventh floor, and the king and queen were overseeing the festival planning when the four of them came in. Almost as soon as they'd opened the doors, servants were bustling past them with arm-fuls of firewood and decorations, murmuring apologies to the royal family as they went. When they managed to reach Samira's mother and father, Aunt Sanya and the king embraced with big smiles and the queen and Uncle Lyam bowed to one another. "Danny, it's so good to see you!" Sanya exclaimed.

"You too," the king replied, smiling more than Samira had seen in a while. "Can you believe this is happening already?"

"No," Sanya said firmly. "You should never have let her get so old."

"I know," he said, shaking his head. "I should lock her up in the Astrium for her own protection." He was still grinning at his sister, but Samira almost wished he was serious. Mason squirmed at her side, like he was thinking the same thing. King Daniel then turned to Lyam and shook his hand firmly as he said, "You've braved the Skytower again, I see."

"Anything for family," Lyam managed to say, with a wry smile in his wife's direction. "But I have to say your hunting woods look much better to me than your tower."

"My land is yours," the king said. "Hunt tomorrow morning if you like. I'm trapped here with cooks and butlers, but that's the burden of the parents of the Declared. Mason would go with you, I'm sure?"

"Sami too," Mason suggested. "She's got to be going mad in here all day." Samira frowned at him, a little irritated he had just signed her up for dirt roads and violence against innocent deer, but the plea in his eyes when they locked onto hers kept her quiet.

"Why not?" the king said. A servant brought him a long scroll then that he unrolled and stared at like it had insulted him. "This final guest list won't offend anyone, will it, Marida?"

The queen peered over his shoulder and faltered. "Well, I don't think so, but..."

"I'll help," Sanya offered. "I spend all my time with the snobbiest of the lot."

"I think that's my cue," Lyam said. "I'll join you for supper. Thank you for having us, Your Majesty."

"Call me Daniel, Lyam, please," Samira's father said. "You're my brother by law."

"Maybe, but I'm still a knight of the Horn," he said, and with a respectful nod, he made his way back to the door. Mason motioned for Samira to follow him as he hurried after him, and she left the hall even more confused. When Uncle Lyam saw them close the door, he said simply, "Let's go somewhere quiet," eyeing the servants starting to come up the stairs again.

"The solar," Mason suggested. Samira led the way, wondering why the whole time. The solar was a lounge on the twelfth story of the keep, with plush sofas and high windows that had several staircases leading to the family's rooms on higher floors. It was empty when they arrived. The fire was burning low, but with everything to do for the festival, no one would come in to tend it . Uncle Lyam sat back into one of the large green sofas and bid Mason and Samira to sit across from him.

"What's this about?" Samira finally asked.

Uncle Lyam raised his eyebrows as he looked over at Mason. "You haven't told her?"

"Not exactly," Mason said, shifting his eyes to stare at his feet. "She told me it wouldn't do any good to tell you, so..."

Samira's eyes widened. In the two weeks Mason had been at the Skytower, he'd never said a word about this. "You *told* him? Mason! Did you tell anyone else?"

"No, no one!" he protested. "Sorry, Sami, it was the only thing I could think of."

"Sami, please, I'm glad he told me," Uncle Lyam said. "You can't do this by yourself. Do your parents know?"

"No," she said, feeling more uneasy every second. Her nerves were turning her stomach and making her throat dry. "They're worried enough already."

"I'd guess so," Lyam said, his expression grim. "Mason asked me if I knew anyone still here who would be able to help you, and I do, but there's only so much they could do this close to the festival. I could have gotten you a thousand miles away by now if I'd known earlier, but we couldn't do it right at this point."

"You want me to run?" she asked, surprised. She hadn't thought anyone would suggest *that*.

"This is serious, Sami," he said. "More serious than you think. I'm sure you know the Priests hate the mages, but you have no idea. You won't be hanged, it'll be much worse than that if you're caught. And the Godhead has plenty of mage-catchers in his Temple." She started to feel even sicker and he softened a little. "I'm not trying to scare you. I just need you to know the situation you're in."

"What can I do?" she asked.

"You can come hunting with us tomorrow," he said. "I know someone in Hollisport who'll help you hide it next week. You'll meet her then. But you should also start preparing yourself as best you can for what's going to happen. Magic shows itself the most in dangerous situations, and becoming the Godwife will definitely qualify."

"What do you mean?" she asked.

Uncle Lyam glanced at Mason and said, clearing his throat and shifting in his seat, "I brought one of the Holy texts on the subject. It's probably best if you read it yourself. What I meant is you should start getting ready for the next few months. It will make hiding a lot easier."

Samira nodded slowly, and gingerly set the scroll he passed her onto the table between them. "Thank you."

"Of course. I wish I could do more. We managed to get Loran to the Isles in time, but you'd be much harder to make disappear."

Samira and Mason both stared at their uncle in shock. "Sorry?" Mason asked, his voice faint.

Uncle Lyam looked again like he had said more than he'd wanted to. "Um... yes. Your cousin had the same—problem."

"Loran was a mage?" Samira exclaimed. She couldn't imagine the tall, handsome boy she remembered as anything other than a typical sword-swinging noble. Uncle Lyam nervously glanced at the door, and she lowered her voice. "Sorry, but— how...?"

"He *is* a mage," Lyam corrected. "Living on the Lordless Isles, with some of my friends from before the Priesthood occupied the Horn. And as for how, we don't know. We thought it was my family— my father was a bastard, so who knows— but now that you are too, it's more likely that it's someone in your father's line." Samira and Mason exchanged an incredulous look— to say the Hollis family had mage blood was blasphemy, heresy even. Mages were men, and royals were from the line of Astor and Morra themselves, according to the Holy Book. The blood did not mix— a royal mage was an abomination in the eyes of the Priesthood. And Uncle Lyam was saying she was likely far from the only one. That would get many more than just Samira sent to the gallows.

Uncle Lyam frowned at their reaction and said, "I hope you don't still believe nobility has no magic blood. Most of the courts in the Triad have at least one mage among them. The bastard at Surpoint's mother... well," he said, coughing self-consciously, "I shouldn't say more. I'm going to find a bath before supper. Read that," he added, glancing at the scroll, "and remember to come to the stables in the morning." Mason clambered over to read over her shoulder as Samira unrolled the parchment, but their uncle called out, "Mason, give her some privacy." With an apologetic look, her brother followed Lyam up the south stairwell out of sight. Alone, she took a deep breath, and began to read.

### *The Godhead and the Godwife: The Father and Mother of the New Land*

*When the Godhead of each generation comes of age, His Holiness is soon to take a wife, as the companionship of a marriage was the salvation of the Mother and Father when the world was new ("...and she rejoiced in the warmth the two lights brought the Earth" 2:4)This holy union is to be modeled for all followers of the Duality here in the Triad, as the Godhead is their example of holy life until such time as they become worthy of Father Astor and Mother Morra's return. The Godwife should be of Tol's people, a royal daughter, while the Godhead is of both races, Men and Kings. This will ensure the unity of all the peoples of the Triad.*

*The Godhead is not a role passed from father to son, and if His Holiness were to have children, they may try to claim the holy calling from the rightful heir chosen by the Council upon his death. While he must take a wife, they must not bear children. Of course, this does not mean that they must not lie together, as that would dishonor the foundations of Astor and Morra's Holy Union. Indeed, they must lie together, but there are many ways in which the Godwife herself may be prevented from bearing a child before their wedding night.*

Samira didn't make it to a chamberpot before she was sick.

* * *

When she was up the next morning, with a handmaiden helping her lace her hunting boots for the ride, she was still shaken from what she'd read the night before. Hours later, after dinner when she was alone in her room, she had unfolded the scroll again and read the rest of the text. It had only gotten worse, and more detailed. She was more outraged than ever that her father was just... letting this happen. But maybe he didn't know. She couldn't see how, but she had to give him that benefit of the doubt, if she was going to keep seeing him every morning without being sick.

Roma looked up when she'd finished tying the laces and said hesitantly, "Have fun, Your Highness."

"Thanks," she said, but she felt like she was hardly there in the room with this girl at all. She made her way down to the stables alone, knowing she'd overslept after lying awake until well past midnight but hoping they hadn't had to leave without her. Thankfully, when she rounded the corner in the courtyard leading into the stables, she found Lyam and Mason and the stableboy, and no one else in sight.

"Good morning," Lyam said, as cheerful as he'd been when he'd arrived yesterday, but as Samira mounted the horse the boy gave her, she could see he was watching her closely. "Everything alright?"

"I'm fine," she said, meeting his gaze and trying to seem as strong as she could. The last thing she wanted to do was talk about *that* with a man three times her age, uncle or not. He nodded once and thanked the stableboy before taking off at a quick gallop, Mason and Samira fighting to keep up as they went. It was foggy and damp that morning, and the two of them urged their horses forward so as not to lose their uncle in the mist.

Mason pulled ahead of her before long, and she then noticed that her brother was carrying a bow and arrows, fit to his size, and Uncle Lyam had the same. No one had given her anything like that, and she was both offended and relieved. She didn't want to be thought of as too fragile to hunt, but she really didn't like the idea of it either. Her father had taken her when she was little, once, and she'd cried the whole way back to the castle after they'd shot the deer she had been so fascinated by. That was in front of an entire royal hunting party, which was why Samira thought it was a poor excuse for why she was leaving the keep now, but on they went anyway.

Uncle Lyam slowed his horse to a stop when they'd reached the creek, a runoff of the Den Morra River roaring past the city to the northeast, and he tied his reins to a nearby tree before starting to walk along the bank. Samira and Mason did the same, and curious, they followed him until he stopped halfway across a crumbling stone bridge, stretching across the creek into a much denser part of the wood. When they reached him, he held up a hand to stop them from following, and for a moment all was quiet. Then, on the other side of the water, a woman stepped out of the thick brambles at the creek's edge, wrapped in a thick cloak and shawl. "Farrah," Lyam greeted her. "Thank you for coming."

"What's this about, Sir Lyam?" the woman, Farrah, asked, as she removed her hood. Her face was dark, darker than most of the faces in Hollisport, and she had black hair in a long braid falling over her shoulder and down the front of her thick wool shawl. Her face changed to something wary when she saw Samira and Mason and she bowed slowly. "Your Highnesses."

"This is Samira," Lyam said, and led her forward in front of him until she was just a few paces from Farrah. "She's meeting her husband in a few days."

"Right," the woman said slowly. "May the Mother bless you, Princess."

"Thank you," she said, almost reflexively at this point. She looked in the woman's eyes and saw some measure of sympathy there, not the empty praise and hints of envy she'd gotten from most of the people congratulating her lately. She didn't seem like a noblewoman; that was probably why. Highborns were much more likely to be religious and much less likely to have had Eirosian friends, before.

"Samira, this is Farrah Vance. She's a friend of mine, from a very old family on the Lordless Isles," Uncle Lyam said. So that was why she looked so strange. "She's the best chance I know of in Hollisport to help you."

"Why does she need help?" Farrah asked, narrowing her eyes. She had seemed jumpy the entire time, but it was getting gradually worse. However she knew Uncle Lyam, she obviously didn't really trust him.

"Show her, Sami," he told her. Samira hesitated. She'd never really *tried* to do magic before. It had always sort of... happened to her. But she knew her magic was elemental, naturally based, and they were standing over a creek. So she took a deep breath and leaned over the side of the bridge. Extending her hands, she tried to focus as much as she could on the water below her, and before long, she had managed to create a small swirling vortex, like a drain pulling the creek into the middle of the path it was carving through the wood.

"Stop that," Farrah said suddenly a minute or so into her demonstration. "Someone could be nearby." When Samira turned around again, the woman was staring at her, aghast. "You're... but you're marrying *him*."

"So you see the problem," Uncle Lyam said.

"Yes, I see the problem," Farrah said, rolling her eyes. Samira was fascinated by this woman, a commoner with a foreign face who rolled her eyes at the brother-by-law of the king. Was everyone from the Lordless Isles like her? "What do you think I can do about it?"

"Is there any way to disguise her magic?" Uncle Lyam asked. "Temporarily, I mean. Just to get her through the festival."

Farrah frowned. "Maybe. I could make her a Mother amulet, but it would have to be incredibly strong. I'll need time."

"How much time?"

"As much time as you can get me," she said. "Come to take it at the last possible moment."

"We can give you... a week, possibly," Uncle Lyam said, frowning. "Even that I'm not sure of."

"I'll try," she said, eyeing Samira again warily.

"You're a mage, then," she said, trying to keep herself from getting obviously excited. "Do you think... could you teach me anything? I don't really know how I did that just now— I've never known any-one else who could help me learn..."

Farrah was already shaking her head. "I am a mage, but I'm not what you're looking for. I'm an artificer. You're elemental. I can make you any potion or amulet you could ever want, but the waters don't pay me any mind. And anyway, the more you learn, the stronger your scent will be, for lack of a better word. It'll be harder to hide. And in your circumstances..."

"Right," she said, trying not to be too disappointed. "Well, thank you for this."

"Don't thank me yet," she said. "Send someone to my house in town on the last day before High Spring. I'll do my best to finish by then."

"Thank you, Farrah," Uncle Lyam said.

Farrah pulled her hood back over her head and said, "You know I've owed you for years, Sir. But this... wasn't what I was expecting." Shaking her head, she turned around and crossed back into the line of trees, disappearing from sight.

"It shouldn't be too difficult to find a servant you trust to get out of the castle," Uncle Lyam said. "If the Godhead isn't here yet, it should go unnoticed."

Samira just nodded, despite how uncomfortable she was with the whole idea. Just a month or so ago, she'd been the only one who'd known her secret, and it'd been that way for years. Now, the number had grown to six, at least, and didn't seem likely to stop growing. This was only getting more dangerous. "Why does Farrah owe you?"

"The group of mages that sailed for the Isles," Uncle Lyam told her. "I made sure her sister was among them."

"Oh," Samira said. "Why not her?"

Uncle Lyam smiled in the polite way that meant he was finished talking. "Another time."

"Do you think Farrah could make me a potion that would stop my voice from breaking?" Mason asked, laughing. "I mean, she said she could make anything, right?"

"Magic isn't funny, Mason," Samira said quietly, and he sobered with a grimace.

"Right. Sorry."

"Come on, then," Uncle Lyam said as he mounted his horse again. "We've got to go back having shot something or it'll be suspect." They set off down the well-worn hunting grounds of the outer wood, and Mason managed to shoot a hare soon enough, though not anywhere near through the eye. Samira might have been more sensitive to violence than usual, after spending the night contemplating all the ways the Priests would inflict it upon her, but whatever the reason, every time an arrow was loosed she flinched horribly. And she nearly fell off her horse when the silence of the hunt was interrupted by the piercing sound of a steward's trumpet along the main road a few hundred yards away. They all exchanged looks and rode up to the edge of the wood in time to see a small party of riders making their way into town.

"It's not *him*, is it?" Mason asked. Samira craned her neck to try to make out their sigils, and her stomach dropped when, despite the fog enveloping them, she saw the golden sun-and-moon symbol standing out on their dull leather-plated armor.

"It is," she said miserably. She was *dead*.

"No," Uncle Lyam said, "the Godhead would have much more fanfare. Those are Holy soldiers, but he's not with them."

"The guard!" Mason exclaimed. "Remember I told Dad, Sami? They're sending knights from Astor Post for your protection."

Uncle Lyam swore. "Well, the Godhead might not be here yet," he said, "but no one's leaving the tower without them knowing."

# 7

## Mychal

Mychal was allowed to sleep in his chambers in the hall next to Sir James's room after two days in the infirmary, but leaving the camp for any reason was prohibited to him before the journey. That meant seeing Senna before he left was out of the question, and he didn't dare send a letter to Lady May's with Luke and Graham; they'd probably read it, and then he would really be in trouble. He did ask them to tell her where he was going, hoping she'd realize the danger in it, but when they came back for the night they just said she'd wished him good luck.

It wasn't her fault, he knew, it wasn't like she knew *why* he was so scared of going to Hollisport. But there were moments when he wished *someone* knew. Then he'd think better of it and try to turn his thoughts to, well, anything else.

He didn't think either of his friends would be coming with them, but Sir Callum was ordered by Lord Thorne to go after he had been insufferable at meetings planning the assault on the Canyon, so Luke was attending as well. Mychal privately thought Thorne should send Sir Callum *home* instead, but he kept his mouth shut, like he always did. He'd never talked back to any of the officers, he was too intimidated, but he didn't know how anyone could come away from service thinking that passing down military ranks like family heirlooms was a good idea.

Sir James was given command of the party, as he was from the crownlands and Sir Callum wasn't, and the older knight was infuriated at the slight. Mychal missed most of this apart from what Luke conveyed after council meetings. He had too much trouble getting around to attend that week, but exactly seven days after his injury, he could walk well enough to get himself down to the stables and climb onto Gale's back with all his armor and his sword at his side.

The road to Hollisport would take eight days, possibly nine, and at first it was excruciatingly silent, but eventually the knights and squires started to talk to each other. He didn't know anyone there apart from Luke, though, who was riding with sullen Sir Callum far at the back of the party. Mychal was a squire now, but he'd hardly been at work after the fight at the holdfast, and the others were all highborn and not very willing to talk to a 'tailor's son'. It was mostly Sir James that he talked to. As they rode further along the Holy Road, the knight talked to him about growing up in the Horn.

"I wasn't born in Fen Faris but my family lived there for years when I was young," he said one morning, the fifth day of their ride, when they were close enough to the Stewards' city and on a high enough hill that they could just make out the outline of the buildings a few miles south. "I studied for a bit, but I was never all that bright. I wanted to squire as soon as I was old enough and my parents were perfectly alright with that."

"It looks like a beautiful city, sir," Mychal said, although when he looked down to Fen Faris below them he wasn't thinking about a young Sir James, but Deronn, somewhere in one of the Stewards' halls and probably only months from being crowned a king at 11.

He wished he could find out more about his father, and what the Priesthood was planning to do when the cancer finally took him.

Sir James hadn't stopped talking. "Do you know what Fen Faris means?"

"No, sir." He did, actually, but he wasn't supposed to, he knew enough to know that.

"'Fen' is 'tomb' in the Old Language. The city was founded when Faris was buried there— 'tomb of Faris'. The Stewards founded their order at his tomb because Faris had been building the Skytower to try to reach the gods when he was murdered. They study to finish what he started, in their own way."

"The Skytower's where we're going, isn't it, sir?"

Sir James nodded. "The Hollises are the sons of Faris's legitimate line. His bastard son's sons founded House Halwood in the Hartlands. So if you hear anyone in Hollisport calling the Halwoods the bastard kings, try not to take offense." He seemed like he was joking, but Mychal had heard that before, and had never liked it. He stayed quiet. The knight seemed to understand that and said, "Well, anyway. Can I ask you a question, son?"

Mychal was startled into paying much closer attention then. Sir James had never been that familiar with him. It made him nervous. "Yes, sir?"

"Why did you join us? Sir Callum says most of the Hartlanders have no great love for the Holy Army."

"I... wanted to serve the Godhead, sir," he said, his heart pounding.

Sir James sighed. "It's alright, Mychal. You can speak freely. I only joined because I wanted to be a knight. And Lord Thorne made me one after we beat back the northeast invasions in '87. I'm an officer by now because King Daniel never sent for me and that's that."

Mychal did relax a little then, although he was still a little worried this was a trap, and without lying he still managed to say, "It was the best opportunity I had, sir. I wanted to leave Queenshearth and make something of myself."

The knight smiled kindly. "Well, you're well on your way to that. You'll be a man soon enough, and a knight someday; you might even start your own House."

Mychal managed to smile. *Not likely.* "I don't know about that, sir."

"Trust me. You've had your first kill before your first shave. There's something different about you, Mychal. And you might think I'm a Hornish snob but I think there's great honor in forging your way in the world. I'm proud to train you."

"Thank you, sir," he said, trying not to go red in the face. He didn't like thinking about killing the marauder, it made him feel strange, but he recognized the compliment in what Sir James was saying. Still, that day at the holdfast haunted him the whole road to Hollisport. They were from the Lordless Isles; wasn't that where Senna sent her letters? He couldn't bring himself to consider that he might have derailed some resistance against the Priesthood because they'd thought he was one of them. He'd liked it better when he'd thought they were Daemons.

The morning of the ninth day, a single stone spire pierced the skyline and came into the party's view. Soon after that, another imposing structure, King Haddon's cathedral, emerged out of the fog, and then the sprawling merchant city of Hollisport came to life in front of them. Mychal found himself transfixed by the sheer height of the first spire they'd seen, having revealed itself to be the tallest part of a much larger grand tower. "That's the Hollises' keep," Sir James told him, noting his awe with tactfully restrained amusement. "The Skytower. King Faris's greatest achievement."

"How does it stay up?" Mychal asked, breathless, as Gale whinnied and shook his head beneath him, clearly annoyed at how slowly his master was now leading him along.

The knight laughed a little at that. "The greatest masons in the

Triad at the time spent their lives working on it. That, and some say magic holds the stones together." Invoking magic in a Holy uniform was a little subversive for what Mychal had gotten used to, and Sir James met his surprised expression with a conspiratorial wink. "Come on, then, Orran's Bridge is only a mile away."

The party crossed the Den Morra River on the crumbling stone bridge, at least four hundred years old judging from the namesake, which made Mychal only too glad when Gale's hooves touched solid ground again on the other side. Past the river, it was only a short path through the royal hunting grounds to the northern city gates, and one of the squires blew the trumpet on Sir James's command as they rode up to the main streets of Hollisport.

The gates slowly groaned open when they were close enough to ride through, and when they slammed shut behind them Mychal felt a knot growing in his stomach. When they reached the Skytower, their horses were led away to the stables from the courtyard, and they were left to wait for an escort inside. The might of the Skytower was no less impressive at its base, and Mychal was only one of many soldiers gazing up the steeply sloped walls of the keep. He couldn't shake the terrible feeling he had about coming here, but the tower really was something to behold.

"Brothers," a voice called out from the doorway into the tower. "Welcome to Hollisport." Mychal looked back down to the ground and saw a balding, portly Priest with the usual blue robes and empty sheath walking out to greet them. "I'm Brother Andrian, of Haddon's Cathedral here in the city. King Daniel asked me to welcome you myself and escort you to the Great Hall."

"Thank you," Sir James said, striding forward to greet the priest. To Mychal, he seemed uneasy. "Sir James Reinhold, Captain of the Holy Army and Knight of the Horn. I'm in command of this guard for the duration of the festival."

"May Astor sharpen your swords," Andrian said, bowing his

head briefly and shaking Sir James's hand. "We're grateful for your help, sir. If you'll all follow me to the hall you'll be presented to the family." The entire party followed the priest, and Mychal hurried to catch up to Sir James, though he was more than a little uncomfortable at the idea of a royal presentation. He thought he'd be likely to draw less attention to himself if he was closely following the knight he was squiring-- at least, he hoped.

They passed through the cavernous entrance hall, the ceiling higher than anywhere Mychal had seen in years, if not ever, and saw that servants were already setting cots up along the walls for them. He hadn't known that the castle would know they were coming, although he guessed living in a 300-foot-tall tower made not knowing who was approaching nearly impossible. The party was taken up a very tall spiral staircase that made Mychal a little nauseous, the one time he lost his resolve enough to look down.

The first door they came to opened to the great hall of the keep, and he started to panic, but the only three waiting for them were adults, two women and a man, standing alone in the center of the room. The man was cloaked in the colors of House Hollis, a dark green and ash gray, and he walked toward them with such an air of ease and confidence that Mychal would have been sure this was King Daniel even if he hadn't met him years ago. Sir James bowed in front of him, as did all the other knights, quickly followed by the squires.

"Thank you for coming," King Daniel exclaimed, looking around at all of them, before shaking Sir James's hand. "Sir Reinhold," he said, "thank you for your devotion to my daughter's protection." The king's smile was tight, and Mychal tried not to wince-- he didn't want them there, that much was clear.

"It's an honor, Your Highness," Sir James said., and if he noticed the king's expression, he ignored it.

"I'm sorry to say she isn't here, but she sends her thanks," Daniel said. "She's gone hunting with my son and my brother-by-law. But allow me to present my wife, Queen Marida Dillon Hollis, and my sister, Lady Sanya Hollis Bennett of Watershed Ford."

The queen, a pale woman with dark hair and wide eyes, smiled at them, and Lady Sanya bowed. She towered over most of the squires and half of the knights, and Mychal could tell most of them were a little intimidated—there wasn't a girl within five miles of Astor Post, except for at Lady May's, and this woman, with her own lordship and a warrior's build, made Mychal smile and the other boys squirm. He knew he'd hear about her later, in a variety of ways, but to him there was something excellent about her.

"It is our pleasure to serve you, Your Highness," Sir James told the queen, and Andrian stepped forward from his position to Mychal's left.

"Brother," he said to the king, "should I see them to your captain of the guard or—?"

The doors to the hall swung open again, and Mychal, who had been a little more relaxed than he'd thought he would be, stiffened once more. Another three people entered the hall, this time armed: a middle-aged man and a young boy, both carrying bows and bloodied arrows as they made their way through the soldiers toward the king, and there she was, Princess Samira, following after them.

She looked just like he'd expected, just like she had years before, only with the grace of having coming of age now. They'd both still been children, really, the last time they were together. Samira was even more beautiful today, if that was even possible. Her hunting boots tracked mud onto the stone as she walked past them, and a long plait of red hair trailed down her tunic layered over riding trousers. She wasn't looking at them then, Mychal's one solace in his terror.

The older man laughed and embraced Sir James when he'd reached him, and Mychal took the opportunity to attempt to slink behind a few of the other squires. It didn't work; no one was moving, and he couldn't dare draw attention to himself. When Luke shot him a confused look, he stopped himself from moving any more and tried to calm himself down. Obviously, he looked different now, but *how* different? Was she going to notice him?

"Jamie!" the man exclaimed.

"Hello, sir," he replied, grinning.

"This is Sir Lyam Bennett of the Riverland, though it seems you know each other," King Daniel said, a hint of a smile starting to form on his lips.

"Know each other? I was the one who taught Jamie how to swing a sword."

"Well, I don't know about that, I was fourteen when I met you," he corrected him gently.

"Exactly. Thank the Father someone came along and helped the poor boy."

"Alright," Sir James chuckled. "It's good to see you, sir." Mychal, from his vantage point behind the knight's shoulder, could see Samira starting to survey the room curiously. He tried to crowd even closer to the others in front of him, almost feeling safe in being unseen. This couldn't go on for much longer, could it? He could escape soon?

"How was the hunting?" the king asked.

"Mason shot a hare," Sir Lyam exclaimed, clapping the gangly prince on the shoulder. "We took it to the kitchens, so I expect we'll see it again soon."

"Excellent," King Daniel said, and nodded at his son. The king looked happier around his family, but there was a level of anxiety that never seemed to leave him. He then looked past the two of them and strode over to the princess, who'd been watching the whole affair quietly next to Lady Sanya. He brought her forward in front of Sir James and said, "My daughter, Princess Samira."

"Your Highness," Sir James said, kneeling in front of her. When he knelt, Samira's eyes met Mychal's, caught watching her. He quickly averted his gaze, heart pounding, but as Sir James stood again he could practically feel her eyes boring into him. *Shit.* "I swear my sword to your protection until High Spring passes."

"Thank you, Sir," she said, after just a moment's hesitation. Mychal dared to look at her again and found her bowing her head in respect to Sir James before retreating back into the fold of the rest of the Hollises. She had gone slightly red, and her eyebrows were knitted together, the way he knew all too well. She'd seen. He was dead.

"Well, then," King Daniel said, "yes, Brother, if you could escort them to the watch."

"Of course, Brother," Andrian said, and the priest ushered them out of the great hall and up even more flights of stairs to the sentry tower, a small turret protruding from what would be the tenth story of any normal structure. The captain of the guard was waiting for them there, and the priest disappeared almost as quickly as he'd come once they had all been led inside the cramped military post full of cots, weapons and armor. Mychal started to breathe; at least he'd been able to walk out of the room without everything crashing down.

"Captain Wythe," Sir James said, nodding to the man with the Hollis panther crest emblazoned on his breastplate.

"Sir Reinhold," he replied. "If I'm correct there's fourteen of you?" Sir James nodded and the captain continued, "Then let's have four of you take watch shifts at the door to the family's private rooms at night. We'll conduct perimeter patrols every dusk and dawn starting tonight, and when the festival begins we'll discuss who'll be stationed where. There's the ceremony in the Cathedral, and the feast, and the ball—but we'll see if we really need the men for all that."

"We're happy to help," Sir James said.

"Yes. Thank you," Captain Wythe said, and Mychal thought his smile looked more like a grimace. No one wanted them to be there, he could tell. They were only being polite, and it was making him anxious even on top of everything else. "If you'd like we can have food brought down to the hall for you to break your fast." Excited murmurs erupted from the group and he nodded. "Right, then. Good morning."

"Mychal!" Luke called as they all filed down the narrow stairway, and with some jostling, his friend reached him just as the last of the party was leaving the armory.

"Hi, Luke," he said, trying to keep his eyes and focus forward. All he wanted was to escape somewhere, to think...

"Gods, they really don't want us here, do they?" he asked, laughing a little. "At least it should be easy."

"Hope so," Mychal said, trying to sound as cheerful as Luke.

It didn't seem to work. His friend's expression changed a little as he asked, "What was that back there?"

*Damn.* "What was what?"

"You know what I mean, where were you trying to run away to?" he asked. Mychal glanced back at the other guardsmen, who were thankfully absorbed in their own conversations by now, and then back at Luke, waiting.

"I got nervous," he said, and shrugged as casually as he could. "I didn't want to be introduced. I'd never been anywhere near a king before."

Luke's face became a lot more sympathetic and he said, "Oh. You've never been to a Declaration, have you?"

Mychal figured it would make more sense to say, "No."

Luke nodded slowly and furrowed his brow. "Um... it's sort of hard to explain. I mean... have you read the Holy Book?"

"Yes," he said, patiently, trying to be thankful Luke hadn't asked him if he *could* read. Luke's interactions with him had always leaned in the direction of well-intentioned but a little insulting.

"Okay," he said. "So you know about the race of Tol being kings of Men and all that."

"Chapter 5," Mychal said, nodding.

"Declarations happen when a highborn turns sixteen. It's a sort of initiation into adulthood. Boys have ceremonial trials depending on where they're from, and girls are blessed to leave their father's house."

"So why's the Godhead coming to this one?" he asked him.

"If you have an engagement arranged already, you're supposed to meet at the woman's Declaration. They confirm the engagement right there as adults."

"Right," Mychal said quietly, trying to stay present in the conversation. Luke was noticing the way he was acting, so Mychal quickly changed the subject. "Did you have one?"

Luke took the bait, and grinned as he said, "I had a small one before I enlisted, but remember when I had leave two years ago? I went down to the Golden Forests to meet my future wife. Talia Penn... The Foresters have the best festivals. And it didn't hurt that after the festival we went for a walk and we ended up—"

"All right, Luke, that's enough," Mychal interrupted, and both of them ended up breaking into nervous laughter.

They'd made it back to the ground floor by now, and a long table was set in the entrance hall for them with bread and butter and a tankard of hot cider. Mychal had downed two cups before he knew it; he'd heard about the Hornish orchards, but nothing had done them justice. It was probably the best, sweetest thing he'd tasted in years. It had almost made him forget what they'd been talking about, until Luke looked up from his own cup and said, "I don't know how this one will be different, I've only been to Declarations in the Hartlands. But if the Godhead's coming, I'd guess it'll be a lot fancier than you'd think."

Mychal's simple happiness from the cider ebbed away and he shrugged. "Okay." Now that he'd been reminded, he couldn't banish the look on Samira's face from his mind. He'd been so worried about her seeing him at all that he hadn't processed the look on her face until now. He knew that look—she was keeping it hidden, but she was petrified. And the arrival of the knights had only made it worse. He couldn't blame her-- he didn't think anyone envied her right now-- but he didn't think her engagement was the reason why, or at least not the only reason.

"Hello?" Luke said, and Mychal snapped his thoughts back to the table. "Seriously, Owyn. What's going on?"

"Nothing," he insisted, and thanked the gods he didn't even believe in when Sir James came around the end of the table and approached the two of them at that moment.

"Payne, you'll take the first watch on the family. You'll wake Mychal to take your place at midnight."

"Yes, sir," Luke said, and the knight continued down the table as Mychal's spirits fell even further. Luke didn't look pleased either. "We just rode for nine days and now I have to stand guard for hours before I get any sleep?"

"Sorry, Luke," he said; he was annoyed too. Of everyone in the party... he shuddered at the thought of how high he'd have to climb by candlelight, and even that would be the least of his problems. What was waiting for him at the top scared him a lot more.

They were put to work on the castle grounds that day, clearing the courtyard for the festival and carrying the heaviest of the supplies up and down the stairs of the keep. Mychal was glad to be doing something, but he didn't like constant climbing, and by the end of the day his back ached and his knees were threatening to give out under him. He didn't envy Luke when he saw him marching up the stairs as the others were putting the torches out. The chance of even a couple hours' sleep before his watch was the only consolation he had in his exhaustion.

When his friend shook him awake, what felt like only moments later, he forced himself up and slipped his boots back on as quietly as he could, hooked his sword back onto his belt, and started up the Skytower's many hundreds of steps. He had lost count of how far he'd climbed when he finally reached the Hollis family solar, and was again sore and struggling for breath by the time he finally rested. Mychal began his watch. He sat down on the steps up to the royal family's private rooms, his hand on his sword and his eyes on the door in front of him.

He had thought he was going to have trouble staying awake, but as soon as he'd reached the top of the stairs he was far from relaxed enough to fall asleep. Thinking about everything that had happened that day, it was all Mychal could do not to run down to the courtyard, take Gale, and be miles out from the city before anyone noticed he was gone. His anxiety had reached such a height that he was actually considering it by the time the door behind him creaked open.

He stood up immediately, hand on the hilt of his sword, and spun around to find a young girl recoiling in fear in the doorway. He let go and held his hands up, backing away off the steps entirely. "I'm sorry I scared you. You just startled me."

"...That's alright," she said, slowly easing the door open the rest of the way. "I know it's your job."

"What are you doing out here?" he asked.

She hesitated. "Are you Sir James's squire?"

His face fell, and could feel the panic building in the back of his mind, but he said, "...Yes. Why?"

"Oh good," she sighed. "Follow me."

"What? Why?" he asked, even more wary than before.

"I'm a handmaiden for Princess Samira," the girl said. *Shit*, Mychal thought. Of course she was. He'd been right. He should have left the city hours ago. "Will you come with me?"

Mychal thought again about running for the stables, but he knew it was over. He let out a breath he hadn't known he was holding. "Alright." He followed the girl up the last few steps and down a long stone hallway, each step feeling heavier than the last. The girl opened a door at the end of the hall, bowed quickly in the doorway, and hurried down the hall. Mychal heard the door to the servants' quarters ease shut behind him and he took a deep breath before he stepped into the room. Just like he thought, Samira was there. They were silent for a moment, staring at each other in the dark. Then she spoke.

"...Lyha?"

# 8

# Edris



*TWO YEARS EARLIER*

Edris was a long way from home. He'd had his own Declaration two years before, but he'd never been to another for royalty, and he'd certainly never been further south than Fen Faris before. The rolling hills and vast woodlands of the Hartlands were like nothing he'd ever seen. At home everything was harsh, strong, imposing. It was hard for him to believe the things he'd heard about the people here, the bastard-kings and the heresy trials when he was younger. The castle at Queenshearth was warm and welcoming, too; King Eronn had received them when they'd arrived, but he hadn't seen the princess yet. They weren't meant to see each other before the ceremonies, if it could be helped, and he was told she had gone out to the woods that morning anyway. That didn't surprise him; he'd been warned that Lyha was a little, well, wild.

*Wild is good,* he thought as his steward laid out his formal dress for the festival. *She'll be able to stand up for herself against Father.* It was only when he looked down at his ceremonial clothes that he started to feel truly nervous. He was about to meet the woman who would be his wife, and he had no idea what to expect. Mostly, he was terrified he wouldn't like her. Because it wasn't as if his father would ever release him from the engagement. The very idea of it made him want to laugh. And his mother, with her health, would be no match for King Bastian in a rage. Whoever he met tonight would be his queen, and he was going to have to find a way to manage that.

Swallowing his fears, he got dressed quickly, pinning a silver bear brooch to his navy blue doublet just as a servant came to the door and announced that the court was leaving for the cathedral. Following the flood of guests pouring out of their chambers throughout the keep, he made his way down from their  rooms to the great hall and out into the street. Queenshearth was a crowded, winding city, with cobbled old streets and graystone walls that burned in the summer heat but were growing cooler with the setting sun. Faris's Cathedral was modest for a kingdom's capital, a single open court-yard surrounded by more of the same mortar and stone and benches circling around the altar. The spire towered over the rest of the buildings around it, but it wasn't exactly imposing, just... very old.

Edris's father, along with a brace of advisors, was waiting for him at the doors to the cathedral, and noblemen and women streamed by them as the king of Thorncliffe pulled his son aside. "You are the Prince of Thorncliffe," his father said, clasping a hand on his shoulder with an uncomfortable pressure that felt more threatening than fatherly. "The heir to the House of Caspar. See that you rise to it."

"I will," he said quietly. Edris was unsure whether holding his gaze into King Bastian's dark eyes or casting it away would gain him more respect. But he had never liked looking anyone in the eye anyway, so he turned quickly and pushed open the cathedral's doors.

Most of the Halwood court had already taken their seats, but the Hartlander royal family was still standing on the open floor below. They were retreating, the king and his two younger children, from the altar, where the High Priest of the kingdom waited with a young girl in a wine-red silk gown. She was staring at the altar, wringing her hands together, which made Edris feel a little better about his own nerves. He found the courage to walk the rest of the way to the center of the cathedral and stand with her in front of the altar.

At first glance, Princess Lyha looked for all the world exactly like he'd expected, but the longer he studied her the more he found her inexplicably strange. She was wearing a beautiful gown, in the colors of her house, and had an intricate braid of long dark hair falling over her shoulder down to her waist. She had the olive skin, large eyes and sharp features characteristic of most southern Farisians, and she was as poised and composed as any princess. But she was also tall, only a few inches short of his own height, and while she was fairly thin, she was obviously  strong. A lot of her features were strong, now that he came to think of it—she was handsome, not beautiful. Maybe that was it. He didn't necessarily think that was a bad thing. He thought a lot of the noblemen's daughters looked like they would blow away in a strong wind. Not Lyha.

She was studying him, too, he noticed after a while, as the priest was waxing philosophical beside them. He couldn't tell if she liked what she saw, and for the first time his worries expanded. What if *she* didn't like *him*? The thought hadn't ever really crossed his mind. She had been more of an abstract concept to him than anything else– until now.

"Prince Edris?" the priest prompted, and he snapped back to the ceremony. The priest was holding out a length of torn cloth, and he nodded and took it, wrapping it first around his palm between his thumb and forefinger. He held out the other end to Lyha, who did the same, coming to rest her palm over his. He could feel calluses on her hands, the kind only earned through hard work or long rides, and decided he liked this strange princess after all. He allowed himself a small smile, and searched for warmth in her face. He didn't find any.

"Let these two be joined in the light of the Mother and Father, and let nothing keep them apart until their wedding day comes," the Priest chanted.

"May Astor will it so," the crowd responded. As soon as the binding was undone, Lyha turned away from him, and when the ceremony was over, she walked swiftly down the aisle and out of sight.

Edris started to walk into the crowd, still blinking in surprise, and soon after, he heard a man's voice calling out, "Prince Edris!" He turned and saw that the rest of the Halwood family was approaching him. King Eronn was a tall man, with a build suggesting strength in years gone by, but it had abandoned him by middle age. His eyes were warm when he clapped a hand on the prince's shoulder. "You're sitting with us for supper. Let's walk."

"Thank you, Your Highness," he said, unsure of what to make of the king's friendliness. He was watching Lyha disappear down the road ahead, too far away to catch up.

King Eronn saw where he was looking and cleared his throat. "She's just gone to, er, prepare, I expect," he said. "So! I hear you're captain of the Valleyguard."

Edris frowned. He knew his father would want him to go along, but lying had never worked for him. The truth always ended up coming out. "Uh, no, Your Highness, I'm only a guardsman. I just joined this spring."

"Ah, well, you'll no doubt rise through the ranks soon enough," the king said, and managed a small laugh. Everything was decidedly awkward now. "Have you met my younger daughter Jullia?" he asked quickly, calling the girl walking on his other side towards them.

"No, I haven't," Edris said, and bowed slightly, best as he could while walking. "A pleasure to meet you, Princess."

"And you," Jullia said graciously, bowing her head and looking intently into his eyes. Princess Jullia couldn't have been more than twelve, but she looked much more at home in her position than Lyha had. She was also looking at him like he'd personally been involved in the occupation of Queenshearth, just like her sister, but Edris supposed there was nothing he could do about that.

"And my son and heir, Deronn," the king said, indicating the even younger boy at his sister's side. He bowed shyly and stared silently at Edris for a moment before retreating to his hiding place behind his father.

When they reached the hall, the princess was waiting alone in the entryway. She hadn't changed and looked like she'd been there for some time, to Edris's embarrassment. '*Gone to prepare*', he thought, watching King Eronn hurry past them into the feast. *Right.* They were announced and walked in together, and she stayed stiff at his side all the while.

He watched Lyha curiously from her left hand side as she received congratulations from a line of admirers, cycling past the royal table one by one. Many of them greeted Edris, too, and he made it through the pleasantries by smiling and nodding, still trying to parse what had happened at the ceremony. Was it something about him, or was she just nervous? He hoped things would get better soon; otherwise this was the beginning of a long life of awkward silences. It felt like years before the main course of the feast had passed, the callers had all been seated, and Lyha finally spoke.

"Do you like Queenshearth, Your Highness?" she asked. Her voice was pitched lower than he'd been expecting, and the courtesy in it sounded strained.

"Er, yes, very much. The city's beautiful. Entirely different from Caspar's Dale," he said.

"Really? What's it like there?" she asked, finally turning her eyes to meet his. He glanced back down at the table.

"Well, it's a valley city. Fortified. And colder than here. But I like the keep, and the mountains."

"That's good," she said. "Fortified cities are better. Queenshearth is pretty, but it can't defend itself." *From you*, he suspected was the implication. Valleyguard forces had taken this hall from her mother's loyal men, less than ten years before, and he was sure she remembered it. The thought made him even more eager to say something that would make her come around to him. But before he could, she added, "I'm sorry your mother couldn't make it."

"She sends her congratulations," he finally remembered to say. "She's caught the northern flu."

"But they think she'll improve?" Lyha asked. Edris hesitated, decided to be honest, and shrugged. "I'm sorry," she said, quieter this time. "My mother's gone. I don't wish it on anyone."

"Thank you," he mumbled awkwardly. He'd been accepting premature sympathies for some weeks now, and it wasn't getting any less strange. He also suspected she'd said it to remind him of her, Queen Mina Wright Halwood—another of Thorncliffe's less pleasant deeds.

"You met Jullia and Deronn?" Lyha asked, glancing down the table to her siblings. Jullia was taking her turn receiving her sister's admirers now, and the small black-haired boy was laughing and gesturing wildly as he talked to his father further down the table.

"Yes, I walked with them after the ceremony," Edris said, frowning slightly. "They seemed... quiet."

"They don't really do well at these things," Lyha explained. "Well, Deronn doesn't, anyway." He only had to look down the table to see that wasn't true, but he didn't say anything. "I'll miss them."

Edris felt a pang of guilt at that and, forcing enthusiasm, he told her, "They're welcome to visit any time they'd like in the North, you know. I know our families haven't exactly been friends, but when we get married I hope that—"

"Excuse me," she said, standing abruptly, and before he could ask where she was going she was already flying through the back door and out of the hall. Edris hesitated; he didn't want to make a scene leaving in the middle of supper. But the music had picked up, and no one had noticed her go out, so he suspected he wouldn't be missed either. He hurried after her, down a long, spiraling and worn staircase that let out at the base of Hartshold Hill. He found Lyha sitting against the walls of the keep, with a Morran shrine at her back, halfway to the stables. She groaned when she saw him. "I would appreciate a moment alone, Prince Edris."

"Your Highness, we're going to be married, Edris is fine," he said. He'd thought that would be a kind thing to say, but Lyha only turned away from him. He frowned and asked, "Have I said something?"

"No," she sighed, "it's not— no, you've been perfectly— I mean... I don't know." She looked up to meet his eyes then and said, suddenly and fiercely, "I can't do this. I can't be married, I'd rather die."

Edris's heart started to race immediately, but he tried not to think right now about what his father would say, and instead exhaled slowly and sat down on the moss-covered stone next to her. They were silent for a moment before he asked, "You can't be married or you can't be married to *me?*"

She was already shaking her head. "It's not you. I'm not stupid, Edris. I know you were almost as young as I was when they killed them. I don't blame you for that."

He nodded, thinking. He'd always been told horrible things about the queen and her son, but it had never quite convinced him and being here, where it had happened, only made him more unsure. "I've never thought that was right," he admitted. "No matter what happened, he was still just a child."

"Thank you," Lyha mumbled, like she'd been accepting

condolences her whole life. "It's not that. It's about— well, it's about who I'd be if I went with you."

After a moment, Edris asked, "Who do you want to be?"

For the first time, he saw a spark in her eyes when she said, "I don't know, really. Anything. A knight, a sailor, a lover, an explorer..."

Edris saw the pattern. "A man?" She was quiet, but color rose in her face and she looked away. That was as much an answer as he needed. He struggled for something to say. "There are some people like that. I've read there are lots in the Lordless Isles. Eirosians, too." Brother Spencer said they'd all freeze with Eiros someday. But Lyha didn't look like she'd been condemned. She looked like she had finally found some kind of hope.

"Really? How do they do it?" she asked, eyes wide.

"I don't know," he admitted. "Probably mages." She looked crestfallen, so he added quickly, "But there've been stories forever about girls dressing as boys. They don't always have magic." Looking at Lyha's strong, sharp face, he said, "I think you'd have a fair chance."

She looked at him, eyes shining like he'd never seen, before looking back down to her feet. "I couldn't. Maybe if I was common. But if I left, they'd look for me."

Edris couldn't believe he was saying this, but after a moment he said, "It would have to be now." She looked at him in shock and he said, "There's hundreds of people in there, and they're all drunk. It could be morning before anyone knows you're gone. Tomorrow you're leaving with us and you'll have Valleyguard men watching you for the rest of your life. This is the last chance you're likely to get."

She stared at him and asked, "You'll help me?"

"Yes," he said.

"Why?"

He had absolutely no idea. "Because I believe you," he finally managed. "And because I don't want to marry someone who doesn't want to marry me. I don't know who that would make me, but I wouldn't like being him very much."

She—*he*, he reminded himself—smiled softly. "Thank you."

They were going to have to move fast. "Alright," he said. "We should find you some clothes."

"The stables," he told Edris. "Down there. The stableboy'll be at the feast."

"Perfect," Edris said, and they both hurried down the path. At the stables, they found a tunic and trousers, and Lyha changed, throwing his dress unceremoniously onto the ground. Before Edris could suggest it, Lyha was ripping a length of cloth off the bottom of the gown and wrapping it around his chest, flattening it under his shirt until no one would be any the wiser.

"Well?" he asked, grinning in the oversized riding clothes.

"Wait," Edris said, frowning. "You won't look right without this." He tore another piece of the dress off, balled it up into about the right size, and handed it to Lyha. "Put it down your trousers," he said. "Trust me." He did and looked down, staring in silence for a moment. "What?"

"I like it," he said, and let out a nervous laugh. "Er, does it look right? It feels big."

"No, it's fine," Edris said. "You just have to get used to it, I expect."

"Thanks." Next they found a straight razor, in one of the grooming bags hanging off the stalls, and sheared off Lyha's hair. It didn't take long, mostly being a few major cuts, but Edris managed to cut his ears and neck a few times, leaving him bleeding by the end.

"I'm a horrible barber, but I think it looks all right," he said. Lyha ran over to the water trough and stared at his reflection for quite a while. It touched Edris and he had to force himself to move them along.

"Take the razor with you," he said. "You won't need to shave, obviously, but it'll look better to have it. And if anyone gives you trouble, a blade won't hurt." Lyha stowed it in one of the trouser pockets, and then Edris said, "I suppose you just need a horse then."

"This one's new," Lyha said, walking over to a yearling courser in one of the farther stalls. "Gale. He's supposed to be for me."

"Good," Edris said. "I would go north, if I were you. Don't stay in the Hartlands. Try to find work before winter, you won't want to be sleeping on the road."

"Right," he said. "Thanks." He climbed onto Gale and slung the grooming bag over his shoulder, filled instead with some of the stableboy's food and as warm a cloak as they could find.

"You'll need a new name," Edris added, and Lyha thought for a moment.

"Mychal," he said quietly, and Edris nodded.

"Suits you," he said, giving him a small smile.

"You're a good man, Edris," Mychal said. "You could come with me."

"What?," he asked, startled.

"Well," Mychal said, carefully, "it— sort of seems like you've thought a lot about running."

He flushed red. *Had* he thought about it? He didn't think so... but it didn't matter, either way. "I—can't. I'm the heir to Thorncliffe."

"The Thorncliffe that murders children?" he asked, sharply, and Edris winced.

"I'm sorry," he said. "This is you. That's me."

They looked at each other for a long moment. It was obvious Mychal was disappointed, and it was all Edris could do to stand his ground. "Well," Mychal finally said, "I hope you find your queen someday. I'm sorry it's not me."

"Good luck," Edris said, nodding, and Mychal took a deep breath before he rode Gale swiftly out into the night. Edris walked back up to the castle, shocked at himself. He was almost sure he would tell someone as soon as he got back, but he didn't. Instead, he went to bed, and made sure he wasn't the first to ask where the princess was. They found the dress, and the blood from the razor, in the stables the next morning and most assumed the worst. He suspected Mychal wanted that. By the time the Thorncliffe delegation left the city, Lyha Halwood, to almost everyone in the kingdom, was dead.

## 9

Samira

The young soldier stared at Samira in silence for a moment, just long enough she started to worry she'd been wrong. Finally, he spoke, in a somewhat strained, lower echo of what had been her friend's voice. "Um, hello, Sami." He looked like he was going to be sick. "It's Mychal now."

She frowned. "Well—I know who you are, you don't have to—"

"It's not like that, it's my *name*," he said. The pain clear in his voice startled her. She nodded slowly, still confused, but really just wanting to hear answers.

"Okay," she said, "Mychal, then." She felt touched by the name he was using, and a flood of affection came over her. Everything came rushing back. She flung her arms around him, and he stiffened before eventually hugging her too. "I thought you were *dead*," she whispered. "You can't *do* that."

"I'm sorry," Mychal said as he stepped back from her. "I couldn't risk sending a letter."

"Well, no, I suppose not," Samira said, eyeing the crest imprinted on his chest. "What are you doing here? Actually, never mind that, what are you *doing?*" She gestured flat out to the sun-and-moon stitching on his chestplate then, and he winced.

"I'm Sir James's squire."

"You're in the Holy Army." He looked down at the ground, and she could see color rising in his cheeks and around his ears. "*Why?*"

"Best place for a boy my age to hide," he mumbled.

*But you're not—* Samira thought, incredulous, before she took a deep breath and spoke again. "Maybe... but—"

"I'm not rounding up Eirosians, Sami," he burst out. It sounded defensive, to both of them. He shifted his gaze back to the ground before he added quietly, "I'm *safe* there."

"You weren't safe before? You'd be halfway to being Thorncliffe's queen by now and..." Samira exclaimed, but she saw him wince again, as soon as she said 'queen', and she started to understand. "It's not really about that. Is it?"

"No," he said, cringing. He still really wasn't looking in her eyes.

"Okay," she said, softening her voice, and looking at him standing in her doorway, she was astounded by how much she wanted to tell him. "Come in," she said, and ushered him inside the chambers, shutting the door as quietly as she could behind them. She hoped no one had been awake to see it; that was the last thing she needed to become gossip, this week especially. Once they were inside, she glanced around again and, still not trusting that her chambers were empty, led him out to the balcony. The royal hunting woods, two hundred feet below, swayed gently in the wind beneath the moonlight. Samira sat down on the stone bench near the railing, but Mychal still seemed restless, and he stayed standing while she studied him. Finally, she asked, "Are you alright?"

"I'm fine," he said, but his voice sounded stiff and uneasy. "Just higher up than I've been in a while, is all."

She smiled. "You're still afraid of heights?" He gave her an exasperated look, and she had to stop herself from laughing out loud. It was definitely... *him* (she supposed that was right). But it only made it stranger that he felt so familiar. She remembered playing with that little girl at weddings and coronations and funerals, and running around Fen Faris years ago. But she'd thought they'd be ladies at court together. Now they were both more or less grown-- she'd be officially of age before the month was out-- and that little girl was a soldier, young and, she had to admit, handsome, and ordered to *protect* her. "Okay, tell me everything," she finally said.

He squirmed. "You aren't going to—?"

"I'm not going to tell anyone, but I need to know why," she said, as patiently as she could manage, and Mychal opened his mouth and closed it again. After a moment, he took a breath and nodded.

"Right. Okay, well... I mean, this is always more or less what I'd wanted, you knew that."

*Did I?* She thought. "I knew you were different," Samira allowed. "That you didn't want to marry... a man, I mean. And fancy gowns always made you sick. But you said that was because it was excessive, with the lowborn starving."

"That was part of it," he said. "But really it was just the gowns."

Samira nodded slowly. She guessed she could understand that. She knew plenty of people who wanted a different family, a different title— maybe this was just a little, well, *more* than most. And she couldn't say that this *didn't* sound like her friend from before. "So it's not just for safe travel, then? This is... for good?"

"Yes," Mychal said quietly. "Well, as long as I'm able."

"Okay, then," she said, and tried to smile, as gently as she could. She felt terrible about how positively uncomfortable he'd looked this whole time. But there was one thing she still didn't understand. "I only... you want to be like them?" she asked, glancing past him to the door, where beyond it they both knew the men were sleeping downstairs, the drunken, hateful Holy soldiers.

"I'm not like them!" he exclaimed, looking like he was floundering a little. "I– I'm still me, Sami, I just– this is me, too. But I still... well, you know how I feel about you," he said quietly, and it was her turn to blush. She did. "And I still understand what all this is like for you, like they never could. You see that, don't you?"

The pain in his face was clear, and she instantly felt horribly guilty for causing it, just like she had in the Golden Forests years ago. She wondered if she'd ever stop hurting him like this, and she knew then she had to make a choice to try. "You're right," she said, because she felt it was true. "Whoever you are, you're still my friend."

She thought it'd worked; maybe a little too well, though, as now he looked like he might cry. "Thanks," he managed, and the absolute relief flooding his voice startled her. "I hoped you'd get it."

*I hope I'll live up to that*, she thought, but instead she said quickly, "Tell me how you've *done* it, though. I can't believe you've survived this long! And now you're a guardsman at Skytower?"

"It's really just luck, mostly," he said, "although I suppose it's not as difficult as I thought it was. Edris said there were plenty of people like me, in the Isles, and Eirosia... although those people have magic."

"*Edris* knows about this?" Samira asked. "Edris Thorne?"

"He helped me run away," Mychal said, nodding.

"And he never told anyone?"

"As far as I know."

"Wow," Samira said. "I'd never have thought he'd have the courage."

"I left from the festival and ended up in the Army after a month or so. I was hungry and I wasn't strong enough to work on a farm." But then his eyes widened and he said, "But *you*, Sami, you're really about to marry *Him*."

"A great honor," she said flatly, her face grim, and he pulled himself back somewhat.

"I'm sorry," he said. "Truly. It can't be easy for you."

"Do you know what they're going to do to me?" she asked him suddenly, angrily, angrier than he deserved. It had just come out of her, she'd hardly been aware she was saying it, but she couldn't take it back now. She felt sick, the same way she'd felt when she'd first read about it, but she kept going anyway. "The Godhead can't have children, it wouldn't be *holy*. So the Steward at the Temple has some *procedure* they can do and they—" her eyes welled up with tears and she couldn't go any further. When she looked back up at Mychal, he looked horrified, and completely at a loss for words. "That's just what will happen if they *don't* kill me. And you're *fighting* for them."

"I'm only there until I can—" he started to protest, but then he stopped and frowned, even more concerned. "Wait, what? Why would they kill you?"

So Jullia had been right-- he hadn't read the letter. She looked back through the open window into her chambers, but even though she couldn't see anyone lurking, she was too scared to say it out loud. Instead she said, "The water pitcher on the dressing table, bring it out here." Still confused, Mychal went back inside and took the water from her bedside out to the balcony, setting it on the bench next to her. "Did you see anyone in there?" she asked him.

"No," he said, incredulous. "Of course not—Sami, what in Eiros's—" He fell silent once she held her hand above the pitcher. Slowly, the water drew up and began to swirl around her wrist, presenting itself for her use, not that she knew what to do with it. "Holy Mother and Father," Mychal breathed.

"I know," she said. "I tried to give you a letter... right before your Declaration." He blushed again, confirming what she'd thought. "Jullia told me you didn't read it."

"You talked to Jullia?" he asked, perking up. "How is she?"

*Oh, gods.* "There's so much you don't know," Samira sighed. Her stomach turned and she said, "Ly—Mychal," she corrected herself,

"I'm sorry." He nodded and she said, "I don't know how to tell you this, but your father..."

"I know," he said, grimacing and turning away. She was trying to get a sense of how much this was affecting him, but she didn't feel like she knew how to tell what he was thinking, not anymore. They used to be closer than anyone, but he was like a completely different person now-- in some ways, at least. "I heard at a war council. Nothing's helped?"

"As far as I know, he'll be gone soon," she said. She hesitated, then reached for his hand and held it gingerly between hers. "I'm sorry."

He clearly noticed, but he didn't move away, so she took that as a good sign. She could feel her heart beating practically out of her chest at just the touch of their hands, but she tried to ignore that. "It's alright," he said, "I never expected to see him again anyway. And he wouldn't want to see me like this."

"Still," she said. "I can't imagine losing my dad."

"Even though he's making you do this?" Mychal asked, and she hesitated.

"Yes," she said, and realized it was true.

Her friend leaned back into the wall behind them and asked, "What are you going to do, Sami?"

She shrugged. "I don't know. My uncle had an idea, but I don't see how it would work now."

"What?"

"He knows a mage woman in town, and she was making me an amulet that would hide me from their mage-catchers. But I don't know how I'll get it from her now. You lot will never let me leave without a full guard." She looked back at Mychal, nodding in sympathy, and her eyes drifted down back to the crest on his shirt. That was when it hit her. "No, wait," she said. "I think I know how."

He looked nervous now; his eyes held that same dread they'd had every time Samira had found some new way of abandoning their lessons with the Stewards. "How?"

"I can't leave the keep," she said, "but you could." She could feel the excitement building in her as she added, "And you could help yourself, too."

"I'm going to need details at some point, Sami," he said impatiently.

"The mage woman," she said. "You could go and get the amulet from her. Her name's Farrah Vance. Take this so she knows I really sent you." She reached into her dress pocket and fumbled for a moment before pulling out the Eirosian whiteflower handkerchief her mother had given her. She gave it to Mychal, who still seemed a little shocked, and added, "You said those other people like you, they had help from magic?"

"That's what Edris told me," he said. "But I don't know. I don't think he knew either, to be honest."

"Well, Vance said she could make a potion for anything. If there's magic for this, she can help you." Mychal was obviously trying to maintain a healthy level of skepticism, but she could see that he was starting to get excited. "She's a little... odd, but if you're helping me I'd bet she'll help you."

"...I'll try," he said. He smiled then and she felt warm, comforted somehow. "Thank you, Sami. Really."

"I'll find out where she lives from my uncle and let you know," she said. "She said she'll have it ready the night before the Godhead's supposed to arrive, that's six days away." Mychal nodded, then stood and started to head back into the keep, and she couldn't help herself from adding, "And— I just want to say— I'm glad you're here. It's good to see you." She took a deep breath and said, "That engagement party, right before you left."

He nodded. "Luke Payne and Talia Penn."

"You remember that?" she marveled.

"Not really, until today," he said. "Now I know far too much about—anyway. What is it?"

"I never should have said all that," Samira said, the apology she'd been trying to give him for years spilling out in an awkward rush. But Mychal was already shaking his head.

"No, don't apologize. I had no right to expect anything from you."

"But I was cruel."

"It's alright, Sami," he insisted. But Samira was looking at his eyes, and they looked pained, an echo of how hurt he'd been two years ago, when she'd told him he shouldn't love her, that it was stupid and wrong and they'd hang for it. She'd called him selfish and sick, and when he'd disappeared she'd thought it was entirely her fault. She wished she could take all of it back now. She hadn't even meant half of it then.

Before she could think better of it, she kissed him on the cheek and said, "Be careful. Don't get yourself hanged just for me."

He was blushing, and she could feel herself starting to as well. But he managed to recover fairly quickly and say, "No one's caught me yet." He turned to leave, and the hilt of his sword caught the gleam of the moon behind him. She couldn't believe that he looked so much like her old friend, and still every bit like a noble prince. In fact... she could feel another one of her ideas coming on, and she almost convinced herself to stay quiet this time. But this one was too big to hold back.

"Mychal?" she called, and halfway across the room, he turned around and waited, eyebrows raised. "If you do get the potion... you might think about going home."

He frowned. "I— I can't. I told you, I can't go back to how it was, and they'll just marry me off, or worse—"

She stopped him before he could really start to panic. "No, of course, *Lyha* can't go back." The words felt heavy in her throat, and it was hard for her to force them out, but eventually she made herself look him in the eyes and ask, as loud as she dared, "But what about Prince Mychal?"

# IO

# Mychal

This ridiculous plan was going to get him killed. The fog was still heavy over Hollisport, and it gave him some cover, but every street corner had him jumping at movement from the alleys, seeing soldiers where there were none. Sir Lyam Bennett had pulled him aside on a perimeter patrol that morning and told him to go to the last house on Winding Row after the change of the night shift. He would stand guard in his place. The old knight had looked at him long and hard all the while, and Mychal got nervous about just how much Samira had told him. He was uneasy at the idea of Sir James's friend, of all people, hearing where he came from. They would never make him a knight if he knew—and that would be the least of his problems.

As soon as Luke had gone back to sleep after his watch, Mychal had slipped out the back door to the hall, as quietly as he could with a sword on his belt. He didn't know Hollisport at all, and all he'd gotten from Bennett was that Winding Row was somewhere in the eastern part of the city, near here but on the other side of the

Kingsroad. He supposed that was good, seeing as he only had two hours, but that wouldn't matter if he couldn't find it anyway.

The city was much less lively at night, but it wasn't completely deserted the night before the Declaration. The population had swelled as people came from across the kingdom to celebrate, and inside taverns and inns there was dancing and drinking that spilled out into the streets. There were a lot of taverns and inns in this part of the city. He wouldn't be surprised if some—or most— of them were the same kind as Lady May's. The bright lights and warm laughter were almost enough to draw him inside, but there was no time, and so he kept on.

The further he went down the Kingsroad, the stranger the people passing by seemed to him. What had been mostly happy, drunk Farisian faces started to become younger, sharper, and paler. He sensed he had entered into a mostly Eirosian neighborhood, possibly even one of the partitioned ghettos. They looked at him suspiciously, and as much as he knew he was safer here than Samira would be, he still felt too conspicuous. He was glad that he'd left his clothes bearing the Holy Crest behind. There were other people, too, decidedly not Eirosian, stocky, short, and darker than anyone Mychal had seen before—except the marauders, he realized, the face of the man he'd killed flashing into his mind. These were Islanders. He must be close now.

The larger tavern district petered out until the only buildings were ramshackle rows of houses, many with small gardens behind them full to bursting with wheat, corn, anything and everything to eat. It seemed like these people fended for themselves. There was a small square at the next crossing of roads, with a statue of King Daniel standing tall and proud next to a crumbling little well. The stone king was pockmarked and battered, and when Mychal got closer he saw that his hands were splattered with paint, a thick coat of crimson red.

Mychal tried not to show how uneasy he was feeling; many of the windows weren't shuttered, and he wasn't sure if anyone was watching him. He knew he probably looked like a prime target for robbery, at the very least, if it wasn't for his sword. So he held onto the hilt and kept on the way he'd been going. Why was he doing this again? He didn't even bother with that-- it had been years since he'd seen her, but he knew he'd do anything for Samira. He kept on, anxious and alert, until the sign posted at one of the crossroads stopped him. *Winding Row.*

Winding Row was, of course, the most dimly lit and deserted of all, and it really did *wind*; he followed it down at least three wide curving bends before he could see where it ended, and each time he half expected someone to attack from around the other side. But he saw no one the entire way down to the last house, a small squat cottage, with a thatched roof and wattle-and-daub walls woven from stiff Hornish pines. It didn't smell like the manure and mud it was made of, though; there was something earthy and thick in the air, an almost sweet smell that wafted from the paneless window at the front of the house. He gathered his courage and knocked on the heavy wooden door.

No one came to let him in, and he couldn't hear a thing inside, but he could see through the window there were candles burning and something was cooking on the fire. He knocked again, and when that went unanswered too, he went to the window and hesitantly called, "Hello? I'm looking for Farrah Vance?"

"Go away," a woman's voice shouted from inside. He frowned and peered inside, but still couldn't see her. "What's a Farisian with a sword doing here?"

"The princess sent me," he called back, as loud as he dared. She was silent then, until he heard footsteps hurrying toward the door. It swung open in front of him, and an Islander woman, probably nearing middle age with long dark hair and large eyes, was gazing down at him from her threshold two steps above the street.

She looked him up and down and shook her head. "You're not a servant. What is that, Thorncliffe steel? You're one of the soldiers. I'm not telling you anything, you can bring me in front of the king if you like, but it won't make any difference."

"No, I swear," Mychal said. He fished around in his pocket, which made the woman flinch back from the doorway until he pulled out the handkerchief. "She said this would convince you."

Vance snatched it away from him and stared at it, incredulous. "This is a Dillon crest," she breathed. "The princess gave you this?" He nodded. "From her mother?" He nodded again, although he didn't really know. She looked out into the street, glancing both ways and, inexplicably, above them, too, before saying, "Right, fine, then. Come in. Quickly." She shut the door behind him immediately, and strode quickly across the cottage to a countertop piled high with vials and flasks.

A woodworking table stood in the center of the room, with shavings and carving knives strewn about its surface. There was a pot hanging over her smoke-filled fireplace, and it smelled decidedly not like food. Little labels, intricately written in the tiniest handwriting he'd ever seen, identified the contents of the jars of strange substances stored on shelves all along the wall closest to him. In a corner of the cottage was a bed and a small washbasin, but otherwise the whole place seemed devoted to potions and amulets.

After sorting through the piles of finished carvings, she found a small one of dark blue stone on a simple chain and pressed it into Mychal's hands. "This is the mother amulet. She'll need to wear it whenever she wants to be invisible to detection magic. But they're like to know what it is, so she needs to be careful. Will you tell her that?"

"I'll tell her," he said, studying the Morran moon engraving, bordered by Old Language runes. "Thank you."

"Well, then, goodnight," she said quickly, and tried to hurry him out the door.

He planted his feet, screwed up as much courage as he could manage, and said, "Wait—Mrs. Vance— Samira said you could make a potion for anything."

She narrowed her eyes. "Yes. But I'm not going to help the Army at all, boy, no matter who you are to the princess."

"It's not for the Army," he said quickly. "I need... well, I—"

"Come on, lad, get it out, it's past midnight," she said impatiently, and he forced the words out.

"I'm a *girl*," he said, grimacing. "Or, but, I'm not. She said you'd know how to... help me."

The woman's face softened. "Oh," she said. "Yes, I see it now." He felt his neck turning red and she added, "But I'd guess that's why you're here." She sighed. "I'll give you something. But be *careful*, and don't tell *anyone*. Everything I give out's another chance I get shipped away, lad—what's your name, anyway?"

"Mychal," he said. "Mychal Owyn."

She waved her hand. "No it isn't. You're obviously highborn and you used to be a girl. Who *were* you, before?"

He shifted uncomfortably. "I was born in Queenshearth."

She turned back around from her potions and stared at him. "You don't mean... you're Lyha Halwood?"

"*Mychal*," he insisted, the rest of his face turning red too.

"Sorry. I just... you have no idea how many people are looking for you," she said, still staring at him with an inscrutable expression.

"I know that," he said, his patience thinning by the minute. "That's why I need a potion. I just want my voice to be lower—and maybe if I needed to shave..."

"You'll get more than that from this," Vance said, holding up a small vial of golden-brown, oily liquid. "It'll happen just slow enough to look natural, but you'll look a man in truth by winter. Course, it won't do anything about what's down there," she said, nodding to his trousers in a way that made him feel that same empty uncomfortable feeling he got whenever he thought about it, "but it'll stop you bleeding with the moon, and your chest'll go sometime next year." She walked over to him and said, "I need some hair from you." Vance took hold of a lock of his hair, and without warning, pulled a handful of strands out by the root.

"Ow!" he protested.

"Apologies, Your Highness," she said, with a hint of a smirk forming on her face.

"Don't call me that, please," he mumbled. As he rubbed the back of his head where the hairs should still be, he thought about what Samira had said the other night. "I'm not royalty anymore."

"But you are," she said, dropping the hairs into a few identical vials. "And you could be again. You've been using 'Mychal', have you? That's lucky."

He shook his head, eyes widening. *Her too?* "No. Why does everyone think that's a good idea? I'm not—I couldn't even *look* anything like my brother would have, let alone—"

"A few months with this draught and you will," she said. "It'll make you strong, too, as long as you keep using that sword. And if you'd been raised in hiding, with common people, you wouldn't have been fed as well as most princes. It won't matter that you're small. Only your blood will matter."

He was shaking his head again. "I—*why*? Why can't Deronn..."

"Deronn's just a boy," Vance said. "With the Godhead choosing his regent, he'd be a puppet. You'd be a king."

"They'd never support my claim," Mychal said. "They killed my— they killed... 'me'." He couldn't help remembering his dream, his brother's head in his own hands, staring at him, accusing with his blank, dead eyes. He shuddered. "I'm not who they want."

"No one's saying you should ask them nicely," she said. "You'll have friends on the Isles, if you make that choice. They've seen you coming."

"They've *seen* me?"

"In the godwine," she said, matter-of-fact, like that was perfectly normal. "'*A true son of Faris will pull his fathers' sword from its tomb to unite his kingdom and drive the false prophet from the warlord's throne.*' Ask any mage or Islander, they know the verse."

"A 'true son'?" he asked, doubtful.

"It's not always strictly literal," Vance said. "The Resistance has been looking for you ever since you ran, even when they thought you were a girl." She pressed three vials into his hands. "Drink half of one vial once a month. I'd give you more, but if you're carrying too much of it you'll catch the mage-catchers' notice. By High Autumn you'll need to find another mage." She stepped away and said, "And please. Think about what I said, and call your armies. They'll come."

Mychal felt a strange sensation growing in his stomach, but he clutched the vials and Samira's amulet to his chest and nodded all the same. "Thank you." He wound his way back through the streets up to the castle, all the while thinking about his brothers. Deronn, at first, alone at Fen Faris; would he really be better off for having the crown taken from him? That wasn't difficult—Mychal was sure he would be. The Priesthood and the lords of the Hartlands would fight over him until they tore him apart. No Lord Regent had ever done the kingdom any good, and the installing of one would be its own nightmare. But the brother that haunted him more was his twin.

He'd never meant for this to happen. He'd used his name to honor him, not to *become* him. He couldn't think of anything less respectful of the first Mychal, than to take away even the slightest remaining chance of someone answering for his death. He felt enough guilt already, just for taking his name. To take everything else, too…

*But,* he thought, as the moon began to sink back toward the hills from its high point in the night sky, *wouldn't it honor him to crown him king after all?* If it wasn't justice for him, maybe it was justice for the kingdom.

There was a part of him that didn't think he could do it. So many had told him, his whole life, that he wasn't fit to rule; politely at first, and then, when he stayed too boyish for too long, less so. Mychal was supposed to have been the Princess Consort of Thorncliffe by now, and that was as high as he was meant to rise. He had been educated to be a royal wife and that only; he never learned military history or philosophy or anything of the sort, except for what he'd stolen from the libraries at school. He wasn't born for this.

Mychal reached the gates of the Skytower at what he was sure had to be nearing the end of his watch, and just as he was beginning to sink into a depression about his lot, the sun-and-moon arms of the Holy Army greeted him in rich blue and gold, flapping gently in the wind on the walls, and felt affronted. In his mind's eye, he was seeing the same banner ten years ago, hanging high over the heads of the High Priest, the Lord Marshal, and his brother being forced to his knees at the headsman's block. And he knew he had to make the Halwood sword-and-fire fly alone again on the walls of his castle. Of *his* castle.

With one swift motion, he uncorked the first of the three vials and swallowed half of the golden liquid. It ran down his throat thick and hot, and he couldn't keep himself from smiling as he thought about what the next months would bring. On his way to relieve Sir Lyam, he walked with more confidence than he'd felt since they'd arrived, and after he passed along the amulet, he slept soundly in the barracks. The Godhead was coming tomorrow. Let him come. Soon enough, it would be Mychal riding up to *his* city walls.

# II

# Edris

Edris didn't like the way Astor Post felt as soon as they arrived. It was like someone had lit a match on dry tinder-- there was an inevitability towards violence in the air. As his men rode into the camp, disheveled companies of fifty or so boys each marched past them, and Edris couldn't help but notice that almost none of them looked older than him. The luckiest among them wore plates of boiled leather, but most had no armor at all. They did have good steel, something like his own from what he could tell, but he wasn't confident they knew how to use it.

The ride from the outer edges of the Army's perimeter into the camp proper was quiet; the Valleyguard men had never talked to Edris much, either out of deference or indifference he wasn't quite sure. But the Eirosians were no better, especially not when their fate was about to be decided in the council hall already looming in the distance. Neill hadn't spoken to him since they passed the Thorncliffe border, and it had been a long two days since.

The council's seat towered over the rest of the camp as they approached it; it was more of a manor house than a real castle, but it was by far the largest building in Astor Post. The camp itself sprawled across the coast and seemed almost endless. When they stopped in the officers' courtyard, the stables were ready to take their horses, and by the time Edris had dismounted the front doors were opening and a young steward was running out to greet them.

"Your Highness," the boy said, bowing to Edris at the front, and added, "My lords," to the line of captains of the guard behind him. "Lord Thorne is waiting to receive you, Prince Edris. Your men can continue on to the barracks. The quartermaster will see they'll have everything they need."

"Lead the way," Edris said, then added, "My father sent hostages with me from Eirosia." That was a lie, of course; *he* hadn't even been sent by his father. But the boy just nodded.

"We had a rider that told us. They can follow you and wait outside the chamber. The Lord Marshal will decide where they go after that."

Edris looked back toward the six Eirosian knights, and nodded to Neill as he handed over the horse he'd been given and led his men up to the front of the guard. "Your Highness," Neill said quietly when he reached his side. Edris had to stop himself from wincing. Whatever warmth had been starting to show there, he was hiding it well now.

The steward, Edris, and Neill's men parted ways with the guard as they entered. A large receiving hall with a roaring fire bustled with activity in front of them then: messengers, servants, stewards, and officers were coming in and out, and all quickly fell quiet when their party marched through to the stairwell beyond. Edris felt their eyes on him right up until the door closed behind the last of the Eirosian men.

The boy led the way up the thick stone steps, past the open doors leading to a hallway full of officers' chambers, up to the last door.

The council chambers were the only room up in the turret, above the rest of the hall. There were armored guards at the door, and once Edris and the steward had passed, they stopped Neill and his men from going any further. "Wait here," Edris said anyway, as sternly as he could manage, and Neill nodded with a smirk that made him squirm. Dropping his gaze, and feeling he was starting to blush, he quickly turned around and followed the boy inside.

Edris hadn't seen Jonn Thorne for years, but his cousin looked the same as ever, with a mane of wild dark hair and a sharp, cragged face. He wore his thirty-odd years rather poorly, but there was a kind of elegance to him that made up for it and more. He wore the dark blue and black of the Norport Thornes, but Edris spotted a sun-and-moon brooch clasping the cloak at his neck, and his chain of office showed the same. "Ned," he exclaimed, and the beginnings of a smile formed as he stood from the council table.

"Edris," he said, reluctant to correct the Lord Marshal, but he never could stand the childhood nickname. Jonn clasped his hand and smiled in earnest.

He looked him up and down and nodded, one strong motion. "You've grown into the name."

Edris smiled, letting his nerves go as much as he could, and said, "It's good to see you."

"I wish it were at your wedding, not here," Jonn said, "but I welcome your men all the same." He turned to the table and gestured for him to sit. "I heard about your engagement to Lady Nora. Congratulations."

"Thank you," he said, his mood dampening a little at that, and sat in the seat to the left of Jonn's head of the table. "I've brought a thousand Valleyguard men, with fifty knights among them."

"Good," he said, nodding again, "that's very good. We have twenty thousand here already, or as close as makes no matter. And officers to spare, though yours will command their own men, to be sure."

"Right. I would be honored to *meet* these officers," Edris said, looking around at the empty room pointedly.

Jonn coughed. "Most of them have gone to Princess Samira's Declaration. They should return within the fortnight, and soon after that we'll move out."

"The Mages' Canyon?" Edris asked, and Jonn nodded. "You mean to surprise Eirosia? Strike first?"

"No, they're already moving," he said, his face grim now. "We've had reports for months of Daemons near the mountains. But none at sea-- they have no navy, thank the Mother and Father. We'll choke them off at the mouth of the Canyon." His eyes drifted to the table, and Edris noticed a map spread out in front of them for the first time, of the terrain where the battle would be. The high ridges of the Canyon's far side were littered with red wooden Xes, and the greener valley on the side of the Horn held a greater number, but only just, of blue moons. They were separated into three larger sections, and each had an officer's name painted on its side. Jonn saw him looking and said, "I'll be in the middleguard cavalry. James Reinhold is leading the van, once he comes back from Hollisport."

"He's leading the vanguard but he's not here?" Edris asked.

Jonn smirked. "I thought he should stay, too, but he wanted to take his new squire to his first official function. Some common Hartlander boy called Mychal. Did you know those people name their children after the Heretic?"

Edris hoped none of his alarm registered in his face. There was no way-- but he *had* been gone long enough to be a squire by now. And the military was probably one of the safest places for him, but... a squire? Did he mean to be a *knight*? Edris didn't know how he felt about that-- maybe that was too far. Maybe now was when he could fix this, and go back to Brother Spencer with some kind of proven loyalty. All he had to do was tell Jonn...

Tell him what? That he thought someone mentioned in passing

*might* be someone he'd actively aided in treason? How would that do anyone any good? There had to be at least one boy born in the Hartlands named after the prince. He was sure there were dozens of Edrises in Thorncliffe. And what's more, he couldn't imagine Mychal had maintained his story for so long while staying in one place.

He wouldn't say anything to Jonn. When Sir James and his squire came back, he'd see for himself if it was really him. For now, he only shook his head and said, "Gods. Well, I suppose they wouldn't have known when he was born."

"Yes. Well, anyway. Sir Callum Roth will be his second in command, and I'll have officers with me and in the rear as well. Your men would be useful in the vanguard, at least some of them, but most can join the middle and rear. We'll need the numbers at our backs, but it wouldn't be right to put them in front of us."

"And you want me with them?" Edris asked.

The Lord Marshal glanced at him out of the corner of his eyes, and, turned towards the map, said, "Ah, no, I'd like you to hold Astor Post in my place."

Edris's face darkened. "You had a letter from my father, didn't you?"

Jonn grimaced and called for wine. "Ned, I don't mean to offend you."

"You know as well as he does that I'm more than old enough to fight. I'm nearly twenty-one years old, half your *men* are younger than me!"

"You're his *heir*, he can't risk your life," Jonn said. "He told me he didn't even send you. You left without his leave."

"Of course I did! He tells me all the time that I need to prove myself and fight, and then he won't let me leave the bloody city!"

"I need you to hold the outpost, and I won't disobey the King. I'll hear no more about it." He poured himself a cup of the new wine and added, "You have six Eirosians outside my door, I hear."

Once he had composed himself, Edris said, "Yes. They claim King Silas is alive, a prisoner in his own castle."

Jonn nodded slowly and after a moment he asked, "And what do you think?"

Edris paused. "I can't imagine why else they would come all this way when they must have known we wouldn't be eager to help."

The Lord Marshal considered this, drinking his wine and staring down at the map in front of him. "I can't say I appreciate this being brought to me, with so much in the balance of this battle already."

"My father was following His Holiness's orders in that," Edris said, hoping the defensive tone edging into his voice would be interpreted as Holy offense on behalf of the Godhead.

Jonn sat up a little straighter and muttered, "Very well. Is there a leader among them?" Edris nodded. The Lord Marshal stood and said, "Bring him in."

Edris went back to the door, opening it to find the Eirosians had been pressed back further from the door by the Army guards and were now standing a good ways down the corridor, with Neill at the front. With a look, the knight stepped forward into the chamber. Even with his wrists bound, he seemed immovable, and Edris couldn't help but admire him as he met Jonn's gaze gamefully while the men examined one another.

"Your name, sir?" Jonn asked.

"Sir Alexander Neill, my lord," he said. "Councilor to King Silas."

"So it's true that he lives?"

"Yes, my lord."

Jonn returned to examining the map, seeming suddenly uninterested in a way Edris suspected was rehearsed. "I've never known the Daemon King to take prisoners."

"Not in the Triad, my lord," Neill acknowledged. "But holding and keeping Eirosia was a difficult task, and he saw no other way to quell the resistance against them than to keep us alive."

The Lord Marshal smirked, and Edris watched nervously as Neill grew more frustrated. "The sacking of Illon's Fast seemed to us an unmitigated slaughter from a demented horde."

"There was an art of strategy to his plans," Neill said. "Avery Dearril may be cruel, but he is not stupid." Edris was startled to find he had never heard the name of the king of the Daemons before. It unnerved him, to think that a monster like that had a name.

Jonn paused for a moment before he responded, and the silence hung heavy in the room. The steward had slipped out several moments ago, and Edris could hardly blame him. If he could have, he would have, too. Finally, the Lord Marshal said, "I admire your capacity for survival, sir; whether or not what you say is true, an Eirosian of your rank standing here today is a testament to your ability. But I fail to see why you're *here*. What would you have me do?"

"My king calls for aid," Neill said, drawing himself up to his full height and holding himself with a gravity Edris hadn't seen in him since the Spire. "The Daemons have slaughtered my people. They are your enemies as well as ours, my lord, and they will look to the Triad next. Send your forces to Illon's Fast and stop Dearril before it's too late." Edris saw him looking at the map on the table, and he had to admit it did look like the Army had the men to do it.

That is, if they abandoned the idea of taking the Canyon.

Jonn seemed to understand this too. "We are at the precipice of turning these monsters back from our borders once and for all. You would have me squander that opportunity to come to the rescue of a land of heretics and sinners, and for what? And into the heart of Daemon-held territory, no less. I'd call that a trap."

Neill was growing desperate. "My lord, I swear to you, on my honor as a knight--"

"Don't presume to talk of honor in front of me," Jonn snapped. "Your countrymen disgrace the very idea of knighthood. I would have you executed for trespassing on the Godhead's lands, but His Holiness has seen fit to send you here and keep you alive, and so be it. Leave us. You'll be kept in comfort as befits a knight of your status, Sir Neill, as *we* have honor at Astor Post."

The knight looked ready to draw his sword, but the two men only stared at each other, each daring the other to move first. Finally, fuming, Neill turned round and marched back through the door. When it slammed shut behind him, Jonn grimaced and collapsed back into his seat. "Eirosians. The gods are testing me today."

"I believe them, Jonn," Edris said, watching his cousin warily.

"It doesn't matter if I believe them," Jonn snapped. "They're not why we're here." He called for the steward, who emerged from a door in the corner of the room and began to clear away the wine as the Lord Marshal stood up. Edris did the same. "They'll show you to your quarters. I'd have you walk the camp with me tomorrow and inspect the forces, if you're amenable."

"Of course," Edris said, when really he felt almost as angry as Neill had been. Pomp and circumstance. Here, just like in Caspar's Dale, he could see he'd do nothing of importance.

Later on, long after Astor was finished pulling the sun across the sky to the west of the tower, Edris's restlessness got the better of him and he found himself knocking on the door to Neill's chamber. The young knight smiled ruefully when he saw him. "Your Highness," he said, a perfunctory greeting and nothing more, as he fell back for him to enter.

Edris looked around at the straw-stuffed bed, tended fire, and recently used bath and said, "Nicer than the Eye, to be sure."

"Oh, sure. Just like my time on Silas's council," he said, with a hint of something ironic twisting his smile. "Only here I wouldn't make it down the hall to the privy before someone would haul me back in."

"I'm sorry about the Lord Marshal," Edris said. "He's... difficult to persuade."

Neill looked at him, clearly suspicious, and asked, "What did he tell you?"

He scowled. "I'm not allowed to fight. He's just giving me charge of the outpost."

Neill chuckled. When Edris glared back, he said, "No, I'm sorry, just-- the problems of a prince."

"Well, it's just incredible!" he exclaimed, finally letting his frustrations boil over. "They expect me to be king of the largest kingdom in the Triad, but I can't fight, can't command, all I can do is --*marry*. It's like I'm-- well, it's like I'm a *woman*," he huffed, resisting the urge to hit something. He couldn't believe how confined he felt.

"Everyone's compelled to marry, Edris. I was married once, just before the war. I'd never met her before the wedding. It wasn't so bad."

Edris knew better than to ask where his wife was now. He looked up suddenly and frowned at the knight. "Before the war? How old *are* you?"

Neill laughed. "I'm not so old, I'm near to thirty. I married very young, for a holdfast that didn't prove all that useful anyway." He glanced over to him and asked, "How old did you think I was?"

"Not too much older than me," Edris admitted. But he supposed now, looking at Neill, he saw twenty-nine years rather plainly. *It might have been more hope than thought*, he told himself, then frowned. *What did that mean?*

"Well, don't worry, Your Highness, perhaps I've aged well but you're still the pretty one." He really blushed then, and felt something strange flipping his stomach, different than sick. Better. But as embarrassed and confused as he was, it reminded him of his other question.

"And you were married to a woman? I thought..."

For a moment he thought Neill had almost actually rolled his eyes. "We don't all *only* love men, you know. We just don't think that's something to be ashamed of. You don't decide a thing like that. Haven't you ever...?"

"Never," Edris said, emphatically. For an instant, inexplicably, Mychal's face as he rode out of the Queenshearth stables flashed through his mind, but he shook it away.

"Right," Neill said, though he didn't seem to believe him, and smirked the same way he had outside Jonn's chambers. "Anyway. That wasn't what you came to talk about."

"No?" Edris asked. He wasn't exactly sure why he'd come himself. And he could feel his heart pounding now, especially when Neill stared at him like this. The feeling had returned.

"No. You can't sleep. Why?"

Edris shuffled his feet where he stood. "You saw the map. What do you think?"

"Truthfully?" The prince nodded. Neill looked away. "They might stand a chance. Maybe. But I wouldn't have much hope."

"Why?" Edris asked, feeling his stomach sinking even as he heard himself getting defensive. "They have more men."

"That's what they think," Neill said. "Daemons are cunning, it's hard to know when and where they'll appear. And even if the Army does have more, it won't matter if they aren't good fighting men. *And* besides that, they'll have to go in too far to meet them."

"So what should we do?" Edris asked.

Neill's eyes burned into his then as he told him, "Tell your Lord Marshal to call off the attack. Or his men's blood will be on his hands."

Edris reacted in kind. "The Holy Army is the Godhead's force against Eiros. They won't lose. Eirosia doesn't stand a chance."

Neill's eyes narrowed. "*Eirosia's* already gone. The Daemon King's who they'll meet at the Canyon. He killed my people. He'll kill yours."

Edris's confidence seemed to evaporate under the man's gaze. Just like it always did. "And I won't be with them," he muttered, blinking back hot tears and trying not to show just how furious and sick he felt. He wished then he could be anyone else. Anyone, even damned and lonely Mychal; at least *he* could do what he would.

"Edris," Neill said. Everything about the knight had softened, his voice lower, and he was standing much closer to him now. Edris forgot how to breathe.

"*Prince* Edris," he insisted, feeling hot and very... *seen* under his gaze. He started for the door but Neill stopped him with a gentle hand on his arm. *Thank the gods.*

"*Edris*," he repeated, just as firm, and calmly turned him around and kissed him, gentle but sending a shock through Edris nonetheless. Everything in him told him this was mad, wrong, that he should stop him, but he found after a moment that not a single part of him wanted to do that.

He practically melted into the knight's arms, who soon broke away and, smiling softly, led him to the cot. Something in him had started listening to Neill. The knight laid down, and Edris quickly followed. Neill kissed him again, strong arms flexed tight as he held himself above him before shifting to one side and caressing his face, his neck, his chest.

"So it's true, about Eirosians," Edris managed to gasp, as the touches moved lower. He could hardly breathe.

"It's alright," Sir Alexander said softly. "There's no shame. You've wanted me for too long not to know that."

Edris knew.

# 12

# Samira



*Dear Lyha,*

*Hi. I know that you probably don't want to hear from me, but I had to try to write to you, to-- explain some things. I wouldn't blame you if you don't ever want to see me again but I do want to see you, if you'll have me. I'm so sorry for screaming at you like that. I don't know why I did it. I'll try to explain why below, but just to make sure you see: I'd like to see you tonight. Alone. Is that alright? I know you're leaving in the morning and I just-- need to see you first. To talk, and also, I'm so sorry, but I need your help. Can we meet outside, maybe at midnight? By the Morra shrine. I'll be waiting for you.*

*About that night. First of all, I told you I didn't share your feelings and I suppose that's not quite it...*

Queenshearth felt more daunting now than it had the last time

"

Samira was here, eight years ago now, and that visit was for a funeral. The royal procession south from Hollisport was on its fourteenth day when the city came into view, and she had thought she'd be excited for a break from the ride. But all she felt was anxiety. Her best friend-- former best friend?-- would be Declared tonight, and would leave for Thorncliffe in the morning. Samira only hoped she would want to see her first.

Lyha hadn't written her since the last Declaration they'd attended together, and she didn't blame her. That night in the Golden Forests was enough to make anyone distance themselves, she knew that. She wished she could explain what she'd really been feeling underneath all that ire. She'd tried, in the pages of the letter tucked into her cloak.

She gripped the straps on the walls of the carriage she was riding in with her mother and brother, as the wheels of the wagon hit the rocky path up to the gates. Mason had his face pressed up to the glass, eager for a view of the city he'd never seen before, while her mother had started to stare at her, frowning. "What?" she asked, instantly self-conscious.

"What's wrong, dear?" she asked, not unkindly. "You've been quiet all day."

"Nothing, Mom," she said, looking away. "Just not sure I want to be around all these people."

"You used to love parties," the queen reminded her, trying for a smile. Samira shrugged. "Well," her mother sighed, "what do I know? You're a mature young woman of fourteen and six months now."

"Mom."

"Sorry, love."

"Are you worried for Lyha?" she asked, and Samira's head snapped up. Her mother gave a kind of sympathetic, knowing smile. "Of course you are. Leaving home and growing up is never easy, and of course I'm sure she'll be nervous. But really, darling, your friend will be fine. I've heard Edris Thorne is much kinder than his father."

"Yeah," Samira muttered, "he'd kind of have to be." But that wasn't what worried her. Or maybe it was, but in a kind of round-the-bend way. She couldn't understand why the marriage was going forward at all, after what she'd told her in the Forest. *She told me she could never love a man, never marry. What is she doing?*

Even then, she chided herself, knowing on some level that wasn't fair. *It's not like you want to marry Riyan Duane. Or anyone, really.* She really didn't. She'd tried, sometimes, to understand what the other girls meant when they talked about some handsome serving boy or squire in the Academy, but she never really got past pretending in hopes something would stick. She'd always been relieved that she was betrothed, so she didn't really have to think about it. Until that became far too real and far too fast approaching, too.

But Lyha's day was here. *Doesn't that mean she'll want to see me?* Samira asked herself, hopefully. *In the stories they always want to see their true love before they leave.* The thought shocked herself into silence for the rest of the ride. She'd called herself her...

But so had Lyha.

The royal carriage passed the city gates and Samira heard the fanfare outside, saw the cheering crowds as they rode through the Hartlander throngs waiting for each arriving noble party. It was all a bit too much, especially in the state her mind was in lately. She was obviously preoccupied with her and Lyha, but there was something else that was quickly taking precedence.

It had only been a few weeks ago when she'd found out. She and her handmaidens had been swimming in the creek, and one of the girls took a bad fall off the bridge, into the more rapid foaming water ahead. The rest of the attendants had shouted for help and gotten out of the water, but without even thinking Samira swam straight for the girl, and carried herself along the current far too fast to reach her in time. She also knew, knew, that she'd pushed the rapids back into the both of them to get the girl out of the rocks. Only the two of them had noticed, and she was sure the girl was equal parts grateful and terrified enough to be silent about it, but it was certainly enough for Samira.

She was a mage. And she had to marry the head of the Priesthood in less than two years' time.

When she'd thought about who to turn to, she'd considered her parents, but she never wanted to burden them with all they had to endure already. Her mother had already lost her entire family in one horrible summer, when Samira was small, and she couldn't imagine causing her to worry about losing a daughter, too. And deep down, she knew they were powerless to break the engagement to Duane. It was a spoil of war, as much as it disgusted her to think of it that way. As was Lyha's to Thorne. Her stomach turned at the thought of having to watch tonight.

But the only person she really wanted to run to was Lyha. She'd always been her greatest comfort, at school and ever since. Even a letter was usually enough to brighten her whole week. And as much as she knew she probably didn't deserve it now, she needed her more than ever. So her magic was in the letter, too. Maybe it would change things.

"Daniel!" The King of the Hartlands was waiting for them when the horses slowed to a stop, in the courtyard of Hartshold Keep along the northeast bend of the crumbling city walls. Samira's father stepped out and embraced his friend, while her mother and Mason followed after him. Cautiously, Samira pulled herself off of the bench and peered through the doorway. Was Lyha here? When she stepped out, though, she didn't see her. It was the king and his councilors alone.

"All this for us?" her father asked, and Lyha's father coughed.

"Er, no, we're expecting the prince at any moment," he admitted, with a sheepish smile. "But between you and I, I'm much more glad to see your faces." The two men laughed and Eronn glanced over to Samira.

"Hello, Princess," he said, and she bowed with a polite smile to mask her trepidation. Why had his face fallen when he'd seen her? "Er, Lyha's in the hunting woods. She said she needed some time to herself before the ceremony. My apologies."

Samira tried not to let herself go red in front of all these people. She was sure King Eronn knew much more than he was letting on about the state of their friendship, but she managed to say, "Of course," in a somewhat normal voice. They were just about to be led inside when a trumpet sounded and another, extensively guarded royal party came riding into the courtyard.

Prince Edris Thorne was looking down his nose from the moment he climbed off his horse. He was riding an actual white stallion, which a stableboy led away while he brushed dust off his perfectly spotless silver armor. Samira smirked as she remembered something her Uncle Lyam had told her once: *Men with no marks on their armor don't put themselves between anyone and a blade.* This boy-- or young man, she supposed, five years older than her, though he hardly looked it-- certainly never had.

This was who Lyha was marrying? Samira couldn't imagine it. She didn't want to imagine it, she realized very suddenly when calling a picture of their wedding to mind made her feel in an instant like she was going to be sick. She told herself it was because she felt horrible for her friend, knew this was nothing like what she wanted. She wanted to turn away.

"Your Highness," Eronn was saying. "Welcome to Queenshearth. I'm Eronn, it's an honor to meet you at last. And your father will be joining us...?"

"Any minute now, sir, yes, thank you," the young man replied, the high airy vowels of the most posh Northern accent Samira had ever heard making every word grate against her ears. "And is your daughter here?" Horribly, he looked around until his eyes landed on *her*. He smiled with relief, and Samira grimaced and tried to look to her mother for help. "Princess Lyha. You have a beautiful home--"

"I'm not Lyha," she blurted out, interrupting. Her mother stilled, and she winced, knowing she would hear a lecture on deference later. "I'm Samira. Hollis. Sorry."

"Ah, right." He took a small step back, blushing bright red. "Apologies, Your Highness."

"My daughter is taking the air in our woodlands at the moment, Prince Edris," King Eronn jumped in. "I do hope it isn't too much trouble to ask you to wait for an introduction until the time of the ceremony."

Edris looked a little baffled, but nodded. "No problem at all. Er, and when will the ceremony be?"

"Four o'clock, Your Highness, if it please you. In the King's Cathedral. Someone will show you to your chambers in the meantime."

"Yes, we'll retire till then as well," Samira's father interjected quickly. "Afternoon." He whisked their whole family away, and Samira stole one last glance at Edris, who was watching her curiously as she went. She shot a final glare in his direction and followed her parents and brother inside.

"What was that, young lady?" the queen asked once they were alone, climbing the keep's stairs up to the solar and the guest chambers beyond.

"I'm sorry," she grumbled. "I'm not feeling well."

Her mother hesitated, and frowned at her, examining her while Samira squirmed. "Rest, love," she finally said with a sigh. "It'll be a long feast."

"Mason, come with us," Daniel added as they turned the corner into their regular accomodations. "We're going to have a talk about proper feast ettiquette. You're too old now, the running round screaming's not charming anymore." The door closed behind them and Samira was alone.

She still had the letter. What would she do with it? Slip it under Lyha's door? No, she was too terrified a handmaiden would read it. She considered going into the chambers herself and waiting for her to come back, but she knew if she reacted badly she'd never be out of trouble with her mother again. No, she would wait until it was almost time, and knock. She'd have to see her. Wouldn't she?

She laid on the bed in the guest bedchamber, staring at the ceiling with the letter between her folded hands and her chest. One of Lyha's handmaidens came in and helped her wash in the basin in the corner, and she suffered through a long conversation about how she had been since Fen Faris. The girl was still talking excitedly when she was already back in her chemise, drying off. "I can't wait to see your gown," Mara said, grinning. "Lyha's wearing the prettiest one I've ever seen her in, actual silk and velvet with a coat and everything, and she's wearing stays, can you believe it?"

Samira froze. "Lyha's dressed? She's back from the woods?"

"Yes, Princess. She's just across the hall."

She blinked, heart suddenly pounding while Mara stared, raising her eyebrows. "Help me get into this," she finally said, rushing over and pulling the green velvet monstrosity out of her bags. "Quickly."

It had only been ten minutes by the time she'd been dressed and her hair had been styled enough to be seen in public, but Samira was still worried she would be too late. She rushed across the hall, leaving Mara behind, and started pounding on the door to the rooms Lyha shared with her sister. "Lyha!" she called, when there was no reply. "It's me. Please open the door?"

There was no answer, not for a long while. Finally, just when she was about to give up, the door creaked open. Her hopes were dashed as quick as they'd begun when Jullia stepped out into the hall instead. The little girl, who couldn't be more than eleven, smiled awkwardly and hugged Samira after she closed the door firmly behind her. "You look beautiful!" the girl told her.

"Thanks, Jullia, you, too," she said quietly, already a little resigned. They stood in awkward silence for a moment before she asked, "She's... not going to see me, is she?"

Jullia bit her lip and looked down at her shoes. "No."

Her heart felt like it was pounding in her ears, in her chest, making her feel faint. "Jule. Please. Just let me in. I just need to talk to her for a moment."

"I don't think that's a good idea, Sami, she's really upset. This is a really important day for her," Jullia started rambling nervously. "I'm really sorry for whatever's going on between you two but maybe you can write to her in Thorncliffe or something."

"That'll be too late!" Samira exclaimed, then cringed, ushering Jullia closer to the wall as guests making their way down to the Cathedral started to stare. "I need to see her before she goes."

Jullia crossed her arms, and though the girl's voice shook a little, she held her ground. "I'm sorry. I can't let you in. She said not to."

Samira felt herself starting to cry and wiped furiously at her eyes as Jullia watched her apologetically. "Okay. Okay. Well, could you just-- could you give her this?" She handed Jullia the letter, and she took it, looking uncertain. "Please."

The girl sighed. "I can't promise anything."

"That's okay. Just... give her the letter. Thanks." Samira turned to go.

She met her family in the solar and they went down together, to sit on the cold stone and watch the ceremony. The seats filled with hundreds of guests, milling about and talking about nothing whatsoever important. She couldn't stand it. She was about to lose her best friend forever, to some posh horrible evangelist prince who'd never set foot in the south before in his life. He wasn't even here yet, just standing awkwardly in the antechamber she supposed, with his horrible father.

The doors opened then, and everyone stood. She wasn't tall enough to see the far end of the aisle by the doors from behind everyone else in the crowd, but she knew Lyha had entered the Cathedral. When Samira stood, she felt her knees start to go out, her heart picking up mercilessly again just at the prospect of seeing her. She almost gave up and sat back down, but she felt a hand grasp hers strongly and support her from her right. Her mother held onto her firmly, staring straight ahead along with the others.

Lyha was walking stiffly down the aisle of the Cathedral, sharp jaw tightened as she forced herself forward-- that was how it seemed to Samira. She felt herself almost smile, at the sight of her friend again, despite how miserable and uncomfortable she looked. The gown didn't suit her at all, no matter what Mara said. And she looked like she would rather be anywhere else. She looked up into the stands and suddenly her eyes met hers.

The two of them stared at each other in silence for a long moment. Samira tried to smile, feeling herself well up with tears again, looking into Lyha's wide dark eyes for the first time in months. She almost saw softness in them, too, and maybe also tears. But soon she looked away, and turned to face the opposite side of the crowd. Samira deflated, and her mother let go of her hand as the crowd returned to their seats.

Samira tried not to watch for the rest of the ceremony, after Edris walked in and the Priest started his horrible recitations. She couldn't help but stare in blank horror at their handbinding, feeling sick rising in her stomach again all the while. As soon as it was over, Lyha bolted from the hall, with a fleeting glance Samira's way that she tried to catch but couldn't. She was gone again. Her only consolation was that Edris looked just as slighted as her, blinking in confusion next to the altar.

Dinner was just as horrible. She sat by her mother and brother, watching Lyha recieve admirers and congratulations at the high table with Edris by her side. She absolutely refused to go with her parents to join the line, not able to stomach the idea of pleasantries being their only interaction. But the feast dragged on and on, with no end in sight, and Samira found herself watching the timepiece carved into the wall, moving the moonlight along the notches. Was it midnight yet? And would it even matter? Was she coming to meet her then?

She looked back up at the table and could see that Lyha and Edris had started to speak. She would give anything to know what they were talking about. She didn't look happy, that was certain. Maybe she was telling him she wouldn't go through with the match--

"Princess Samira," a voice interrupted her brother and broke her out of her thoughts. She looked up to see a young man in a green velvet doublet grinning at her from a polite distance away from the table. He bowed to her father and added, "Your Majesty. My name is Cavan Moran, I'm a squire to Sir Jason Baylor. May I have the honor of a dance with your daughter?"

Daniel took a long drink from his mead and said, "My daughter can answer that for herself, young man."

Samira restrained herself from groaning. The Morans and the Baylors were both lords of the Horn and sworn to her father. She essentially had to say yes. "Of course, sir."

Cavan brought her into the dancing floor in the center of the tables, as the band started a long, emotional Hornish ballad she would have rather died than dance to. When their hands touched, she tried not to recoil. He didn't dare put his hand on her actual waist, but rather hovered it over the cinch of her gown, and she glanced down and tried to rid her face of the grimace she knew she wore.

Samira looked around as they swayed awkwardly in step with the other couples, many young girls like her laughing and talking with boys just like Cavan. Were they better at pretending than she was? How could anyone possibly enjoy this kind of thing?

Would she like it better if she were dancing with Lyha?

Cavan spun her around at a swell in the music and they floated far too close to the high table. Before she could hurry them away, Samira saw Lyha see them among the dancers. *Shit.*

Lyha stood up and fled from the hall, out the side door that went to the stables. After a moment, Edris, clearly rattled, rushed out after her.

"Is something wrong?" Cavan asked, and Samira turned back to him, trying not to show her hurt on her face. *Did she think I did this on purpose?*

"No," she said. "No, I'm alright. Um, tell me about you, Cavan. You're from Greenfield?"

She talked with the boy until the song ended and excused herself graciously, returning to her seat in a haze. "Are you alright, dear?" her mother asked her, looking concerned. "You're pale."

"Yes," she mumbled. "Er, yes, I'm alright. I'm just, er, going to take some air. Excuse me." She'd caught the time on the wall as she returned to the table. Five minutes to midnight. Maybe Lyha would be waiting to meet her after all.

Samira slipped out the same door Lyha and Edris had gone out from, but there was no one at the shrine. There was a light in the stables just ahead, but she didn't see anyone in the doorway there. So she sat, and waited, under the graystone goddess that stared facelessly out at the night.

She waited until midnight. Then till ten minutes past. Then twenty. Finally, she started to cry, really cry, believing for the first time that she really wasn't coming. Had she even read the letter? Samira didn't think so. She couldn't believe, even after everything that's happened, that Lyha would leave her to deal with the death sentence of her magic alone.

She was about to go back to the castle. And then she heard something.

There was a commotion coming from the stables; she could hear muffled voices, and possibly hoofbeats on the path. Maybe Lyha had gone there, she thought, and started to stand. She could run down there, plead her case, tell her she'd finally figured things out, that the only one she ever wanted to dance with was her...

A lone rider left the stables. A small, cloaked figure, a boy-- she thought-- *someone* with dark curls and wide, dark eyes, leaving on a yearling courser with a satchel slung over his shoulder.

Samira watched Lyha until she couldn't see her anymore, until she and her horse had disappeared into the night, leaving her behind.

# 13

## Mychal

Luke was right, Declarations in the Horn were different from the ones he'd seen in the Hartlands. They were much more formal, for one, and just setting foot in the King's Cathedral was intimidating enough. Though that might have been because of who he was walking in with.

They were told not to speak to the Godhead once the ceremony began, but they were all presented to him outside the Cathedral beforehand. Mychal was there at the end of the line, trying not to be sick, standing at attention next to Sir James. As the Godhead moved down the assembly of knights and squires composing the honor guard, Mychal tried to strain to get a better view of him. He only managed to see the outline of a tall, thin man in resplendent blue and gold before Sir James told him to keep his eyes straight ahead.

He knew the knight only thought he was innocently curious, but inside Mychal was close to panicking. He was so conscious of the vials from Vance in his pocket that he felt like they were burning a hole through the fabric. The mage-catchers worried him-- he knew one of the worst of them, Jacob Denastor, was with the Godhead's party now-- not just for Samira, but for himself. If they sensed potion on him, he didn't even want to think about what they might do. But it hadn't seemed any safer to leave the vials in his bedroll, thrown into an antechamber full of cots in the lower floors with all the others. Between them, and his chain with the Halwood crest hidden with them, it was all he could do not to noticeably sweat here in sight of Riyan Duane himself.

"Sir James Reinhold, Your Holiness," the knight said, when it was their turn, bowing deeply. Mychal saw the man nod in his peripheral vision, before Sir James added, "And my squire, Mychal Owyn."

The Godhead stepped in front of him, and Mychal managed to bow deeply and slowly as James had done. When he raised his head again, he met the gaunt figure's eyes, just for a moment, but it was enough to make him flinch. The man's eyes were clouded over, like he was blind or cursed, but Mychal could tell he could see him. He inclined his head and smiled politely before moving on. Something in the eyes gave Mychal a chill down his spine.

Once the Godhead was gone, the rest of the entourage passed him by without a second glance, including the mage-catcher, and he began to breathe again. They took their places in front of the cathedral doors, and the party formed a line directly behind Duane. Sir James led Mychal to their place, Sir Callum and Luke and several others behind them. There were six more on the party's other side, and walking behind the entire procession. "Isn't he...?" Luke breathed when Mychal took his place behind him.

"He's thin," Mychal said quietly. Luke started to turn and frown at him, but was corrected swiftly by Sir Callum. Mychal was again taken aback when he snuck another look at Duane, supposedly Astor's messenger on Earth. He looked more sickly than anything else. It was difficult to remind himself to be afraid.

The doors were thrown open then, and the Holy Army procession marched into the Cathedral.

They approached the altar in the middle of the cavernous stone structure, slowly, regally, and a hush fell over the audience as their attention openly abandoned the Declared already standing in her place. But Mychal remained focused on her.

Samira was gorgeous, there was no way around it; he tried not to feel guilty for thinking it, staring at her burnt-red ringlets and long velvet gown. The green and gray of House Hollis had always suited her, but she looked more beautiful today than he had ever seen. He felt a pang in his chest, an ache that reminded him of long nights spent at Fen Faris, dreaming alone. He saw her eyes search for and land on his, and he thought she relaxed, just a bit, when she saw him. At least he could do that for her. He tried to smile at her, but found that he couldn't, not once the Godhead had reached her and taken her hand.

The priests, the ceremony, the words said while they bound Samira to her future, it all blurred together for Mychal. He stood at the edge of the open area of the cathedral, guarding her from the masses, which struck him as funny considering how much more danger she was in from the people standing there with her. It felt like forever before the pronouncements stopped, and when the Guard followed both of them from the cathedral he couldn't have told anyone what exactly had happened. In his mind, he was far away from here and a long time before tonight.

He loved her. He'd loved her for years, and he'd thought he could forget when he ran, but now he knew it was hopeless. It had always been her.

As soon as they crossed the threshold, Sir James led him out of the crowd's path and said, "His Holiness brought his personal guard and said they'll be sufficient for the festivities. We'll be off duty for the feast, at a table close to the dais."

"Yes, sir," Mychal said, and heard Luke calling him back to the rest of the guard.

"Go on, then," Sir James said. "I've got to discuss with the other Officers." Mychal turned away and made his way over to his friend.

"Well, what'd you think?" Luke asked.

"About what?" he asked, still a little dazed. "The ceremony? It was alright, I suppose."

"I'd think it'd be a lot to take in," Luke said. "I mean, I grew up in a castle but even for me, that cathedral is really something else. Haddon Hollis was mad, but maybe in the right way."

"Oh yeah, everything was beautiful," he said, going a little red. He didn't like the position it put him in when Luke started talking about his birth. It made things harder to keep straight. He wondered how Luke would react if he ever found out who he was. Or who he was deciding to be.

"First time?" one of the other boys said. "The feast'll be even better. Ever been to one of those, Owyn?"

"Er, once, but just the tables outside," he said. He hoped that made sense. He'd seen something like that going on outside of his own Declaration.

"It's a different world inside," the boy laughed. "And the *girls*. Girls and wine. Come on. We'll have fun." Mychal let himself smile and be taken into the group while they walked with the rest of the city up to the Skytower.

The hall they'd been sleeping in that week was unrecognizable when they returned. Tables filled most of the space, decorated with glass oil lanterns and overflowing plates of every kind of food Mychal had ever seen, and some he hadn't. He'd been royalty in the Hartlands, but the Hornish royalty were *royalty*. He had never seen anything like it. Doors were flung open to the outer courtyard beyond, where Mychal could hear music and dancing starting to pick up. Inside the hall, there were already hundreds seated, and by the time they reached the table set aside for the Army, the roar of laughing voices was nearly deafening. Samira and her family entered last, with the Godhead, "His Holiness Riyan Duane and his betrothed Princess Samira". Mychal reached for the wine.

The drinking flowed freely, but Mychal only drank enough to ease his mind, not anywhere near enough to be careless. When Luke was paying attention to him, he made himself seem drunker than he really was, an act he was used to from Lady May's. Luckily, though, in the Halwoods' place the Hartlands had sent the Lords of the Golden Forest, and Luke was soon thoroughly distracted by his bride-to-be Talia Penn.

Mychal suspected Luke had talked to the other squires at some point about manners, because they were much friendlier to him than they had been before. They in fact seemed determined to show him a good time at his 'first feast', and as much as he appreciated the thought, he couldn't stop glancing at the high table to make sure all was still well with Samira. She looked rigid and distant every time he managed to spot her, sitting high on the dais, between Duane and her father. But no one had arrested her, so the amulet seemed to be working okay.

It was much later that night, after an exhausting conversation about the serving girls with a very drunk boy, when he noticed that Samira was missing, and the Godhead too. "Excuse me," he mumbled quietly, before he made for one of the doors leading outside. His heart was pounding, and the sudden burst of lively music and stomping feet when he made it outside didn't do his anxiety any favors. He started to scan the crowd and sighed in relief when he found Samira right in the center, dancing-- and with Luke, no less. Mychal tried not to roll his eyes as he pushed his way through the crowd to stand somewhere she might be able to see him.

He caught her eye just as the dance ended, and she smiled at him. That would have been enough for him to go back inside, satisfied she was alright, but when Luke whirled her around one last time, he ended up seeing Mychal too. Grinning, his friend strode towards him as the guests spilled back out into the rest of the dancing area, and Samira followed.

"Mychal, I was wondering where you were! I know you're not much for dancing but it's only old men left in the hall," he said, slurring his words only slightly. Remembering himself then, he drew himself up, despite the intoxication, and said, "Your Highness, this is Mychal Owyn, squire to Sir James Reinhold."

"Pleasure to meet you, Mychal," Samira said, grinning breathlessly.

He forgot how to speak for a moment before saying, "The pleasure's mine, Your Highness," and bowing low. "Congratulations." The smile in her eyes faded when he met them again, and he regretted saying it.

"Does your friend want a dance as well, Lord Payne?" she asked Luke, and Luke's eyes widened as he looked at Mychal with eyebrows raised.

"I don't know any of the dances they'd be doing here, Your Highness," Mychal protested, starting to blush again, and Samira shrugged.

"It's my Declaration. What dances *do* you know, Mychal?"

Luke grinned and walked away tactfully, bowing to the princess, as Mychal looked back at her, trying to tell her why he was hesitating. She quietly said, "It's alright. One dance, as a thank you for my protection-- it won't stand out."

He nodded and said awkwardly, "I'm from the Hartlands, Your Highness. I know 'The Lady of Lake Royal'."

He thought he saw her breath catch before she smiled and said, "I'll tell the band." She disappeared for a moment and Mychal tried, without much success, to compose himself. He heard the band start the first chords on the lute, and the fiddle came in high after that, mournful in a major key. Partners started to dance all throughout the courtyard, and Samira found her way back to him just as the bard was starting to sing.

*"I met my love at the end of the river, where Lake Royal turns Brookbridge blue..."*

"Where's His Holiness?" he asked, when they were far enough away for no one to hear.

She rolled her eyes. "He had to rest before our private audience later."

"What private audience?" That wasn't a part of the Declaration Mychal was familiar with. He frowned.

"Didn't you have one?" she asked.

"I don't know, I ran away before we made it that far," he said, and she hushed him quickly, but he saw her laugh in spite of herself as the dance picked up and she spun away from him. The lake dancing in the Hartlands was quick, light, and energetic, and not at all too close for propriety's sake, but something about this was giving Mychal the pang in his chest all over again. Maybe it was the song, but then, that had been the point.

*"I left my love at the end of the river, while the goddess watched me go..."*

He saw Luke dancing with Talia, and some of the other squires with girls he didn't know. He saw Samira's brother Mason dancing with one of her handmaidens and her uncle Lyam slowly swaying with his wife Lady Sanya, ignoring the steps of the dance entirely. He felt almost too sad to continue and he would have walked away if he didn't know this was the last time he'd see Samira for a long time, possibly ever.

"I'm alright, Mychal," she said, the next time no one would be able to overhear. "It's working. Thank you."

"It wasn't any trouble," he said, trying to keep his smile on his face.

"Did you get what you wanted, too?" she asked.

*Not half of it*, he thought, looking at her, but instead managed to say, "Yes."

Her smile seemed even wider then, and took his breath from him in an instant. "Oh, thank the gods. I really am happy for you."

"Really?" he asked.

"Of course," she said, and even though everything in him distrusted anyone understanding him as *him*, he did believe her. As the song drew to a close, they parted again, and he forced himself to memorize everything about her in that moment. His best friend, grown up and beautiful and still, for the moment, belonging to herself.

> *"All my nights with naught but my heart and the Mother's light*
> *Would all fade to gray, oh, if ever you were mine."*

When the song ended, he bowed respectfully and she walked away, both of them very aware of the eyes on them. It was acceptable for them to dance, he supposed, but only just. He had the feeling a few observers had noticed the way he'd been looking at her, and he hoped for her sake they'd just see another squire infatuated with the princess. It might have been safer, but the thought made his face burn as he returned, still dazed, to the hall.

That night, he had the watch second, but he couldn't fall asleep for even the short time he had, knowing that *he* was with her in the keep. What was going on? He didn't want to speculate but he couldn't help himself. He only hoped she was alright. When Luke came to wake him up, he didn't help things by adding, "His Holiness is in there, so when you go up make sure you're at attention."

"Okay," Mychal said, getting dressed again as quietly as he could.

"I didn't hear anything, but if you do, make sure to tell me," he said, grinning from ear to ear, and Mychal grumbled something noncommittal. "How was your dance?" Luke asked, suddenly livening even more, and Mychal wished he could lace his boots faster.

"It was... brilliant. It was great," he said, doing his best not to let his face flush again.

"Dancing with the princess, not bad for--for you," Luke said, going a bit pink, before he clapped him awkwardly on the shoulder and said, "Goodnight, mate."

"Night," Mychal said, relieved when Luke finally made his way to his cot.

The climb up to the family's rooms hadn't filled Mychal with so much dread since the first night. Luke hadn't helped things, but he'd been dreading this moment long before that. Nothing, however, prepared him for the panic he felt when he opened the door to the Hollis solar and found himself face to face with the Godhead and his personal attendant. "Um, hello," Riyan Duane said. His voice was strangely quiet. "Are you the new watchman?"

"Yes," Mychal forced out, blinking rapidly.

"Well, you really should change shifts without leaving the chamber unguarded at all. Someone should just wake you up. You should tell them that."

"Yes, sir-- um, Your Holiness."

Duane shrugged. "I know it's not your fault, it's alright. But I want her to be safe. Goodnight, er... I'm sorry. I thought I knew it, but your name's lost on me." He left the room without another word.

Mychal, through his shock, almost laughed as he thought that it was probably better if he remained unremarkable to someone like that. Duane took the tension in the room with him when the door shut, and Mychal sat down at the base of the stairs, trying to ignore the sea of dark thoughts flooding his head.

"Mychal?" A young girl's voice interrupted his wallowing and he looked up to see the same handmaiden that had come for him earlier that week. "If you want to see her..."

He was standing in a heartbeat. "Yes. I do."

Samira was still wearing the Declaration gown, though she'd let most of the petticoat layers fall in a fluffed pile to the ground and all that remained was the Hollis-green silk outer dress, draping over her legs in a way that made Mychal almost look away. She'd let her hair fall down around her shoulders, too. He entered the room and the handmaiden shut the door behind him, and then it was just the two of them. She looked like she'd just been crying, but he knew she'd never admit that. "It went alright?" he asked carefully.

"It was fine," she said quietly. "He was quiet." She looked down and admitted, "He scares me."

"Of course he does," he said, slowly moving in and sitting down beside her on the sofa. "You know what him being here means. I was scared, too, when Edris came." They both knew it wasn't the same. A heavy silence hung in the air. "The amulet worked, then."

"Yes," she said, exhaling sharply. "That went right, at least." She looked at him, smiled a little, and said, "So. You're going to be a man."

He shrugged a little. "Mostly so far I've just been hungry and tired. But that's what Farrah said." In truth, that wasn't quite right either; he was starting to understand the way he felt about Samira was so different from the others that he had no idea *what* he was anymore, other than in love.

"What are you going to do with it?"

He looked up, daring to meet her eyes, and she looked like she was hanging on his every word. He paused before he said, as sure as he dared, "I'm going to take my crown."

She smiled. "Good." A glint of mischief appeared in her eyes then, and she said, "You'll have to go back to Astor Post now, I expect. But my father told me to get out of Hollisport for a while, he thought it'd be good for me. So I'm thinking of going down to Queenshearth... and seeing some of the holy sites in the Hartlands." He looked at her, confused, and she added, "You know, like the Pool of the Mother, in *Brookbridge*." Oh. The Paynes. "The Golden Forests and Fen Eiros." The Penns and Allyns. "The Landing at Surpoint." The Wrights and the Great Forge. "Anyone-- I mean, anywhere-- I'm missing?"

Mychal smiled widely then, beaming at her. "You should take Jullia with you. You can trust her. Tell her the truth."

"I will," Samira said. "I might not be with you but I'll make sure your lords are."

"Thank you, Sami," he said quietly. He could feel all his feelings, from all the years of wanting, threatening to make themselves known. "I wish I could help you."

"I don't want to marry him, Mychal," she suddenly said, her voice breaking, and he couldn't take it anymore.

He felt the ache swelling in his chest again. "If I'm ever strong enough to protect you from him, I will," he promised. The words were tumbling out of him now, before he could really think about what he was saying. "If you move quickly I might have the men before it's too late."

Samira looked overwhelmed. "You promise?"

"I do." He took her hand then, and held it tight between them. She looked down at it and back up at him, and he felt his face burning but for the first time he didn't care at all.

"Mychal," she said slowly, "what you said. Back at Talia Penn's Declaration. Did you mean it?"

His eyes welled up with tears and he tried to push the feeling down. But it didn't matter. She knew him "Every word." he said, nodding, and without warning she leaned over and kissed him fiercely, bowling him over onto his back. When he was finally set free, he propped himself up on his elbows and gazed up at her, dazed and completely lovesick. "Sami... you're about to be--"

"I know," she said, pulling back, just a little and he could see the pain in her face. "I know I can't be yours but–"

"No," he said, fiercely. Something came over him, and his words came easy and breathlessly, looking right in her eyes and without the least bit of shame. "You're not mine and I love you *because of it.* You're your own, you're my best friend and the love of my life and my *queen,* if I had what I wanted. Sami, I've always loved you, before I was ever this. I loved you as a girl, as the girl I was, and I love the woman you are, as..." He laughed a little and said, "As whatever I become."

"Mychal..." she breathed, eyes wide, and he smiled, with the pure joy of hearing her speak his real name. "I love you, too."

He kissed her, fiercely, burning with a kind of heat and hunger and happiness he hadn't ever felt before.

She took a deep breath when they separated and said, "And I want it to be you. ...First. Not him. You."

She kissed him again, and he pulled away long enough to say, "I-gods, Sami, *yes,* but, I mean you know I don't-- have..."

"I don't want it to be like *that,* I just want... you," she whispered. "Is that alright?" He was looking at her, looking at him like he had always wanted her to, and he made his decision. He'd made it years ago.

"Yes," he said, "of *course.*"

* * *

It wasn't like what he'd imagined, it was much better. And anyway, he hadn't really known what to imagine. Samira was more than he'd ever dreamed, and every moment made it harder to leave now.

He knew that he had to. He also knew he'd do whatever he had to to keep her safe– including risk everything, for this new name and place in the world.

She fell asleep afterwards. Just in her shift. Mychal was pulling his shirt back on over his binding, getting ready to wake the next watch, but he found that he couldn't leave her– not yet. He sat watching her until the last possible moment, gently singing 'The Lady of Lake Royal' to himself.

# 14

# Samira

The road to Queenshearth from Hollisport was short, especially traveling in a small party like Samira was. Her mother had tried to convince her to go in a litter or coach, but she'd wanted to ride. Only two of her father's men had been sent with her, and Uncle Lyam had promised her they would be sympathetic if she couldn't hide her powers from them. It wouldn't have mattered if they hadn't come at all, as far as she could tell, because she was dressed like any common girl from the city, and most of her was hidden under a long, dark cloak. Her horse could have given her away, though; a Declaration present from her parents, Kit was a strong brown stallion, and he was too pretty to have come from anywhere rough. He made the ride easy, even though Samira could never get him to stay in one place long enough to tie with the other horses before he wandered off. She'd found him a good ways away from their camp more than once, sniffing curiously around the woods.

The men-- though they were more like boys, really-- were nice enough, but too terrified of her to really make conversation until more than a week into the journey, when they were almost there anyway. They had crossed the border into the Hartlands the day before, and were coming down the royal road to the capital city when the one on her right, Dominic, asked, "Have you ever been to Queenshearth, Your Highness?"

"Not since I was too young to really remember," she told him. "I've always wanted to go back."

"Hollisport's the only city I've ever seen," he admitted. Dominic was tall, with the strong, stocky build of a lot of the Horn's farming people, and looked much older than he seemed when he spoke. "I've never left the Horn until now."

"I have," the other one said, Harry, the smaller and older of the two. "I went to Astor Post for six months before I got called back to Skytower."

"Astor Post *is* in the Horn, Harry." Harry glared at Dominic and pulled the reins back on his horse, so Samira rode up on Kit between them.

"There's the city," she said, pointing over the crest of the hills ahead. The Hartlands' capital was a great walled fortress when it was built, with guarded turrets at every turn of the stone. But the centuries had worn down the walls until they were easy to pass through now. Queenshearth was built circling a hill, Hartshold Keep the crowning jewel at its peak. The castle, standing on the highest ground for miles, was much more exposed than the rest of the city would be if the walls were repaired; *not a bad place for a siege*, Samira thought, *but with catapults--or Daemonfire-- there wouldn't be much to be done.* Memories of the last time she was there, what must have been ten years ago now, all came back to her at once. Suddenly, she was thinking about the little girl she met then, her quiet, kind playmate who'd just lost her mother and brother.

Mychal had been gone when she'd woken up the morning after her Declaration. She'd known he would be but it still left her with some quietly painful feeling. She wondered where he was now, if he was back at Astor Post yet; she guessed not. They had both left Hollisport on the same day, and she was almost certain her road was shorter. If he was back, though, he'd be going into battle soon. She couldn't help but worry. He seemed every bit the soldier now, and she didn't want him to think she didn't have faith in him, but she wished she had a way to get a letter there when it was over, just to know he was safe.

When they rode further up into the highlands, they started passing groups of travelers, mostly old men and women but a good number of boys her age and young mothers too, all wearing some kind of blue and marching toward Queenshearth. With some distaste, she realized they were pilgrims, winding their way up the hills to Faris's Cathedral. She started to pull Kit's reins back, but Harry fell into line with them and said, "Safer to travel with them, Princess." So she resigned herself to being led into the capital by her future husband's devotees. They had always made her uneasy.

They had some trouble at the castle gates. The Halwoods had been told she was coming, but she knew she was never quite what people expected, and eventually the sentries brought down one of the men that had been with Mychal at Fen Faris to confirm who she was.

"That's her. Welcome, Princess," he said immediately, and the sentries stepped aside, looking a little embarrassed. Kit was led away to the stables, with some snorting reluctance that clearly unnerved the stableboy, while Dominic and Harry dismounted and followed her inside. "I'm sorry about that," the man said. "We haven't been letting almost anyone in lately."

"Why not?" she asked, as her eyes explored the entrance hall, covered floor to ceiling in tapestries and painted portraits of Halwoods, and the oldest Farisian bastard-lords before them. The hall seemed a bit small to her, for a royal keep, but then, so did everything else after the Skytower. More than anything, the castle felt *old*.

The man's voice dropped to a whisper, so low that Samira thought even Dominic and Harry likely couldn't hear. "His Majesty is in his final days. There's a Priest with him now."

Samira's face sobered and she nodded. "I understand. I came to see Jullia, if I could."

The man raised his voice again and said, "Of course, Your Highness. I'll take you to her." They passed through huge oak doors at the back of the hall into a large receiving room, and then up spiraling stairs to the Halwood family solar, where the man cleared his throat and knocked twice on the door.

"Yes?" Jullia's voice rang out, clear and confident, and Samira couldn't help but smile.

"Princess Samira to see you, Your Highness." They heard quick steps bounding up to the door then, and Jullia Halwood threw open the door herself, beaming when she saw her.

"Sami!" she exclaimed, and hugged the older girl as soon as she pulled her inside. Samira's guards closed the door discreetly behind them as Jullia added, "I had no idea you were coming until yesterday. You need faster riders."

"It was a little sudden," Samira agreed, laughing. Jullia was three years younger than her, but the Halwood middle child had always been old for her age, and they got along quite well. "You've gotten so tall!" she exclaimed, realizing she was of a height with the girl.

Jullia frowned. "Yes, well, I can't end up too tall. I hear Paul Baylor's still shorter than his mother."

Samira grinned. "He was at my Declaration, he's taller than me at least."

"That's not saying much," she said, smirking. "Well, he'll keep growing, and it's a while yet before *my* Declaration. But how was yours? Did you talk to *Him*?" A kind of awe had settled over Jullia as she spoke, and Samira's stomach started twisting in knots again.

"I'd rather not talk about Him," she said quietly, and the girl seemed to understand. She went over to the armchairs framing the fireplace and gestured for Samira to sit, too. As she did, she looked carefully at Mychal's sister, wondering how in all hells she was supposed to say what she came here to say. When she was quiet for a moment, Jullia frowned.

"What is it? Why *are* you here, anyway? I mean, I am happy to see you, but..."

"How's your father?" Samira interrupted, and tried not to feel bad when Jullia's face fell even more.

"It's getting much worse. The Stewards all gave up. They said the cancer is in the blood that's supposed to protect him, so he gets sick all the time and it's worse than it should be when he does. He has pneumonia now. It's probably going to end soon."

"I'm sorry," she said. The girl's face had gone a bit blank, but she nodded absently when she heard.

"Deronn's with him all the time now," she said. "Father's telling him all about what to do when he's king. It's really kind of scaring him."

"Deronn's here?" Samira asked, raising her eyebrows. "I thought he was still at Fen Faris."

Jullia nodded. "We sent for him last month. It was pretty clear Father wouldn't be around much longer." She sighed. "He's too young to be king."

Samira saw the opportunity and took a deep breath. "Jullia," she finally said, forcing her voice to stay steady, "he might not have to be."

"What?" she asked, and she saw her go still, like she was preparing for news the way Samira had seen her own parents do. She felt a sudden wave of sympathy for Jullia. The Hartlands didn't have a queen anymore; it seemed like most of that responsibility had fallen on her.

Everything came out then. Samira told her all of what Mychal had told her, and what he was doing now; she told her about the mage woman, too, and where she was really going after Queenshearth. When she finished, Jullia stared at her for another moment or so, until slowly she started to nod. Samira frowned. "What?"

"It's just... not that surprising," Jullia said, before she suddenly burst out laughing. She covered her face as she tried to stop giggling, and Samira didn't know what to make of any of it but she felt herself starting to grin. "I'm sorry," she managed, a little while later, "it's just... a lot."

"I know," Samira said. "That's alright."

"Oh, Holy Mother and Father," Jullia said, "that's... incredible. She's– oh, *he's* a squire? Brilliant." She giggled again and suddenly asked, "Do you want me to come with you?"

"He thought that you should," Samira said, smiling properly now. "But if you need to be here, I'd understand–"

"No, I should go," she said. "Lord Payne won't listen to a Hornish messenger, no matter who it is. He's a really proud, cranky old man."

"Okay," Samira laughed. "You're not worried about getting found out or...?"

Jullia shook her head, solemn now. "The queen was my mother too, Sami. And L-- *Mychal's* some of the only family I have left." She giggled again and exclaimed, "*Fucking* hell, this is *perfect*." When she saw Samira's startled face, she glanced sheepishly at the door and mumbled, "Er, sorry."

"I'll take my things upstairs," Samira offered, grinning, and opened the door to let Dominic in with their things.

Jullia, composing herself, nodded. "The guest chambers are on the next floor, there should be a bath drawn for you if you want to wash up. Come down when you're ready and we can see my father after we eat."

"Oh, I don't want to disturb him," she quickly said, but Jullia shook her head.

"No, no. He wanted to see you," she assured her. "I'll see you for supper."

When Samira reached the guest chambers, she recognized them from the last time she was in Queenshearth. Back then, they'd seemed open and inviting, but now they felt smaller and were gathering dust. She wondered if Jonn Thorne or the High Priests had used these rooms when they came to execute Queen Mina and... the *first* Prince Mychal, at least. She and Jullia would have to think of something to say to explain that day, if it ever came to that.

"Your Highness? If you're okay here..." Harry interjected, and she saw the two of them hovering at the door awkwardly.

"I'm fine," she said, nodding, "go ahead and find your quarters." With two quick bows, the guards were gone. She'd hardly had time to sit down on the bed before there was a knock on the door. "You don't have to knock if you just left, Harry," she called, laughing a little, but when the door opened, she was looking at a woman she'd never seen before. Samira quickly stood again as the woman, a greying Farisian in wine-colored Steward robes, bowed and smiled at her.

"Your Highness," she said, "I'm sorry, I didn't mean to startle you. Your guards let me pass. I'm Petra Keaton, the High Steward here at Hartshold Keep." Samira began to relax. She remembered Mychal mentioning a Petra, a long time ago at Fen Faris.

"You're the king's advisor?" she asked, offering her a seat in the armchair facing the bed. Petra nodded, and Samira said quietly, "Jullia told me he doesn't have long."

"No," she agreed, "he doesn't. We've tried to prepare Deronn as best we can, but I'll have to leave soon. The regency won't want anything to do with me. The Godhead will choose the council." Samira heard bitterness creep into her voice and Petra quickly added, "Meaning no offense, of course."

"Please," she said, "I'm not offended at all."

"I only meant he's your fiance..."

"All the more reason," she said sharply. Here, at least, she wasn't going to pretend. "I've met him. He's not a god, he's a man, and not very much of one at that."

Petra did seem surprised by this, but it didn't soften her at all. "When you have the power he does, you don't need much else," she said, her voice grim. "Don't underestimate him. He hasn't been in the Hartlands for ten years and we're still living in fear."

Samira nodded, trying not to show on her face how much that had struck her. *She really has no idea what's about to happen*, she thought. *But if we can get Mychal his army–* But she didn't know how much Jullia trusted this woman, so she only asked, "Why did you come to see me?"

Petra frowned. "Well, frankly... I wanted to know why you'd come. I thought the Priesthood might've sent you, but I can see you're not their creature." The woman narrowed her dark eyes and leaned forward in her chair. "So why *are* you here, Your Highness?"

Again, Samira wasn't sure how much she should say, so she dropped her eyes to her shoes and said, trying to sound as downcast as she could, "I wanted to see Jullia and... I wanted to do something by myself. Before I left." She let herself trail off, hoping it was enough to satisfy Petra.

The Steward didn't necessarily seem convinced, but there was sympathy in her eyes when Samira looked up again. "I can understand that," she said kindly. "It's very hard to leave your family. My son's at Surpoint, and I haven't seen him in two years. Castor's grown, but it still isn't easy."

Samira's breath caught as she remembered something Uncle

Lyam had said, the first night he'd arrived. She couldn't quite stop an excited smile from forming on her face as she asked, "Castor Wright?"

Petra nodded hesitantly. "Yes, Your Highness. My son is Lord Wright's bastard."

"My Uncle Lyam told me– well…" she searched for the right words and eventually settled on, "He said you might have known my cousin Loran… and his friends."

Petra's expression didn't change, but Samira thought she saw the slightest flicker of something go through her eyes before she asked, in a very even voice, "And why did he tell you that?"

Wordlessly, Samira kept her eyes on the other woman as she pulled the mother amulet out of her dress and let it drop down again in front of the roughspun cloth. The markings, engraved in enameled stone, caught the light and glimmered as Petra stared in shock.

"Put that away," she finally whispered, when she had recovered several seconds later. Samira quickly hid the amulet, and a long, heavy silence passed between them before the Steward finally asked, "Are you trained?"

"No," she said, feeling her hopes building.

"Well, that's one saving grace at least," Petra said.

Samira deflated. "I was sort of hoping that you would be able to teach me."

"Only if you want to be killed," she said. "The mage-catchers aren't looking for latent talent, they're looking for the more– refined."

"Like you?" she asked, her voice starting to edge towards irritation. "The Stewards train their mages, don't they? Why haven't you been found?"

To Samira's utter shock, the woman pulled her *own* mother amulet from under her robes then. She tucked it back as quickly as it had come, and sighed. "Why do you think I came to Queenshearth?

There was never much of a mage population here, so there are almost no mage-catchers, and certainly not in the castle. King Eronn has his faults, but he's never allowed that sort of thing to go on in his city."

"What sort of thing, arrests?" Samira asked, frowning.

"Arrests. Deportations. And worse," she said.

"Worse?" Samira could feel her stomach turning once again.

"I've only heard rumors. As like as not, the mages are wherever the Eirosians are."

"You mean Eirosia?" she asked, thoroughly confused now.

Petra smiled a grim smile and said, "No, Your Highness. No one's in Eirosia." The Steward stood up then, drew herself up to her full height, and said, "I won't talk about this anymore. The more you know the more danger you're in."

"Please, Lady Keaton," Samira said, and the woman cut her off, shaking her head.

"I'm not a Lady, Your Highness," she said. "You can call me Petra." Her eyes softened when she bowed again and said, "It was good to meet you. The prince and princess will expect you soon for supper." And with another nod of the head, she slipped back through the door and was gone.

Samira, finally alone, tried not to get angry as she undressed next to the steaming basin of water and sank into her first bath since she left Hollisport nine days ago. Petra's warning had disappointed her, but there was also some small consolation in it— she was safe in Queenshearth, at least. Curious, she let her hands linger at the surface of the water, and soon enough two small spirals formed in the bath below her wrists.

Slowly, making an effort to breathe normally, she raised her hands, and thin streams followed them up into the air. She brought her hands over her head, and as she worked her fingers through her hair, the streams started to soak the strands. She worked out the subtler rules of controlling the water quickly enough, and before long she had washed her hair without ever touching the pitcher left at the tub's side. It wasn't until she heard footsteps passing the door that she let the water fall, heart pounding. Whoever it was passed without stopping, but it still scared her. She finished her bath as quickly as she could.

Once she had pulled a comb through her hair and gotten herself into a nicer dress than the clothes she'd been riding in, she hurried downstairs, tailed at a cautious distance by guards all the way. When she found Jullia and Deronn, they were alone in the great hall at a long dark table, with only a kitchen servant running dishes in and out of the room. Jullia waved her over when she saw her, and Samira sat across from the other princess as she said, "I half expected the whole court."

"We thought you wouldn't mind this after the feast you came from," Jullia said, and Samira nodded gratefully. She couldn't imagine *another* reception in her honor. She barely survived the last one.

"Most of the court left when Father stopped getting out of bed, anyway," Deronn said. Samira turned her attention to the boy, picking listlessly at his food at the head of the table between them. The youngest Halwood looked remarkably like Mychal did now. He had the olive skin, dark features, and sturdy frame of a Farisian king, but the chair he sat in was far too big for him, and his voice was still higher than his sister's. She felt a pang of sympathy for him and looked down at the plate being set in front of her.

"Mason told me to tell you good luck," Samira said, and Deronn met her eyes then. He smiled a little.

"Thanks. I miss Fen Faris." He looked behind him, and saw that the servant was gone, before he added, "Good luck to you too. Is your magic elemental or artifice?"

"Deronn!" Jullia hissed. "How do you even know about that?"

"Mason told me they read the letter, it's okay," Samira said, although she had felt her heartbeat pick up. "Um, elemental, I think. I can do things with water, but I don't know what else. I guess artificing is stuff like potions?" Deronn nodded. "So yeah, elemental, then."

"That's interesting," he said. "Sorry. I was just curious."

"That's alright," Samira said. "I hope it helps me more than it hurts."

"You made it through the Declaration," Jullia said, with a smile that looked a little forced. "It might turn out better than you think."

Samira frowned and nodded. Deronn seemed even less convinced than his sister. After a brief silence, the young prince asked, "Does the Godhead look addicted to the godwine? I wondered because the Stewards say if you drink it before you're grown-up--"

"Deronn," Jullia warned.

"What? I'm only asking," he protested. "I mean, I guess he'd be in withdrawal by the time he got to Hollisport. Did he seem annoyed or maybe faint or–?"

"Deronn!"

The boy glared at Jullia and pushed his plate away. "Fine. I'm not hungry." He ran out of the hall, and Jullia put her face in her hands.

"I'm sorry," she said.

"It's really fine," Samira said, glancing at the door he'd gone out of, a little concerned.

"He just... still wants to be a Steward. Studying everything all the time. He's angry at pretty much everything that reminds him what he actually has to do."

"I understand that," she said softly, and they ate silently for a while before Jullia stood up.

"I'm finished. We can see my father now if you're ready," she said, not really looking at Samira.

"Let's go," Samira said, nodding, and let the younger girl lead her through the corridor down to the second tower further back in the castle, where two dozen or so steps led them to a guarded entry-way. The men stepped aside for Jullia and she eased the door open, peering inside quietly.

"Father? She's here," Samira heard her say, as she studied the tapestry hangings lining the walls around her. To her left was Caspar burning the boats at the Landing, and to her right, Haddon Hollis and Artur Halwood making peace at Lake Royal. Both scenes were beautiful, but she was drawn to the fire on the left, and the cold Northern eyes of Caspar watching it burn. She couldn't help but shudder as she turned back to Jullia holding the door open for her.

When she went inside, she immediately noticed the stench in the chamber: it smelled like doctor's mixtures, old age, and something sickly strong and desolate– carefully masked decay. Thankfully, the Priest had been replaced by a doctor, mixing some kind of paste at a table next to the Hartlands' dying king. King Eronn looked nothing like she remembered. The strong, smiling older man from her child-hood, tall and laughing loudly with her father, was gaunt and pale now, a poor approximation of the man he'd been. He coughed into a handkerchief as she approached, and smoothed the fading white tunic he wore as he tried to straighten himself against the pillows he leaned against. "Samira," he said, with a thin, weary smile, and his voice was hoarse and quiet. "It's been some time. How's your family?"

"They're all well," she said, trying to smile. "My father sends his love."

Something between a laugh and a cough came out of the king, and he said, "Daniel's a good man. Tell him to make sure our sons stay friends. Deronn needs the Horn. Gods know he won't have Thorncliffe." She nodded, and he coughed a little more before he said, "Congratulations on your Declaration."

"Thank you, Your Majesty," she said, hoping it didn't sound as rote as it felt.

"Sami and I are going to Brookbridge," Jullia told him, and he looked up at his daughter, brow furrowing.

"Oh? When?"

Jullia's face changed and she quickly said, "We don't have to go just yet. We'll wait–"

He smiled softly. "Don't worry about me, darling. I'll most likely go before you do."

She shook her head, and Samira felt very much like she was intruding. "You don't know that, Father, don't say that."

"Oh, I think I do." Another coughing fit racked the king, and the doctor came hurrying over as the coughs became erratic wheezes. He eased him down to a less upright position, and the king looked around until his eyes met Samira's. "I wanted to see you because you were Lyha's closest friend," he said softly. "By rights I should see her before I die. But she's gone, and my wife and eldest son too. A father shouldn't see his children buried." He started coughing again, and looked gravely at the doctor. "Would you go find my son?" he asked, and the doctor nodded and left the room silently.

Samira was reluctant to say anything, but when she glanced at Jullia, she saw conflict in her eyes too. Someone had to tell him. Finally, Samira went over to the side of the king's bed and quietly said, "Lyha's not dead, Your Majesty." She glanced back at Jullia before she said, "We're going to Brookbridge to... help... her."

If King Eronn noticed the hesitation, he didn't show it. He stared at both of them for a long moment, before a serene kind of smile spread across his face. "Thank you. *Thank you.* You should go, then, as soon as you can." He looked at her suddenly and asked, more desperate than Samira had ever heard him, "You're *certain?*"

"I am," she said, smiling as much as she could. It felt a little like lying, but it was better than telling him nothing, and it seemed to have given him some kind of peace.

He nodded, leaning back and sighing slowly. "Good. Thank the gods. Tell her... I wish I could see her again." His eyes widened again and he asked, this time to Jullia, "What are you doing at Brookbridge?"

Jullia glanced at Samira before she said, "Calling the armies."

Samira had never seen as many emotions play across a man's face at once as she saw in King Eronn then. Finally, just as the door opened again, he nodded, and, in a fierce, low whisper, said, "*Give them a real fight.*" He then struggled to sit up and smiled as wide as he could at the solemn little boy being led inside. "There's my son," he said. "Come sit by my side, both of you." He took Jullia's hand when she approached, squeezed it, and said, "Don't cry, Jule." Samira slowly retreated to the doorway. As she slipped through, King Eronn's eyes met hers and he managed another thin smile before she closed the door behind her.

Samira stayed up in the Halwoods' solar until well into the night, wondering if she had done the right thing. She reassured herself as she sat by the fading fire, waiting for Jullia. But she didn't see her again that night, or Deronn, and she had already guessed why when the bells started ringing at the Cathedral. By quarter past midnight, it seemed like all the bells in Queenshearth had joined in, tolling all together, telling the city their king was dead.

# 15

# Mychal

"Mother *Morra*," Luke exclaimed when they finally rode over the crest of the hill that brought Astor Post into view. "What's going on?"

Mychal couldn't blame him— the town was almost unrecognizable. The usually bustling streets were almost entirely empty; even from this distance, they could see armored sentries directing the long, winding lines of shuffling men, women, and children up the northern road, in wagons, on horseback, or on foot. "They're evacuating the city," Sir James said. "And not a moment too soon, I'd bet. We'd all best be prepared to ride straight into battle." Mychal could see the man's jaw tighten and eyes narrow as he urged his horse forward. He kept up as best as he could on Gale, but it wasn't until they entered the city streets and were slowed into a sluggish march with everyone else that their party congregated again.

As they rode past the townspeople, he could hear people shouting up at them: lots of "Astor protect you!" and "Defend the Horn!", and one brave soul yelled, "Die well, boys!" before disappearing into the crowd. Mychal would have thought it was funny if he wasn't so afraid. He'd only just begun to think about the future-- he couldn't very well go and die *now*. He tightened his grip on Gale's reins and kept his eyes on Sir James ahead of him as they made their way to camp.

On one of the last roads, they were stopped behind the civilian lines, and Mychal noticed a wagon full of young girls in identical cloaks, sitting among stores of food, gaudy furniture, and a comically large barrel of wine. He squinted at them curiously until he realized who they were, and without thinking, he broke off from the guard and galloped over to the wagon, calling out as he went: "Senna!"

The other girls from Lady May's were giving him dirty looks as he slowed to a stop next to the coach, but before long the girl he'd been looking for poked her head out from between two of the others. Senna looked like a deer blinking in bright light. "Mychal?"

"I--" he realized he wasn't quite sure why he had run after her. It wasn't as if they could talk about what he needed to *here*. "I would have so much to tell you if we had time," he managed, a kind of apology, and she nodded, with a rather sad smile.

"Well, if you don't fancy dying," she said, "there are people in the mountains. Ride north from the Canyon and tell them you know me. Otherwise, good luck. Don't die. I'm getting out of here."

"Where are you going?" he asked, still breathless from the ride. She shrugged.

"Wherever there are men who'll pay for a dance." Senna shifted to steady herself as the wagon lurched back into motion and the line started moving on. "Hope I'll see you again. Go, before your army misses you."

"Goodbye!" he called, grinning, earning more looks from the other girls, and rode back to the irritated column of knights and squires waiting for him.

"What was that?" Sir James asked, raising an eyebrow. Mychal blushed.

"Er, nothing, sorry, I--"

"Mychal, your birth didn't change, but your station did. You can't go running after a... *dancer*-- at least not in broad daylight." Sir James seemed like he was trying not to laugh, so Mychal didn't feel quite so embarrassed when he said, "That girl will be fine. Let's worry about ourselves now."

"Yes, sir," he said, and looked pointedly at a snickering Luke to his left as the party traveled on. He didn't care about the looks he was getting. He had a way out now, and the battle didn't feel quite so terrifying anymore.

The party rode into the camp, which was in even greater chaos than the town, and managed to make their way past the throngs of worried soldiers and last-minute drills to reach the council hall. As soon as they dismounted, a steward brought all of them up the stairwell and into the war room. The Lord Marshal stood inside, poring over his map of the continent, and several of the officers that had stayed at Astor Post surrounded him. Lord Thorne looked up as they entered and his lips twisted into a tight smile. "Reinhold. Good." Mychal couldn't help but notice Sir Callum deflate at Luke's side. "You're leading the van tonight."

"Tonight?" Sir James asked, his voice betraying his unease.

"Yes, tonight," Thorne said briskly, returning to his map. "We've only been waiting for you all. We cannot waste another minute. The Daemons have already been sighted in the peaks. So we'll have bowmen to watch for, but Sir Edward will lead our own into the hills to contend with them. We've already sent scouting parties to start routing them. The greater part of the bastards will be coming through the Canyon, though, and you'll meet them there." He finally addressed Sir James directly and said, "My cousin Edris brought a thousand Valleyguard men. You'll take three hundred to add to your force." Mychal froze. *Edris?*

"Prince Edris is here?" Sir James asked.

"Yes. He won't be fighting, of course. But I believe he wanted to speak with you. I'll send for him." Mychal's heart started pounding, and suddenly the room seemed very small, like the walls were closing in around him. Edris was coming *here?*

Thankfully, some of the other knights started asking questions, and as soon as the noise in the room reached a steady buzz of activity, he found Sir James and, hopefully calmer than he felt, said, "Sir, I was wondering if I could go."

The knight frowned. "You don't want to hear the plans? You always have before."

"I just thought I might be able to practice a little more before..." he said, not even convincing himself. But the knight smiled kindly.

"Alright, lad. Be here at sundown, that's when we leave."

"Yes, sir," Mychal said quickly, and darted out of the council without another word. He hurried down the stairs, through the hall, and out into the camp before he heard the beating of hooves coming from the other direction. Panicking, he found a group of infantry boys to stand behind and watched as the prince and his guards rode up to the gates.

He looked almost exactly like Mychal remembered, only a bit taller, with the same blond curls and wide, almost gray-green eyes. He had no idea how Edris felt about what they'd done at his Declaration years ago, but he didn't want to find out, not now when it would be a disaster to be discovered-- and not only for him. When the horses had gone, he began to breathe again, and decided to look for a place to rest, and hide, before they had to ride out.

Sundown came too soon. The ride to the Canyon was hours, not days, and Mychal knew by midnight he'd be fighting for his life. Still, he felt oddly calm as he met Sir James in the yard of the council hall at dusk.

"Sir Callum's men will ride with us," the knight told him. "But we'll be mostly Hartlanders, actually. Eighteen hundred of them, six Hornish, and three from Thorncliffe." *Of course*, Mychal thought, *my people have always been disposable to Thorne*, and surprised himself. They were *his* people to him now?

Sir James looked Mychal up and down, and asked, "Are you ready, son?"

Mychal tried to swallow the lump in his throat, but his mouth was too dry. Even so, he managed to say, "I'm ready," and the knight nodded and started to ride.

The battalions fell into formation as the Army rode out of Astor Post, and at the front of it all, Mychal turned around and craned his neck to see the thousands of men all marching to the Canyon. He was shaking, and was glad of his horse then; Gale's feet were much surer than his. He let him carry them over the foothills until they could see the mouth of the canyon below by the sparse torchlight the Lord Marshal had allowed.

The procession halted about a mile away, and Sir James turned to Sir Callum on his left and said, "It'll be just us for a while now." The other knight nodded, his face grim, as groups of men silently peeled off from the back of the force to meet the scouting parties and attack the Daemon archers on either side.

Sir James looked over at Mychal, who was already watching him, his palms sweating and clutching Gale's reins as tight as he could. "If you ever have to give a speech like this, Mychal, don't talk about kings or glory. You have to make them want to fight for their own sake." With that, he urged his horse forward and rode up and down the line at the front of the great mass of men that made up the Holy Army vanguard.

"All my men!" he shouted, and the great roar of voices fell to just whispers. "We ride first tonight! We'll break their lines until the middleguard comes, and then we'll rout the bastards out of our lands for good!"

Sir James pulled the reins on his horse, slowing to a stop in the center of the line. "The Triad is *ours!* You fight for the Godhead, but for yourselves too! The Daemons want to burn *your* towns. *Your* country. *Your* children. Are you going to let them?"

A loud roar rose out of the crowd, an approximation of *No.*

Sir James smiled. "Then ride with me!"

And he turned around and charged down the hill, Mychal and Callum and Luke and then all the thousands of the vanguard behind him.

Mychal was urging Gale forward, doing his best to keep up with Sir James, and he could feel his heart pounding as they all poured through the mouth of the Mages' Canyon. The men were all shouting at once and the beating hooves of the horses only added to the noise; he stopped trying to hear anything after a while and focused only on keeping Sir James in sight. Luke was nearby, he knew that much, and Mychal could tell he was trying to say something to him but it was lost in the roar of the charge.

When Gale's hooves hit the rough rock of the pass, it sent a jolt through Mychal's spine that spiked his blood and had him riding even faster.

It wasn't until Sir James pulled his horse to a sudden stop that Mychal slowed down too and watched the knight frown and scan the narrow road ahead. Some men rode on, others noticed and stopped, and the vanguard slowly turned into a mass of confusion, choked off at its head. "Sir?" Mychal asked, frowning at the look on Sir James's face. "What is it?"

"They're not here," he said quietly.

"Reinhold! What's going on?" Sir Callum shouted from a little ways behind.

"Where are they?" Sir James called back. "We've ridden in at least two miles. Where's their army?"

"Perhaps we arrived first," Sir Callum said, with a satisfied smile. Sir James was already shaking his head.

"Even if they haven't charged yet," he muttered, "we should be able to at least *see* them by now." Mychal squinted at the road ahead, and something strange soon caught his eye: piles of large stones, sitting in the middle of the road. They didn't look like they had fallen off the walls of the canyon; they were too far away from the cliffs and too neatly arranged for that. Sir James saw where he was looking and, riding much more cautiously now, approached the nearest of them. Mychal followed, and as he strained to see ahead of him he saw Sir James recoil seconds before he also realized what they were.

Heads. There were at least forty human heads on the floor of the canyon, heads of soldiers, severed at the neck and tossed into bloody piles. Many of them were still wearing helms with sun-and-moon crests– the kind they gave the archers.

Horrified, Mychal pulled Gale back as Sir James turned around, and before he could say anything, the knight confirmed his suspicion: "The scouts," he said, with all the color drained from his face. Suddenly, he started racing back to the men, waving them back the way they'd come and shouting as he went. "Fall back! FALL BACK! It's a trap!"

He and Mychal had hardly made it back to the front of the line when they heard the first crash. Still turned back toward the forces, Mychal saw the barrel hit the ground in the middle of the vanguard, with a heavy crunch followed by a splash as its contents went flying. The men around it shouted and recoiled as they were spattered with a thick, black sludge. Another crash resounded through the canyon from the other side, and before long a dozen more barrels had fallen on the Army, mostly at the back of the charging forces.

"That's pitch," he heard Sir Callum say, in a faint, quivering voice. "Morra have mercy."

"FALL BACK! NOW!" Sir James was still screaming, but hardly anyone could hear him now; the men were already panicking. Some were starting to run, but the mouth of the canyon was narrow and a barrel had broken open right at its entrance, and it was slow going at best. The knight swore and looked around wildly until he saw Mychal. "Get to the walls!" he shouted, and when Mychal hesitated, still staring at the chaos, James rode up to him and turned Gale around with a firm pull on his reins. "*Now!*" Sir Callum and Luke followed them, and a few other men who'd managed to hear, but there was only so much room under the shelves of rock jutting out from the walls.

"Reinhold!" Sir Callum shouted. "What do we do?" Before Sir James could answer, a flash of firelight caught Mychal's eye up at the top of the opposite cliffside. The panic grew on the ground when the men saw the torches being lit all along both the canyon walls, and before long a deadly hush fell over the Army as a wave of flaming arrows arced over them and fell to the ground. Most of the arrows landed in the middle, and men, especially those that had been hit with the pitch, ran like madmen to both sides, but it wasn't long before enough arrows hit their mark.

And, with a horrible roar, the canyon went up in flames.

Fires raged on all sides back at the front of the pass. Even where Mychal was, soldiers were running wildly away from the blaze, and it was already becoming oppressively hot on the ground. With his jaw tight and eyes hardened, Sir James rode as far out into the middle of the Canyon as he dared and shouted, "FORWARD! FOLLOW ME!" He quickly dashed back to the rock shelf and said, "We're going to have to fight our way out on the other side. There are paths up to the top of the walls, we can attack their archers from behind."

"What are you talking about, man? We need to retreat!" Sir Callum sputtered.

"You're welcome to try your luck that way," Sir James snapped. Mychal dared then to glance back at the wall of fire behind them, and heard burning men screaming as the lucky ones ran blindly through the smoke toward the remaining forces further inside. Sir Callum looked down at the ground, reddening in silence. "Boy," Sir James said, and a young cavalry soldier nearby nodded, uncertain. "Follow the wall and get back to the hill. Tell the Lord Marshal the middle and rearguard *can't* charge this way, you understand? They need to come up through the mountains and meet us at the top." The boy nodded, and Sir James said, "Go." With a terrified look behind him, the young soldier turned his horse and urged the protesting animal back to the mouth.

"Sir, I'm your squire, I can go," Mychal protested, bristling at what seemed to him a slight.

Sir James rode up to him and, quietly enough that the other men didn't hear, said, "Mychal. The odds of that boy making it back..." He sighed. "Stay with me, you're like to live longer." Mychal swallowed hard and nodded, watching the young rider disappear into the smoke. "We have to move now. That fire will spread."

Sir James took off toward the path far ahead that Mychal could just barely see winding up into the side of the cliffs. As they raced for the last way out of the canyon, the smoke billowed up and filled the air around the hundreds of men that had followed them. Mychal had no idea how many the fire had swallowed, but he could tell there were far fewer with them now. The horrible, acrid smell of the pitch and burning *everything* filled the air and scorched his lungs, and he started coughing and hoped it wouldn't turn to retch.

Before they reached the pass, though, Sir James stopped his horse and swore again. "Astor above," he muttered. "That idiot Thorne's killed us." Mychal heard them before he saw them, but before long he too felt the hope he had left wither away. Hundreds of Daemon cavalry soldiers were charging down the hill in front of them, ready to close off their last escape. Sir James turned around, looked at the terrified men he had left, and shouted, "With me! Around the sides! Charge!" And they surged forward, the charging Daemons meeting the first of them with a violent clash.

Traveling along the walls had proved useful, as they were starting to effectively flank the Daemons, but just as Mychal was meeting the charging soldiers, he heard more crashes behind him. He didn't have to look to know what it was; he could feel the heat from the new burning pitch at his back now, the leather of his jerkin intolerably hot against his skin. The fire was everywhere, it had finally caught them– there was nowhere left to go. It was all he could do not to lose Sir James, and Mychal rode behind him as the knight cut his way through the cavalry, avoiding the enemy until he couldn't any longer. One charged straight for him, and he felt his heart leap and his hair stand on end as he steadied Gale and readied his sword.

The soldier he clashed with was no great swordsman, but the long and lithe figure of the Daemons made his reach much longer than Mychal's. He was swinging wildly, just like the marauder had done, and Mychal managed to block all of the slashes of his blade until Gale stumbled on something, a rock, a head, a body, he didn't know. Gale screamed in protest and kicked his front legs up, spooking the Daemon's horse enough to force them apart, and another passing Army soldier slashed through the Daemon's neck as he rushed by. Mychal recoiled as the body slumped forward and almost hit him as it fell to the ground. He heard the Daemon crash onto the dirt as his panicked horse abandoned him.

"Mychal!" Sir James was shouting then, and he turned to find him there, sword locked in a bind with a much bigger Daemon wearing heavy plate. "Find Roth and get as many men out as you can. There ought to be caves somewhere around–"

It was then that the Daemon's sword sliced through the knight's armor, cutting boiled leather as if it were cloth and spearing him all the way through and out his back. His eyes, still meeting Mychal's, bulged somewhat in shock, and with a heavy grunt the knight managed to thrust his sword up to slash into the Daemon's side, who took his sword with him as he fell. Red blossomed out through the hole it left, and Sir James slumped forward over his horse. His eyes had never left Mychal's, but there was no life in them now. The horse ran off, carrying its master with it for several yards before the body fell off and was quickly trampled.

Mychal blinked several times, trying to understand what he had seen; his ears were ringing, and he couldn't hear the battle as clearly anymore. It was only when Luke crossed his path that he woke up. "Where's Reinhold?" his friend shouted, one hand up to cover his eyes the best he could from the smoke.

"He's dead," Mychal managed, and Sir Callum behind them heard.

"Then we're all dead," he moaned, and Mychal instantly felt furiously uninterested in what the man had to say. He pulled Gale's reins around, ready to leave, before he remembered what Sir James had told him to do.

"Sir Callum!" Mychal shouted. "He told me to tell you to find as many men as you could and--"

"The men are on *fire*, boy! The *world's* on fire!" he shouted. "Eiros take Reinhold, if he thinks I'm going to--"

Another assault of pitch barrels rocked the caverns, and a mass of riders escaping the closest one rushed like a wave over the three of them. Luke's horse, always a little excitable, finally lost its nerve and reared back, kicked him off, and rode away with the others. Just then, a small band of Daemons broke loose from the battle and made right for the shelf where they were sheltering. Luke's eyes widened and he looked to the knight. "Sir!"

Sir Callum looked at him, then back at the Daemons, and with a jerking, miniscule shake of his head, turned his horse around and raced into the smoke back the way they had come. The Daemons kept charging.

"Luke!" Mychal shouted, and his friend scrambled to climb onto Gale's back before they took off along the canyon wall. The most well-preserved hundred or so men of the vanguard had been driven back into a corner of the cave, and as Mychal and Luke rode towards them, Mychal spotted a break in the cliff face, a small opening that had been blasted clear by a falling barrel. The cornered soldiers, mostly infantry, watched them as they came, and when Mychal, making the decision in an instant, shouted, "WITH ME!", they followed him. When they entered the cave, the searing world of the battle turned cool and black, and only a dozen or so of the Daemons made it in after them before another barrel caught fire at the entrance, sealing them inside.

Six Army men died before the twelve Daemons lay dead at the mouth of the cave, and suddenly Mychal found he had ninety-odd men, battered and bloody, watching him as he brought his horse to a stop. They could hardly see the entrance now, and he had no idea how far the cave stretched on, but anything was better than the hell outside. When he and Luke dismounted, he tried to soothe the frightened Gale, but found after a moment it was better to leave him to sort himself out.

"You're Reinhold's squire," one of the boys nearer to him finally said. "Owyn. Graham's friend."

"Is Graham here?" Luke asked hopefully.

"I'm here," their friend said, pushing his way out of the crowd, his face grim and covered in soot. "What do we do now?"

Luke turned to Mychal. "This was your idea," he said, quietly.

Mychal looked at the soldiers around him. They were more boys than men, really, but none of them looked like they'd have much of a problem running from the Army. That was good. He thought about what Senna had told him, about people in the mountains, and weighed that unknown with the known danger of meeting Thorne at the top. He nodded, took a deep breath, and said, "We'll go up into the mountains when the fighting stops. There are Resistance fighters there who can help us."

Shouting erupted instantly, and Luke looked at him, aghast. "Abandon the Army?" a voice finally broke through above the others. Mychal turned to look, and saw Graham staring at them, his armor singed and his face incredulous.

"The Army who sent us to die?" he challenged. Feeling a kind of confidence building, he went on, raising his voice louder. "They were either too stupid to see this coming or they didn't care if we all burned. Do you want to go back to them?"

"But why would the Resistance help us?" Graham asked. "We're the Godhead's men."

Mychal steadied himself. It was time. He sent one last prayer, not to the gods, but to the ones *he'd* always prayed to: *Mother, Mychal, forgive me, please, and be with me now.* "You could be," he said. "Or you could be mine." He turned to Luke as he reached into his pocket, hoping his chain was still there. He felt it inside, warm in his hand, and took it out to show to his friend. "My name's not Owyn," he said. "It's Halwood. Mychal Halwood."

A heavy silence rippled through the room, and he felt all the eyes on him, even more than before. But he focused on Luke. A host of different emotions passed on Luke's face, one after the other, as he stared at the sword-and-fire chain, silent. Awkwardly, Mychal started to say, "I'm sorry I couldn't tell you..."

Suddenly, Luke knelt, with his right hand on the hilt of his sword the old way, and said, "My sword is yours. My house fights for yours, it always has, and Eiros take the Army. I'll follow you. My prince."

Mychal wanted to smile, but found that he couldn't. The weight of the moment was too heavy on him, and his face stayed solemn as he raised his eyes to the soldiers around him. Slowly, Graham first, then others, and finally all the boys in the cave knelt too, the ninety men of his first army.

# 16

# Mychal

Mychal's new army had been marching into the Holy Mountains for about ten days when the food ran out.

No one had brought very much to the battle. The Lord Marshal had called the supply packs unnecessary burdens. So while a week's rations had been sent along with most as a precaution, none of the soldiers that had defected with him, Luke, and Graham had any more than that. Their first attempts at foraging had produced a little, but most of Mychal's forces were squires, young boys almost all of them. None of them knew how to live off the land, and he knew that if they didn't learn fast, his campaign would be over before it started.

"Could be worse," Luke said on the tenth night, as Mychal paced around their fire, lightheaded from the hunger. "We could still be stuck in that cave."

"Gods, don't," Mychal groaned. "If I retch I'll have wasted the last of my bread." The smell of the Canyon, and the stale air of the cave that had only made the burning worse, still haunted him. Still haunted most of them.

"Where's that boy?" Graham asked, lying on his back across a felled log and staring up at the stars. "The one you sent over the hill. Sam?"

"He was supposed to be back by now," Mychal said, running a hand through his hair. "But who knows what happened to him. He's only thirteen."

"Maybe he found food and won't be coming back," the other squire said darkly, earning looks from both him and Luke. "What? Meaning no offense, Owyn, but it's not like I wouldn't be tempted myself."

"He's not Owyn," Luke was quick to correct him. "He's your prince. 'Your Highness' or 'Prince Mychal'."

"Right," Graham said, sounding a little nervous, while Mychal turned a little pink. "Sorry. Er. Your Highness."

"Don't worry about it," Mychal mumbled. "You've known me another way for the better part of two years."

"Can I see it again?" Luke asked, a little quieter suddenly, and Mychal's heart picked up as he handed over the livery chain he'd hidden in his things since he'd run from Hartshold Keep. He hoped the other boy wouldn't have known enough to notice he'd had his brother's chain altered on his twelfth birthday to drop as a pendant over his ceremonial gown, the clasps different and the shoulder buckles gone. He'd changed it back as best he could on their second night after the Canyon, but soldering iron alone at a dying campfire was hard work, and he'd never gotten to learn forging from his mother's family the way he would have, if he'd been born this way.

Luke didn't appear to notice. "Gods," he breathed. "I really can't believe it. My mum always thought you were out there, somewhere."

Mychal blinked. He'd heard something similar from a few of the boys sleeping in the camp in the hills behind them. "Really?"

"Yeah, of course," he said, nodding. "Loads of the queen's loyalists believed you survived. At first, I mean. Most gave up, but Mum never did. She's gone to Cor Hara now, three years past."

"I'm sorry."

"It's okay," Luke said. "I mean, I suppose you know how it feels. D'you remember your mum?"

Mychal's heart seized, like it always had when he thought of his mother. He'd been telling everyone Mrs. Owyn was happy at home with his tailor father for so long, just to not hear condolences for a while. So the familiar feeling was new again, too. Coming home to himself-- nearly-- was full of strange moments. "Yeah. I do. It's hard."

"Well," Luke said, clapping him on the shoulder, "we'll make them proud, right? I believe they're watching, gods willing. My sword is yours-- wherever we're going next."

"Thanks, Luke. I know." There was a little tension in the silence that followed, and Mychal knew both his friends were waiting for him to tell them where that was exactly. Graham smiled, a little tightly, and they both sat and followed his gaze back toward the clouds.

Mychal wished he knew what to tell them. All he'd been able to say was 'north', into the mountains where Senna had said there were Resistance fighters waiting. But they hadn't seen any, not yet, and the mountains were only getting sparser the further into Thorncliffe they got. They'd passed the Downs yesterday, and over the border, he didn't have much hope for hunting while the snow still stuck even halfway into the fourth month now.

"You sure we aren't heading toward Eirosia by mistake?" Graham asked after a moment. Pointing up toward the constellations above, he said, "I thought Aria's Arrow goes east."

"No," Luke argued, "it's west. She's aiming for Caspar. We're going to Thorncliffe."

"But if Tol's Pot is below the arrow--"

"Both of you shut it," Mychal mumbled, trying to laugh. "Neither of you know your stars half as well as you say. And it's west."

"I just don't fancy running into the Daemons up here," Graham said, sounding serious now.

Mychal brought his knees up to his elbows, feet crossed at the ankles, letting some of the pressure off of his chest binding. It had started to hurt, and he suspected the potion was to blame. He looked over at his friend, still staring at the sky. He felt very responsible for all of their safety now. "I know. But we left first, we're ahead of the Daemon army."

"And they went east from the Canyon," Luke added. "We went due north."

"We didn't see them ride out," Graham said, shaking his head. "If the Canyon's open now... they could've gone anywhere. Caspar's Dale, Fen Faris..." Mychal flinched when he sat up just enough to look at him and say, "And Queenshearth will be next."

"I know," he said, staring at the ground.

"So is your father going to do something?" Mychal heard the challenge in the boy's voice and understood that he meant *this time*. His own anger about the executions agreed, but he did still feel some loyalty to the man who raised him.

"My father's dying."

"Right," Graham said. He glanced nervously at Luke before he met Mychal's eyes again and asked, "So are *you* going to do something?"

An uproar started in the camp then, and a boy rushed into the firelight to call out, "Sam's back." Mychal broke from Graham's gaze, with a nod to tell him he understood. They put the fire out and followed the boy back to camp.

The soldiers' camp had woken up quickly, eager for news, and many shouted out to Mychal as they passed, excited to catch a glimpse of him. They were camping in lean-tos, sleeping rough on the rocks with their cloaks as blankets, the horses all tied at the creek where they were doing their washing. There weren't too many fires burning-- most of the boys were still afraid of the flames, for now. Sam had gone back to his own camp, toward the north side of the hill, and a crowd was gathering as Mychal made his way there.

Sam, Hornish with an Islander family, was a gangly, wide-eyed boy that had eagerly volunteered to go find signs of life in the hills ahead two days ago. He bowed when Mychal approached, and grinned when he gave him his own waterskin to drink from. "Thanks, sir."

"What'd you see, Sam?" Mychal asked, trying to hope.

"I found fires burning last night in a ravine not too far from here," he said, between gulps of the water. "There's some kind of traveling party down there. I think maybe twenty or more. And it didn't look like soldiers."

"Maybe that's who we're looking for," Luke told him, while the crowd whispered amongst themselves. Mychal frowned. Maybe...

"No one saw you?" he asked. Sam shook his head. "Good. Thanks for your help."

"Are we going?" one of the men asked from behind the scout, as he hurried back into the crowd. "Maybe they can help us."

Mychal had been hoping for them to find someone, but now, in the face of it, he felt terrified, having almost nothing to go on. "We don't know who they are. We're in Thorncliffe, they could be Valleyguard."

Luke pulled him aside then and whispered in his ear, "Mate. They're only going to get hungrier."

He looked up and out at the waiting men, and saw then that they had started to look panicked. Shit. He was right. They didn't have any other options. "Alright. But only a few of us. I'm not putting everyone in danger yet."

"Let me go," Luke immediately said, and Mychal nodded and held up a hand to stop the many volunteers that followed.

"Luke and Graham will go with me."

"You're going?" Sam asked, aghast.

"Of course I am," Mychal said. "I'm not asking anyone to do anything I won't. We'll leave tonight and be back as soon as we can."

The crowd broke up when he walked away, and within the hour he was following the trail Sam had shown them, trying to breathe. The path was too treacherous for Gale or any horse, so the three of them were on foot. He didn't like that; at least riding made him feel like he could run, if he needed to. He hadn't been parted from Gale since he'd left home.

The Holy Mountains were bare this time of year; the snow wasn't melting yet, and the pines were frosted with not much growing in the brush. The incline was steep as they wound around the creek where their camp had stopped, but soon when the treeline broke into a slope they got to start walking downhill. They were looking for a ravine that arced sharply west at a landmark tree, and Mychal and the other two scanned the horizon constantly without any luck for hours after dawn had come and passed.

His stomach growled, louder than ever with the new hunger of the potion's first effects. Luke was right. They were going hungry. They'd found some roots, nuts, and fish by the creek that had helped some, but the meat and cheese was long gone. Mychal had no idea how these people, whoever they were, survived up here. The roads through the rocks were well known to be unforgiving to travelers. *But*, he thought as they walked on empty stomachs, *maybe that was why they could go undiscovered.*

By the afternoon, all he could think about was his hunger. It had started to feel even worse than the last days before he found the Army. He had gone without food for four days then, but he had assurances that he'd be fed once he reached Astor Post. These people *might* give them food, but he couldn't be sure. And now he felt all the hunger of a boy of seventeen, and the empty gnawing in his stomach was killing him.

He took the same approach he did when his blood each month would double him over during drills, and absolutely refused to think about it until he couldn't feel his body anymore. It helped some. But every time Luke or Graham spoke, he was pulled back to the present and the pain. At least the potion had taken *that* ordeal away-- it should have been happening now and both trials at once would have been far too much. He could only hope it was gone for good.

Finally, suddenly, Luke hauled both of them off the path behind a tree trunk and silently nodded toward the cliffside to their right, sloping into a clearing where Mychal could see a sod-roof cottage and signs of fires burning. "That's got to be them," his friend said, pointing to the tree Sam had described. "What do we do?"

"Luke," Graham said quietly, and both turned to look at him. He was pale white and backing slowly into the brush. Mychal followed his eyes and turned around quick toward the path the way they'd came.

Shit.

Two archers, bows nocked and ready, were coming out of the trees on either side, training their weapons directly at Mychal and the others. "Gods!" Luke exclaimed, jumping and backing into the tree.

"Evening," one of them said, nodding to them, sounding stiff. "You with that little boy from yesterday?"

"Yes," Mychal said, making an instant decision. Whoever these people were, they weren't Valleyguard. So he took a leap. "We're Army deserters. Are you Resistance? Senna Baker sent me."

The archers stared at them for a long moment, while Luke and Graham looked at him in horror. Finally, the one who'd spoken before lowered his bow and laughed. "Not Resistance, not exactly.

But come to the fire. Enemies of the Army are friends of ours." The men made room for them to join on the path, and Mychal took a deep breath and started to walk, keeping his hand firmly on the pommel of his sword but starting to trust a little that they'd be alright. When Luke and Graham stayed rooted to the spot, he turned around and raised his eyebrows. "Are you coming?" he prompted, and they both quickly ran to catch up.

"They listen to you," the archer commented, as he led them through the brush down to the clearing. "You a lord of something, boy?"

"Not exactly," he said, and supposed it was true, but the man caught sight of his chain jostling under the jerkin and peered closer.

"What's that crest?" he asked, and Mychal inched away.

"I'd like to speak to whoever's in charge first," he said. "Sorry."

The man looked at him oddly, but nodded. "Fine. We don't really have someone in charge," he said, "but the preacher will see you if you want."

Mychal froze. "Preacher? Like a Priest?"

The archer shook his head, pushing aside the last of the branches to break the tree line into their camp. "No, lad. Not a Priest."

He glanced back at Luke and Graham, who both looked back helplessly. That was fair. He'd made their bed fully himself this time. He turned back around and nodded, and the men led them into the clearing.

There were about forty or fifty people moving about the camp, between the cottage and a few large tents, with a cook fire burning bright in the center. The group was mixed company, what looked like a gathering of families to Mychal, all ages, races and men and women alike. He couldn't see any crests, but most of the people seemed to be wearing some sort of blue. A few turned around when they entered, and soon the entire group went silent and stared as the archers led the three of them straight through and into the cottage.

As soon as they passed through the doors, Mychal was overcome with the smell: *food. Real* food. There was a stew bubbling in a large basin hanging over the fireplace inside, and the aroma of it was wafting through the whole cottage. His stomach started growling, so violently he almost fainted. Instead, he walked as confidently as he could behind the archers toward the woman bent over the fire. There were a few children peering around a corner, watching them with wide eyes, and the two guards as well, along with a small group in a hushed, tense conversation in the next room. The dark, cool soil packed into the walls made the warm firelight cover everything around them. Mychal could almost relax in the first reprieve from the elements they'd had in weeks, if it weren't for all the eyes on him.

"Sister," the archer said. Mychal blinked when the woman turned around at that. She's the preacher? "Found these boys. They say they're deserters. The little one wants to talk to you."

The woman was younger than he was expecting, maybe thirty or thirty-five, with long hair falling over her shoulders and a sky-blue cotehardie dress laced with black cord. He heard Luke and Graham react to her eyes just as he noticed them himself. They were clouded over, the pupil indistinguishable in the fog from the iris, creating a strange, gray film over dark blurred eyes. They looked like the Godhead's.

"He does?" she asked, tilting her head and looking Mychal over curiously. After a moment, she gestured to the fire and said, "Sit at the hearth and have supper with me."

Mychal had never heard something so tempting in his life, but still braced himself and said, "I'm not eating until my friends do."

She smiled. "They're welcome, of course."

"Oh, thank the gods," Graham muttered, and he and Luke rushed over to the hearth. The last of Mychal's hesitation stopped him for just a moment, unsure about taking food from this strange woman, even if he was starving. But he couldn't wait any longer. He sat as the woman gave them all generous bowls of stew, and ate so ravenously he felt sick when he finished. When he looked up, the woman was staring at them, eating much more reservedly across the fireplace. The state of her eyes made it difficult for him to read her expression.

"Why are you so hungry, boys?" the woman asked, not unkindly. "Didn't you take rations when you ran?"

"We left from a battle," Mychal said, quiet as he looked around the room at the others in the cottage. The whole room stilled when he said, "The Mages' Canyon. Eleven days ago now."

The preacher woman turned around to the whisperers behind her, something darker in her face now. "The smoke. It *was* the Army."

Mychal nodded, shuddering as he remembered the first week of their march, the sun blocked for most of the day by the thick haze the battle had produced. So it had spread as far as this, at the beginning. He couldn't imagine what people in their homes had thought, watching the black air roll in. "Daemons," he said, and heard the horror in the gasps around him. "It was a massacre."

The woman bowed her head, and a couple of the others did as well while she muttered, more like a chant than any prayer Mychal had ever heard, "Mother and Father protect us. Morra, place a shield over your people, Astor, lend us your sword--"

"Right," Mychal said sharply, and maybe it was the days of hunger, or just the quicker temper he'd acquired since the potions started their work, but he couldn't stomach a service now. "That's all fine, but we came here because of the *real* Daemons *actually* coming--"

"Mychal," Luke said, eyes widening, before he realized what he'd done and quickly ducked his head down to look intensely at his soup instead. The woman had turned around and was once again staring deep into Mychal's eyes.

"What did he call you?" she asked.

He opened his mouth, but no sound came out. He had no idea what to say. Was it safe to tell these people? He still hadn't figured out if they were Resistance. "He's got a chain," the archer from the path said, approaching him as he started to stand, hand flying instinctively up to his chest. "Wouldn't let me see it."

Everyone in the cottage was watching him now. Mychal took a deep breath. He supposed they'd come this far. He pulled the livery chain out from under the leather and let it hang, turning to the woman. Her eyes were clouded, but he saw them recognize the crest.

"Welcome to Thorncliffe, Your Highness," she said, voice betraying very little emotion. "You're a long way from home."

"Yeah, well," Mychal said, breath coming quick as the others put the pieces together and started to react. "I don't think you've given me *your* name."

"My name doesn't matter," she said. "We're all the gods' children here."

"Are you Resistance?" he asked, starting to hope. "Senna Baker sent me. She thought--"

The woman held up a hand. "We don't know your friend, lad. We're not the Resistance."

"Well then who are you?" Luke asked, before he panicked again. Mychal gave him what was supposed to be an encouraging look, but his friend had already turned red and looked away from the preacher.

"We started as pilgrims," one of the others said. "But we liked it better out here."

"We're deserters from the Godhead too, in a way," the woman said, with a ghost of a smile. "We no longer wished to live in his kingdoms. So we wait."

"Wait for what?"

She blinked slowly. "The Son of Faris."

Mychal's heart picked up. "Right. And that's--"

"Do you know the story?" the woman asked, still spooning mouthfuls of the stew as she spoke.

He shrugged. "I know who Faris was."

"The youngest son of the son of the gods," she said, nodding, and Mychal tried not to show his annoyance on his face. She was preaching now, to the rest of the room. "His brother Caspar gave him Farisia to rule and his sons broke it apart after he was killed by his middle brother Amon. Or so the story goes."

"Yes," Mychal said, patiently. "And the Horn and the Hartlands--"

"Belong to his son and his bastard son, respectively," the woman nodded. "And their sons after them. The legend says one of their heirs will bring the kingdoms together once again. One Farisia. And drive the false prophets away. We think Riyan Duane is as false as prophets come. Many believe the time of the Son of Faris is coming."

Mychal could feel his heartbeat stuttering through his binding. He'd never attempted to claim this part of the plan, not yet, but... "I've been told--"

"You are a contender, yes," she said, still smiling with more than a little amusement now. "But just that." Deflated a little, but still waiting, Mychal nodded, watching her as she continued. "Though perhaps not for much longer with no food and how many men?"

He tried not to blush. "Including us, ninety-seven."

"Quite." The woman turned behind her and told the others, "Send them with the salted meat. Enough for a few days, at least."

"We couldn't," Mychal said, even as Graham and Luke bustled excitedly at his side. "You have children here."

"We have no need for it, now that spring has come," she said. "We've been supporting ourselves here for more than a year now, young man. You're just starting."

"Thank you," he said. "Truly. I won't forget this, when I get my crown."

"That might be sooner than you think," she said quietly. "I see dark words from home coming for you this spring."

Mychal clenched his jaw and tried not to think about it. "Yes."

"Whatever your fate, we are honored to have broken bread with you, Prince Mychal. May the Mother and Father bless you."

The meeting was over, he could tell. They all stood. "I wish you good fortune," he said, the closest to prayer he could manage. She nodded graciously. The guards from before started to move them toward the door, and before they left, he couldn't help himself and asked, "*Is* the Resistance in these mountains? Where can I find them?"

"If they are," she said seriously, "I expect they'll find you. And young man? One more gift." She nodded to one of the others, who brought her a bundle that she handed to Mychal and he opened to find a plant he hadn't seen in years, long red tendrils of snarling vine. It smelled like home. "Madder root. Mix it with iron."

Before the hour was out they were back on the path, on their way back to camp laden with crates of salted venison and jerky that they'd only stopped once to break into. Mychal walked several paces ahead, watching the moon rise as they went. The stew and now the strips of salted meat meant his hunger was gone, and it left more room for his mind to wander. It seemed it had done the same for Luke. "Did you say Senna back there?"

"Yes," he said, as his friends both rushed to catch up to him, flabbergasted. "She's Resistance."

"Are you joking?" Graham asked, then very seriously added, "Are *all* of May's girls Resistance? Because I told Alyce a *lot* about my sister, she waits on the princess and--"

"No, Graham, I think just her," Mychal said, though he winced at the allusion to Samira. He hadn't let himself think about their night, not since the Canyon, but when he slept it all came back and left him sick with worry and wanting every time. It was hard not to turn the march around and go back for her, even though he knew she was already gone from Hollisport. He was so scared of running out of time.

"That was mad," Luke said. "Did you know there were people like that? Pilgrims in the woods? And waiting for you?"

"No," he said, honestly. "I didn't."

"Do you think there are more of them?"

Mychal felt the hairs raise on the back of his neck as he nodded. "Yeah. I do."

They trudged on for a while, until they got close to reaching camp again. Graham spoke first. "What do we do now?"

He had no idea, in the long sense. But he did know how to start. "When we get back," he said, "find three barrels and fill them with water."

They did. All ninety-seven of the Halwood army came together around the barrels, sharing the venison hungrily as they did, and pitched their Army tunics into the water mixed with madder and gunpowder. Mychal woke up to the shirts drying on the branches the next morning, floating with the wind, nearly a hundred all flying Halwood red.

# 17

# Samira

Samira hadn't spoken for a long time when Jullia progressed from shouting to beating on the doors to the cathedral. Despite the growing crowd outside in the street behind them, no one from inside had acknowledged them since they arrived, and the younger girl was growing more desperate by the minute.

"Please!" she insisted, when she'd grown frustrated and her palms had started to turn red. "He's my brother! As Princess of the Hartlands, as *heir* to the Hartlands now, I demand to see Deronn!"

"Er, princess," one of the men interjected, a courtier of King Eronn's with one foot out the door and a member of the congregation of nobles Samira could best describe as 'snivelling', "actually the Hartlands would pass to one of your cousins should some misfortune befall the king--"

Jullia whirled around and shot the man a look that even Samira would bend to, as Petra Keaton ordered the man away without a word. There was a long silence as the court stood there, waiting for an answer from the Priests.

Deronn had been whisked away in the hours after the king's death, and no one had seen him since other than the Priests in the King's Cathedral. This was fairly normal, considering the circumstances; princes often held vigils for their fathers, and everyone had expected the Priests to grasp for power with the need for a regency until Deronn came of age. But whatever was happening inside, Jullia wanted him out.

Samira couldn't blame her. It had been two weeks now, and there were plenty of urgent matters that Deronn had to be present to attend to, now that he was acting king. The Godhead had just sent word to wait to crown him until he could make it to a formal coronation, but until then, though unofficial, he was Eronn's son, and there was nothing anyone else had the right to do. She and Jullia were holding things together as long as they could, delaying their trip to the lords' castles until Deronn returned.

There was an arrival today, though, that had been the last straw-- a messenger from the Holy Army, about the battle at the Canyon, with strict orders not to speak to anyone but the king. So Jullia had brought both of them in a palanquin through the city to the holy men's doorstep, and now they would wait.

"What should we do if they don't let him go?" Samira asked Petra quietly.

"I have no idea," she admitted. "My first thought would be to write to Lord Wright. He might come, he's the boy's uncle..." *And your lover*, Samira amended privately, but she knew the woman was probably right.

"Lady Keaton," one of the courtiers said sharply. "Perhaps this is not a discussion for guests."

Samira rounded on the man. "Excuse me? And who are you?"

The man did not flinch. "A knight of the Hartlands, Princess. Meaning no offense, but I find it difficult to believe you stand in opposition to your betrothed's loyalists here."

She took a step back, genuinely surprised. "I... I'm no Priest. Gods bind the idea."

"Right," he muttered. She turned back around, fuming, but still heard him say to another, "It's positively chilling. She would have been our queen, as of two weeks ago. Like a ghost, the prince's betrothed haunting the halls. What's she *doing* here?"

Samira reeled, remembering as she sometimes suddenly did that she had been engaged at birth to the original crown prince. Not for the first time in the past weeks, she wished *her* Mychal was here.

Finally, the huge cedarwood doors of the Cathedral creaked open and a younger Priest stepped gingerly into the daylight. "Good morning, Princess Jullia," he said, bowing his head to her. "I'm Brother Fabian. The king is waiting for you inside."

"Deronn?" Jullia called past him, nearly bowling the man over to pass into the temple. Petra gave him a cursory thanks and followed behind, and Samira trailed both of them. She could feel the mother amulet hanging over her heart under her dress and thanked Farrah silently for the protection as she glided past Brother Fabian without more from him than an ordinary leering glance.

The inside of Queenshearth's cathedral was different from Hollisport's, the marbled cobblestone rougher-cut and older than Haddon's buttressed graystone. Samira stared up as she walked the antechamber, hung with Priesthood sun-and-moon banners underneath the bell tower and the spire, until the ceiling opened up to bathe the meeting space and altar in sunlight. Deronn sat on his knees in front of the slab of rock, deep in a book, with hair still wet from a bath in brand-new clothing. Samira exchanged a look with Petra. She wondered what shape he'd been in before they'd found out his sister was on her way.

He looked up as Jullia rushed to him and eagerly jumped into a hug, sounding stripped of air when he managed to say, "I'm okay."

"What have they been doing with you?" she insisted, but Deronn gave her a look before glancing around and Jullia seemed to understand. "Let's go home."

"I... yeah," he said, but he still seemed a little unsure. "Let's go." He set the book down and Samira managed a glimpse of the cover before they left: *The Last Days of the Brothers.*

"You'll be leaving us now, brother?" Brother Fabian asked as Jullia marched Deronn quickly past and up to the waiting palanquin.

"Yes," he said, hurried and calling over Jullia's shoulder. "Thank you for the books!"

Samira and Petra climbed in quickly and Jullia shut the door. The coachman drove the horses down the street immediately, and they were on their way back to Hartshold Keep.

"Thank you," Deronn said, sounding tired. "Can I sleep when we get home?"

"I'm sorry," Jullia said, "but we need you for a moment first." He nodded, resigned. After a second she asked, "Did they hurt you?" Her voice sounded choked, but Samira could tell she was trying to be brave for him. Her heart ached for both of them.

"No, Jule," Deronn said, "honest. It was a vigil for Dad, mostly. They want to bury him today."

"About time," Petra muttered, and Jullia nodded.

"And the rest of the time they mostly just talked about the gods. I started asking questions so they gave me lots of books. It was kind of nice, actually. But I wasn't allowed to talk to anyone who wasn't a Priest. And they all started calling me 'brother', which was... really weird, you know. I've only ever heard them call Dad that."

"Yeah," Jullia said quietly. "Well... okay. But listen, Deronn, you're king now. You don't have to go anywhere you don't want to. Next time, tell them you want to stay."

The boy looked at his sister for a long, quiet moment. "Doesn't work that way," he finally said, and the rest of the ride back to the castle passed in silence.

Samira had felt trapped the entire chaotic past two weeks here, but now she felt it especially acutely. She was still here, both to help if she could and in hopes Jullia would be able to come with her soon, to Brookbridge and then on to the other great houses, but King Eronn's death had thrown everything into the air. She wondered if Mychal had heard yet. They hadn't heard about him. Only that the battle had happened, and no one knew how it had ended, not yet. But maybe this rider would change that. They'd see.

*I wish you were here,* she thought to him, though she knew he couldn't hear. She'd been talking to him, privately, lately, and it helped, a bit. She felt a little stranded without him, after the Declaration night. *Your brother and sister need you. But I'll do my best.*

When they reached the keep, much of the rest of the court had already made their way back, and Jullia marched straight into the reception hall, bringing Deronn along with her. Samira followed, sitting on the advisors' bench on the dais next to Petra as the Halwood children directed the beginnings of petitions for the day. If the castle staff or any of the councilors had thoughts about Deronn's sudden return, no one voiced them. The first visitor begging an audience was brought through the doors not long after, and the procession began.

It wasn't long before the messenger from that morning passed through the entryway and Samira and Jullia both jolted up in their seats. Deronn looked at them, confused, before he said, "Approach, sir."

"Your Majesty," the soldier said, the sun-and-moon crest glinting in the sunlight streaming through the long hall windows. Turning to Samira and Jullia, he bowed quickly again. "Your Highnesses. I come from Lord Thorne at Astor Post with urgent news."

Deronn nodded, glancing at his sister. His voice came out quiet and quivering, and Samira felt awful. It felt like watching a child wear his father's clothes. He had no business doing this. "Right. Er, what is your message?"

"The Battle at the Mages' Canyon," the messenger said, and the whole room stilled. He cleared his throat, glancing around at the court, and continued. "It did not go as hoped."

Samira braced herself. *He's going to be okay. He has to be.* Deronn glanced nervously back at the two of them, again, and Jullia gripped the armrests of the throne tight but spoke loud and evenly. "What happened?"

"The vanguard was met with immediate resistance from the Daemons. There was..." The man looked at Deronn and Jullia hesitantly, then said, gently the way one would speak to a child trying not to scare them, "There was much fire. Perhaps half the forces perished in the blaze."

"Did you say half?" Samira couldn't help but exclaim. "Meaning *ten thousand?*"

The messenger looked horrified himself, but nodded. "Yes, Your Highness. Possibly more."

"Gods above," Petra murmured at her side while the whole hall reeled with the news. Samira couldn't stop the ringing in her ears. *Mychal had to have been in the van. Does that mean he's...?*

"I am sorry to hear that," Deronn said shakily after Jullia whispered in his ear. "What does Lord Thorne ask of the crown here?"

"Well, Your Majesty, Lord Thorne asks that your remaining standing forces report to Astor Post as quickly as possible."

Samira raised her eyebrows and looked to Jullia, who scoffed and met her with the same expression. Petra was the first to raise her voice.

"What right does the Holy Army have to ask that of us?" she asked. "We've already sent 8,000 men to Thorne's camp, many of whom I am sure were the first to be sent to the fire." The messenger glanced away at that and Samira's blood boiled a little more. "Why should we send a single man after he was so stupid as to kill them all in one fell swoop?"

"My lady," the messenger bristled, "you are speaking about the anointed commander of the military arm of the Faith."

"Yes, I am, gods help us."

Jullia stifled a smile while the messenger stood there, clearly at a loss. "I was asking His Majesty King Deronn, not his High Steward." He turned to the boy, who looked terrified to speak. "Sir--"

"No, you were not," Petra interrupted. "His Majesty has not yet been appointed a Lord Regent. He will not come of age for five more years. It would not do for him to command troops without guidance."

"So what would you have me do, my lady?"

"Leave. Now." Petra and the soldier stared each other down for several long moments. Finally, the man turned tail and stalked down the aisle toward the doors.

"Wait!" Jullia shouted after him. He stopped and turned around, looking hopeful. But Samira knew she wasn't going to speak about forces. "Do you have a list of the dead? Is my--" She watched as the girl caught herself, eyes wide, but quickly recovered. "Our cousin, Luke Payne. He's a squire there. Is he alive?"

The messenger deflated. "We don't know, Your Highness. Not yet. But many squires are missing." He left the hall.

Jullia bowed her head. "Thank you, Petra," she muttered. The woman nodded, but Samira saw her peering at the girl curiously and she coulld guess why. The Halwoods and their cousins weren't close. It wasn't as seamless a cover for asking after Mychal as they'd thought. But Luke and Mychal *had* been practically joined at the hip, at her Declaration, so not having his body was a good sign. And what had he said? Squires were *missing*?

*Maybe he ran.*

"Can I go?" Deronn asked, clearly distraught, and Petra nodded.

He bolted from the hall, into the back door leading directly up to the keep. The court was still dealing with the news, and many had walked out with the messenger. Samira shook her head. They'd all desert Deronn soon. She and Jullia had to start as soon as they could.

* * *

They interred King Eronn privately, after the public procession from his body's vigil chambers in the Cathedral up to the castle on the hill. The Halwood family crypt lay under the royal chapel, a small dirt-floor shrine with an altar and two stone benches where Jullia stopped to pray. She went with her and Deronn down the stairs that opened at the back wall as Petra directed the attendants down with the body.

Samira didn't want to look. The dead had always disturbed her, but the Hartlands felt differently, and there was no cover obscuring the view of the king. She mostly avoided the sight, but caught a glimpse of his folded hands over the black robes he would be buried in as he was carried past. For Jullia's sake, she braced herself and continued down into the crypt.

There was no natural light this far underground. Torches had been lit for them earlier that day, bathing the long, narrow halls to the burial vaults in warm orange light. It didn't help. Samira stepped past the altar carved into the floor, slipping her boots off with Jullia and Deronn as they went, and didn't stop at the benches on either side that stood here, too. She wondered what they were for; at the moment they were only gathering dust. They followed the attendants down the Hall of Kings, bypassing the family vaults on either side.

The chamber opened up when they reached the end of the passageway, into a huge circular room lined with statues and headstones of fallen Halwood kings. Samira recognized the emblem of

Faris on the panel for the grave across from the doorway, the sword and waves of the Farisian crest. He wasn't buried here, but under Haddon's Cathedral back in Hollisport; this was, surely, Hart's way of honoring his father and his house's lineage nevertheless. The others fanned out on either side from the empty grave, and the attendants brought the body to an unclaimed panel of the wall, where a newly-cut stone chamber waited to receive it.

When they laid Eronn inside, the attendants quickly departed, and Petra hugged Deronn and Jullia before whispering something and leaving the chamber. Samira examined the nearby statues, trying to give them their privacy, until she heard Deronn speak.

"I'm scared, Jullia."

She heard Jullia inhale sharply and wipe her eyes on her sleeve. "I know. Me, too. But everything will be alright."

"How can you say that? He's gone, and we're the only ones left, and I'm not old enough so it's only going to get *worse*."

"We're not the only ones left," Jullia said, like it had tumbled out before she'd meant it to. Samira looked sharply back toward them and met her eyes in a panic. What would they say now? They'd agreed Deronn was too young to understand about Mychal.

Deronn blinked and looked from one of them to the other. "What?"

Jullia took a long, deep breath, and Samira held hers. "Mychal's alive, Deronn," she whispered, and Samira's eyes widened. *Gods. He'll never forgive this, when he's older.* "He's coming home."

The little boy stumbled back a bit, immediately incredulous. Pointing back towards the other halls, he stuttered, "But then-- who's-- who's buried in the Hall of Princes? I've seen him!"

"Someone who died to keep the secret. It's horrible, I know."

Deronn still looked shocked, but he was starting to follow. "Where's he *been?*"

"He's been in the Army. But we're calling our men together to bring him home. Samira and I have to go for a while, but we'll be back soon and then he'll come."

The boy's lip quivered and Samira almost had to turn away. "So... I don't have to do this?"

"Not forever," Jullia said, pulling her brother into a hug. "Just hold out until we get back. Okay?"

"Okay," he mumbled into her shoulder. They hugged for a few more seconds before he pulled back, wiping his eyes quickly. "I, um," he said, hiding his face from them, "I sat with him this whole time, can I go now? I don't want to be down here anymore."

"Sure, Deronn," Jullia said, smiling gently, and he practically ran from the chamber. Jullia sighed and sank to her knees in front of the grave, groaning and squeezing her eyes shut tight. Samira wasn't sure what to say, so she knelt next to her and waited. After a long while, the girl spoke.

"Please don't judge me too much for that."

"Never. I couldn't imagine being in your place." And at thirteen, too. Samira had seen cause every day for weeks now to wish Jullia could still be a child. As it was, the girl rested her head on her shoulder, and Samira squeezed her hand. "We are going to need to work out what to say," she added, as Jullia collected herself. "Where has he been? We'll need a story for all of that."

"Right." They sat in silence for another moment, until Jullia said, "The message from the Battle. Do you think... he survived?"

"Yeah, I do," Samira said quietly. She'd convinced herself about that, hours ago. Now she felt oddly at peace in the face of it, here in the crypt of the Halwood dead. "He's alive, I know he is. If he wasn't I would've felt it."

Jullia turned and stared at her, stunned into silence for a moment. "Oh, Sami," she said softly, after a while. "I had no idea."

Samira would normally have felt embarrassed, or at least on the spot, but she didn't here. "I didn't either, until a little while ago."

The girl covered her mouth with her hands. "Are you still going to New Astoria?"

She smiled a little, trying not to let too much hope in about that part of Mychal's promises. "I hope not."

Jullia took a deep breath again; Samira appreciated the restraint. "Alright." After another pause, she asked, "Does he still look... like my sister did? At all?"

"Yes and no," she said. "You'll recognize him. But they'll believe it. And he has some kind of potion for that now."

"Really? So other people have done this?"

"Yes," another voice said. Both girls turned quickly to the entry-way, and Samira's heart stopped when she saw Petra, looking like a specter in the torchlight carrying her own lantern and bouncing shadows off her robes. "They were called Sons of Morra, in the old times," she went on, ignoring their reactions. "And speaking as the one who for all intents and purposes, raised you children, do not count me as shocked in his case."

"I thought you'd gone back up," Jullia finally managed to say.

"I was in the Hall of Queens," the Steward replied quietly. "Lighting a candle for my friend Mina. Before your mother died, she made me swear to protect her children. So it seems we are going to Brookbridge."

# 18

# Edris

"The sun's going down," Edris said, as their horses trotted up onto the first steady ground for miles and the horizon came into view. "Should we stop for the night?"

Sir Alexander's face had been unreadable ever since they'd gotten news from the battle and set out from Astor Post, about two weeks ago, but now it twisted into something almost frightened. "We're across the border now, and past the Canyon," he said quietly. "This is disputed territory. I say we keep going until we get somewhere safe."

"Safe?" Edris asked, raising his eyebrows. "Half the bloody Army's gone, I don't think anywhere's--"

"*Safer*, then," the other man snapped, then looked away and sighed. "I'm-- sorry, Your Highness. I just-- you know that if I'm captured..."

"I know," Edris said quickly, trying to meet his eyes, but the knight wouldn't look at him. "Your Highness," he said, and forced a small laugh, trying to tread carefully. "You, um, haven't called me that for a while now."

"What would you prefer I call you, Your Highness?"

Edris frowned. "Xander, what's wrong?"

Xander was looking at the horizon now, the ever-growing peaks of the Holy Mountains jutting up between them and the more settled part of Thorncliffe, and he exhaled slowly, like something had deflated him. "He's going to send us back, isn't he? Your father?"

Now he did meet his eyes, but Edris found he couldn't keep them there. He stared down at his horse as he said, "I don't know. When we get back to Caspar's Dale and tell him what happened, we'll see. But the Mages' Canyon decimated us. We can hardly defend ourselves, let alone--"

"The battle was a disaster because you don't know how to fight the Daemons!" Xander suddenly exclaimed. Several of the ragged remaining Valleyguard men ahead of them turned to look, and Edris felt prickling embarrassment at what they were seeing as Xander continued. "Silas does! He could help you!"

"Silas got captured!" Edris protested. "You're the ones asking *us* for help!"

"He held his castle for *three years* with 500 men and one mage," Xander said. "The Holy Army didn't even last a day!"

Edris didn't know what to say to that, so he said nothing, his face burning under Xander's furious gaze. After a moment, he turned to the men and said, "We'll camp here for tonight. Start north again at first light." He dismounted, ignoring Xander's aggrieved expression, and made for a shaded spot below the face of the rock stretching up behind them to help the men set up his tent. He expected he'd be camping alone tonight.

They had guards on all sides of the camp, but Edris couldn't help but notice later that night as he was going in to sleep that Xander was still wide awake, hand on his sword, keeping watch with the other Eirosian men nearby. Quietly, careful not to stir any of the sleeping soldiers, he made his way over to him and sat down, trying to read his expression. "You really should rest."

"I won't sleep tonight," he said. "Not here." Xander was staring east-- toward the flatter, whiter landscape far in the distance where Edris knew his home lay-- and his eyes were blank, unfocused, like he was lost in deep thought.

Edris sighed. "I know you think it's dangerous here," he said, "but we have sentries posted and you need to sleep."

"No, thank you," he said firmly. "When I die, I want to do it standing, with my sword in my hand. Not burnt to a crisp in my sleep by some Daemon scouting party." The man's attention seemed to come back to the world around him and turned to Edris. "I shouldn't have shouted at you in front of your men. I'm sorry."

Edris shrugged. "They're not really *my* men, are they?" he asked, trying not to sound as bitter as he felt. "Someone else led them into the Canyon. I marched them down the Holy Road to their fate, but I wasn't *there*."

There was a long silence, and then Xander asked the question he'd been dreading. "Why aren't we going back by the road we came?"

Edris, once again, tried not to seem as embarrassed as he felt and said, "I'm worried we'll be taken back to Astor Post if we do. The Godhead will be going south soon for Deronn Halwood's coronation, and just seeing him might make the men think to go back."

"And you're afraid?" Xander asked. Edris grimaced and he quickly added, "That's alright. So am I. I'm *glad* I wasn't there, Edris. I know they've told you what they saw, but you have no idea. Most of the ones who saw the worst of it aren't even here to tell it."

"I still... isn't it mad? I still wish I'd been there," Edris said.

"I thought I'd made you see sense that night," Xander said. There was a suggestion in his voice that made Edris go red once again. "You blush about as much as a little girl, you know that?"

"You can't talk to me like that!" Edris exclaimed, trying to sound genuinely indignant, but the knight just chuckled. After another long, heavy pause, he hesitantly asked, "So you are like Silas?"

Xander shrugged. "Not quite. Silas only ever had eyes for men. Well, really only for Perin. There was never anyone else, after he died." Edris nodded. He'd heard about the Eirosian king's husband his entire life, not very favorably of course, but he'd always been struck in the stories he'd been told by their obvious devotion to each other. His lifelong compassion for them, despite what he'd heard, made more sense to him now. "But I've never troubled myself much one way or the other, honestly," Xander continued. "If I want something, I want it. That's that."

Trying not to go red again, Edris asked, "You're not... worried about...?"

"About what?"

"Divine retribution," he said, laughing to hide how serious he was, and how much he needed to hear his answer.

Xander laughed a little, too, but his face was solemn when he said, "I don't think anyone's keeping score, rewarding or punishing people either here or after... I've seen too many things that no one could count fair."

Edris stared at the sleeping soldiers as he thought about what he must have meant. "There's hardly a third of them left," he said quietly. "Do you really think Silas would know how to help us?"

Xander's eyes came alive again, more than he'd seen them in weeks, when he said, "Yes. I do."

"How would we get to him?" he said slowly. "*If* we were going to."

Xander looked around and asked, "I'm assuming you're not planning to go home for more men from Thorncliffe?" Edris shook his head. He couldn't even imagine going to his father about this. If this were to work, they would have to abandon going home first. He felt a kind of thrill when he thought about it, but he wasn't sure he'd be able to bring himself to... to what exactly? Lead a rogue force of

Valleyguard in deserting Thorncliffe to stand with *Eirosia?* it was insane. But he wanted to hear what Xander would say. "We don't have enough to take Illon's Fast here. We'd need more men. Eirosians."

"I've heard there's a colony close by," Edris said. "Near the border, further north. We might be able to--"

Xander gripped his arm suddenly then and hissed, "Edris. There's someone coming." Edris turned around to face the path, and had just enough time to hear the footsteps of a marching force growing louder before one of the sentries shouted, "Daemons!" and steel clattered together just out of sight. Edris scrambled back to his tent and drew his sword from its scabbard at the entrance, standing his ground with his heart pounding as the shadowy figures charged into the camp. *He was right,* Edris thought miserably. *We're going to die because of me.* The sleeping Thorncliffe men were waking in the midst of the attack, and not nearly enough of them were ready to defend themselves when the invaders reached them.

Edris crossed swords for the first time with a brutal, rattling clash, and the excited blood rushing through his veins was enough to keep him light on his feet, alive, for several terrifying moments. It was only when their blades locked and Edris was fighting for purchase on the rocks under his feet when he saw the moonlight glance off a sun-and-moon crest on the man's chestplate. He looked up with horror and met his attacker's very human eyes.

"Stop!" he shouted, stumbling back from the man. Xander broke from his own opponent to give the man a solid shove with all his weight into his shoulder, sending him flying away from them for good. *"Stop!"* When no one heard him, he shouted again, desperately, "STOP! We're fighting ourselves!" He saw the men around him respond, break apart, and a ripple of confusion ran through the camp. The fighting stopped altogether when one or two of the men on the other side told their own to fall back, and seizing the momentary silence, Edris yelled, "I'm Edris Thorne of Thorncliffe! We're Holy Army men!"

"Why aren't you dead, then?" a harsh voice called out in the darkness. It was still hard to see anyone's face in the dim light of the moon, and Edris was searching for a clear leader to speak to but found no one.

"Why aren't you?" he shouted back.

"We're not His army anymore," the same voice said. "We're Halwood men."

Edris hadn't been expecting that. He found himself searching for something to say, blinking rapidly and staring at the crests on the men's armor. Finally, he said, "You're going the wrong way, then. Hartlands are south of here."

"We're exactly where we're supposed to be," someone called from the throng of shadows in front of them. This voice was different, loud and coarse like a boy's when it was breaking, and came from a figure obscured in shadow on one of the few horses they had. Edris's heart nearly stopped when the men parted for the rider and he came close enough to see familiar dark eyes staring down at him. He looked older, and there was something undeniably different about him now, but there was no doubt that it was Mychal. "I'm Mychal Halwood."

One of the archers to Edris's right nocked an arrow as shocked whispers broke out throughout the camp. Edris turned to the archer and said, "Stand down." He lowered his bow, eyeing Mychal warily, and the men around the boy visibly relaxed.

"I would speak with you alone, Prince Edris," he said. His expression was betraying nothing, despite what Edris was sure was clear on his own face. So he'd been right, back at Astor Post. He couldn't say it gave him much satisfaction. After a long pause, Edris nodded and stepped back to let him dismount. Another boy tried to follow, but Mychal stopped him and said quietly, "It's alright, Luke. Come find me later." As they were walking toward Edris's tent, the men parted for them, and Xander's eyes followed them all the way inside.

Within the canvas of the tent, and the wide berth the soldiers were giving it, they would have a while to speak in private, and Edris got a better look at Mychal than before. His hair had grown out a bit, falling down in waving curls all around the crown of his head, and it seemed like very recently he had dyed his Holy Army uniform tunic a deep, Halwood wine-red. He wore the chain of a crown prince, too, the sword-and-fire family crest woven into the Surpoint iron links. Mychal saw him appraising him and laughed a little. "I reckon I've changed a bit."

"You *haven't* been telling people you're Mychal Halwood," Edris began, the only thing that he could manage to say. "Or, the *real* one, I mean."

"Not the whole time, of course not," he said, a redness creeping up into his cheeks. "Just since the battle."

"Why?" he asked, still at a loss.

"What do you mean, why?" Mychal asked, frowning. "I'm claiming my crown."

Oh, *gods.* "It was never *your* crown, Mychal."

"It's mine more than it's the Godhead's," he said, eyes blazing again, just like they had years ago in Queenshearth. "Why shouldn't I take it?"

Edris was finding it difficult to argue with him, but he couldn't tell whether it was because he was making sense or it was just too insane. "You and your, what, 100 men? Fewer?"

"So far," he said, defensive.

Edris narrowed his eyes. "What *are* you doing here?"

Mychal shifted his gaze and said, somewhat too casually, "Looking for aid."

"You won't find it in Thorncliffe," he said, frowning, and when

Mychal looked up at him again, he understood. "Oh, gods, the Resistance?"

"Well, who else?" he exclaimed.

"If you're Mychal Halwood, you have lords that would follow you. Soldiers," Edris pointed out.

"We're working on that too," he said. "Edris, I don't need you to tell me how to do this."

Why *was* he telling him how to do this? Edris paused, then let out a long breath and said, "I can't believe you've been able to keep it up this long."

He shrugged. "It suits me, I suppose." His voice was breaking again; Edris took that as as good an opportunity as any to ask.

"How are you doing that?"

"What?"

"The voice. And, well, you're thinner, you know, where you ought to be. You've got a... sharper frame. You know what I mean, Mychal, *how* are you doing it?" Edris asked, trying not to show his embarrassment again.

The other prince smiled a little. "Really? You noticed?" He unbuckled one of the pouches on his satchel and opened it just enough to show Edris three small vials, with thick golden liquid filling two up to the brim and swishing around the bottom of the third. "I had some help."

"So desertion, treason, and now magic too? Brilliant," Edris muttered. "I almost told the Lord Marshal about you, you know. When I heard you were a squire."

Mychal stiffened, and he asked, his voice terse, "But you *didn't?*"

"No, I didn't," Edris said. "But I might now. This is getting out of hand, Mychal."

He paused, then shook his head. "You won't tell anyone," he said firmly, eyes narrowing, looking confident now.

"Why?" Edris asked, swallowing hard.

"If you tell them about me, you'll also be telling them you kept it from them for years."

"I could have only just found out," he protested. Mychal raised his eyebrows, and Edris swore quietly. He was right. "What do you want from me?"

"Safe passage," he said, all sincerity now. "That's all." He coughed and added, quieter, "And maybe some food." As they stared at each other, each seeming to be looking for the right words, the tent flap pulled back and the boy who'd been riding alongside Mychal entered but hesitated at the threshold. Xander was behind him. "Luke?"

"Sorry for interrupting, Your Highness. This man wanted to meet you," Luke said, eyeing him suspiciously. "He's an Eirosian."

"Um, alright," Mychal said, nodding, very matter-of-fact, which seemed to quell the consternation on Xander's face-- a little. "What's your name?"

"Sir Alexander Neill," he said, bowing his head as he did. "My men and I came to Thorncliffe to petition King Bastian on King Silas's behalf."

"I heard about you," Mychal said, nodding. "The Lord Marshal said something to the man I was squiring for, weeks ago. They didn't believe you." Xander nodded, and he said, "I'm Mychal Halwood, rightful Crown Prince of the Hartlands. Tell me what you told them."

"Your Highness." Xander bowed his head again, but it only took a moment for Mychal's words to register with him and he turned to look at Edris, brow furrowed. "Crown Prince? But--"

It hit Edris then, too, and he stared back at the knight for a moment until Mychal broke the silence. "What is it?" he asked, clearly confused.

"I thought you knew," Edris said quietly. "But I suppose you couldn't have-- the rider only got to Astor Post after the Army marched out."

"What?" he insisted, but Edris could tell from his tight jaw and the demand in his voice that he must have some idea.

"King Eronn died, Mychal. More than a fortnight ago," he told him, as gently as he could.

Edris watched the moment he'd dreaded all his life, the moment of becoming a king, play out on someone else's face; he saw the grief, and the shock, and then the crushing weight of realizing that the death of his father meant something else entirely. Mychal looked like he had been transported thousands of miles, back home, in an instant and all he could do in the tent was nod, slowly, just once.

"Alright," he finally said, barely louder than a whisper, and ignoring a shocked Luke, turned back to face Xander. "What did you want to say, Sir Alexander?"

"Your Majesty," Xander corrected himself, and Edris watched Mychal stiffen to keep from recoiling. As conflicted as he was, as much as he thought he ought to have the stomach to ride back to Astor Post right then and declare the deception for the Lord Marshal and all the Godhead's men to hear, Edris also truly felt for him now. He was already living in fear of the day he became a king, and he had been prepared for it his whole life-- Mychal hadn't had that luxury. Not to mention the way the Canyon-- and Xander-- had played out had thrown everything he'd ever thought he knew firmly into peril. So he stayed rooted to his place, and listened.

"My men and I escaped from Illon's Fast in the last month of the year, and came to Thorncliffe on foot seeking aid for our captured king. Silas Dillon and what remains of his court are hostages in the castle. The king of the Daemons rules Eirosia, and after his victory at the Mages' Canyon, it's only a matter of time before he crosses into the Triad." He glanced at Edris briefly before he said, "Prince Edris has been... kinder than his father. But my king still suffers."

"I met the Daemons at the Canyon," Mychal said. He looked sincere, but Edris still saw the uncertainty written on his face. It was clear he was very new to command. "I understand. What would you have me do?"

"Go to Illon's Fast," Xander pleaded. "Help us take our kingdom back and we'll help you win yours."

Mychal hesitated and turned to study Edris's face carefully. "I thought he was your prisoner."

Edris let out the breath catching in his lungs and shook his head. "I haven't decided."

The boy smiled, in a knowing way that made Edris nervous. Was he really so transparent? He turned back to Xander. "I have fewer than a hundred men, sir. My forces in the Hartlands haven't gathered yet."

"We have three hundred here," Xander said. "And we're on the way to an Eirosian colony now to find more. Numbers won't be a problem, they hold the castle lightly."

Mychal looked back at Edris. "Your men will follow you?"

"Some of them, maybe," he said, doubtful. "I can't be sure."

He nodded, and faced the knight again. "We'll go with you, Sir Alexander," he said. "That is if Edris agrees."

Xander's eyes widened a little, and Edris couldn't tell he hadn't thought it would work. "Thank you, Your Majesty," he said quickly, and bowed before exiting the tent.

"Luke, go tell Graham and the others," Mychal said.

"Are you alright?" Luke asked him. "I know you didn't really know your father, but..."

"I'm fine," he said. "Go. I'll be out soon." Luke bowed his head and left the tent.

Edris was still unsure what exactly had just happened. "Mychal, I still haven't said we were going," he said. The smile was back, this time with a little bit of a laugh. "What's funny?" he demanded.

"You didn't yet, but you will," Mychal said. "Because it's the decent thing to do, and you've already done that much for me."

"You have more faith in that than I do," Edris warned.

"That's fine," he said. "If you need to sleep on it, that's fine. We'll leave in the morning." He looked down then and said, "I have to tell my men my father's dead, and write to my sister. It's... good to see you, Edris." And with that, Mychal ducked out through the tent flap and Edris was alone.

He stared for a while at the spot where Mychal had been standing, dismayed; his mind couldn't make sense of what his one decision years ago had come to. If he had known then that this would happen... well, he didn't know if he would have done anything differently, if he was being honest. If he hadn't helped him then, Edris would have a miserable wife in Caspar's Dale and everything else would be the same. He had never thought the Priests killing the first Mychal was right to begin with. The crown was that boy's birthright, whatever his mother might have done. Why did this Mychal deserve it any less?

Edris still hadn't made a decision when he got restless an hour or so after trying to go to sleep alone and went for a walk through the camp. The Halwood men were set up at a cautious distance from the Valleyguard, closer to the road, and he saw their fires still burning brightly and heard singing and shouting floating over to the Thorncliffe side. While he was watching, one man called out, "*Long live King Mychal!*" and several others took up the cry.

He stood there for a long moment, thinking. Then he walked over to his officers and told them to get word out that any man still here in the morning would be marching to the border with Mychal Halwood. He slept better than he had in weeks that night, and when he woke the next morning, there were still two hundred men there with him.

The men that had stayed watched him walk through the camp to the others at dawn, and Edris felt much less harshly regarded than before. He was looking for Xander, but the knight found him first.

He stopped in front of him, gratitude written plain on his face and maybe something more, and said softly, "Thank you, Edris." When the sun had risen in earnest, they marched out, three hundred strong, northeast to the border where Xander's people were waiting.

# 19

## Samira

"Traditionally, the man himself would come to ask for my support." Gerron Payne, the rather large, irritable, and aging Lord of Brookbridge, was staring suspiciously at the three of them from his seat on the dais of his reception hall, framed by his family and attendants. "Forgive me if I have a hard time accepting that a dead man is asking for my help if he isn't here."

"Lord Gerron, I understand it sounds unlikely," Jullia said, still patient as ever. Samira was glad the other girl was the one speaking. She wouldn't have kept her composure this long.

"Unlikely? I should say so," he said. The lithe white wolf on the banner of House Payne hung on the wall over the scene, a stark contrast to the image of the rough man they called the Old Dog. "I was there that day, Princess. He looked dead to me."

"That wasn't him," Jullia said. "My mother snuck him out of the city before the Godhead arrived. He was raised on a farm in the crownlands. We always knew he was alive. I met him two years ago, before he went to the Army." The story they'd devised spilled out of the girl so naturally that Samira almost believed her herself.

Lord Gerron wasn't as convinced. "And why would he do that? The Army are the ones who killed him, after all." The Old Dog seemed to think the whole idea was funny, which was getting under Samira's skin and, she was sure, Jullia's too. But she pressed on.

"He had to learn to fight," she said. "And he would be here if he could, but he's with the Army, defending the Triad. He *is* alive, Lord Gerron, I promise you that."

"Are you sure he still is?" he muttered. "The battle at the Canyon was a massacre. We're still waiting for word whether my younger son survived." Samira took a deep breath as she tried not to hear what the lord was saying. They had no idea if Mychal was still alive, but she refused to entertain the thought of him being dead. It was too much to bear. *I just got him back.*

"We got word from him just last week, just before we left," Jullia lied, the picture of confidence nonetheless. They'd heard nothing after the messenger at Queenshearth of the battle. What was left of King Eronn's court dissolved almost overnight after he was interred, and they'd left for Brookbridge with only Petra and a small guard two days later, a full two weeks after she'd arrived. *Wasted time.*

Lord Gerron sighed. "Your Highness, do you think I've kept my head this long by throwing my lot in with everyone who's asked?"

"No, my lord. We have great respect for you. I'm asking you to take my word as a Halwood. This is about a free Hartlands," Jullia said.

His eyes flickered over to Samira. "So then why is the Godhead's wife here? Sounds like a trick to me."

Samira's blood rose then, and before Jullia could stop her she said, "I'm not his wife, not yet. My loyalty is with Mychal, for as long as I have a choice."

She thought she saw the hint of a real smile on the Old Dog's face when he said, "I see. Young love. He's certainly set on committing heresy left and right, isn't he?" He turned his eyes back to Jullia and said, "I can respect that. But I'm still not convinced I won't hang for this."

"They're telling you the truth, my lord," Petra said suddenly. The Steward had been silent up until that moment, standing back behind the two princesses, but she'd stepped forward now, holding her ground in front of Lord Payne.

He now looked more annoyed with her than anyone else. "Yes, so you say, Keaton. Because your mistress says. I've never understood why Stewards are permitted in closed audiences-- why are you in my city?"

"I– to serve my princess, and to see my son, when we reach the Forge," Petra said, clearly startled.

"Abandoning a sinking ship, more like," he muttered. "Though I wouldn't say the one you've jumped onto now is in any better shape." He looked back at Jullia. "Your Highness, I hope what you're saying is true. But even if he is alive, the Godhead will crush us. I've given the Army my second son. Why should I give you my armies?"

"Because the Hartlands are *ours*!" Jullia exclaimed. "They came here and said it was theirs, and *killed* my mother. Your daughter-by-law, Grandmother," she added, addressing the lord's sister, the Queen Mother Katheryn Payne, sitting in quiet contemplation at the far end of the dias. She stirred and nodded slowly at Jullia, and Samira felt drawn to this sad but sharp-looking woman. "I love Deronn," she continued, turning back toward Lord Gerron, "but he's too young to do this. They'll tear him apart. Mychal's our *only* chance. The Paynes are our oldest allies, with the largest force in the Hartlands. We need you. Will you help us?"

Lord Gerron was quiet for a long time. He looked at his eldest son, sitting at his other side, and when he met his gaze, he paused another moment and nodded slowly. "Alright, Princess. I'll help your brother. Provided I see him for myself, and he asks me the old way, face to face."

Samira had half a mind to slap him, but her hopes began to rise all the same. "If he goes to Surpoint, will you come to see him there?" she asked.

Lord Gerron smirked. "Yes, fine, I'll meet your farmboy king at the Forges. Now pray let me rest. I'm an old man and I've been in this hall for six hours now. You're welcome in my castle, but Astor help us if a Holy man hears you conspiring..." He stood up and his heavy steps echoed as he left through the archway behind him, grumbling to his advisors as they went.

"That wasn't so bad," Jullia said cheerfully, and Samira stared at her, incredulous.

"Are you serious? I nearly killed him."

"I know," she said, smiling. "You could be a bit more serene, you know, as the Godhead's fiancée."

Samira narrowed her eyes, but before she could say anything back, a new voice interrupted them: "Welcome to Brookbridge, Your Highnesses." When Samira looked, she was greeted by Lord Gerron's eldest son, a stocky, smiling young man, who was approaching them from a polite distance. He bowed when they turned to look at him.

"Lord Devonn," Jullia greeted him.

"I'm not a lord, Your Highness, not yet. But thank you," he said. "Please forgive my father. He's a very honorable man, deep down, but... he's seen a lot in his time."

"Of course," Jullia said smoothly, before Samira could reply. "I'm glad we could come to an agreement."

"I hope I'll be swearing my sword to your brother soon," Devonn said. "My own brother Luke was at the Canyon too."

Samira jumped at the mention of Luke Payne, and told him, "If Mychal's alive, then Luke must be, too. They were both at my Declaration, and they were inseparable."

Devonn smiled then, and she saw a spark in his eye that hadn't been there before. "Really? Thank the Father. I mean, I hope you're right."

Another voice echoed across the hall then: "I can't believe it's really you, Jullia. I haven't seen you in years." The little old woman from the dais was striding up to them now with a remarkably youthful step, and Devonn stepped aside for her.

"My father's sister, Queen Katheryn," he said.

"Grandmother, it's wonderful to see you again," Jullia said, and they hugged, the thirteen-year-old princess towering over the tiny woman. When they broke apart, the dowager queen bowed her head and smiled at Samira.

"Welcome to Brookbridge," she said. "I don't think we've met, Samira, but I've known your father since he was a boy."

Samira bowed her head respectfully and said, "I'm sorry for your loss, Queen Katheryn."

She nodded solemnly and said, "Yes, thank you. Eronn was my only son." Turning to Jullia again, she said, "But I've been blessed with wonderful, brave grandchildren. And apparently one more still with us than I'd thought." She looked around the room once, her eyes flickering from one attendant to the next, and said, "We heard you were on a pilgrimage, Samira. Was that only justification, or did you want to see the Pool of the Mother? I could be your guide, both of you-- and we could talk privately," she added in a lower voice.

Samira, curious if nothing else, said, "Of course, Your Highness. Thank you."

"Well, then, we'll waste no more time standing about here," she said. "Devonn, would you go find your father and keep him from doing anything too rash while I'm gone?" With a nod toward Jullia and Samira, Devonn excused himself and the three of them started for the doors.

On their way out of the hall, Petra stopped Samira and told

her, "Be careful. There are mage-catchers in Brookbridge. Keep your amulet round your neck and don't speak to Holy men."

Fifteen minutes later, Samira was back on Kit, riding through cobbled streets where people bowed as they passed--to Katheryn, though, not to her or Jullia. They didn't seem to have any idea who the princesses were, but they obviously had a deep respect for the Paynes. Dominic and Harry rode behind her, carefully scanning the crowd, and Samira found herself truly grateful for the first time that she'd brought guards along. Brookbridge was a loud, crowded city, not too big but with far too many people for its size. If someone was following her, she'd have no idea.

"The Pool of the Mother is just beyond the temple for the Holy Sisters," Katheryn said, who was riding a horse on her own and easily keeping up with her much younger companions, even though she rode sidesaddle in all her skirts. "We'll pass through there."

"Sounds lovely," Jullia said quickly, before Samira could answer, and the Queen Mother, or, Samira supposed, the Queen Grandmother now, led the way through the streets down to the quaint stone temple that sat at the banks of the Den Morra south of the city. The hooded blue-cloaked pilgrims Samira had seen on the way into Queenshearth were here too, and they parted for them as they rode past. They were even more disturbing to her now than before, after Petra's warning; she imagined there were Holy men among them and likely some who knew how to detect magic. She fought the urge to clutch the amulet hanging below her neckline, and kept riding.

The road leading to the Pool from there was nearly fully deserted, though she could hear singing inside the walls of the temple. "What did you want to speak to us about?" she asked Katheryn, as quietly as she could manage, while Jullia hurried on ahead.

"Not here, Your Highness," she said gently, and as they passed the temple, Samira strained to see through the open doors inside. The sunlight streamed in from paned windows stretching almost from floor to ceiling on either side of the building. The tiered seats built into the walls around the space were empty except for the occasional pilgrim, praying in silence. The singing was coming from a chamber in the back of the temple, where the musicians seemed to be practicing. Samira thought she remembered the same song playing at her Declaration; it sounded cheerful, but it still had that uniquely *Priesthood* tinge to its chords that would always sour it for her.

"The first Paynes built the temple with Artur Halwood's blessing," Katheryn said, smiling as Jullia also craned her neck to see inside.

"It's beautiful," Samira said, just as quietly, as she tried to keep Kit moving without leaving the others behind. Dominic and Harry seemed very taken in as well, and she began to think they would never make it to the Pool.

"I expect it's nothing like Haddon's cathedral," she said, smiling, and Samira nodded, searching her expression for some kind of hint about what she was going to say. She had no patience for this kind of thing. Between whatever the old queen had to say, and her anxiety about the mage-catchers, she couldn't wait to get out of there.

They kept riding soon after, and Samira was only too glad. Every minute they spent riding through crowded streets at the outskirts of Brookbridge, she was growing more and more impatient, and when they were finally alone on one of the roads further out of the city, she practically exploded. "What did you want to tell us, Queen Katheryn?"

The old woman slowed her horse, bringing herself back to ride next to them as they kept making their way toward the lake. Samira's guards fell back a respectful distance, and when she was sure they were out of earshot, she said, "I am sorry for the secrecy. You can never be sure, in a court." She looked at Jullia first and said, "Jule, I wanted to let you know we got some word about your brother's-- meaning Deronn-- his coronation is going to be done as soon as they can. Before the end of August, if I'm right. Does he know about what you're doing here?"

"Yes," Jullia said. "We told him just before we left." She frowned then and asked, "Have they chosen a regent?"

"No," Katheryn said. "Not that Gerron has heard. Whoever it is, the Priests will have a tight hold on them. And that means it certainly won't be my brother." She turned to Samira next and said, "I've also heard the Godhead's going to take you with him on his way here from Astoria Bay."

"Alright," Samira muttered. "Doesn't matter when." *Let him try it.*

She looked at her, seeming unconvinced and said, "In any case, I thought you should know. Because of the rumors, about King Silas, there's been talk among the Priests..."

"What rumors?" Samira asked, blinking.

Katheryn frowned. "Well, that he's alive. Edris Thorne left Caspar's Dale with hostages from his court asking for aid to rescue him from the Daemons. With them marching on the Canyon suddenly, it seems too neat a coincidence to ignore."

She felt a little lightheaded. "My uncle's alive?"

The old woman shrugged. "Who knows? But the rumors are enough to spark the Priesthood's ire. There'll be more raids for Eirosians soon."

Samira felt her heart seize as she asked, "My mother...?"

"Should be safe, for now, but if it goes on much longer, it could become difficult for Daniel to protect her," she said, her face grim.

"What about Mason?" she asked.

"The prince? He'll be alright if he swears his faith for the High Priests. Even if they did come for your mother," she said.

Samira shook her head. "He's never been good at holding his tongue."

"I wouldn't tell him what you're doing, then, if I were you,"

Katheryn said. "He'll be questioned, if anything comes of this. The war's not going well and it's making people scared, and when people are scared they get violent. I'm sorry I can't help you any more, that's all I know.. I hear things from Gerron, who hears them from the ships that come down the river, but I don't leave the city anymore unless I'm planning to stay out. I am seventy this year, after all. So that's the best I can do for you. I hope I'll get to see Mychal again, though, one day. *King* Mychal," she corrected, smiling a little.

"Thank you, Grandmother," Jullia said, and bowed a little as they brought their horses to a stop.

"You should be able to walk to the Pool from here," the Queen Mother said. "It really is a sight. I'll give you a moment alone with it." They were stopped on an overlook, with a sloping bank carving a path through the last line of trees before a break in the canopy ahead. Samira and Jullia dismounted and they started down the path alone, the guards waiting with the old queen on the road.

"I'm sure Mason will be alright," Jullia eventually said, with an encouraging smile that almost looked genuine.

"He could tell them about my magic," she whispered.

"But he wouldn't do that, would he?" Jullia asked, but Samira was already shaking her head.

"He's so young," she said. "They could torture him."

"Sami, why would they--"

"I have to be more careful," she said abruptly, cutting off the wide-eyed girl trying to console her. Samira couldn't believe how reckless she'd been before. As scared as she was of being caught, she had still used her magic far too often-- once just to *wash her hair*. She couldn't use it anymore. Not unless it was a matter of life and death. She wasn't only putting her own life in danger; now her family's lives were on the line, too.

"*Gods*," Jullia breathed then, and Samira was brought out of her head and saw that they had arrived. She had never been a very religious person-- except that obviously, everyone had to be, after the Priesthood took hold. But she had never really thought or cared deeply about the gods or fate or any of it. Looking at the Pool of the Mother that day, she finally felt what seemed to her was what religion was supposed to make her feel.

The sunlight was glittering like a million crystals on the surface of the water. The pool was still, serene and untouched, unmarred by mills or ships or swimmers the way the rest of the waters that Samira had ever seen always had been. The colors on the leaves reflected in the pool were changing for the summer, growing a darker, lusher green, and when she got close enough, she could see herself reflected perfectly in the clear blue water. She looked sadder than she'd been when she started riding from Hollisport. She looked away.

"This is where Faris spoke to Morra herself," Jullia suddenly said, then went pink when Samira looked at her. "Um, or where they say he did." She looked back out at the water and, somewhat wistfully, asked, "How long are we staying?"

"Long enough that the court believes it's why we're here," Samira said, glancing back up the way they'd come. She felt very self-conscious now about the reaction she'd had to this place, and tried to put it out of her mind.

Jullia nodded, and then, staring down at her feet, she said, "I know you don't go in for this kind of thing, but I'd like to pray for a while if that's alright. I'll just be over there." The younger princess departed to the far side of the bank, where she sat on the beach and closed her eyes with a soft smile.

Samira didn't really know what to do with herself after that. She started pacing back and forth along the water's edge, trying to ignore her reflection, and when that didn't work she sat down on the rocky shore and stared out at the water in contempt. *It's just another bloody pond*, she thought, fighting the urge to disturb the water for Jullia's sake. Besides, she knew if she got any closer the water would start to respond to her, and if there was ever a place where she was likely to meet a Holy man, this was it. Glancing nervously around the Pool, she couldn't see anyone else, but she still knew she could never be too careful.

It wasn't long before she realized this was the Lake Royal from the songs-- from the one she'd danced with Mychal to. She felt her eyes welling up the longer she thought about him, and about the two of them together, only a distant dream until now. The thought came to her, stronger than before, that he very well could already be dead, burned alive by the Daemons at the Mages' Canyon like most of the rest of the men from the first charge of the Army. And before she knew it, she found herself whispering, "Please let him be safe. I don't know who's right about you two, and if it's the Priests then I'm sure we're all damned anyway, but– just let him live. I didn't even know I loved him until that night, and now I can't lose him."

Just as Samira was starting to feel stupid, talking to a pond, she heard dismayed horses whinnying in protest at the top of the hill and stood up in alarm. Her hand flew up to her amulet, checking that it was still tucked safely under her dress, and when she was sure that it was she started running back up to Katheryn and the guards, Jullia hurrying after her. As they got closer, Samira slowed down and held up a hand to stop Jullia, trying to peer through the branches before they revealed themselves. There was a boy on a horse, in a damaged and dyed-red Army uniform, insisting, "I'm only carrying a message."

"If it's just a letter, why didn't you leave it at the castle?" Harry asked, clearly suspicious and poised to draw his sword at any moment.

"I was told not to give it to anyone but Her Highness," he said, sounding like he had said it several times before. "The castle told me she was here."

"Me or her?" Jullia asked, pushing through the branches before

Samira could stop her. The boy's eyes widened as Harry and Dominic whirled around, just as shocked.

"Your Highnesses," Dominic said, reddening, "we're sorry, we told him you weren't to be disturbed--"

"It's alright," Samira said, looking only at the messenger boy. "Which one of us is the letter for?"

"Er, Princess Jullia, Your Highness," he said, and looked from one to the other, rather lost. Jullia stepped forward and he exhaled and smiled. "Thanks, Your Highness. It's from your brother."

"From Deronn?" she asked, frowning. "I don't remember you from the castle guard."

"No, sorry, Your Highness. From Mychal," he said, and Samira's whole body flooded with relief. It wasn't just *about* him, either, it was *from* him. Wherever he was, he was alive at least. When dismounting was met with hands on hilts, the boy stopped, slowly trotting his horse forward instead and handing down a neatly folded letter. "I have to be getting back now."

"Back where?" Jullia asked eagerly, but when the boy looked at the guards, uneasy, she said, "Never mind. Thank you."

"My pleasure, Princess. Begging pardon, Your Highnesses," he said, bobbing his head in Queen Katheryn's direction, then Samira's. "Long live King Mychal." The words sent a shock down Samira's spine. Though she supposed they were technically true, they still felt strange and illicit to be saying out loud. Not even Dominic and Harry were getting in the way of the boy's enthusiasm now. He grinned and turned his horse around, galloping off toward the main road.

"We'll be back in a moment, Grandmother," Jullia quickly told Katheryn, who nodded, still watching the messenger disappear.

"Soon," the woman warned them. "The sun's setting. You always want to be seen coming and going, so no one will suspect you when you need to slip away." Jullia smiled and pulled Samira back through the brush down to the shore, well out of their earshot. She then ripped open the letter and started to read aloud.

*Dear Jule,*

*I hope this reaches you. I still don't know my men very well, and I'm not even sure you'll be at Brookbridge when this gets there, but if Sami did what she said she would, you'll be reading this. Luke Payne is here with me, make sure his father knows.*

*First off, I'm sorry I didn't tell you I was alive. You were too young when I left for me to know it would be safe, and I had to leave. I suppose you understand why. And I'm hoping you're going to help me. I just found out our father's dead. I'm so sorry I wasn't there. (The men are all calling me king now. It's a strange feeling.)*

*I'm alright, by the way, after the battle. A hundred or so escaped with me from the vanguard, but the rest I think are all dead. It was a massacre, absolute hell. I won't tell you any more, I don't want to scare you. But I'm lucky to be alive. And luckier that they deserted with me. I've met some other soldiers who are hopefully going to help us. We're going to Eirosia once we have the men, to get King Silas's aid. The rumors that have been going around about him are true, he's alive. Once we find him, I'll come to gather my armies myself. Surpoint will be the easiest to reach without going through the Holy Roads, so if you meet us there we can join forces then.*

*I should have three or four hundred with me by morning, and more before we go east. As long as the Priests don't start to suspect, I'll be alright, but if they find out, they'll finish us before we've started. Keep yourself safe, though, and Deronn, if you can. I don't think they'd hurt him, but they'll want to take him from you. Make sure he's protected if they do.*

*I love you both, and I hope I get to see you soon. If all goes well I'll be at Surpoint before summer ends. Give Samira my love. And tell her I might be able to keep my promise.*

*Mychal*

Jullia breathed deeply and said, "It's really him. That's a relief." She then frowned at the end of the letter and looked up at Samira, curious. "What promise?"

She looked away and said, "We should get you to Surpoint soon, then. Make sure Lord Wright's ready to receive him."

"What promise?" she insisted, and Samira hesitated.

"To protect me," she said. "From... Him."

Jullia's eyes welled up again. "Gods. Okay. Right." The girl collected herself, and said, "Well... stay at Surpoint with me." She was starting to smile. "The Godhead won't know you're gone until it's too late!"

"No," she said quietly. "You heard what your grandmother said. I have to go with Him to the coronation. If I don't, he'll know something is wrong and then we'll all be in danger."

"Then how will you get to us?" Jullia asked.

Samira stared at her feet and said, "I'll work something out."

"Alright," Jullia said, and when she looked up at her again, she was smiling. "At least we know he's alive. And your uncle, too, in Eirosia? Mad."

"Right," Samira said, and looked back out at the water as she spoke. She was suddenly overwhelmed by a feeling of peace, and couldn't explain why but she felt like something was *with* them on the beach. She'd never really known what to believe or not, but she'd asked and received, within minutes, and if that wasn't some kind of sign... *Just don't let him die,* she found herself thinking, to Morra or whatever it was she could feel with her then. *You let him live, now keep him alive. You owe me that much, at least, if I have to go back to Riyan Duane.*

"Sami? We should get back to them," Jullia said, and Samira nodded and started to follow her back.

"I'll go with you to see the Penns," she said. "But then I have to go home, if I'm going to be there when he gets there. You'll need to deal with the Wrights on your own."

"I'll have Petra with me," she said. "I'll be fine. Deronn, though, I don't know if I'll get back there. Do you think he's going to be alright?"

"I hope so," she said. Whether he would be or not, he would have to face it soon. They all would. The messenger had made things more real to her than they'd been even hours before. There were hundreds of people marching in Mychal's army. There was no going back now.

# 20

# Edris

*"Well, I'm no great lord, and I'm no great knight*
*Though perhaps I'll be when I'm older,*
*But I'll carry my sword and I'll march all night,*
*Oh, Ma, I'm a royal soldier!*
*I come from the Horn or a Norport Thorne, but it makes no matter truly,*
*Cause I fight for the king and come next spring what girl could ever refuse me?*
*I've got no gold, yes truth be told, I'm a poor boy sir, I've no old name*
*But the prince or I, we'll fight with honor or die together the same!*
*No, I'm no great lord, and I'm no great knight*
*Though perhaps I'll be when I'm older,*
*But I'll carry my sword by Astor's light,*
*And I'll be a royal soldier..."*

Edris walked away from the fire and the men singing gaily around it, and approached the edge of the overlook's ridge to watch the lights of the village below. He had never been to any of the colonies his father had started, but he'd imagined them as morose, crowded places, far from any kind of real civilization.

He wasn't far off, from what he could tell at their vantage point about a mile away, although he couldn't see why it had been built into the side of a mountain. The rows of huts with the glow of candlelight from inside were like little blinking lights to them, but they could see patrols marching around the perimeters, and there was a tunnel drilled into the rocks where they could see people going in and out. He imagined the officers' quarters were in there, or some kind of supply stores.

They were firmly in Thorncliffe territory now, very far north, probably into his uncle's lands surrounding Norport. Their camp was hidden from view by a few higher slopes, but there were very few fires burning, by Mychal's orders. They'd sent a scout out when they'd arrived that afternoon. It was midnight by now. He hadn't come back.

"At least it's a clear night." Edris turned around to find Xander standing beside him, and felt himself grow nervous at the other man's unreadable expression. The knight nodded toward the colony and added, "It rained the whole way here. I was worried we wouldn't be able to see where we were going."

"Well, it's almost High Summer. You'll miss the rain soon," Edris said, trying to keep his eyes trained ahead at the faraway lights.

It was quiet for a moment. Then Xander gently put his hand on Edris's arm, and every nerve jumped to attention. "I just wanted to say that I... appreciate that you decided to come here."

"It's no trouble," he mumbled, trying not to show how much he was preoccupied by the simple touch.

"No, it is," Xander insisted. "You'll be called a traitor for this, don't think I don't know how much you're giving up by being here, and by helping Mychal."

"That's not what I'm doing," Edris said, jerking away from him.

"I'm not helping Mychal, I'm helping *you*. When this is over I'm... going straight back to Thorncliffe." He'd made the decision the night before. This was the right thing to do, rescuing Silas, but the rest of this madness he wanted no part in.

Xander took a small step back. "Oh." He looked away for a moment, then met his eyes again, ever the braver of the two. "Why?"

"Mychal's committing treason," Edris said, knowing he was stammering a little now. "You're serving your king. I'm comfortable helping with that, but Mychal's situation isn't the same."

"Of course it is!" Xander exclaimed. "We're taking our kingdom back. That's exactly what Mychal's doing."

"It was never meant to be his," Edris insisted. He immediately knew how that sounded and cursed himself for saying too much.

Xander looked at him, appalled. "Yes. It was. Do you agree with the Priests? Did he lose his right to the crown by being a child with a mother who loved him?"

Edris struggled with himself for a moment, whether to tell him what he'd really meant by that. But there was no easy way to explain it, and Xander wasn't in any kind of mind to believe him. He looked away and said, "No. You're right about that. But-- it's more complicated than that, more than you know. And I can't help him."

"Edris," another voice called out from behind them, and they turned around to see Mychal himself, waving them over to the command tent. "Council."

They both started towards him, avoiding each other's gaze as much as they could. Eventually, Edris muttered, "You can't talk to me like that."

He could have sworn he saw Xander roll his eyes. "My humblest apologies, Your Highness."

When they reached Mychal, he regarded them both with the kind of restrained smile that passed for his being happy these days. It seemed false to Edris, like he was nervous about every movement now. He suspected it had something to do with whatever magic he was using to change himself. Since the moon changed last week, his voice had been breaking even more violently than before, and it was as if he was trying to appear kingly in every other way to compensate for it. Edris hoped he would get past it soon. "Our scout's back," he told them. "Undetected."

"And late," Xander said, sounding wary.

"True," Mychal said. "He's inside." They all walked in, finding Luke Payne already inside, along with the other of Mychal's trio, Graham, another former squire and a Hornishman to the point of parody. Both were sitting on the bench at the back of the tent with a smaller boy between them. He looked to be from an Islander family, and he was dirty, dressed in common clothes, and drinking greedily from a large flask. All three of them stood at attention when Mychal entered the room.

"Your Majesty," the boy squeaked. He sounded even younger than Mychal did, but that wasn't all that remarkable among the Halwood 'men'.

"What did you find, Sam?" Mychal asked.

"I don't think we're going to be able to find a quiet way in, Your Majesty," he said, still struggling to control his breath. "It's going to have to be a straightforward attack. And the man I met said they'll use the Eirosians against us."

"Who?" Xander asked from where he stood near the entrance.

"A Lord Carroll, sir."

The man looked at his feet, eyes blinking in shock. "My father served him," he said quietly after a moment. "I had no idea he'd survived."

"Why would they fight us?" Luke asked, frowning. "We're trying to help."

"Under pain of death, sir," Sam told him quietly.

Xander turned to Edris and asked, in a low, flat voice, "What kind of colonies *are* these, Your Highness?"

Edris wanted to ignore him, but quickly noticed that everyone else in the tent was looking at him, too. "I don't know," he managed to say. "No one ever told me."

"They're work camps, Your Majesty," Sam told Mychal, breaking the uncomfortable pause that followed. "They have mines in the mountains."

Xander's eyes betrayed something darker than annoyance at Edris when he said, "Of course they do."

"Mining for what?" Edris sputtered.

"Steel, Your Highness," Sam said. "For the war."

Mychal's eyes darted down to the sword on his belt, and with a tinge of disgust, he asked, "Just men?"

"Women and children too, Your Majesty," he said, avoiding looking at Edris now. "Not as many, though. Not everyone's working the mines, it's a proper town, but... they're all starving."

"How many Valleyguard?" Mychal asked. Edris felt his head starting to spin. There were *Valleyguard* men running this horror?

"It's hard to say, Your Majesty, but it's not a big colony. I'd say there're probably about a hundred," Sam said. "One for every five or so Eirosians."

"Then we outnumber them," he said. "As long as the Eirosians don't fight. Some likely will, but..."

"I tried to tell them about you, Your Majesty, but I think they've been here too long to believe," Sam said quietly. "Lord Carroll, though, he said he'd get everyone that he could together to refuse to fight."

"That's good, Sam. Thank you. You can go." With a quick bow to Mychal and a frightened glance at Edris, Sam gave the flask to Graham and disappeared out of the back of the tent. As soon as he was gone, Mychal's eyes were on Edris. "Will your men fight Valleyguard?"

"I don't know," he admitted.

"I have to decide if we even *can* attack, Edris," he said. "If they won't fight, what do we do?"

The consternation on Mychal's face was too much for his nerves, and Edris turned away. That was a mistake; he met Xander's eyes next, and the look he was giving him was even worse. "A moment, please," he said, backing out of the entryway. "I need a moment to think. Excuse me." The night air was cooler outside the tent, and he felt less like he was suffocating, but he was starting to feel rather sick. He was looking at his sword, his breastplate, all the steel in the Thorncliffe camp-- wondering where it came from.

"Where did you think they were sending them?" he heard Xander ask him. The knight had followed him out, and was now standing a few paces back. Edris didn't want to imagine what he must think of him now. "Holiday on the Islands?"

"I didn't know," he insisted.

"I believe you," Xander said. "That's why I'm angry."

Edris whirled around. "What does that mean?"

"A man can be blind if he wants to be, Edris," Xander exclaimed. "Did you think every cheap sword in the infantry was Surpoint steel?" Edris's face was burning, and he didn't dare look at him. After a moment, Xander sighed. "This doesn't do us any good. If it helps, I don't blame you for the position we're in now. Valleyguard won't fight Valleyguard, I understand that."

Edris froze. He couldn't believe he hadn't thought of it right away. "You're right."

"Edris?" Xander asked, but he was already moving past him, back into the command tent. Mychal was pacing the length of the tent, now strapped into his full armor, but stopped when he saw him.

"Well?" he asked.

"We're not going to have to fight," he said, trying not to get caught up in his own excitement. Nodding at Mychal's chain and colors, he added, "You're going to have to lose the... royalty."

Not even an hour later, the three hundred men of their combined forces were arrayed in regiments of fifty, marching one after the other behind Edris and Landiss, the only Valleyguard captain that had stayed. There should have been at least one more officer, with the numbers they had, but Edris hoped the colony wouldn't notice. Mychal was somewhere among the marching men, wearing one of Graham's shirts and a jerkin from one of Edris's smallest men. He hadn't liked taking the boy's protection, but all of his own clothes had been dyed Halwood red.

Edris brought the march to a halt at a short distance, and as loud as he could, he shouted down the road, "*Long live King Bastian!*"

It was dead silent for several of the longest moments of his life. Then, a single sentry's voice called out from one of the guard posts ahead. "Who's there?"

"Prince Edris Thorne!" he shouted back. "On orders from my father. We're relieving you."

Another long pause. "We weren't notified of this," the same voice replied.

"We're sorry about that. We've had to send all our auxiliary forces to the Army and there hasn't been time. Can I speak with the captain?"

The gates stretching over the main road creaked open, and Edris turned his horse around, lowering his voice. "If anyone gets in his cups and tells them why we're really here, I'll hang him myself," he warned the men behind him. Xander, his Eirosian face hidden behind his helm, nodded, and Edris thought he might even be smiling.

Edris rode slowly through the gates into the dilapidated colony, with soldiers running to the square ahead of them, surrounded by barracks and huts on all other sides. Waiting for him, in the middle of the square, was a wiry older man, a true Casparian with blond hair turning white at the roots. He bowed when Edris dismounted, though something in the man's eyes told him he wasn't convinced just yet. "Your Highness," he said. "I'm Captain Abbott. I have to say I'm surprised a member of the royal family would come here."

"I'm only leading the men here after our service in the Holy Army," he said, trying to sound as confident as he would be if he actually were given this mission. Two months ago, all he'd wanted was to be an officer in the Valleyguard. He couldn't believe that now it was so hard to look this one in the eye. "I'll be returning to Thorncliffe once I establish a chain of command."

"We've never been relieved all at once," Abbott said, frowning. "Did His Majesty provide a written decree for us?"

Edris, focusing on keeping his breathing steady the way Xander had advised, raised his eyebrows. "I would almost think you were questioning me, sir."

Captain Abbott was not as quick to quail as the younger guardsmen outside. He flinched, but didn't look frightened. "My apologies, Your Highness, but these are dangerous times. We heard about the horrible loss at the Mages' Canyon. I'm sure it won't surprise you that we, as guards of mages, are suspicious of everyone these days."

*Mages?* Edris thought, and felt a knot forming in his gut. He wasn't sure anymore that this was such a good idea. Could they control them once they were freed? "Of course," he finally said, and produced a small roll of thick parchment from his saddlebag. He hoped it would hold up to scrutiny. He'd done his best with his father's signature, but he didn't think Captain Abbott or anyone else assigned to guard a mine would have seen the royal seal much anyway.

Captain Abbott read the decree closely, then rolled it up and handed it back to Edris. "Welcome to the Norport Mine, Your

Highness," he said. "Your men can ride in. They're trained in guarding mages, I trust?"

"Yes, sir," Edris lied. "Of course."

"Good, then. We'll make ourselves scarce and march out in the morning."

He felt his knees start to buckle as the rush of the moment left him, and steadied himself with a hand on his horse. "Thank you, Captain. May Morra bless our efforts."

"And Astor sharpen our swords," he said, rote and tired. Captain Abbott seemed a hard man, but rather glad to be going back to Caspar's Dale. Edris got the feeling he'd probably wanted to believe them. He started to hope his father wouldn't punish them too harshly when they found out they'd been tricked, but his sympathy dwindled to nothing when the Eirosians started to peer out from doorways and windows around the square. The faces were gaunt, with bloodshot eyes, and many of them were covered in soot or stricken with large burns. He had to look away, and turned to watch the others march into the colony instead.

Edris was horribly nervous all night long, knowing one wrong word to the wrong person and it was over. He looked for Xander once most of the original guards had left their posts, but he couldn't find him anywhere. It was just as well, he told himself; he had probably gone to speak to his own people, and he couldn't blame him. Besides, Edris didn't think it was likely he wanted to see him anyway. Eventually, he forced himself to find a bed to lay down in, and the improvement from the rocky ground he'd been sleeping on as of late put him to sleep within minutes.

* * *

Mychal was the one to wake him up the next morning, what felt like only seconds later. "What is it?" he mumbled, struggling to sit up.

"They're gone. My men are getting the Eirosians gathered in the square," he said, his voice rougher the higher it went from excitement. He was wearing his royal chain again. "You've done it, Edris. Five hundred freed without a drop of blood."

"Right," he said, avoiding looking him in the eye as he dressed and felt around for his own chain in the pockets of his satchel. They walked out of the barracks together, and found a crowd amassing in the square before them. They were watching Mychal with a kind of awe that was not extended to Edris. He could hardly blame them, after what Thorncliffe had done, but it still unnerved him, hundreds of mages staring at him with dull, angry eyes.

"I already spoke to them," Mychal told him quietly. "If you'd like to say something..."

"That's alright," he said. "They don't want to hear from me."

Mychal looked at him, in that perceptive way that never failed to make him squirm. "You did a good thing, Edris. They'll see that someday, even if they don't right now."

"Sir Neill should speak," he said, as they approached Xander and his five men standing in a tight knot of colonists and Halwood soldiers. He looked up at the sound of his name, and the conversation died out around them.

"Sir," Mychal greeted him.

Xander bowed his head for a moment. "Your Majesty," he said. "This is Lord Elliot Carroll." One of the older colonists turned to regard both of them; he was a serious man, with thinning gray hair and dark blue eyes set deep in a lined old face.

"Are you the leader of these people, my lord?" Mychal asked him. Lord Carroll looked at him for a long moment before answering.

"Not officially. But they often look to me, yes," he said. "I'm the man your scout spoke to last night." The old man's voice was not as commanding as Edris had expected; he spoke softer than Xander did, with a slight accent that he hadn't known the other Eirosians to have, but there was something still oddly intimidating about him. Maybe it was the way he was looking both Mychal and Edris directly in the eye, without any of the usual deference.

"Are all of you here mages?" Edris asked, as he looked over the people in the square nervously.

"Did you say something?" Carroll asked. When Edris turned around, he said, "I need to see you when you speak, young man."

Edris frowned, and looked over at Xander, who said, "He's deaf, Edris, he needs to read your lips."

He stared at Carroll for a moment, shocked. He'd never met a deaf man who could speak, certainly not that well. He couldn't believe he'd remained in line to inherit his family's title; that would never have happened in Thorncliffe. The man chuckled when he saw him staring. "I'm hardly a world wonder, just an old man," he said, and Edris reddened.

"Sorry," he mumbled at the floor, then remembered he had to face him and raised his head as he repeated, "Sorry. I'm Edris Thorne. Are all of you mages?"

"Not quite," Carroll said. "Many of us though. I am. They tried to send us all here, but I'm sure there are more in the other mines. Or the Hollisport ghettoes, perhaps." Edris's head was spinning. There were *more* colonies like this one?

"Will you come with us, sir?" Mychal asked him.

"I will," he said after a moment. "But I can't speak for them." He gestured out to the waiting crowd, and said, "You've given them their freedom. But many of them will only follow one of their own."

"Sir Neill?" Mychal asked, and Xander nodded. He stepped out into the center of the crowd, and the noise in the square fell to a low buzz of confusion. All the Eirosians' eyes, and the hundreds of Edris's and Mychal's men's as well, were on him.

"People of Eirosia!" he shouted. "My name is Alexander Neill! I was in the court of King Silas at the Fall and I have been imprisoned these thirteen years since. The Daemons still hold our castle. King Silas is alive and captive inside." A flurry of shock exploded throughout the crowd, and Xander waited for it to die down before he spoke again. "Mychal Halwood is a stranger in his own lands. The Priests of the Triad have taken his home, his birthright from him. He will take it back, but first he has promised to help us take ours."

Edris looked over at Mychal, who for the first time looked very much like a king to him, watching Xander speak in calm silence with his sword and regalia completing the picture. "You've been told your magic is a mark of evil. It's not. It's a *gift*. We've suffered terrible injustices, but we are the only ones who can save our kingdom now. Will you follow me?"

There was silence in the crowd, but Edris saw hardened resolve on many of the faces he could single out. Slowly, quietly at first but growing louder, a roar of feet, staffs, and anything else the people had beating against the ground rose in the air around them, until it was deafening, a gesture that meant nothing to Edris but was bringing tears to Xander's eyes.

"Whoever wishes can make for the mountains west of here. You'll find aid from those resisting the Godhead's rule in the Triad. But the rest of us leave for Eirosia at sundown." He paused and said, in a voice choked with emotion, "Thank you." The rattling solidified, became rhythmic and universal, and when Xander returned to his men, they embraced him as the noise filled the square, like the loudest drumbeat Edris had ever heard.

# 21

# Samira

The Horn felt different somehow when Samira went back. Riding into Hollisport, she recognized everything around her, but it just didn't seem like home anymore. She was no safer there than anywhere else, and any day now the Godhead would be coming for her. Even though the Skytower was much taller, the spire of the King's Cathedral seemed to cast it in shadow as they rode through the gates.

As she rode, she remembered the last night she'd spent here, and the man she'd been promised to then. Their audience still haunted her, in the strangest of ways. She didn't want to be afraid of him, but she was; how could she not be? He was the enemy. The Holy Court had ordered the deaths of thousands of mages like her. But the most frightening thing about Riyan Duane was that she would never have been able to tell by looking at him.

He was a sickly, strange young man, for the most part, with eyes clouded from godwine that repelled and fascinated her. He'd been perfectly polite, which had been nothing but unsettling to her. "I've heard tales of your beauty, but you put description to shame," he'd said to her, this man who was supposed to be the mouthpiece for the gods.

She had to laugh thinking about it now, knowing the things Mychal would say to her hardly an hour after. He'd found description enough. She was sure he would like to know that, and with a wry smile, she knew that no man's attention was ever going to feel like his. It would always be him, the only one who'd love her for more than her name.

Her Declaration had been months ago now, and there was no evidence of it left in the entrance hall. There was, however, still a Priesthood banner, the sky blue flying next to the Hollis green and gray. She resisted the urge to pull it down as she made her way through to the stairwell. The  ancient worn steps dipped in the center, making her journey harder, but it felt like home to her, even with the invasion of her fiance's colors.

Dominic and Harry were still trailing behind her, but they broke off their own way when the path diverged to the armory and barracks, with a quick final bow. Both of them had been good enough not to ask questions about the message from Mychal or what it meant, but they had heard more than enough to start spreading rumors among the Hollis soldiers. *Good,* Samira thought. There was no harm in that, as long as they didn't reach the Holy men. And if the soldiers at home hated anyone, to a man, it was Priests.

The doors to the great hall didn't reveal her parents upon opening, so Samira kept climbing until she reached the family solar four stories higher. That was empty, too, but from there she could hear faint voices up in the family apartments. She followed the sounds down the narrow halls of the keep, past her room and Mason's and the servants' quarters, until she found the closed door to the king and queen's bedroom. She was about to make herself known when she heard her mother through the door, stifling a sob. Samira frowned then, and careful not to make a sound, she pressed her ear against the door.

The first voice she heard was her father's. "Marida, my love, please don't cry. I promise you, you won't be in any danger as long as I live."

Between her tears, the queen, her voice strained and unsteady, replied, "I'm afraid for the children, Daniel."

"I'll be alright, Mom," Mason said, sounding very uncomfortable. *Mason?* Samira thought, frowning. Wasn't her brother supposed to be back with the Stewards by now? "I'm not even really Eirosian, anyway."

That didn't help; in fact, it only made Samira's mother cry harder, and she could just picture the look their father was giving Mason. "He will be fine, love," the king said gently. "He'll be right here with us."

Samira couldn't stand it anymore and eased the door open. The three of them were all sitting on the bed, her father holding her mother as she cried and Mason sitting awkwardly on the other side of the mattress. All three turned to look at once when she entered, and her mother let out a sigh of relief between sobs and hurried over to her. "Oh, Samira, sweetheart," she sighed, and pulled her in close, practically suffocating her.

Over the queen's shoulder, Samira asked, "What happened?"

Her mother returned to the bed as Samira walked around to stand beside Mason. The king, after a moment's hesitation, said, in a careful voice, "A Priest from the Holy Court came to speak to your mother. They said they were investigating all converted Eirosians still living in the Triad. Apparently, the guards at a refugee colony in Thorncliffe were deceived into abandoning their posts by an organized force claiming to be Valleyguard. It seems to have been resistance activity. All five hundred or so of the mage colonists disappeared overnight."

Samira tried to focus on her mother, rather than the colony story; that had Mychal written all over it. Instead, she let herself get angry over whatever had been said to put her mother in this state. "They can't really think Mom was behind that."

"There's very little that's beyond these people, in my experience," her father muttered. Looking at both of his children now, he said, "I need the two of you to understand something now. You may have been born here, and you may be royalty of the Horn, but you also come from Eirosia. They won't forget that. You shouldn't either, not only because it's your history, but also because they will use anything they can to take your birthright for themselves."

"Dad," Mason exclaimed, eyes wide. Samira was just as surprised. Their father had never said anything quite so blatantly seditious.

"I'm only saying this because no one else can hear us here. You *must* be careful about what you say and who you say it to. And realize that you are very lucky. Most of the people this investigation will hurt are not as fortunate as you." He turned to Samira and said, "You must be especially careful, once Duane comes for you."

She felt her heartbeat start to pick up, but all she said was, "Right." She rather appreciated this new honesty from her father, but a part of her wished that her position would have angered him as much before as a Holy officer questioning his wife had now.

The king sighed. "It's good to have you here." With a pointed look at Mason, he added, "*Both* of you." Then, he stood up and said softly, "I have to meet with the High Steward and the generals. I'll see you for supper, Marida?" She nodded and he kissed her and squeezed her hand before he started for the door. At the last minute, he turned back and said, "Mason, you should come too. I'll test you on the officers' names afterwards." Mason sighed and got up to follow him.

"You're still here," Samira said to him as their father left the room.

"Yeah," he said. "I don't think I'm going back to Fen Faris at all. Dad said he needs me here." *Of course*, she thought, trying not to be bitter. *He needs his heir. Not me.* In a low voice, he added, "I'm more worried about Mom, though, honestly. I'll see you later, Sami."

Once Mason had followed the king out the door, Samira tried to move closer to her mother as tactfully as she could. Eventually she sat cross-legged in the middle of the bed and watched as the queen wiped her eyes with a whiteflower handkerchief, same as the one she'd given her on her birthday, what felt like years ago. When it had been quiet for a while, she asked, as gently as she could, "Mom, are you alright?"

Her mother didn't respond for a moment; she just sat, staring down at her hands, for a long moment before she spoke. "Everyone here thinks they need to handle me delicately," she said slowly, with the same bitter undertone Samira recognized in herself. "I know I don't speak in court much, but I'm quite bright, actually. I just learned a long time ago that no one wanted the opinion of someone like me."

"A woman?" Samira asked, nodding.

"An Eirosian," she corrected her. "But yes, that too." After a pause she said, "Certainly not the hangers-on that surrounded your father when we were first married. They would never tell him what he was doing wrong, who he was failing. I did. And everyone had something to say about it. An eighteen-year-old girl, a Dillon's daughter, new to the Horn, what could I possibly know?" She wiped her eyes. "They hated me for it. But Daniel didn't."

She smiled as her eyes shifted away from her daughter's, into a long-past memory. As she came back to the present, she said, "The Priests won't like you either. They won't trust you. You've never set foot in Eirosia, but to them you might as well have crossed the mountains yesterday. They're going to do everything they can to work against you."

Samira blinked, more than a bit taken aback. She understood that, but she hadn't been expecting to hear it from her mother.

"What should I do then?" she asked, staring at the queen. There was a confidence and a fierceness in her that she hadn't often seen before.

"You need to have Riyan Duane on your side," she said, and Samira grimaced. "I know, darling," she sighed. "But what you really think of him doesn't matter. If you're going to have any kind of life, he needs to think well of you. Get him to care for you and they can't touch you, no matter what happens to me."

Samira blinked again, startled. "What? Mom, what do you think is going to happen?"

"Nothing," she said, but her voice had an edge to it now, different than before. It sounded more like the white lies she'd told when Samira was small. "Don't worry about me, sweetheart. You're going to have to start worrying about yourself."

She took a deep breath and stood up. For a moment, she thought about telling her everything, but how could she, when she was already worrying so much? "Okay, Mom. Thank you."

As she turned toward the doorway and started to leave, her mother's voice stopped her. "Samira," she said, and there was a tone of warning in it that froze her in her tracks. "They have the best mage-hunters in the world in New Astoria."

Her eyes wide, she whirled around to stare at her mother's carefully composed face. Samira was stunned and for a moment the two women just stared at each other. Finally, she managed to ask, "You knew?"

"Earlier than you, even," she said quietly, nodding. "You were around nine when we noticed the signs."

"*We?*" Samira exclaimed.

The queen nodded again. "Your father knows, too. If we'd have known earlier, we would never have agreed to the match, but by then--"

"I was already supposed to be his," she muttered, nodding. "I know."

Her mother's lip quivered, almost imperceptibly, but Samira noticed it and it struck her more than she'd expected. She felt much more compassion than she had before for her parents' decision in that moment. "You're not anyone's but yourself," the queen said, her voice breaking, and Samira ran back to her mother and hugged her tightly.

*Not anyone's.* Mychal had said that, too. Standing there, crying with her mother, she wondered if she could believe it was true. At the very least, when Samira finally left her parents' chambers she felt strangely calm about the engagement, like it was more surmountable. Her mother had done that much for her, anyhow.

Of course, she still had no intention of actually marrying him. She was going to Surpoint as soon as she could-- *if* she could, that is. But now, at least, she knew her family would be with her, if she did find a way to Mychal's side.

That was enough for her to make it through the rest of the day, but after a tense dinner where her father said almost nothing, she grew more and more anxious until she couldn't stand it anymore. Once her parents went to bed, she said goodnight to Mason and slipped downstairs to the armory, where she found the master-at-arms at work over the fire. She knocked on the open door, and he jumped, putting down his tools and bowing as best he could in the cramped weapons forge. "Princess," he said, clearly startled. "How was your trip?"

"It was... fine, thank you," she said, and tried not to show him how nervous she was when she spoke again. "Er, Wythe, I was wondering if you knew where Dominic is?"

Wythe frowned. "Well, some of the boys went into town, but I think Dominic's still in the barracks. I'll walk you, Your Highness."

"Oh, no, that's alright, I know the way. Thank you again," Samira said quickly, and darted back out of the armory before he could argue. She heard his hammer start to beat against the anvil again before long and relaxed as she made her way down. She had known most of these men all her life, but she still had no idea who she could trust with what she'd been doing for Mychal. Telling as few of them as possible seemed like the safest option.

When she had almost reached the barracks, she started hearing music and singing; it seemed the soldiers that had stayed were also enjoying themselves. By the time she could see the door, she could make out the lyrics, a simple drinking song being sung in the round:

> *"I'd like to be prince of the Valley up north,*
> *I'd like to be prince of the sea,*
> *I'd have loyal knights and a kingdom by rights,*
> *And sweet Samira sitting on my knee."*

Lovely. She thought now was as good a time to interrupt as any, and started through the door. There was a hallway between her and the men, though, and they got through most of another verse before any of them saw her.

> *"My gold would shine brighter than Astor's sunlight,*
> *Kept under guard, key, and lock,*
> *I'd have friends with me there, enough wine to share,*
> *And sweet Samira sitting--"*

"Your Highness!" someone shouted suddenly, for which Samira thanked the gods, and whoever was playing the music immediately stopped. The men all shot to their feet, some swaying drunkenly as they did, and all of them bowed after a prolonged moment of awkward silence.

"Is Dominic here?" she asked. Her face was burning red, and she couldn't exactly figure out why. They were the ones who should be embarrassed, she knew that, but something in her felt so... *exposed* that she couldn't think of anything to say or do to make her discomfort go away.

"I'm here, Your Highness," Dominic's voice called out from the far wall of the barracks. The young soldier stumbled awkwardly out of the crowd and bowed to her, asking, "Did you... need something?"

"I'd like to speak with you," she said, trying to keep her eyes fixed on him and not on the shocked faces of the rest of the guards. "Out in the hall?"

"Er. Yes. Of course," he stuttered, and followed her out while the others all stared at them. When the door was closed and they had made it a good distance away, Dominic said, "I'm so sorry, Your Highness, I wasn't part of that but it's just something they like to--"

"It's alright," she said, knowing as she did that she didn't even sound convinced herself.

"It isn't," he said. "But I won't speak about it if you don't want to."

Samira considered this, but found she couldn't help herself saying, "They do know I only just came of age, don't they?"

Dominic coughed. "I reckon they do know, yes, Your Highness." She didn't want to think about all that *that* meant-- particularly not about how long the song had been in rotation. "Again, I'm sorry."

"Right," she said, trying to calm herself. With a deep breath, she stopped walking and turned to him. "I need to go out into the city. Would you go with me? It shouldn't take very long."

Dominic blinked, clearly surprised, but after a moment he said, "Of course, Your Highness. Where are we going?"

"Winding Row," she said. "I need to see a friend of my family's." Dominic's eyes widened and she frowned. "Is that a problem?"

"N-no, Your Highness," he said quickly, "I only... a friend of your family's lives on Winding Row?"

She narrowed her eyes. "Yes, why?"

"Nothing," he said. "I'm just... it's good you aren't going alone, is all."

Uneasy now, Samira nodded and said, "Alright, then. We'll go down to get horses."

"I wouldn't, Your Highness," Dominic protested, as they started to climb down to the entrance hall. "Horses in a place like that-- it'll be like a sign round your neck that you've got things worth stealing. It's not far on foot."

"Then we'll walk," she said, getting more impatient by the minute. She wasn't sure this was such a good idea anymore, but she was already almost out of the castle, so she steeled herself and marched on through the hall and out the rear doors in the kitchens. At the final gate, she pulled the hood of her cloak over her head, hoping she would look inconspicuous enough, like any other figure in the darkness. Dominic was at her heels all the way, with his hand on his sword, and though he was well over six feet tall and practically twice Samira's size, he jumped every time so much as a rat or pigeon crossed their path.

After they had been walking in silence for a while, she turned to him and said, "I'm sorry if I put you and Harry in a bad position."

He frowned. "How d'you mean, Your Highness?"

"In the Hartlands," she said. "You probably have questions about what you heard there."

"No, Your Highness," Dominic said firmly. "I was there to protect you, that's all." After a minute, though, he added, "I met Mychal when he was here. We worked on the festival together. He seemed nice enough. Wouldn't say he seemed like a king, but..."

"Does anyone really *seem* like a king?" Samira asked, and Dominic looked down at his feet.

"No, Your Highness. I suppose they don't, not right away." He paused, then added, "King Daniel does. But I expect that's just from having done it so long."

Samira nodded, but her attention was elsewhere; while they were talking, they'd reached a town square of sorts, with a pockmarked and vandalized statue of her father at its center. It had clearly been pelted with rocks, and his hands were stained with red paint, several coats over, the blood on Daniel's hands shining in the moonlight. She pulled her cloak tighter around her as they pressed on, and felt the clasp to make sure there was no Hollis panther on the brooch. She knew Dominic would protect her, but she found herself wishing she had a sword, too, not that she would have known how to use it.

Finally, as the roads grew rougher and the noises in the dark more frightening, they happened upon a street sign that read *Winding Row*, and turned down the narrow road and kept walking until they reached a dead end. When they did, Samira took a deep breath as she faced the last wattle-and-daub cottage on the unlit street. "Last house on Winding Row. This is it," she told Dominic. "It's probably best if you wait out here."

He looked at his surroundings, grimaced, and said quietly, "Of course, Your Highness. I'll be right here when you're ready to go."

Samira pulled down her hood and knocked on the door, timid at first, then louder when there was no response. After a long silence, Farrah Vance's voice rang out through the door, shouting, "Who's that?"

"Lady Vance?" Samira called out. "It's Samira. I need to talk to you." Moments later, she heard shuffling footsteps and muttering behind the door before it jerked open and the mage she'd met in the hunting woods peered suspiciously out at her. After a moment, the woman sighed and stepped aside to let her in, shutting the door quickly behind her. The house was everything Samira imagined a mage's workshop would be. It was difficult not to get distracted by the countless potions, diagrams and other indiscriminate magical objects surrounding them.

Vance, however, was not distracted. She was in fact fairly

annoyed, from what Samira could tell. "First of all, I'm not a lady. I wouldn't be living in this bloody place if I was. My name is Farrah. And second, what in Mother Morra's name are you doing here? Is something wrong with the amulet?"

"No, no," she said quickly. "It's been working fine. Thank you."

Farrah's eyes narrowed, and she said, not unkindly, "Well, out with it, Princess. I can't imagine you're meant to be here right now."

"My uncle told me your sister left with my cousin Loran because they fought against the Priesthood," she said. Farrah stayed quiet, so she pressed on. "Does that mean you know anyone here who's still fighting?"

"Why?" she asked, wary as ever.

"I can't marry him," she said, feeling as she said it how true it was. Farrah just stared at her as she said, "I just can't. I need help getting away from him."

Farrah looked out the window. "Do you trust that man out there?"

"I think so," she said. "But I don't know him very well."

"Well, he can't stand out there, someone will notice. Bring him in." Samira opened the door and motioned for Dominic to come inside. He was hesitant, but he did, and the woman wasted no time saying, "I'll thank you to sit in the back garden, young man, and try not to listen at the door."

"I wouldn't, milady, honest," Dominic said, and with a quick nod she ushered him through a back door. When they were alone again, her attention returned to Samira.

"You were going to marry him when I first met you. What's different now?"

"I'm worried about the mage-catchers. More than before," she said. "No one's training me, but I'm learning more than I'd like to on my own, I have to think I must be getting more noticeable. Not to mention I'm Dillon on my mother's side, and now that my uncle might be alive they're investigating us. And... I met him... he scares me."

Farrah sighed. "Princess, if I had a silver for every girl who's scared of her betrothed..."

"It's not just-- even besides all that, there are a lot of-- other factors," Samira said. She was starting to get frustrated, but she knew she couldn't upset this woman. Farrah was, as far as she could tell, her only option.

The mage woman looked at her for a long moment before she asked, "Do you know who that boy you sent to me really is?"

"Yes," she said. "Mychal's marching to Surpoint with his men right now."

"He is, is he?" she asked, with a small smile. "So he took my advice. Good."

"Your advice?" Samira frowned. "What advice?"

"The resistance fighters believe the Son of Faris myth," she said. "I told him he'd be wise to use it. That *is* why he's going to Surpoint?"

"No," she said, "he's going to meet the rest of his army. What else is in Surpoint?"

Farrah glanced out the back window toward Dominic and made sure the glass was firmly shut before she started rustling through the papers on the work table behind her. She handed a scrap of parchment to Samira. "If the stories are true, Faris's sword is in the Forges there."

Unrolling the paper, Samira found a long script written in verse, with a lead sketch of a longsword in the traditional style enclosed in rock and iron. She looked back up at Farrah and said, "I have to meet him there."

The woman stared at her, looking exasperated. "If you know who he is-- and who he really *was*-- you'll know that you disappearing and turning up at his side will put him in danger. People might connect two missing princesses."

Samira had to admit she hadn't thought of that, but it didn't matter. She pressed on. "He *asked* me to meet him there. If it's dangerous, that's his choice." Farrah shook her head, turned away and said nothing. Reining herself in as best she could, Samira tried to calm her voice and said, "I'm not asking you to risk anything for me. I'm going to Prince Deronn's coronation with the Holy Court, and I'm leaving for Surpoint from there. What I'm asking for is a name, or a safehouse, anything in Queenshearth that could help me. That's all."

Another long pause passed between them before Farrah spoke. "Alright. I know somewhere you can go. The Holy Sisters have a poorhouse on the cathedral grounds in the south of the city, called the Warren. I'll let a friend know you're coming, and he'll meet you there. From there on, I can't help you."

Samira tried to contain her excitement as she said, "Thank you. Truly."

Farrah was back to rooting through the papers and materials cluttering the room by then, and she received the thanks with an absentminded wave. When she emerged from her workspace again, she was holding a very small stack of papers bound with twine that she pressed into Samira's hands. It was hardly larger than the palms of her hands, and she stowed it away in the pocket of her cloak. "What is it?" Samira asked.

"A bit of reading for your trip," she said, dryly. "It'll help you with what I'm about to show you. I've got one more useful thing for you." She moved Samira gently by her shoulders until they were standing face to face and said, "If you're going to run, or especially if you don't, you need to be prepared. Duane and his men are either mind mages or they're damn close to it. The godwine they all drink means that it doesn't matter whether they were born to it or not. They trade in visions, stolen thoughts and memories. You'll be dead within days if they find out almost anything going on in your head."

Shaking her own head a little in disbelief, she said, "You're going to need to practice locking away those thoughts. And, obviously, they can't know that you're doing it either."

"So what do I do?" she asked, nervous now.

"Construct another story for yourself, one that you'll let them see instead," Farrah said. "And be ruthless with what you think about while they're questioning you. Nearly all magic is in your mind. Willpower and discipline."

Samira frowned, unconvinced. "Will that really protect me?"

"If you do it right, it will look like the only story your mind has for them."

"How will I know when they're trying to see?" she asked.

"You'll know," Farrah said. "It feels like this." And suddenly, Samira felt searing pain, burning deep inside her head between her temples. But that wasn't the worst of it-- she also felt *horribly* exposed, like the feeling of being watched a hundred times over. When the pain finally ebbed away, she rubbed her temples, dazed, and looked cautiously back at the mage.

"What did that do?"

"I followed the trace left by the most emotional memories you have. It's a common shortcut into the mind," she said. "For example, I know you had a religious experience at the Pool of the Mother, and that you slept with our runaway king." Samira's face flushed and Farrah warned, "Things like that will get you killed just the same as your magic."

"It wasn't some indiscretion," she said, her face hot. "I love him."

Farrah looked at her for a long moment. "You sound just like Darya," she muttered, rolling her eyes, but Samira heard something fond in the groan that followed. "Right, then, in that case you *really* need to practice. I noticed that you tried just then, but you'll have to do better than that to evade them. Let alone to do it without them catching on."

"You said they use godwine to do it," she said, still trying to get her bearings again. "So how did *you* do it? I thought you were an artificer."

"I've had plenty of godwine in my life," Vance said, and her tone did not encourage further questions. "I wish I could teach you more, but again, the more magic you know the more danger you're in."

She nodded, and glimpsed Dominic then, pacing listlessly outside through the back windows with Farrah's sheep nudging at his knees. "We should go." She went to bring him back into the cottage, and he walked right through to the front door with only a polite nod to Farrah. Dominic really was very good at seeing nothing. Maybe she could keep him in her service when she left.

Samira was about to follow him out herself when the mage said, "I hope you make it to Surpoint." She turned around, a little surprised, as Farrah continued. "If you do reach him, the two of you could heal the wounds the war left, centuries ago. Unite Farisia once and for all."

Samira couldn't help smiling a little. It was a nice thought. "Thank you, Farrah."

"May the gods protect you, Princess," Farrah said as she shut the cottage door, and for the first time in a long while, Samira appreciated the prayer.

# 22

# Mychal

Mychal could feel that Eirosia was different from the moment they crossed the border. It wasn't that it looked all that different from the rocky mountain passes in Thorncliffe, but the air was colder in the east, even though High Summer had come and gone while they marched. Not to mention something about their surroundings felt instantly unfamiliar and unsettling to him.

Of course, the Eirosians with them were more at ease than ever, apart from some of the children who'd been born in the Triad. Sir Neill was like a king among them, as was the old mage Lord Carroll. They bowed to Mychal, too, and to Edris, although the Thorncliffe prince was met with a sticking suspicion by most of his father's former prisoners.

Illon's Fast itself was a coastal fortification, according to Neill, and their combined forces, eight hundred or so strong, marched dutifully on for weeks to reach the eastern side of the kingdom. They traveled only by night and carefully followed the path deemed safe by the scouts they'd sent ahead. They didn't see any Daemons at all for a week or more after they crossed the border, or humans. The first ghost town Mychal rode through made him shudder, but he learned to steel himself against the worst of his imaginings after that. There were many more empty villages between there and King Silas's castle.

"Does *anyone* still live here?" he finally asked Neill one night, as they tramped through abandoned fields and passed the charred foundations of a farmhouse. "Has Dearril left you anything?"

"I don't know, Your Highness," Neill said. "But we never heard from anyone after the siege on the castle started."

"What did you ask him, Your Highness?" Carroll asked, calling out from his own horse at Neill's other side. "I only saw Sir Neill saying he couldn't help you."

"I asked if anyone was left in the villages," Mychal said, turning to face the old man directly.

His eyes took on a sadness then that answered the question before he did. "No, Your Highness. Not that I know of. We had to run for our lives, and many of us ended in camps like the mines. The ones sent back to our land are long dead." The old man ventured a glance at Edris, riding behind them, and the prince averted his eyes when he did. Edris had been very quiet since they left Norport. Mychal didn't like it. He wanted to trust him, but he always kept himself apart from the others, and it was starting to make him nervous.

"Why did they attack?" Mychal asked them. "I've never understood that. It can't have been that they needed the land. They're not here."

Neill and Carroll shared a look, neither answering for a moment, until the knight finally asked, "What have you heard?"

"Close to nothing," he admitted, and with a grimace, he added, "The Priests said it was a Holy cleansing."

Neill quelled his anger faster than Mychal would have been able to, given the circumstances, and said, "The Daemons wanted the humans gone. They had land in the north, but they wanted to expand. It hasn't been possible, after they burned so much of the country, but they did it all the same. Some say they were created to conquer and kill."

He didn't look convinced of that, but this was the part of the story that Mychal knew, so he asked, "By Amon?"

"So the legend says," Neill said, with a dry smile. "The black sheep of the Three Brothers. He built himself an army and had them slit his brothers' throats. But then Faris's bastard killed him," he said with a pointed look at Mychal, the only Halwood, and descendant of said bastard, present, "and the Daemons got pushed up north by Amon's people."

"But then you... well, they kept worshiping Eiros," Mychal said, trying not to blush. He didn't think it made him look very kingly. "The god of death. Why?"

"He's not the god of death," Neill said, patiently, like he had explained this a thousand times before. "He's the god of the Chill."

"The Chill killed everything," Edris interjected, and Neill moved aside to let his horse into their line. He quailed a little at Neill's raised eyebrow, and Mychal made a note of that. Odd. He went on anyway, though. "Astor was the only one that could stop it."

"Yes," he said simply. "Balance. That's the point. And now that High Summer's past, the Chill's days are coming. Until Astor drives them back again, just like every year." Mychal saw the same look on Edris's face that Neill did, and the knight quickly deflected. "But I was never very religious. I'm not the best person to explain this to you."

"We're close now, Your Majesty," Carroll called out to Mychal then. "I lived in the capital. I remember this road."

"We should come another way then," Mychal said, feeling his stomach start to twist in knots at the thought of facing the Daemons again. He knew it was his only way to Surpoint, but he couldn't keep the memories from the Canyon out of his mind. Every time they mentioned Daemons, he could smell the burning flesh from that day. He didn't think it would ever leave him. "We have to get off the road. They'll see us miles off."

"Agreed. We should ride along the coast," Neill said, with a firm nod. He fell back and began directing the soldiers off the main road, while Mychal brought Gale to a halt on the well-traveled dirt.

"Ready to rough it again, boy?" he asked him. The horse snorted in response, and Mychal patted his head with a small smile. He wondered if Gale had nightmares about the Canyon too. It must have been even worse for him, to not even know what was coming and then be plunged into fire.

The patter of hooves trotting past brought his attention back to his men, and he looked up just in time to see Luke riding up to him. His friend bowed his head when he reached him, but he was smiling too. "Sir Neill said we're getting close to the castle."

"Lord Carroll thinks we are," Mychal said, nodding. "How are they?"

Luke looked behind them at the rows upon rows of Halwood men, with Edris's after them and the Eirosians in rear. "Scared," he admitted. "We're going to have to try something different from the Lord Marshal's plan."

"I know," Mychal said, frowning. "I'm still working on that."

"You'll think of something," Luke said, with a small smile. His friend looked earnest enough, and Mychal was grateful for the faith in him, especially when he didn't have it himself.

"You know, a few months ago you thought I could hardly swing a sword," Mychal said. "What happened?"

"You're my king," Luke said, all sincerity, but laughed at the doubtful look on his face. "And you're better than you were. I've seen it." It was true; Farrah Vance had been right, training had gotten easier. He was stronger, faster, and was starting to look it. He thought some of it might be that thanks to the potion, the bindings on his chest were getting looser and he could breathe better now, though he still had to wear them and he was still anxious about being seen. But there really was something real changing about him-- he even thought he had grown an inch or two. His shirts from before were starting to feel tight at the neck and shoulders. When he caught his reflection he could see the difference, too. He felt closer than he'd ever been to who he'd always wanted to be.

The men started to move at Neill's direction, south toward the coastline on the horizon, and Luke and Mychal rode down alongside them. As they fell into line with the Halwood forces, Luke asked, "Why didn't you ever tell me who you were? I know it would have been a risk but... I'm your cousin, you know. I wouldn't have told anyone."

"You were in the Holy Army," Mychal said slowly, trying as he always did to avoid lying if he could. Of course he knew he was his cousin-- it was why he had sought him out, when he'd first arrived in Astor Post. He'd taken the gamble of not being recognized to be able to have someone there who felt a little like home. He wouldn't have done it now, it had been reckless-- but he was glad that he had. "I didn't know how you felt about the Priesthood. I didn't trust you. I'm sorry, Luke, I should have."

"No, you're right, I understand. I don't know if I would have either. But I think you have more friends than you realize. I don't know anyone who thought what they-- well, I suppose what they *tried* to do to you-- was right." He glanced back at the other officers and muttered, "Excluding Thorne, maybe."

"Edris isn't so bad," Mychal said gently.

"Why do you trust him, Your Majesty?" Luke asked.

"I don't," he said. "Not completely. But... he helped Lyha." His old name left a sour taste in his mouth, like lying but also doing some kind of harm to himself. He knew he would have to reckon with this forever, and he felt a kinship with the person he'd been, always, but there was too much pain there still for Mychal to think fairly about it now. It meant he had to struggle to maintain a neutral face while talking about his 'sister'.

"What? You mean helped her go missing?" Luke asked. "I don't know if that helped her." Mychal nodded, not really trusting himself to navigate this conversation smoothly. Unfortunately, Luke was still talking about it. "Are you going to look for her?"

"I don't know," he said, hoping his discomfort would pass for normal concern. "I want to find her, obviously, but I don't know how much hope there is. It's been more than two years now."

"Well," Luke said, with a kind of enforced cheerfulness, "you turned up."

Mychal laughed. "Yes," he said, then added quickly, "but I had help."

Luke smiled, in that awed way he did at times that made Mychal uncomfortable. "You'll have to tell me that story someday."

"Someday," he agreed. *When I've had time to think of it, or find out what it is,* he added to himself. He supposed Samira and Jullia had to have told his lords some kind of story, and he would ask for it when he saw them at Surpoint. But first there was Illon's Fast.

The two of them rode together the rest of the two hours remaining before they stopped along the southern coast, with all eight hundred of their party-- but most of those were undertrained boys or completely untrained women and children. If he only considered trained mages and soldiers of fighting age, he had gained two hundred from the mines, according to Neill and Ward at council that night.

"So that's five hundred for the attack," Mychal said, in his tent on the beach where they lay in wait as midnight came and went. If he walked outside now, the shadow of Illon's Fast would dominate the northern skyline. The ghost of the capital city stood in ruins around its walls. "Will that be enough?"

"It has to be, Your Majesty," Neill said.

"I'm asking so I know if we can charge or if we have to be ready for a siege," he said, trying to be patient with Neill's clear eagerness for vengeance. With a grimace as he remembered the castle's history, he added, "But Illon's Fast won't fall to a siege anytime soon."

"It wasn't the castle that kept them out," Neill said. "It was Perin."

"The Grand Mage?" Mychal asked. That was some relief at least; there were no mages, at least not human ones, guarding the castle now.

Neill nodded. "Silas's husband. It was a wonder to watch him work. He was the shield between us and the Daemons, but when they killed him it was all over."

"So how will they defend it?" he asked. "Fire?"

"Yes," Neill said. "But they have magic beyond that, too. Some of it we don't even understand."

"The fire will kill us faster," Edris said, a fear creeping into his voice that made Mychal nervous. He wasn't sure he wanted him leading men into battle. In fact he was fairly sure Edris had never been in a battle. But he needed the Valleyguard, so he just glanced over to him and nodded.

"We can't make the same mistake the Lord Marshal made," Mychal said. "And we can't just fall back every time they send fire. It'll show them we're afraid."

"We could stay here on the coast," Neill suggested. "Send archers to fire on their walls, see how much damage can be done that way first."

Mychal had stopped listening at the word coast. And something Neill had just said, about a shield... He knew vaguely that Edris was arguing the finer points of Neill's strategy, but his own idea was taking shape and suddenly he stopped pacing the room.

He was remembering his mother, one night very soon before she'd died. Mychal didn't remember why she had said it, some bedtime story that had led him to ask questions, maybe. But clear as day, he heard Mina Halwood's voice ringing through the years like she was standing right in front of him: "A king might be the sword for his people, but the queen is the shield."

Mychal wasn't a queen, had never been meant to be one. But he had listened.

The others grew quiet after a moment as he pieced his plan together, and once he was sure, he looked directly at Lord Carroll and spoke to him with a small smile. "Your mages have elemental magic?"

"Most of them, Your Majesty," he said.

"Good," Mychal said, starting to get excited. His next question was for everyone. "How much water can the horses carry?"

About an hour later, he was marching the last mile up to the castle, on foot, with his and everyone else's men around him, leading laden-down horses by the reins. Even Gale had been turned into a pack-horse, with heavy pouches of water slung over his back, and though he'd protested, he went with the mage he'd been assigned to without much fuss. Mychal hoped he'd be alright. He had no idea if this plan was going to work, but it was the best idea he'd had, and no one else had a better one. So here they were.

Soon enough they had reached the castle green, the sloping hill up to the gates of the keep beyond the bailey, and the sentry towers manned by archers, arrows trained at their lines. Illon's Fast was the last structurally sound building in the capital, with the wreckage of the town surrounding it from all other sides. Its singular tower, jagged and severe, rose ominously into the nearly starless sky, and the rest of the castle, sprawling rough-hewn stone walls with barred slits for windows, seemed to crawl with movement from an unseen enemy force. There was a deadly silence.

Mychal, spotting Neill a little ways to his left, walked to his side and asked, "If we get past the gates, do you know where the king is?"

"I can get us there," Neill said, nodding. The knight didn't seem nearly as intimidated by the castle as Mychal was, but he supposed that made sense. He was only coming home.

"We need Silas Dillon if we're going to hold this castle," Mychal said, eyeing the dark tower nervously.

A hushed dismay rippled through the men behind them, and when Mychal looked up at the sentry towers, he saw them alight with torches and pit fires, arrows being lit at each station. "Hold the line!" he called out, as forcefully as he could, and he heard others echoing the same. He was again amazed when they actually listened to him. No one moved.

Mychal thought about making a speech, like Sir James had told him he would someday, but most of the men here had heard the knight speak then and it hadn't done much for the vanguard. As he stared at the flames flickering in the darkness ahead, he could see the knight's lifeless eyes again as the Daemon's sword left his body. He hoped Sir James would be proud of him now. Finally, after another long silence, Mychal turned to Neill again and gave him a nod.

Without another word, Neill raised a banner, hastily painted overnight, black with the whiteflower crest of House Dillon emblazoned on both sides. "*Long live the king!*" he shouted, loud enough that Mychal was sure those inside Illon's Fast could hear. And only seconds later, he saw the Daemons nock and draw their flaming arrows.

"Now!" Mychal shouted, and all two hundred of Carroll's mages lifted the water out of the horses' packs and brought it down over the men's heads.

The sudden assault of cold, *cold*, nearly freezing water was enough to send blood rushing through Mychal's body, shocking him awake to every nerve even more than he had been before. As the fire rained down on them, the mages formed a wall of churning waves above their heads, too, and the few flames that did manage to break through found no purchase on the soaked men below. Emboldened, no longer fearing another Mages' Canyon, the Halwood men charged eagerly up the hill, and the other forces followed suit. Mychal ran with them, exhilarated and honestly shocked that it had actually worked. The Daemons continued to pelt them with fire, but all they managed to burn was the stalks of tall grass in the fields around the edges of their forces.

He'd given his men that much, a shield. As he charged with the others, he wondered if his mother was watching him, in Cor Hara or wherever the dead really go. He hoped he'd finally given her a reason to be proud of her *strange, sweet child*. That was what she'd always called him. *Never daughter*, he realized as he ran. Maybe she'd known him better than he'd thought.

Neill had drawn his sword already, and was running nearby with all the determination of a true knight toward his king's castle gates. When he saw Mychal watching him, he smiled and looked up at the waves of water above them. "They'll write songs about this, Halwood," he said, and Mychal believed it was the first time he had seen genuine hope on the man's face.

He grinned and drew his own sword as they came closer to the gate. "Where's your man?" he asked, and Neill glanced behind them.

"Coming up now!" he called back, and just as he did, the crowd started to part for the Eirosian soldier sprinting to the front of the line. There were two other men with shields and a mage holding the water above all four of them, attempting to protect the man who was now drawing a large part of the Daemons' fire. They knew what was coming.

Mychal saw him reach the inner gate and strap the petard to the doors, which was when the fire really started to rain down with the full force of the castle's defenses. The water kept most of it at bay, but rocks were coming now too, and the wooden shields were barely holding together. Mercifully, though, it only took him seconds to light the gunpowder inside, and as soon as the match was struck the Eirosians were racing back to the line. They hadn't quite made it to Mychal and the others when the explosion sounded across the field, but they were close enough, not to be blasted back through the front lines like Mychal had worried.

The gates, wooden double-wide doors with iron crossbars, were blown off their hinges easily, and when the smoke cleared, the gate was ablaze but clear. Cheers erupted from their side, but Mychal could hear shouting and rushed footsteps coming from the Daemons on the walls. "Men!" he shouted, and Neill turned to him then. "Get ready!" Mychal looked to the open doorway, and the knight understood.

"Get into the courtyard and hold all the passages!" Neill called out. "Don't let anyone start picking you off from the walls! I want archers defending our position!" After a moment's hesitation from the men, he shouted, "Now!" And the combined forces all charged toward the open gate.

As the men rushed past them, Mychal struggled back through the press of the crowd to Neill's side and asked, "Who do you need with you to find Silas?"

"I need you," he said. "And Edris. They need to think the whole Triad's come down on them. We should have a mage too, Carroll probably. And some fighting men."

"Yours?"

"No. My knights should stay here, lead the Eirosians," Neill said. "Valleyguard would be best."

"I'll find Edris," Mychal said, and rushed after the army, now flooding into the courtyard of Illon's Fast and meeting very little resistance. Neill was at his heels, and as soon as they crossed the threshold he started directing men up to the walkways surrounding the walls of the courtyard.

"If you don't hold these, the Daemons will! Take the highest ground!" he was shouting, and Mychal left him there, following the brightest gleam of armor that he knew would lead to the Thorncliffe forces. He pushed his way through the waiting soldiers until he found the prince where the crowd was thickest.

"Edris! Neill needs us!" Mychal shouted, but his breaking voice was easily lost in the chaotic din of the courtyard. Edris had noticed him, but he was still a ways away, and the press of hundreds of men around him wasn't making it easy to move. The air was thick with the smell of dust and water, and the soaked soldiers around him looked even younger and less formidable than before with their clothes plastered to their skin. But none of them were burnt alive just yet, and for Mychal that was a victory.

"They're going to start attacking here soon!" Edris shouted when he had managed to push through the mass of men between him and Mychal.

"Yes, they are, but we have to find Silas!" he said. "Neill's near the gates. He wants us with him, and Valleyguard men!"

Edris frowned, clearly uneasy, but he turned to one of the men nearby and said, "Find Landiss, tell him he's in command for a while. I need six men with me, now!" The closest several in Thorncliffe blue and brown followed them as they wove their way back to Neill and the gates.

When they found him, he had already found Carroll, who still had a good deal of water swirling around his arms and gathering at his wrists. It made Mychal think of Samira, and he found himself wondering where she was now and if she'd made it to Surpoint yet. He shook the thought out of his mind and came back to the present just as soldiers started to shout warnings down from the far ends of the walkways and the Daemons entered the fray. The night came alive again with fire and the clash of swords, and Neill strode confidently past them toward the second set of doors into the castle tower.

The rest of them caught up with him quickly enough. Neill turned to Edris when he reached them and, grinning wickedly, said, "Well, Your Highness, it looks as though mages and Eirosians saved your life tonight."

Edris looked tense, his eyes darting around the courtyard with his hand ready to draw his sword. He went red, but wasn't even looking at Neill when he managed to say, "Not quite yet."

"Where would the king be?" Mychal asked, deciding to ignore whatever just happened-- for now. Something had been going on with the both of them, ever since Norport or maybe even before, but he didn't have time to wonder about it right now.

"They always kept him in the tower, just in here," Neill said, indicating the doors they stood in front of, "but they could have moved him down to the dungeons."

"We'll try the tower first, then," Mychal said, and even though he was feigning the confidence it took to command, no one questioned him. He couldn't imagine himself ever getting used to giving orders and having them followed.

"We may have to fight our way up," Neill warned, and Mychal looked back at Carroll, standing at the ready.

"Douse us again, sir," he said, and the old mage raised the water high above them and let it rain down on their heads. Blinking and shivering with the cold, Mychal wiped the water out of his eyes and held his sword at the ready. "Let's go," he said, and they walked into Illon's Fast and plunged into darkness.

# 23

# Edris

Illon's Fast had looked small from the outside, at least compared to other castles Edris had seen, but once they were inside the tower, it felt like nothing less than a labyrinth. It bore no resemblance to the wide, well-laid halls in Caspar's Dale, and there was something cold and dank about the air around them that went beyond just the chill from their drenched clothes. He tried to convince himself it was only his imagination, but he had a terrible feeling as they walked through the entrance hall, like it wasn't stone at all, but the mouth of some cavernous beast.

Xander was leading the way, and he seemed confident enough, but he had hesitated noticeably before turning the last two corners and Edris was starting to worry. Lord Carroll was especially unsettled by the dark, clutching the sleeve of one of the Valleyguard toward the back of the group. Eventually, Edris heard the knight stumble at the front of the group, and everyone else stopped in their tracks. "Xander?" he asked, his voice tense.

"I'm all right," he said, in a low voice. "We found the stairs, is all."

They all carefully started forward again, each of them feeling for the first step before they began to climb.

As they felt their way up the long, winding steps, Mychal appeared out of the darkness to his right, and in a voice barely louder than a whisper, asked, "Did you just call him Xander?"

Edris paused. He was thankful, just for the moment, that no one could see him because he was sure he was blushing already. "I suppose so, why?" he whispered back, hoping no one else could hear.

"That's friendly," the young king said, almost too casual. "For a hostage."

"He's not a hostage," Edris said, trying to sound gruff and hoping it would put Mychal off. "After tonight he's free to go."

"Alright," Mychal said, still with the casual tone. Edris wished he could see if Xander was listening. The knight had been acting oddly toward him the last few weeks of the march. He seemed both more and less comfortable around him, and it changed nearly every day. He'd meant to ask him what was wrong when he'd gone to see him in the camp last night, but there hadn't been much conversation. There was no doubt Xander had gotten quieter the closer they came to the castle. But tonight he was all bravado and charm-- which didn't seem quite like him either.

Mychal wasn't finished. "What about me?" he asked, and Edris grimaced, knowing what was coming next. "Will I be free to go too?"

He hoped his voice sounded calm enough when he replied, "I'm not sure I know what you mean."

"I'm not stupid, Edris," he said. "If you brought me to your father now, everything that happened at the mine would be forgiven. So are you going to let me go to Surpoint?"

Edris took a deep breath. He tried not to imagine the look that must have been on Mychal's face. Finally, he said, "I won't stop you, Mychal. But I have to go back to Thorncliffe." He felt it was the right choice, when he said it out loud, but he still wished there was some easier option.

There was a pause, and then Mychal asked, "Even after what you saw in Norport?"

"I can't just *leave*," Edris hissed, in a last effort to keep his voice low. "I can... change those things when I'm king. It'll be different." He couldn't deny that the mine had shaken him. But he couldn't just *not* go home. No matter what his father had done, he was still the crown prince. He had responsibilities and he didn't think it was right to just walk away-- *not that Mychal would understand that*, he thought sullenly as they kept marching further into the dark.

Mychal scoffed, and Edris grew even more frustrated. "Good luck."

"It's different for me!" he exclaimed. "It's not like it was for you."

"Do you think I would have left if I'd had a choice?" Mychal asked, his voice sounding barely but carefully controlled. They were venturing into territory that would endanger both of them if any of the others repeated it, or gods forbid figured out what it meant, so Edris didn't answer that.

"I hope you make it home, Mychal," he said quietly. "Really."

At that moment Xander stopped moving. The two of them almost collided with him at the top of the stairs, and the others halted on the steps below. "This is it," Xander said. "We'll have to make it through the reception hall to get up to the keep. There's another set of stairs there that leads to the dungeons, so if he's not in the tower we'll go down that way. Now let's hope there's some light." Edris heard the door creak and ease open, and moonlight spilled into the hall from the windows ahead.

He wished it hadn't.

The reception hall looked like it had been left in a hurry. The courtiers' benches were overturned, and an abundant banquet had been abandoned, wine spilled and food strewn about the room. The first thing Edris had noticed, though, was the smell. Death. He was certain of it. And when they stepped inside, the dais came out of shadow and he suddenly saw why.

A man's body was propped upright on the throne with a vicious gash across his throat. His eyes bulged and his limbs were limp, and he had been dead long enough to start to decay. A sign hung around his neck, wood with crude writing in black ink and clean of all blood. *THE KING OF EIROSIA, ON HIS THRONE AGAIN.*

"No," Carroll breathed, shaking his head, and Xander stood frozen in place. Edris turned away from the body, feeling himself start to be sick, and approached him as Mychal reeled and the Valleyguard men stared.

"Xander?" Edris asked, hesitant. The knight was still staring at the body.

"That's not Silas," he said, his voice choked and breaking. Edris hesitated– he supposed the body's face was somewhat obscured by the decay, and maybe that was on purpose, but he couldn't imagine who else it could be, or why it wouldn't be Silas.

He put a hand gently on the man's arm, trying to offer some kind of anchor-- he looked likely to collapse. "I'm sorry, Xander."

"No, it's *not* Silas. That's a *glamour*, it's a *spell*. That's what they *do*," he insisted. There was a dangerous edge to his voice now. "They knew we would come here. We have to keep moving!"

Before anyone else could speak, something whistled past Edris's left ear and speared through one of the guardsmen's eyes. He fell to the ground with the spine of an arrow protruding from his skull. "Get down!" Mychal shouted, and everyone dropped to the floor as more arrows flew past, right where their heads had been seconds before. Soon after, four Daemons emerged from the shadows at the corners of the room, armed with bows and arrows and daggers glistening in the light. Edris had never seen a Daemon, but in the dim light he could make out their figures, almost human but a good deal taller with gray hardened skin and blue-black eyes. He froze, and Xander shoved him into the middle of the circle that the remaining nine of them had formed, huddled together on their hands and knees.

The guardsmen rushed the Daemon soldiers as soon as they were within range, and two of them made quick work of the first they assaulted, but a third Thorncliffe man was stabbed with one of the Daemons' knives. The other two guards cut clean through the two remaining archers, and the final Daemon made a fair stand with his dagger before Xander stood and slashed through his back with his sword. The knight sheathed it when it was done and said, "Keep moving. Be careful turning corners and passing through doors."

Edris's ears were ringing as he stared at the Valleyguard man on the ground in front of him, and the dead Daemons surrounding them. It took Xander's outstretched hand to pull him out of his head and off the ground. The man didn't look at ease, exactly, but Edris knew he was having a worse reaction himself, and he was quickly becoming embarrassed. He had never been in a real battle before, and the fighting outside had been bad enough, but that was his own man that'd died right in front of him. A man he'd ordered to be here. His voice coming out weaker than he'd have liked, he asked Xander quietly, "We're still going on?"

"We have to," he said, his face stoic, determined.

"But we know it's a trap," he protested.

"Doesn't matter," Xander said. "We go." He walked on to the door at the end of the hall, and everyone else picked up and followed him. Edris marched on behind, trying to stop himself from inventing in the shadows even worse things than they'd already seen.

The next door revealed more stairs, but no Daemons, and no more light either. "How long until we reach the tower?" Mychal asked. He sounded like he was doing better than Edris, but not by much.

"Not long now," Xander said. The rest of the climb was silent. When they reached the top of the stairs, a small arrow loop in the side of the stairwell let in enough light to illuminate the door to the royal chambers.

When Xander opened the door, they entered a room that looked like it was once a solar, but was now a ruin. The floor was stained with blood, old and new, and the furniture was, for the most part, torn, toppled, or utterly destroyed. At the back of the room, in front of the fireplace, stood a tall and lithe Daemon, his skin more blue than the gray Edris had seen in the soldiers. He was wearing no armor, but a velvet doublet of gray and white spattered with new, red blood. But all of Xander's attention was on the human man at his feet, on his knees with his head bent and his hands tied. When they entered, the man looked up, and they saw a face nearing forty, weathered and hard, with pale skin, jet black hair and blue eyes, almost eerily bright. His face was battered and bruised, and his hair hung limply in long, dirty locks, but Edris knew instantly this must be Silas Dillon.

Xander went down on his knee in front of Silas, bowed his head, and whispered in exhausted relief, "My king."

The Daemon laughed, a low, easy rumble, taking pleasure in every moment. "Thank you for your fealty, Sir Alexander. I must admit I wasn't expecting it."

"Not you," Xander said sharply, raising his head and staring daggers into the Daemon's eyes.

"Why not?" he asked, a glint in his eyes as he gave Silas a sharp kick in the square of his back, sending him fully flat onto the ground. "I'm the king in this land. I have been for some time now."

"You're the Daemon King?" Mychal asked, then quailed when the creature looked at him, as if he were surprised at himself.

He grinned wickedly at Mychal and said, "Do I not look the part? My name is Avery Dearril. The King of Eirosia."

"The King of the Daemons. The Eirosian Usurper," Xander spat, and Dearril shrugged.

"What's the difference?" he asked, and Silas jerked his head up, glaring at the Daemon King. "I must say, Sir Alexander, for all your devotion to Silas here, you've caused him a lot of trouble."

"Whoever he is to you, he is a king," Xander said, brimming with anger, and Dearril laughed again. "He looks close to death."

"You should have thought of that before you ran," he said. "I understand why you would run, mind you, any coward would. But I can't imagine why you would come *back*."

"I'm here for my king," Neill said. "As he asked of me."

"Oh, he *did* tell you to go?" Dearril asked. He spoke to Silas then in a menacing hiss. "I thought we'd agreed he ran away on his own. Have you been lying to me?"

"No, my lord," Silas mumbled, and Dearril kicked him once again.

"Another lie. Well, Silas, your rescue comes a little late, no? Thirteen years is nothing to me, but to humans..." He shook his head and *tsked* at the party, still smiling tightly as he did. "And it wasn't wise. The rest of my men will be here soon."

"You don't have any more, not anywhere near here," Xander said, sounding more confident than Edris could believe. "I saw two hundred out there. That's your entire garrison for twenty miles at least."

"Who are your friends?" Dearril asked, ignoring that. "Well, not the common ones. We won't trouble with them. In fact--" And with a flick of his hand, arrows of pure flame came flying out of the fireplace and straight into the chests of the four Valleyguard men. Carroll's water and magic had done its job, and at first they couldn't find lasting purchase on the soaked leather. But then, with a sigh, Dearril snapped his hand up and Edris heard screams behind him, even though he didn't dare look as the fire rose to their necks. He heard them slump onto the ground, and could smell it too, the burning that he'd heard Mychal describe and knew he'd never forget.

In the silence that followed, Dearril looked at Carroll and said, "You first, old man."

"Elliot Carroll," Xander said. "Lord of Carroll's Pass. He's an Eirosian and has a right to this land just as we do."

Dearril looked annoyed, but waved him off. "What about him?" he asked, looking to Edris, who forgot how to breathe.

"I'm Edris Thorne," he managed to say, with no idea where the courage came from. "Prince of--"

"Thorncliffe!" Dearril said, with a wide, surprised smile. "Thank your father for me. I wouldn't be standing here if he'd come to the siege all those years ago." Edris felt his stomach turn as the Daemon moved on. He was right, though; his father regarded it as a point of pride that *he* had brought Eirosia down. "And who's the little one?"

"I'm a king too," Mychal said, and when Edris looked he could see he was talking more to Silas than Dearril. "Mychal Halwood of the Hartlands."

The Daemon King narrowed his eyes and said, "You're supposed to be dead." Mychal met his gaze and Dearril drew in a deep breath and smiled. Suddenly, Mychal was clutching his head, doubled over, and Dearril was nodding. Edris didn't know how, but he knew he had looked into his mind. "I smell power on you. Is it the potions in your pocket or something in your future?" Mychal paled, and Edris started to panic. Would Xander believe Dearril if he... but *did* he really know?

"No matter. I could keep you once your friends are dead. You can bear my son." He knew. Mychal reached for his sword and Edris shot him a look to stay still. Xander looked puzzled, but his eyes had never left Dearril's, and Edris suspected he was too full of fury to have thought too much of that. "And I'll send Thorne back to his father in one piece, as a thank you for my kingdom. The rest of you? I'll put your heads on spikes."

"No," Xander said, taking another step forward. "You won't."

"I won't?" Dearril asked, his voice more dangerous now and his expression darker. "Even if I don't kill you all, my army will. Your drowned rats only have one trick," he said, nodding at the dead guards on the ground, "and it doesn't last long."

"No," Xander repeated, and as he did he moved to the center of the room and drew his sword. "We'll end this now. You and me, with no magic. You always said you were the best sword in the North. Let's fight for the castle, and for Silas too."

"And if I yield you'll let me go?" Dearril laughed.

"Yes," Xander said, as sincere as he had always been. "You'll have clear passage back to the North."

"Back to that freezing hell," Dearril snarled. He had drawn his own sword now. "I don't think so. You always were too smart with me, Neill. I'll kill you slowly when this is over." He let go of Silas and started stalking toward Xander.

Edris scurried back, and dragged Mychal and Carroll with him. They stood with their backs to the wall near the door, and despite Xander's terms, Edris was ready to run for his life if Dearril won. The two swordsmen circled each other slowly, neither willing to make the first move and surrender their initial control. The Daemon King had a longsword made of a gleaming white high-ore steel, with ice blue inscriptions in the Old Language in a long line along the center of the blade. The way the moonlight reflected off of it made it seem sharper than any steel Edris had ever seen. Xander was strong and steady, and he didn't seem afraid of Dearril, but he looked small compared to this towering figure.

The first time the blades clashed, Edris jumped, and he saw Mychal wince at each blow. Xander was fighting in near-perfect form, but it still looked like the Daemon was only playing with him.

Dearril's strokes were quick and powerful. No matter how much the knight weaved and dodged his attacks, he was losing ground all the time, and when they next broke apart, he almost fell back into the far wall. "He's going to lose," Mychal whispered, and Edris hardly dared to watch.

Xander managed to rush in and clash with the Daemon's sword before it bore down on his head, but the power of the thrust sent him rocking back on his heels, and Dearril tripped him when he did. He fell and Edris winced before he rolled expertly away from the coming strike, and managed to knick Dearril's ankle as he stood back up. That only made him angry. "You're only making it worse for yourself," he warned, and advanced again.

Edris was desperate to do something, but he knew Xander would never want him to intervene, and what could he do anyway against someone like Dearril?

"Edris!" Mychal suddenly shouted, and he turned around just in time to stumble out of the way of a Daemon soldier's swinging sword. Edris drew his own, but the soldier was already racing back down the dark spiraling stairwell. He wasn't alone. Silas was gripping his chains, trying to break free, as the soldier dragged him down the stairs and out of sight.

Before anyone else could react, Edris was rushing after them, plunging himself into darkness and shouting for Carroll and Mychal not to follow him. Someone had to be there to save Xander if he needed, but Edris knew all his knight would care about was saving the king. Before long, a flash of fire raced past him up the turn of the stairs, setting the wall hanging to his left ablaze at once. "Don't come any closer," the soldier growled.

In the light of the burning tapestry, Edris saw that this particular Daemon looked strong and was much taller than him. He was also glaring at him with a menacing snarl that held a hint of challenge. Daring him to engage.

He took the bait. "You need your fire to protect you against one human soldier?"

The Daemon almost laughed, and looked down at Edris's shining chestplate and intricate Thorne insignia, probably all steel from the Norport mines. "Don't look like a soldier."

"You're right," Edris said, "I'm not a common soldier." He had to make him angry, get him to use his sword and let go of Silas's chain. So channeling the worst of his father, he held himself up and, voice dripping with disdain, said, "I'm the prince of Thorncliffe. And I'm here to send you abominations of Eiros back to the hell you crawled out of."

It worked. Silas's chain hit the stone floor and the Daemon charged, his sword raised high in the air. Edris had to bring his own sword up quickly to keep his head from being sliced in half– that would have been embarrassing, right in front of a king– but it did knock the soldier off-balance enough to keep him alive. The Daemon was bearing down on him with furious zeal, his pallid skin growing redder with each passing moment. Edris hoped that didn't mean fire was coming. Dearril had accepted the terms of Xander's challenge with honor, but he didn't know this Daemon.

He managed to push the soldier's blade off his with one surge of wild strength, but every moment after that was a very real fight for his life. The landing they had stopped on was still in the turret of the stairwell, so there really wasn't anywhere to retreat to, and each time Edris was pinned against a wall he thought he was done for. But he had trained in Caspar's Dale with the best of the Holy officers, including the Lord Marshal himself, since he was old enough to swing a sword. He'd never done this before, but even so, it felt familiar to his body. For that, and only that, he thanked his father.

It was in one of these moments of muscle memory that he recalled the only trick he'd ever really mastered for an opponent with a longer reach. He had to wait until the Daemon bore down on him from above again, though, and he would have to be quick. Flushed with exhilaration, as he braced for the soldier to charge again, the old axiom of the Holy Army came to him with spiritual clarity: *"May Astor sharpen our swords."*

The Daemon's sword came flying at Edris's neck from the left, and he was ready; he blocked it with as much momentum as he could manage, enough to send it down to his cross guard. Praying for his armor's endurance, Edris brought up both of his arms even higher, and felt the flat side of the sword pressing against his gauntlet, only boiled leather standing between that and losing his hand. He stepped forward, following through with his whole body as he pushed the blade away from his arm as hard as he could and gripped the Daemon's wrist. He pulled his enemy's sword down and past him, the soldier's far reach the only thing protecting Edris now. He held it there, struggling to keep control, while his right hand swung his sword down, in a lucky, perfect arc, right into the Daemon's throat. The hardened gray skin cracked inward as the sword beheaded the soldier and he fell, black blood spilling out onto Edris's blade as he went.

The body slumped to the ground, and Edris collapsed, wheezing and coughing, into the wall behind him. Slowly, he saw Silas Dillon stand, walk cautiously up to him, and offer his hand. Edris let the man pull him up, and met his eyes with some reservation. The king was staring at him and, despite his treatment, seemed to be in less shock than Edris was. "Thank you," he said. Silas seemed to notice the state he was in then and asked, "Have you ever killed a Daemon before?"

Edris, still struggling for breath, shook his head. "I've never killed anything before."

Silas took the Daemon's sword from the ground beside them and cut through his chain until it fell, snaking down to the ground at his feet. "We should go," he said. "Neill may need us."

The duel had grown more desperate by the time they returned. Dearril didn't seem to have much of a fighting style beyond overwhelming force, but with his size it was more than enough. Xander had started to sense his next move, though, and he was now dodging at the right moments for the Daemon to be as off-balance as possible. It wasn't long before he took advantage. One perfect feint sent Dearril stumbling onto the ground, but before Xander could swing his sword downward the Daemon slashed wildly at the air behind him, slicing a fine line into the knight's right shoulder.

Xander cried out in pain and Edris saw Dearril grin as he took his time standing up again. "That's only the beginning," he promised, and brought his newly bloodied longsword swinging around, meaning to finish removing the arm. With a horribly pained grimace, Neill brought his sword up with the injured arm just in time to block the blow, and in the moment of surprise when Dearril was distracted, he kicked him in the stomach and his legs went out from underneath him. The Daemon was on the ground now, but their blades were still locked together. Xander was gripping his sword with both hands to keep it steady, but he was determined, and there didn't seem to be a way up for Dearril. The swords fought for ground, the upper hand changing each second.

"Yield!" Xander shouted, grimacing through the pain. Edris could almost feel it himself, watching his shoulder bleed.

Dearril's snarling glare faded back into a smug smile then, and he said, "You can have this castle. I'll take it from you again." And in the next second, he was gone. There was no flash of light, or rush of wind, or anything Edris had imagined happening when Daemons vanish to announce his going. He had just disappeared. Xander fell forward onto the ground, his sword clattering down as he tried to catch his fall with both hands. He rolled over onto his back, cursing and breathing heavily. Slowly, in the silence, Silas Dillon stood and walked over to where he lay.

"My friend," he said, and extended his hand to help him up. When Xander was standing, he embraced him, and the two stood there for some time, hugging each other tightly and crying. "Thank you," Silas finally said, and they broke apart then.

"I knew you were alive," Xander said, stiff as he pulled himself back together. Silas, with tired, bewildered eyes, looked at each of the four of them in turn and landed finally on Edris.

"The prince of Thorncliffe," he said, amazed. "You saved my life. I never imagined my plea would actually work."

"It didn't," Xander said. With a sunny smile in his direction, more than he felt he deserved, he added, "Edris is here of his own will."

"Yes, Your Majesty. I am," Edris said, with a rather awkward bow. He paused then before he said, "I can't begin to apologize."

"You mustn't," Silas said. "These weren't your sins." Even ragged and beaten, he carried himself like a king, something that still eluded Edris— he worried it always would. This man, even as an abused prisoner, demanded respect merely by deserving it. "If you're unwelcome in Thorncliffe now, I would be honored for you to remain in Eirosia."

Edris looked over to Mychal, who was watching him closely. He looked at the Valleyguard men on the ground, and then down to the mines' steel of his sword, his armor, everything that declared his allegiance to Thorncliffe. He turned back to Silas and said, "For as long as Xander needs me. But I have to go with King Mychal to Surpoint first."

Silas turned his attention to Mychal then, who was beaming at Edris in a way he didn't feel worthy of. The older king approached the younger, and they both bowed their heads. "Neill, could you cut me free?" As the knight released his hands from their bonds, Silas said, "It's an honor to meet you. I can't thank you enough for being here."

"My kingdom was taken from me too," he said. "I was glad to help."

"I'd be glad to help you as well," Silas said, quirking a small smile as he studied him. "I have no army, but what's left of my navy ships are at the harbor. If you're going to Surpoint, you'll need them."

"Thank you, Your Majesty," Mychal said, with an awed reverence that Silas met graciously as he nodded to him.

"Send word when you know where your court will be," he said. "When I'm strong enough, I'll sit on your war council."

"You will?" Xander asked, with a small frown.

"Yes," the Eirosian king said, looking back at the knight. "And when I do, I'll name you castellan." Xander went still with utter shock as he continued, "You fought for this castle. I would have you hold it."

"I will," he said, bewildered, bowing deeply once more. Edris grinned when he met his eyes again. He felt nothing but pride when he looked at him, this wonderful man he couldn't believe had ever even looked his way.

"Have your shoulder seen to," Silas added, and said, "The Daemons will have gone when Dearril left. I should speak to my people. Mychal, will you come?" With another shocked smile, Mychal nodded, and the two kings left the keep together. Carroll trailed behind them, and Edris helped Xander wrap his shoulder before they followed too.

The blood, the body in the banquet hall, none of it remained, and he supposed the magic had gone with the Daemon King when he left. He didn't want to know how any of it had been done, he was only glad to be alive. But he did worry about when Dearril would come back, and what shape Illon's Fast would be in when he did. They held the castle now, but for how long?

When Silas emerged into the courtyard, the enemy army was gone just as he'd predicted. The soldiers' cheers were deafening and he threw his chains to the ground while they watched and shouted even louder. They cheered for Mychal too, and Xander was watching with such joy that Edris had to say, "Thank you," as they stood on the steps behind the kings.

"For what?" he asked, confused.

"For bringing me this far," Edris said. He could hear the emotion in his voice, and he didn't dare to elaborate. He knew his eyes might start to fill with tears if he did.

Xander shook his head. "No, Edris. You did that on your own." He turned to face him now, with his hands gently grasping Edris's arms. Edris felt every nerve he touched come alive at once, just like the first time and every time after. "That hate and fear, it's like a disease in your mind. You have to cut it out before it takes over. It's not easily done, and I know how hard it was for you to--"

Edris couldn't help himself anymore. He stepped forward and kissed him, gently at first and more confidently as he grew braver. He could practically feel the eyes on them, but he didn't care any-more. He knew he could probably never go back to Thorncliffe now, but that was alright. He didn't want to. He knew what he wanted.

When they broke apart, Xander didn't hesitate. "Stay with me."

"I will," Edris promised. He felt like he was floating, and he knew the cheers of the crowd were for Silas, but it felt like they were for them. "But first there's Surpoint."

# 24

# Samira

"From The Book of the Harvest," the High Priest of Queens-hearth announced, as a small serving boy held up a gilded and over-sized missal of the Holy Book. With the reading, the coronation of the new King of the Hartlands began.

*"Morra brought forth Tol, the first man. And they together, with the clay wetted by Morra's waters and baked in Astor's light, created a people for Tol to rule. And Tol's children forever were the kings of men."*

As the boy shut the book, Samira raised her head and noticed that Deronn looked like he might be about to cry. She tried to meet his eyes to encourage him from her seat at the front of the crowd, but he was clearly trying to avoid looking at the Godhead, sitting at her left. She couldn't blame him.

The heat was bearing down on the coronation guests without mercy. There were rows and rows of them, highborns from all over the Triad including the young boy's newly minted court, and the heat radiating from the crowd itself wasn't helping either. It was bad enough summer was ending with a last gasp of sweltering heat, but coronations were always held at midday, when Astor was strongest, and outdoors. And of course, with the Godhead present, nothing would stand in the way of tradition.

As if he'd read her mind-- maybe he had-- Riyan Duane leaned over to her and whispered, "We just rode for days in this heat, you'd think the Father could give us one afternoon." Samira nodded and managed to laugh quietly, but she didn't look at him. He had leaned in a little too close for her liking. Since she'd joined the Holy procession when they came through Hollisport nearly two weeks ago, her betrothed had been warmer than polite, maybe even what you could call romantic, in his own very strange way. It was unsettling to Samira; she wanted so badly to hate him, but his kindness was throwing her off. She had to remind herself every so often that she could be executed for half a dozen things if she even so much as thought about them in his presence at the wrong time.

The attendants around them had noticed when he'd whispered to her; Samira could feel their eyes on her everywhere. But no one dared say anything disapproving, ever, to the Godhead or his bride. That kind of untouchability was new to her, and she couldn't say that she hated it. As she was quickly discovering, royalty was one thing, but religion was something else entirely.

Although she wouldn't have known from the coronation ceremony. Samira hadn't seen a king crowned since her father, and she'd been almost too young to remember then, but she suspected the Priesthood had changed the rituals considerably. This was a very religious affair. The priest had circled around now on the raised dais where Deronn sat and cloaked him in a long wine-red coat of heavy fur and velvet. Just watching made Samira feel faint; she could see the boy starting to shine with sweat already. "What is the name of the one who comes before us?" the High Priest asked then, the question ringing out powerfully across the green.

Deronn's voice was high, and not so confident, but he projected well. "Deronn of Halwood House."

"And who was your father, Deronn of Halwood House?"

The boy was a little quieter this time. Samira could still hear him, but she wasn't sure about the back of the crowd. "Eronn of Halwood House, from the line of Faris and Tol before him."

Satisfied, the priest gestured to the apprentice with the missal once again, and as he read, he paused now and then to anoint Deronn, rather ungracefully, with water from the Den Morra River.

"From the Book of the Princes. *One day, the three sons of Tol's sons went to the Mother and Father. The three brothers, Caspar, Amon, and Faris, were bade to approach the Holy Thrones. Astor commanded them to travel across the Mother's widest sea to spread the Holy Kingdom across all the Earth. They were told never to return until they had died, but their children would one day see Cor Hara living. And so the brothers set out in holy purpose, and only the dead looked on Cor Hara from that day onward.*"

He closed the book again and turned to Deronn, who looked even more terrified than before. "Do you swear to protect the kingdom of the Hartlands from evil, provide for its people, and rule in righteousness till the end of your days?"

Deronn opened his mouth to speak, but nothing came out. He cleared his throat and tried again. "I do," he managed, softer than ever.

"Do you swear to defend the Faith under the guidance of His Holiness the Head of the Church of the Duality?"

Deronn glanced down at Riyan and Samira, and answered, slightly louder this time, "I do." Samira had never prayed harder in her life than she did at that moment that none of the mage-catchers were trying to see into *his* mind. He must have been thinking about Mychal. She remembered his shock and relief at the idea of his brother coming to take the crown away from him, that night in the crypt all those months ago, and felt for Deronn again instantly.

She still wasn't comfortable with the fact that they hadn't told him which twin Mychal really was, though. Jullia had decided that it would be too dangerous, and held to her judgment weeks later on the road when Samira had asked. She did understand it had been the safest choice, but her heart hurt for the boy, still thinking his sister was gone. Not to mention the first Mychal would be a stranger to him. The executions had only waited until Deronn was weaned.

"And do you swear that, should it be your fate to face the Last Days, you will lead your people to paradise in Cor Hara, on the path of the enduring faithful?"

Deronn needed a moment before that one, too. "I do."

"Bring the crown," the Priest announced, and four squires marched down the aisle between the guests, carrying the crown of the Hartlands on a pillow of red velvet. Samira had never seen it. The king only wore it on occasions of state. It was a beautiful piece of metalwork, she assumed crafted in Surpoint, with bands of polished steel weaving and rippling together around in a delicate ring. Spades of steel rose from the ring as well, all around the crown like fire licking at the air above. It shone brightly in the summer sun and even Deronn watched with awe as the squires carried it to the dais.

The Priest, with careful hands, picked it up gingerly and lowered it with reverence onto Deronn's head. It was nearly too big, but it came to rest around the middle of his forehead and the boy could see again once he had swiped at his hair once or twice, tucking it up into the crown or behind his ears. He was blinking, looking a little in shock, as he watched the crowd stand and then kneel, showing fealty to their new boy king. Samira started to kneel, too, but Riyan stopped her. "We don't bow," he whispered, not unkindly, in her ear, and she stayed standing at his side.

The Priest stepped back and gently motioned for Deronn to stand, which he did, somewhat unsteadily as he got his bearings under the weight of the crown. "King Deronn of Halwood House, Defender of the Holy Faith and Sovereign of the Hartlands! Praise to the Mother and Father!"

"Long live King Deronn!" the crowd exclaimed, and Samira joined in. Riyan didn't, but politely clapped during the thunderous applause that followed while Deronn was led off the dais and into the castle. Hartshold Keep was calling to Samira too, and the cool bath she was longing to recover in before the banquet, but she knew it wouldn't be *holy* to run back to the guest chambers and push through the rest of the crowd.

"I thought that was lovely," Riyan said, when the roar of conversation reached the point where they wouldn't be overheard. "I was worried it would be, er, rather quaint. Hartlands, you know."

"Right," Samira said, still watching the train of the Deronn's formal robes dragging along the grass for several feet, far lower to the ground than usual, behind him as he went. "Yes. It was."

"Are you alright?" Riyan asked, touching her arm as he spoke, gently but still enough to shock Samira. She wasn't used to *anyone* touching her, not since her birthday, other than her handmaidens-- and Mychal, once.

"I'm fine," she said, managing a smile. "Just a little overheated, is all. I'd like to find a cold bath..."

"I'm sure we can find that for you," Riyan said, smiling back. "I know what you mean. And you do feel a bit warm." At that moment, his expression changed into something neutral, serene, and she knew that meant someone from Riyan's court had appeared behind her. Sure enough, as she turned she found herself face to face with Jacob Denastor, one of the Holy Court's inner circle and the leading player in Samira's worst nightmares. The mage-hunter was long and lean, with a high brow and very little chin. His small dark eyes made it difficult to discern what he was truly thinking, and though they were too dark to tell, Samira knew they must be cloudy from godwine. "Jacob. What is it?"

"Your Holiness," he said, and then turned and bowed quickly to Samira. "Apologies, Your Highness. Your Holiness, the council would like to speak with you before the feast this evening."

Riyan nodded, his expression unchanged. "That's fine. Only I was just going to escort Princess Samira back to the castle."

Samira watched Denastor's eyes flicker over to her again and thought she saw annoyance there. She remembered her mother's advice, and in a moment of either courage or stupidity, she spoke in front of the mage-hunter for the first time. "I could come with you, Your Holiness. It's no trouble."

Riyan frowned. "Princess, you said you weren't feeling well."

"The council is no emergency," Denastor interjected. "We'll wait for you to return first, sir."

"Thank you," Riyan said, and led Samira away from the older man and into the stream of guests making their way back to the center of the city. The Holy Guard surrounded them, creating a kind of moving eye of a storm within the crowd, and the two of them walked there undisturbed. "I'm sorry about that. I know it must seem like I'm ignoring you..."

"No, it really doesn't," Samira assured him, hoping he would miss the sarcasm. That was just for her.

"Well, anyway. I have to go back there and feign *serene wisdom*," he muttered. "It's what they expect. I almost envy kings. At least they're allowed to get angry."

"What do you have to be angry about?" Samira asked, trying to sound as sweet and innocent as possible. She wasn't sure it worked, because he just smiled a tight, bemused smile.

"Nothing. Well, we'll see, after this council."

"You'll just have to tell me all about it," she said, turning to look directly into his cloudy blue eyes. The Godhead looked back at her, too, and smiled.

"I'm sure it will bore you. But it will be something to talk about at supper," he said. "Try to rest while I'm gone." When they stopped at the door, he took her hand in his and squeezed it before he departed. When she saw the faces of the women who'd been closest in the crowd, staring in shock, Samira couldn't help but feel scandalized too.

The Holy Guard had gone with Riyan when he left, and as soon as they did she heard her name called at the threshold into the entrance hall. When she turned to look, she saw the tiny dowager queen, Katheryn Payne, shuffling gamefully toward Samira and smiling widely. Back in Brookbridge, she had hardly betrayed an expression at all. "It's good to see you again, Your Highness," the old woman said, brightly. It was starting to verge on unsettling.

"Queen Katheryn," she said, bowing her head. "I hadn't heard you were making the trip."

"I'm here to stay," she said, and Samira must have looked more surprised, because she added, "I wouldn't miss getting to be Queen *Grand*mother, after all. And the poor boy hardly has any family left."

"Of course," Samira said. "And even Jullia couldn't be here," she added, rather enjoying the conspiracy in the absence of the Holy Court.

"I know," Queen Katheryn said, shaking her head. "She only goes to visit her uncle, and then sends word there's a plague in Surpoint. That must be why no one from the south showed their face in the capital today." Samira could have sworn the old woman *winked* at her. "In any case, I must go prepare Deronn for the feast. They're announcing his regent, after all."

"It ought to be you, Your Majesty," Samira said, smiling.

"Well," she scoffed, "we'll see who has the gall to oppose me. Deronn's never had a mother, and what's a boy king without a scheming dowager? Whoever it is will have to contend with me before they lay a finger on the lad. Enjoy the feast, Princess." She shuffled closer to embrace her, and Samira let her, even more confused, until she heard the woman whispering in her ear. "Lord Gerron says if you're in his camp by dawn, he'll take you with them to Surpoint."

"Thank you," Samira whispered back, and with a friendly wave, Queen Katheryn hobbled away back to the Payne guards waiting for her across the hall.

The feast was far less exciting than her Declaration had been, and the long line of courtiers swearing themselves to Deronn before the high table made excusing herself impossible. Samira suffered through hours of dignified silence until the food had been cleared away and the crowd began to get livelier. She was watching Riyan speaking softly with a Priest to her left, and was just about to ask him what the meeting had been about, when the Priest turned to the hall and bellowed, "ATTENTION!" With the exception of a few guests who were already drunk, within seconds the noise had fallen to near silence. The Priest smiled in satisfaction and said, "His Holiness would like to make an announcement."

Riyan stood, and all eyes turned to him. Samira tensed, and she started searching the room for quick escape routes; what if they'd told him about her? Maybe she could make a break for the stables if she hurried... It wasn't until she saw Deronn's eyes, wide and watching Riyan eagerly, that she realized what this must be and relaxed. "My council and I have deliberated and we have chosen a Lord Regent for King Deronn. His uncle, Lord Reval Wright of Surpoint, will be called to serve until His Majesty reaches his Declaration day."

The applause from the guests was muted, and Samira saw the

grumbling start; the only family not here and they got the honor of Regent. The Hornish guests were especially displeased, always shocked by anything that smelled of upward mobility. But they weren't the only ones. Deronn was lucky that the Paynes had already thrown in with Mychal, or they would likely have been seriously offended, and a good many of them were already seriously drunk. Reval Wright was a strange choice, and Samira had to wonder why it was made as her fiance returned to his seat.

The crowd went back to their drinking and laughing eventually, and Deronn stood up and walked slowly over to them, still trying to balance the crown on his head. "Thank you, Your Holiness," he said, inclining his head as much as he dared. "But it's nearly midnight. I'll be going to bed."

"Of course, Deronn," Riyan said, smiling. "You can call me Riyan, you know. You're a king now. Congratulations."

Deronn nodded, but he still looked uneasy. He managed to smile shyly at Samira before he said, "Goodnight," to both of them and left the hall, his regalia dragging behind him.

"Was that what the council was about?" Samira asked when he had gone. "The regency?"

"No, we'd decided that weeks ago," Riyan said, with a kind of tired tone she'd heard her father's voice take on in his most stress-filled moments. He hesitated and said, "I wouldn't want to scare you, Samira."

"What is it?" she asked, letting her concern show, knowing he would think it was for him.

"I've been seeing strange things in the godwine this summer," he said. She could have sworn that his eyes clouded over even more as he spoke. "Surpoint, and Daemons, and... a Halwood king riding against my army." *Shit.* Samira made herself perfectly still, gripping her hands to keep them from shaking, and focused intently on clearing her mind the way Farrah had taught her. Riyan continued on, not even noticing the change in her. He was gazing into the back of the hall now; she might as well not have been there at all. "I thought it was a warning about letting Deronn grow up with too much power. That's why we chose a man like Wright-- I had almost been convinced Queen Katheryn would do. But..."

"There's something else?" she asked. She hoped her voice still sounded steady.

He nodded. "There's no plague in Surpoint. I don't know what's going on down there, it could be nothing... but after what happened at the Mages' Canyon, I can't risk ignoring a problem. I gave the order for the Holy Army to go down, they should be there in a fortnight or so. And then we'll see." He sighed and leaned back in his chair, oblivious to Samira's panic. "You'll think I'm mad about this next bit. I *hope* I'm wrong. But there have been rumors... were you there for the executions in 489? The prince, and Queen Mina?"

"No," Samira said, as her stomach sank, and Riyan shrugged.

"I was," he muttered. "It looked real to me, but..." He stood up suddenly then and offered her his hand. "It's no matter. You should get some sleep, Princess," he said. "I'll see you in the morning."

Samira let him help her up as her mind raced, and smiled as sweetly as she could. "Goodnight, Riyan," she said, and processed down the center aisle, making sure the guests saw her go up the stairs to the keep just as Queen Katheryn had advised. It might matter later, when they were questioned by the Holy Guard, that they would be in positions to deny her escape.

She laid awake that night, waiting, listening until she heard Riyan going to bed in the chambers just down the hall. After several minutes of silence, she rose quietly and dressed again in a plain dress and cloak, with only necessities in the satchel she swung over her shoulder. She prayed there wouldn't be guards at the end of the hall, and thankfully, Deronn's new and scrambling court meant that no one had yet been appointed to watch the guest chambers. She made it down the back steps and out through the kitchens, like Jullia had suggested, and within minutes she was outside the castle walls.

Samira wasted no time making for the Warren, the poorhouse at the back door of the King's Cathedral. She could see its tiled roof from her vantage point on the castle grounds atop the city's hills, with the chimney with smoke still climbing up to the sky even then, at least an hour past midnight. She hoped that was a sign that Farrah's friend really was waiting for her there. But she heard drunken soldiers in the front courtyard of the keep then and stopped. Did she even have to go to the Warren, or could she just go and find Gerron Payne? Maybe it would be easier to bypass the resistance fighters altogether. But then, if anyone saw her in the Payne camp, the Holy Guard would be after them the very next morning. And Mychal would need the resistance someday, if anything did come of this meeting at Surpoint.

She was still trying to decide when a looming shadow, which she had thought to be a coronation guest pissing on the castle wall, started to make its way closer to her path. There was no way she could risk running into someone who very well could recognize her. She had to keep moving forward. Whoever was waiting at the Warren, she was sure they could help her get back to the camps before morning.

The streets between the castle and the cathedral were wide, paved, and inviting at first, and Samira had walked them only hours before. But the further she got from the castle, the more different the roads felt at night. The revelers filling the nicer streets were replaced by much less savory lurkers, few and far between to be sure, but their faces looked mean and hungry. Maybe it was just her imagination. But still, she worried about how much longer the walk would be.

After she turned down her third side street, she noticed the shadow from before walking on the opposite side of the road, several steps behind her but keeping pace all the while. She got more nervous when he turned down the fourth street with her, and on the fifth she started to look for an escape. She couldn't see the cathedral's spire anymore-- all the buildings were far too close together here and two or three stories tall at least. She felt like a rat in a maze, and was about to turn and run in the opposite direction when she heard someone hiss, "*Hollis!*"

She was so unaccustomed to being addressed by her last name that she whirled around immediately, and saw an old man, wearing what looked like Stewards' robes, peering out at her from the alleyway to her right. He jerked his head toward her and with a final glance at the shadow, still only walking but picking up pace now, she followed him into the alley. The old man scurried away as soon as she started to follow him, and she had to run just to keep up with his stride. "Who are you?" she whispered.

"Keep your hood up," was all he said to her, and she did, looking behind her as much as she dared while they ran. She couldn't see the shadow anymore, which was a blessing, but also meant he could be anywhere.

Finally, the man stopped at the doorway to an old two-story structure, wattle-and-daub with a flat clay-tile roof. As he unlocked a heavy wooden door and pulled her inside, she looked up and saw that the building was built up against the back walls of the Cathedral. She had made it to the Warren after all.

There were no candles in the room they had entered, and no windows either; when the old man shut the door they were plunged into darkness. "A light, we need a light..." she heard him mutter, and after a moment she could hear him fumbling with cabinets and drawers.

"You're the one I was supposed to meet here?" she asked. "Farrah Vance told you about me?"

"She did. She also told me you were reckless," he muttered.

"Good thing I went ahead to find you. You could have brought a guard, you know." Samira *had* thought about bringing Dominic and Harry along, as she had brought them to Queenshearth, but there hadn't been time to explain and it didn't feel right to force them to run away too.

"Who was that?" she asked, shuffling further from the door.

"I have no idea. I hope we never find out," he said. His voice was gruff, and he went right to the point when he spoke, but there was something kind about him, and she began to breathe again. "Ah. Here we are," he said, and in the next moment a candle filled the room with warm light.

Samira jumped and pressed her back against the wall when she saw the man in the light. The first thing she noticed about the old man was his face; a good deal of it was scarred, burnt and mottled pink, and the splotches spanned all the way across his neck and down under his robes. The second was the robes themselves: they weren't Stewards' robes, they were blue, with a gilded belt and empty scabbard secured round the middle. "You're a Priest," she exclaimed, disgusted.

He chuckled. "I have to say most people mention the maiming first."

She narrowed her eyes and appraised the burns as he remained calm, his face unchanged in the candlelight. "Daemons?" she guessed.

"Mages," he corrected. "For my sins. I was the one leading soldiers against them, after all." He watched as she stared at him, blinking, and said patiently, "I've changed more than a little since then. I make a terrible spy anywhere but here, so identifiable. But the resistance was so thoroughly chased out of Queenshearth that they hardly even look for us anymore."

"You're going to help me escape?" Samira asked, still uneasy with the idea. "Why?"

The old Priest paused. "Do you believe in the Mother and Father, Princess?"

Samira's thoughts drifted back to the day at the Pool of the Mother and she said quietly, "Yes. I didn't think so but... I do."

"And yet, you're helping Mychal Halwood. You mean to break a holy engagement. You do not recognize the Godhead's authority."

"I don't think any man has the right to tell me what the Mother and Father would think of anything," she said hotly, and then paused, expecting a reaction. But the Priest just nodded.

"I agree. The concept of a Godhead is blasphemous in and of itself. But the Priesthood wanted power. And we didn't want to wait for a king to decide to give it to us. You heard the new vows at the Coronation. They want Riyan Duane to be the Last King and lead us all to salvation, but you know that won't happen."

"Yes," she said slowly, frowning. She still couldn't see what any of this had to do with Mychal.

"The people I work with, many of them Priests like me, we feel the same way. We would back your friend's claim to the throne under one condition," he said.

Samira started to get excited, in spite of her instinct not to trust anyone in Priest's robes. "What condition?"

"His claim is not to the Hartlands."

She frowned again. "Then where?"

She saw a spark in the man's eyes as he replied, "Farisia. One Farisia. *That* will be the Mother and Father's will fulfilled on the continent. Not Duane. Restore the kingdom that human wars severed. And who better to do it than the child they claim to have killed for the sake of the Faith?"

Samira stared at the man for a long moment. She wasn't entirely sure he wasn't crazy. But it did sound something like what Farrah had said to her back on Winding Row. She was starting to see that this was what the resistance had always meant when they were looking for 'Lyha'. But she felt a knot in her stomach when she realized why he was telling her all of this. "What would you have me do, then?" she asked, already guessing at the answer.

"Don't go to Surpoint. Return to the castle and marry Duane. And then, when the time is right, kill him. No one else would even get close."

Samira started to panic as she struggled to speak, shaking her head. "No, I... I can't marry him."

"You must," he insisted. "If you leave here tonight, Duane will have months to plan to attack and a real justification for doing so."

All she could do was keep shaking her head. *No, no, Mychal...* "I can't just *kill* him."

"Of course you can," he said. "Anyone else needs a weapon, a way inside the temple. You'll already be in his bed. And all you'd need is water."

Samira glanced down at her hands, then back up at the maimed man in horror. "I can't," she insisted, and he stepped closer. She flinched and he backed away, raising his hands.

"I won't decide for you," he said, still backing away. "I'll take you wherever you decide to go tonight. But I can't tell you how many lives you will save if you stay."

As she struggled to respond, someone began to bang on the door from the outside, and another bolt of panic shot through her. "What do we--" she whispered, before the old man held up a hand and she fell silent. Without another word, he gestured at two large barrels along the wall behind him, and she hurried across the room to duck behind them as he opened the door.

The shadow from before, a younger man in a newly polished Holy Guard uniform, sauntered into the Warren, hand on the hilt of his sword. "Can I help you, sir?" the Priest asked, and the soldier pushed past him.

"Where is she, old man?" he asked.

"Who, sir?" he replied. From her vantage point, Samira saw him glance surreptitiously at her and then up to the tops of the barrels. She looked up and saw spigots on her side, each held in place by just one large cork. Easy-- if she dared.

"You know who I'm talking about," the man barked. "The princess! I followed her here, what's she doing with you? I'll have your head for hiding her. She's to be the Godhead's wife."

Samira winced as she braced herself against the wall. With a deep breath and a quick prayer, she ripped the spigot loose and kicked the first barrel as hard as she could.

The great wooden thing burst when it hit the stone floor, and water rushed across the ground, flooding the room and drenching Samira head to toe. After a yelp of shock, the soldier began to smile a sinister grin. "That was stupid, Your Highness," he said. He raised his sword up to the old man's throat, and with a final desperate look from the Priest, Samira screwed her eyes shut and snapped both of her arms up in one violent motion.

The water in the room rushed up toward the ceiling, gravity forgotten, in one large pillarlike wave and soaked the soldier from head to toe. He stared at her, eyes wide, for a moment before he sputtered, "You just... you'll die for that, you witch!" Samira wasn't sure what to do next. She turned to the old man, who swirled his hands around each other in a small circle. She had to stop herself from recoiling.

"No, I can't," she pleaded, and the soldier looked from one to the other, clearly lost.

"If he tells them, they'll kill you," the Priest warned, and Samira took another deep breath and nodded. She knew. She pulled the water back toward her and copied his motions, forming a circle in the air in front of her chest.

The massive wave surged forward, a loosely held dripping ball of water that she pushed toward the soldier until it completely engulfed his head. She couldn't see inside it very well, but she did see his eyes bulge in horror before he started thrashing wildly, trying to pull it off his head and stumbling around the room. She kept the water around him, swirling it to keep her barely mastered creation from falling down around his shoulders until she could tell it was finally almost over. The water was clear enough for her to see one last terrified look on the man's face, and grimacing in disgust, she pushed the water forward again, down his throat, finishing his death. The drowned man slumped to the ground, and Samira, breathing heavily, let the water fall with him.

The maimed man walked slowly over to her, put a gentle hand on her shoulder, and said, "Like I said, he would have had you killed. It was the only choice you had."

Samira didn't answer him. She was trying to force herself to look at something, anything, but the body in front of them. Her wandering eyes finally landed on an old, fraying banner hanging on the far wall, wine-red and midnight blue and intricately composed. It took her a moment to recognize the crest, and when she did she looked back to the Priest.

*Mychal, forgive me.*

"Would you be able to carry a message for Mychal to the Paynes for me?"

The maimed man smiled. "Yes, Your Highness."

"And could you get that to him as well?" she asked, gesturing to the banner behind them. He smiled wider and nodded. "Alright then," she said, trying to keep her voice steady. "I'll need a quill and ink. What should I do when I get to the Temple?"

"We have people in New Astoria that will help you," the old man said, as he searched for an inkwell for her. "A girl named Senna, in a house of ill fame run by a Lady May. All of our messages will go through her."

"Thank you," Samira said softly, and she sat down to write on the other side of the parchment Farrah had given her. When she had finished, she rolled it up and gave it to him, and together they walked back to Hartshold Keep. With her bundle in his arms, the Priest continued on to the Payne camp, and Samira walked back to her hidden door alone. Her hand flew up to the amulet round her neck when she entered the castle, and she clutched it tight as she snuck back to her chambers and waited for morning to come.

# 25

## Mychal

The shores of the Triad had been in sight almost the entire time they'd been on the boats, but that didn't really make things much easier for Mychal. He had never been at sea before, and he already knew he didn't like it. It had only been a week aboard the ships, but he felt like no matter how long they sailed he would never get his bearings. The *Queen Aria* was a beautiful ship, with waxed wood to guard against Daemonfire and a carved prow of the Dillons' mythical foremother leading the way, but she was quite old now and rocked more than Mychal would have liked. He didn't like looking clumsy around his men, so he spent most of his days in his cabin. But when the ships spread out enough that he didn't think anyone could see the deck, he managed to get himself up to breathe fresh air, even if he did have to grip the bow for support. They were meant to reach Surpoint today, and landfall couldn't come soon enough.

"They want to know if you're coming back to the council," he heard Luke say from behind him, and turned around to watch his friend walk with much surer step up to his side.

"No, I don't think so," Mychal said. "I want to watch the harbor come into view."

"Shouldn't be long now," Luke said, nodding. It was quiet for a moment, and then he added, "Just as well. Thorne and Neill, they're being very..." Mychal raised an eyebrow at him as he struggled for a word and landed on, "Eirosian."

Mychal smirked. "Luke, you can just say they're sleeping together. Everyone knows that."

Luke went pink and sputtered, "I know..."

"And honestly I don't see why it's such a terrible thing–"

Luke cut him off, insisting, "I didn't say anything!" Mychal laughed as the other boy kept blushing. After a moment, he said, "It's just a little odd that Thorne, I mean, *Bastian Thorne*'s son..."

Mychal shrugged. "I don't know. I think anybody can love anybody."

There was another pause before Luke asked, "Were you really in love with Senna? Back at Lady May's?"

He laughed. "No, we were friends. I let you believe what you wanted to."

"Right. Just, because, that was alright when you were just Mychal Owyn, but..."

"Yes," Mychal said, trying to stay lighthearted about the whole thing. His mind was moving to more serious places the longer they talked, and this close to Surpoint, he wanted to stay hopeful.

But Luke didn't relent. "Well, have you ever–?"

"Yes."

"Really? Who?"

Mychal sighed. "Well... you met her. In Hollisport," he said, his discomfort clear in his voice, and it didn't take long for Luke to put the pieces together.

"Samira Hollis?" he asked, eyes wide. "I mean... you know she might already be married."

Mychal blinked, realizing as he did how strange it was to him that *that* was the only problem Luke saw with what he'd said. He was allowed to love her now, even if it meant treason. Changing had changed that much for him, as odd as that felt. It *was* odd. He'd thought he'd have to hide this forever, ever since he was small.

"She's not married," he said firmly, turning to look at Luke directly. "She's going to be at Surpoint."

Luke nodded slowly, eyes still wide. "Wow," he finally said. "I... I hope there's thousands there, then, or we really are all going to hang."

"Or worse," Mychal muttered, trying not to flinch. He couldn't imagine what would happen to him if they lost now. But they'd come much too far already, and there was only one path forward.

"I think that's it, Your Majesty," Luke said suddenly, and Mychal snapped out of his thoughts and looked out at the haze over the horizon. The gray mass of the shore in the distance was coming to a point on the far edge of their sightline, and as they moved closer, the outlines of a town and rocky cliffsides began to take form.

"You're right," Mychal said, feeling the excitement beginning to bubble up inside him. "That's Surpoint. Get the others." Luke ran off, and Mychal moved carefully to the front of the boat to tell the Eirosian captain to call the fleet back into formation. He watched his ships drift closer together, a hundred from King Silas's navy, some already carrying his men and many more ready to transport the Hartlanders. The navy formed tight lines around their flagship while he waited for the others to come up.

A few moments later, he heard the steps up from the galleys rattling and his small band of councilors emerged: Luke and Graham, the last of their group of squires who'd survived the Mages' Canyon; Lord Carrolll, the old mage commander; and Alexander Neill, with the least likely of all of them, Edris, standing stalwart by his side. "Your Majesty," Neill said, nodding to him.

"Surpoint's just there," Mychal said, indicating the town on the horizon. "We'll land soon enough."

"And what happens then?" Neill asked.

"My sister's already told them we're coming," Mychal said. "I suppose they'll send a boat out to meet us, or a welcome party at the harbor." Neill exchanged a look with Edris, and Mychal frowned. "What?"

"We should pull back, Your Majesty," Neill said. "Let scouting ships go in first."

"Why?"

"You don't know what's waiting for you there," the knight said.

"My uncle's waiting for me there," he said, trying and failing not to sound incredulous.

"It's not a small thing you're asking for, Mychal," Edris interjected. "And, I mean... have you ever actually met him?"

Mychal could feel his anxiety start to rise, and he took a deep breath. "No," he admitted. "Alright, fine. Scouts go in first."

"Captain!" Neill shouted, as Edris sighed in relief. "Fall back!"

The fog cleared as they got closer to the shore, and sooner than they'd thought, they had reached the South Bay off the coast of the Hartlands. Surpoint shone like a jewel at the height of the cliffs, a fortress of a city ringed by iron and steel gates perched on its famous quarries and the Forges that were the envy of the world. The sheer face of the rocks plunged down into the bay some two hundred feet below, sleek and ash gray and shining in the sun. The port was lively with markets and piers, and plenty of ships were already anchored on the shore, which Mychal took as a good sign that maybe his armies really had come. He tried to steady himself as he watched the tower in the center of the city grow larger, the keep where his mother's brother, his sister, and, if the gods were kind, Samira too, all waited for him.

He was still gazing up at the city when the *Queen Aria* lurched to a halt, and he started to hear shouting coming from the other boats around them. The rest of the council looked just as concerned as he was, and he turned to the captain, just a few paces away. "What's happening?" he asked.

"They've dropped a net over the harbor, Your Majesty," the man said, pointing ahead to where the two ships leading the fleet were stopped as well. If Mychal looked closely enough, he could see loose netting tangled on the ships' prows and draping in a long sagging line across the entire entry into the bay.

"I thought they knew we were coming," Edris said.

"They do. They should," Mychal said, and the nervous feeling in his gut only grew stronger. Had Jullia even made it to Surpoint? He hated being in the dark, he had his whole life, but this was especially infuriating.

However worried he was, though, Neill still seemed to outdo him. "Maybe it's a trap. Should we turn back?"

"No," Mychal said firmly. "We wait." They had nowhere else to go, anyway, except back to Eirosia where the Daemons would inevitably attack again. Surpoint was their only option. And so they waited. And waited and waited, while the men got more restless and the sun dropped lower in the sky. Standing at his watch on the flagship, Mychal saw the pier empty of all life before the sun had even set. Something was wrong here.

Once it had gone dark on the water as well as in the city, a flicker of movement at the westernmost pier caught his attention. When he squinted, he could make out a small wooden fishing boat, paddling gamely out to meet the armada before her with a small white banner flapping off a pole at her rear. The scouts started shouting at the flagship, and Mychal waved to show he understood. "Get closer," he told the captain as the fishing boat approached, and Graham, the only one of the council left on deck, ran to get the others. Slowly, the *Queen Aria* creaked forward until her shadow loomed over the little boat in its path. The net, still raised, stretched across the water between them.

For a moment, all was silent. Then, a voice called out from the fishing boat. "*Long live King Mychal!*"

Mychal wanted to relax, but he was still cautious as he leaned over the prow and shouted back, "Who are you?"

"Castor Keaton Wright," the man replied. "The heir to the Forges."

Mychal heard a ripple of relief go through the men around him, almost palpable, but he still wasn't satisfied. "Why is your father refusing us entry?"

"There's a situation at our gates," Castor said. "My father asked me to bring you ashore myself, Your Majesty. I'm sorry it had to wait until nightfall."

Mychal hesitated. This was clearly his only way into the city, but something was still off about all of this to him. At any rate, he wasn't going alone. "How much room do you have in your boat, Castor?"

"Room for yourself and two more," he called back.

Mychal moved away from the prow and faced his council. "Alright. Who's coming?"

"I should go," Luke said immediately. "I'm the only other Hartlander here."

"And I can explain the Dillon banners," Neill offered.

Mychal nodded. "Fine. Good."

"Mychal--" Edris protested, but stopped at a look from Neill. Mychal went over to him and placed a hand on his shoulder, a distinctly manly gesture that still felt foreign to him at times, but it did get the prince's attention.

"I need you here with the men. If something goes wrong, you need to take command. There's something off about this."

"Then don't go," Edris argued.

"These are my men," Mychal said, stepping away. "They're here for me." The captain lowered them down in a tiny ranging boat off the port side, and when they reached the water they approached the net cautiously until Castor swung his boat around and they climbed through one of the wider holes in the barrier. Mychal liked these smaller boats even less somehow, but he tried to tell himself they were only minutes from shore. He settled down as best he could behind Castor, as Luke and Neill climbed in behind him.

"Welcome to Surpoint, Your Majesty," Castor said amiably as he rowed them back to the harbor. "I'm sorry about the circumstances." When he turned around to flash him a cheerful smile, Mychal was struck by just how familiar he looked. He could see the family resemblance immediately in the dark eyes and thick dark hair they shared, and while Castor was probably half a foot taller than him, he looked almost exactly the way Mychal had pictured his twin would look if he were alive today. He couldn't decide if that comforted him or made him self-conscious, and he tried to remind himself that Castor was nearly twenty-five and no one expected him to look that mature.

When they reached the shore, four of the Wrights' household guards greeted them, chest plates displaying the smith's hammer on a blood-orange field that Mychal remembered from long ago as the crest on his mother's things. The guards were silent and walked with purpose, escorting their party across the deserted pier and into the mouth of a cave in the cliffside. Castor led them up wide, crumbling steps, further and further into the caverns, opening higher and higher still as they went. When they had almost reached the top, Mychal had to grip the wall for balance as the rocks beneath them shook violently. It was just for a second, but long enough to disturb him and to send Luke tumbling into the steps in front of them.

"What was that?" Mychal asked, still a little shaken as Castor and the guards continued on like nothing had happened.

"Sorry, Your Majesty. Work in the quarries shifts the rocks around," he explained, far too flippant for Mychal's liking, and they pressed on. He knew they were technically still underground, but each flight of steps climbed only reinforced the feeling of *height* that always so disturbed him, and he wanted nothing more in that moment but to reach their destination.

The passage narrowed as they climbed from that point on, and eventually split into two paths. The one they followed ended in a great metal door, cold and rusting with an ancient steel lock. Castor produced a key and with one great turn, the door cracked open with a loud snap. Two of the guards pushed on it slowly, straining under its immense weight, and they saw that they had been led directly into the reception hall of the Keep of the Forge.

There were twenty or so people standing around the hall, all whispering intently to each other. Someone had draped thick black curtains over the windows, so the only light in the room came from the torches and the hearth on the wall opposite the doors. The passage had opened below a window on that side, so when they stepped in most of those present had to turn to look at them. It grew very quiet when Mychal stepped into the light.

One of the onlookers, a tall black-haired man wearing a linen black doublet in the sun-conscious southern style, crossed the room with confidence and embraced Castor. "Thank the Father, you're safe," he said, smiling, before stepping away from him and regarding the other three. "You must be my nephew," he said, his voice softer than before, when his eyes fell on Mychal.

"Lord Reval," Mychal said, bowing his head. "It's an honor to meet you at last."

The Lord of the Forge smiled again, the ghost of his mother's grin shocking him a bit as he did. "The same to you, Mychal." He turned back to Castor and said, "Well, I had my doubts, but look at him. I suppose we have one fewer family tragedy after all."

"Mychal!" a young girl's voice called then, and from behind Wright, his little sister Jullia came running. She jumped on him when she reached them, hugging him tightly until he thought he might suffocate, and as she did she whispered to him, giggling, "You look great!"

"Jullia!" Mychal exclaimed, finally starting to buckle under the girl's weight, and she released him, grinning from ear to ear. "Gods, you've grown so much." It was true; his sister, at thirteen, was practically of a height with him now. He saw the lords behind them chuckling and told her, smiling too, "That wasn't very ladylike."

She raised an eyebrow, and he hoped she'd leave it there. He'd gotten the point-- not much room to talk. "That's alright. They already love *me*," she said. "It's you that has to win them over now."

He sighed. She was right, of course, but his own charm had always needed work. "How close are we?" he asked in a low voice.

"The Old Dog needs some convincing," she admitted, quiet enough that only he could hear. "Think honor and tradition." Raising her voice, she added loudly, "Most of us have been here since last month for you."

Mychal's eyes lit up as he remembered the other reason he'd come. "Is Samira here?" he asked, scanning the room for her face. Before Jullia could answer, an older woman in Steward's robes presented herself to him, and when she'd finished bowing, he recognized her and panicked. Petra Keaton, his father's High Steward, looked in his eyes and he immediately froze.

The woman was staring at him, with a kind of sad, stunned expression. He knew she recognized him, if she hadn't already been told. Would she keep his secret here? Mychal fought to keep himself calm, and asked very carefully, "And you're the Steward Jullia's told me about? I'm sorry, I... don't have very many memories from the castle."

Jullia had appeared at Petra's side, and placed a gentle hand on her arm, which seemed to bring her back to herself. "Er, yes," she said. "Apologies, Your Majesty. You... look so like your twin sister."

"I've heard," Mychal said, exhaling sharply with relief. He wished he could tell her how grateful he was. "I hope we find her safe someday."

Fortunately, at that moment an older man, with thinning hair and a Golden Forests brooch on his cloak, cheerfully interrupted them. "I'm Donnan Penn, Your Majesty, it's a pleasure to meet you." Mychal managed to smile in sincere thanks again to Petra before he was led around the room to meet the many lords of the Hartlands. He was horribly paranoid the entire time, especially after Petra had recognized him, that someone else would know him from some feast or other years ago, but the consensus seemed to be that he was clearly a Halwood, so he was also clearly the lost prince.

Gerron Payne stood apart from the others, a short and stout man with a permanent expression of suspicion, and the delegation approached him last. "Lord Gerron," Mychal began, as respectfully as he could, and bowed his head to him. "Thank you for coming. I'm sorry I couldn't petition you at Brookbridge myself."

"Not the best start," Gerron said, nodding, his old man's low rumble sounding just as rough as Mychal's new voice, like rounding the other side of a hill. The Old Dog did bow his head, though, and when he came up again he looked over at Jullia and said, "Well, he's certainly one of you." His eyes wandered to Luke and he smiled, genuinely, at his son. "My boy. I'm so glad you're alive." Luke embraced his father, and the Old Dog added, "Let's hope you stay that way, running with this one."

"Where's Devon?" Luke asked, looking around for his brother.

"He's back at Brookbridge. Someone's got to be lord in my stead. Everyone's fine." Looking back at Mychal, he said, "You have quite the fleet of ships for a farmboy. Though gods know why they have Dillon whiteflowers on their sails."

Mychal glanced back at Neill, and the knight stepped forward. "My lord, I can explain. My name is Sir Alexander--"

"Is this a *long* story?" Gerron interrupted.

"Well..." Neill sputtered, and he held up a hand.

"Another time, then," he said gruffly. "We have other matters."

"Yes, you said there was a situation?" Mychal asked the Wrights, grateful for the distraction.

"Lord Gerron arrived last. He brought bad news with him," Lord Reval confirmed, and Gerron nodded.

"We were held up at Queenshearth. A Holy Guardsman went missing the night of the coronation, and they questioned my men for the better part of two days. Apparently we were suspected because of some nonsense about the regency. But what do I see when we finally march out but a Holy Army force, heading down the coastal road straight for Surpoint."

"If they kept to those roads, they'll be here any moment now," Lord Reval said. "We already had a scout here earlier today, arguing with our sentries refusing him entry. We can't risk the Army seeing Eirosian ships in port."

"They'll see them out in the bay too," Neill pointed out.

"At least we won't be harboring them," Castor argued.

"What do we do, then?" Mychal asked.

"Leave," Lord Reval said, like it was obvious. "Now. There are thousands of men here, and that would cast things in our favor but they haven't trained together. If we fight the Holy Army we'll be crushed."

"The Holy Army is half of what it was," Mychal protested. "I was there at the Canyon. We were slaughtered."

"Jonn Thorne isn't a man to be trifled with, no matter what the numbers are," Gerron snorted. "Speaking of which, I heard his cousin liberated a prison camp on the border. Was that you too?"

"Edris is with us," Mychal confirmed. "But that's part of the long story, my lord."

Gerron's resting scowl tipped up into a smirk. "So your men have fought Valleyguard?"

"No," Mychal said. "But they have fought Daemons." The whole hall fell silent as Lord Gerron laughed. "It's true, my lord," he said. "They call themselves Drowningmen. Daemonfire bounces off their backs."

Lord Gerron's eyes narrowed, and when he spoke again, his voice was full of suspicion, but Mychal thought he heard good humor in it. "What kind of mage king have you brought me, Princess?" he asked Jullia.

"It's not my magic," Mychal said.

"It'd better not be," he advised, "or you'll have a hard time calling yourself the Son of Faris." Mychal froze. Where had he heard *that*? Was Farrah here? He almost asked if Samira had told him, before a guardsman burst in through the double doors and rushed to Lord Reval's side. When the boy had finished whispering, the lord of the Forge turned back to Mychal, his face grim.

"Your men might have to fight Holy men after all," he said. "They're at the gates."

# 26

# Mychal

"Have they attacked?" Mychal asked, fighting to keep himself calm.

"No, not yet," Lord Reval said. "Apparently they'd like to speak with me."

"Then speak with them," Mychal said. "And make it last as long as you can." Raising his voice, he addressed the rest of the room. "We can get all of your forces out on our ships. Give the orders now."

The lords in the room scrambled for the doors, running off to other parts of the tower where their men were waiting. "You'll need these Forges, Your Majesty," Neill protested as they went. "We can't just give them to the Godhead. That's *why* they're here, to take them from you."

"We don't even know what they know yet," Mychal said. "How would they have found out we're here?"

"The order came from the coronation. Maybe Samira told the Godhead what she knew," Castor suggested.

Mychal couldn't stop himself from whirling around at that. "She wouldn't have done that," he snapped. "Where is she? Is she with the forces?"

It hit him then. He could see it in their faces. "She didn't come, did she?" he asked softly.

Jullia bit her lip, and cast her eyes to the ground. "No, Mychal, she didn't."

He felt a horrible wave of bitterness rising in the pit of his stomach, and his heart started pounding and sending his head spinning, but he knew he couldn't deal with it right now. He pushed it away as best he could, and while he'd buried these feelings before, he found it much more difficult than before Hollisport. He still felt lightheaded, but he knew he had to speak to the lords. Mychal took a deep, steadying breath and said, "However much they know, talking to them will give us time. Is there a way to get the men on the ships without them seeing?"

"We'll open the far west side of the harbor," Castor said. "If the ships come in one at a time, the Army still won't be able to see them from where they are."

"Once we do get on the ships, where are we going?" Luke asked, and Mychal paused. *Shit.* He had no idea.

"The Lordless Isles," Lord Reval said suddenly, and they all looked at him, surprised. Lord Gerron, in particular, was staring at him like he'd grown three heads. But the man continued. "The last time the Holy Army came here, the mages left on ships and went to the Isles. Most of the exiles from the Priesthood's rule have found shelter there. They'll support you, Your Majesty."

Mychal thought about it; he couldn't help but be apprehensive when the Isles were mentioned, especially after the marauders had attacked him at Astor Post. The face of the first man he'd killed still came into his mind sometimes, an Islander and probably a resistance fighter. He didn't think he had much of a right to ask for their support after that. But he didn't have very many options left, either, and Farrah had also told him he'd find safety there. "Alright. We'll go to the Isles."

"Good, then," Lord Reval said. "I'll keep them talking for as long as I can. You all should get on board, now." Wright started for the double doors leading to the gates, and Neill and Castor started heading back to the passage.

"Mychal?" Neill asked, pausing in the archway, and he shook his head.

"I'm leaving on the last ship," Mychal said. "If the men end up having to fight they'll never follow me if I leave, and they'd be right not to." He saw Lord Gerron smile out of the corner of his eye, and thanked the gods that at least one of his problems appeared to be solving itself.

"Then I'm staying with you," Luke said.

"Luke, get on the bloody ship, you're not the king," his father barked.

"It's all right, Luke, go. Take Jullia and keep her safe," Mychal said, and his instinct on what to say had been right; his friend hesitated, but after a moment he nodded and led Jullia from the room. They had almost reached the door when an ear-piercing blast from a trumpet wailed through the walls of the tower. It was coming from the gates, Mychal knew, turning the room around in his head. Everyone froze to listen.

"*LORD REVAL WRIGHT!*" a crier shouted. "*His Holiness is calling you to serve as King Deronn's Lord Regent! We've seen the Eirosian fleet in the South Bay. Show yourself and we will help you free your city of these heretics!*"

No one moved as the trumpet blasted again, followed by silence, and within moments, Lord Reval walked slowly back into the hall.

"Castor," he said, his voice weak. "I have to ask too much of you, son."

"What do I do?" Castor asked, hurrying over to his father, at the ready in seconds.

"I need to tell them you've rebelled against me and stolen the city," Lord Reval said. "It's the only way they'll trust me."

"Father, we need you," Castor insisted.

"No," he said sharply. "We need *Deronn*. If it isn't me in the regency, it'll be Charles Thorne, or even Jacob Denastor, Morra help us. I will not give those monsters the Hartlands, not for a single day."

Castor was nodding slowly, even as Petra, his mother, was shaking her head and rushing up to both of them from the far side of the room. "Right," the young man said. "What now?"

"Let me go with them, as a hostage released. And then hold the Forge as long as you can," Lord Reval said. "We'll leave you enough men for a siege. When you've lost, and you will, go to the Isles, or wherever Mychal is then."

"He can't do this, Reval," Petra exclaimed. "He's still so young. He'll have no honor left."

"I'm already a bastard," Castor said, his voice tightly controlled. He wasn't looking at his mother. "I never had much honor to begin with."

Petra's eyes welled up and she said, "I'm staying with you."

"Petra--" Wright began to protest, but a look passed between them and he fell silent. He embraced his son, and then walked back across the hall, ripping his shirtsleeves and dirtying his clothes for the Army to see as he went. When he saw Mychal watching him go, he paused and said, "Queenshearth will be with you, Your Majesty." He passed through the double doors and was gone.

Castor wasted little time after that, running for the passage to coordinate the evacuation. Petra went up into the Keep without another word, and Jullia, Luke and Neill had already disappeared down the passage, leaving very few left in the hall. Mychal, still reeling from the news about Samira, eased himself down on a bench at the base of one of the blackened windows. His head spun even more now that he was able to let it run wild. Had something happened to her? Why hadn't she stayed with Jullia? Had he misunderstood?

He knew that he might never know. He tried to put it out of his mind, knowing he had responsibilities, staring down at his shoes as he heard the drawbridge opening below for Lord Reval. But he couldn't stop thinking about her. He could hear his blood thudding through his ears as his fingers started to turn numb, and he struggled to breathe. He hadn't had a moment like this since he was a child-- in fact, he thought with another pang, since his botched confession in the Golden Forests. He didn't know if he could survive a second severing from her.

"She didn't betray you, boy," someone said, and he looked up to see Lord Gerron standing in front of him, watching him closely, with an attendant trailing him holding a large rolled length of fabric.

"What?" Mychal asked, blinking in surprise.

"Your princess. She gave me this for you," he said, and motioned for the attendant to hand over the cloth. He started to unwrap it but Gerron said, "No, read this first." The Old Dog handed him a roll of old paper with writing on both sides. Mychal unrolled it and began to read, first finding a passage torn from a very old book.

*A true son of Faris will pull his fathers' sword from its tomb to unite his kingdom and drive the false prophet from the warlord's throne. The sword in question is thought to rest under the quarries of Surpoint, awaiting its rightful master. The Sword of Faris, though possibly not actually used by the man himself, dates from at least three hundred years prior to the time of this writing, 450 After Landing. The blade is, if still in workable shape, the strongest steel ever produced on the continent. Drawing included here.*

Mychal took in the detailed drawing of a fairly thin longsword, of the traditional style in the pommel and hilt, and carvings in the Old Language inscripted in the base of the blade. He turned the paper over, and his breath caught when he recognized her handwriting.

*Mychal,*

*I'm sorry. I want nothing more than to go with you, believe me, but there's something I have to do first. I sent along something that might help in the meantime: maybe you could set more than one thing right. And look for the sword. It'll be more convincing.*

*I meant every word that night. All my love.*

*Sami*

Pinned to the bottom of the note, folded tight against the paper, was Samira's whiteflower favour, the very same she'd given him months ago to bring to Farrah. He rolled both tight and tucked it into his pocket, knowing he'd read her words over and over in the next days and weeks. Blinking back tears he couldn't afford to let Gerron Payne see, he unfurled the fabric and broke into a smile. He couldn't believe it, she'd outdone him again.

He was looking at a banner, very old and fraying at the edges, but its design was still clear. The top section was the wine-red of the Halwoods, and the bottom the deep blue of the ancient house of Faris that preceded them. The same sword insignia used by his family to this day was set in front of a roaring wave, and framing the heraldry were Old Language symbols. He couldn't read all of them, but he knew some: *tol* was king, and there in the center were the Old Language name runes for Faris. He knew this crest. Mychal looked up at Lord Gerron, still in disbelief. "This is an old Farisian banner," he breathed. "Where did she get this?"

"I don't know," he said, shaking his head. "But she's right about one thing, you'll need to do some convincing. I like you," he said, rather grudgingly, "but it'll take more than that to get your crown.

Let alone *that* crown," he added, gesturing down at the banner on the ground. "So you'd better look for that sword."

Mychal felt his pulse pick up as he stood, rolling up the banner and tucking it under his arm. "You'll find me if we have to fight?"

Lord Gerron nodded once, chuckling. "I will." He paused for a moment before adding with a smirk, "Your Majesty." That made him laugh more, and Mychal ran for the passageway as the Old Dog watched him go.

It was harder to find his way around the caverns without Castor, but he managed. Going *down* was much better for his nerves than up. He had no idea what exactly he was looking for, though, and soon enough wandering around the caves was getting so frustrating he almost gave up. He tried going the other way at the fork that had led up to the reception hall, but turned around when it started getting lighter in the tunnel and he suspected he was moments from reaching the surface. Climbing down again, he followed the path they had come up, searching the walls for a crack, a side passage, anything.

As he went, the foundations of the quarries started shaking, and rocks tumbling off the walls, cracking in strange places-- a reliable sign of trebuchets pounding the ground. Mychal knew Silas's ships had some equipped themselves, but they weren't supposed to be seen if it could be helped. He hoped Surpoint would survive this.

He didn't find the sword, but before long he did find the hundreds of men being ferried through the smaller passageways out to the harbor. Mychal saw Neill and Castor standing together, ushering people outside, and came to a stop next to them, breathing heavily from all the climbing. "Your Majesty?" Neill prompted, looking confused.

"Neill," he said, trying to catch his breath. He decided asking was worth a shot; Farrah Vance had said mages and Islanders knew about it, so maybe Eirosians, with likely less altered histories, did, too. "Do you know anything about the Sword of Faris?"

The knight furrowed his brow and hesitated before he said, "There was someone... yes, I knew a mage from the Horn who was looking for it during the Priesthood's conquest. But–"

"Who?" Mychal asked, getting more impatient every minute.

"Loran Bennett," he said, and Mychal frowned.

"Samira's cousin?" he asked, and at the same time Castor snapped to attention and said, "It's here."

They both turned to look at him. "What?" Neill asked, clearly bewildered.

"Loran left for the Isles through us. He was *convinced* the Sword was here. He had to leave before he could reach it, but he knew exactly where it was."

"Show me," Mychal said, and the two of them rushed back up the passage. They ran several stories back up toward the fortress until Castor took a sudden right turn and led him into a small cavern, separate from the rest of the tunnels. One of the walls looked like it had recently broken apart, and his cousin slowed to a stop and stared at it, clearly surprised. "What?" Mychal asked, unable to see whatever it was he was looking at from his own angle.

Castor moved aside for him to come further into the cave. "I don't believe it," he said.

"It must have just broken down from the assault," Mychal said.

Castor still looked shocked. "I suppose, but... that stone wouldn't break for anything before. Not even Loran's magic." Mychal slowly approached and before long he could see a long iron case mounted in the wall, with a steel clasp sealing it. The rock around it looked crushed, pressed in on the case with unnatural force from all sides. But enough of the wall was gone now, felled by the Holy Army outside, that Mychal could reach out and undo the latch.

When he eased the box open, he was looking at a longsword,

obviously Surpoint steel, and not especially remarkable other than the fact that it was identical to the one in the drawing on the back of Samira's message. He looked at the inscription in the fuller of the blade and recognized many of the same symbols as the ones on the banner she'd given him. The pommel, faded but still recognizably a dark red and blue dyed leather, was rotting away from the metal, but the sword was still as sharp and shining as if it had been forged yesterday.

Mychal knew this was a moment when most people would pray, but all he could think of now was his brother. *Well, Mychal?* he asked, staring at the sword. *What should I do?*

He knew his twin couldn't answer him. But in that moment, just for a moment, it almost felt like he did.

Slowly, Mychal pulled the Holy Army-issued sword, probably forged in one of the Thorncliffe mountain mines, out of his scabbard and let it fall to the ground. He gripped the Sword of Faris tight, lifted it out of its casing, and turned it over in his hand. It was just the right size for him, as unlikely as that was, and light, too. He felt better about his chances with this blade that with any other he'd held. With one easy motion, he sheathed it at his waist. It was a near perfect fit. And before he could think too much better of it, he pulled Samira's favour from his pocket and wrapped it tight around the hilt. Now she would be with him, at least a little, and for now that would be enough.

When he looked up and saw Castor's face, he knew carrying the Sword would have just the effect he intended. Even his own cousin was looking at him now in a way no one ever had. Now all he needed was for everyone else to know— and he knew just how to come out of hiding.

"Castor," Mychal said, as they started walking back to the mouth of the cave, "I'm going to the fleet now. I need you to open the harbor."

"But Your Majesty, they'll see the ships coming in," Castor argued.

"And if they don't, they won't believe you really revolted, and they'll punish Silas Dillon for attacking you," Mychal said. "And besides, I'm not bringing in the whole fleet. Just one ship."

Castor was still looking at him curiously, but when they got back to the others, he started shouting for the net to be dropped. Neill, watching the last hundred or so Hartlander men going out to the ships, fell in with Mychal as he walked back onto the shore and asked, "Did you find it?"

"I found it," Mychal said, showing him the pommel, and Neill smiled.

"Brilliant," he said, but he still sounded cautious. "What is Castor opening the harbor for?"

"I need them to know I was here," he said, and before he had the chance to explain further they were boarding the last transport ship, sailing out of the west side of the bay just as the net dropped down from the rest of the harbor. "Take us to the *Queen Aria*," Mychal said.

"What's going on now?" Lord Gerron grumbled from his seat on the starboard side, but Mychal ignored him. They found their flagship stalling in the water, waiting for him and Neill with Jullia and all the other councilors on board. When they had reached her, Mychal hurried onto the deck and thrust Samira's banner into the captain's hands. "Raise this," he said. "And move into the harbor, as far east as you can." They paused for a moment as the whiteflower sail was lowered. Mychal watched, heart pounding, as the banner of Farisia rose up on the *Queen Aria*'s mast.

"What are you doing, Mychal? What is that?" Jullia asked, but she went quiet when she saw what it was.

He smiled. "It's a gift from Samira."

The *Queen Aria* was flying into the harbor now, as fast as she could, and when they could just make out the soldiers standing in the field at the gates of the Keep, Mychal ordered the boat swing around until the sail was clearly visible. "Fire the trebuchet, now," he ordered, and the captain, and his council, looked at him in shock. "Do it!" he exclaimed, and the soldier standing by loaded the bundle of thatch and pitch into the catapult and let it fly.

They all watched as it whistled through the air, and when it hit the Holy Army up along the top of the cliffs Mychal felt joy like he hadn't in ages. They could hear the commotion it had caused from all the way down on the ship, and judging by the chaos of the Army's response, he knew they must have seen the banner.

Before even a full minute had passed, a voice amplified beyond nature shouted down from the top of the cliff, powerful and furious. "*MYCHAL HALWOOD!*"

He knew that voice. Edris seemed to too, but before he could speak, Mychal had already turned to Lord Carroll. "Can you carry my voice to them on the air?"

"Yes, Your Majesty," Carroll said. "One of Duane's mages is doing the same." The two of them stood right at the front of the ship, and Mychal's next words carried all the way up to the Holy Army.

"Do you remember me, Lord Marshal?"

Jonn Thorne was silent for a long moment. When he spoke again, his voice was colored with disgust. "Reinhold's squire. All this time you were right under my nose."

Mychal was getting excited now; he had dreamed of the day he could speak to him this way. "I suppose a common serving boy wasn't worth your notice."

That only made Thorne angrier. "You ungrateful traitor! Every moment you've lived since I sentenced you and your mother has been stolen time. And just like then, you've run away again! Deserter!"

"I left the Army of a false god!" Mychal shouted back.

"You are nothing but a heretic and a pretender to the throne," the Lord Marshal sneered.

Mychal shook his head, and with a grin, he said, "I'm the Son of Faris come home again. And the men who fight for you should think about where their loyalty really belongs. Come with us and free Farisia!"

There was no response to that, except that almost immediately, the first responding trebuchet fired from the top of the cliffside. The *Queen Aria* sped away, arrows and cannonballs licking at her heels, and the rest of Mychal's fleet followed. His councilors were just as exultant as he was, and Jullia was beaming at him. The cheering from the other ships around him almost made him forget that the night had felt more like a loss than a victory. He had most likely lost Surpoint, after all, and for now he'd lost Samira. But he was still alive, and he was someone for the Priesthood to fear, and whatever else would come, that was a victory.

He watched the coast of the Triad disappear on the horizon, smiling as they sailed for the Isles. He'd be back.

# Epilogue

Minutes before they were due to make landfall, there was a knock on Mychal's cabin door.

"Come in," he called out, not really paying attention, struggling against the buttons on the wine and gold doublet's breast. He saw Edris enter the room in the reflection of the looking glass.

"We're landing soon," he said, watching him with a smirk for a few moments before asking, "Do you need help with that?"

"Yes, please," he sighed, surrendering, and turned to face Edris as he started to deftly do up the many buttons and hooks up and down the doublet's seam.

"It's not difficult, you know," he laughed.

"I've never had to wear one of these before," he said, feeling himself going red as he spoke. "Lord Penn gave it to me for the landing." Edris nodded. "I've only really been in armor as a... I mean, since I left Queenshearth."

"Right. Honestly, Mychal, looking at you now? It's easy to forget."

Mychal didn't know why, but that didn't sit right with him. He didn't want to *forget*, just... change. He tried to shake it off. Things to think about, when there was time. "Well, I just took the last of Farrah Vance's potion," he said instead. "I'm going to have to find a new mage soon, if any of this is going to last."

"There are plenty of those in the Isles," Edris pointed out. "I'm sure you'll find someone."

"Except that every new person I tell puts me, puts *us*, in more danger."

"I don't think you have much to worry about," he told him, stepping away from the fully secured doublet. "Between Illon's Fast and what you did at Surpoint, you don't have to worry about loyalty."

He knew it wouldn't work like that. But he appreciated what he'd meant. Mychal looked at Edris's earnest expression and said, as gently as he could, "Thank you, for everything."

"It's nothing," he said, clearly uncomfortable.

"It's not. Really, Edris. Thank you." After a moment, he asked, "So you and Neill are sailing back from the Isles?"

"With a few thousand of our closest friends," he said, with a laugh. "Don't worry, we'll leave you enough mages for your Drowningmen. And Silas will come to you sometime in the fall."

"Be careful in Eirosia," Mychal said, allowing himself a small smile. "Try not to get in above your head. You're no match for, well, anyone, really."

Edris scoffed. "I'm very well better than *you* in a fight, Halwood."

"Yeah, well, maybe, but I've seen more of them," he laughed, and Neill appeared in the doorway just as they turned to leave.

"We're here," he said, and the three of them hurried up to the deck to watch the approaching shore.

The *Queen Aria* was coasting along at the front of the fleet, drifting into the harbor of what Mychal assumed was the capital city of the Lordless Isles. He couldn't believe his eyes when he saw it for the first time. The water around them was a clearer blue than he'd ever seen, and to reach the beaches the ship sailed through a grotto with a beautiful limestone outcropping towering over the water. Everywhere he looked, schools of fish darted through the water, weaving among the boats docked in the lively merchants' harbor they entered now.

The trees on the steadily approaching shore were taller than at home, with stiffer, longer leaves. Shaded between them, on wide streets of crumbling cobblestone, were grand halls, markets, temples, and rows of homes, all cut from towering sandstone and lime. The structures were ancient, older even than most of Queenshearth he guessed, and covered pavilions and gardens lined the beach before them where children were playing and families sat eating together in the shade.

"I don't believe it," Edris breathed. "This is Cor Hara."

Mychal could have believed it. When he breathed in he could feel the cool clear air filling his lungs and felt more at ease than he had since... he couldn't remember when. When the captain dropped the ladder down to the beach, Mychal was the first onto shore. The sand felt warm, even through his boots, when he stepped onto dry land for the first time in weeks.

The rest of his council descended next, and the other ships began landing as the people in the nearest pavilion started to take notice. Before long, a group of six, men and women  both and wearing patterned linen clothing in rich colors, began to approach them. Mychal, with his hand hovering cautiously over his hilt, stepped forward in front of his friends as one of the men in the group did the same.

This man was not an Islander. He was pale, with close-cut auburn hair and dark green eyes, and he was wearing a chain of nobility that mirrored Mychal's, though his was linked by the heads and tails of sleek silver panthers. Mychal knew who this was. "Loran Bennett," he called out, with as much confidence as he could muster. "I heard you were here."

"Mychal Halwood," Loran responded in kind. They were only a few yards apart now. "We're glad you've made it. My sister by law told us you were coming." Mychal frowned, lost, until a woman standing at the man's right side, with a hand on his arm, stepped forward.

"I'm Darya. Farrah sends her regards." He nodded, saying nothing, waiting for more.

"How do you know my name?" Loran asked, when the pause had gone on long enough.

"I found something you were looking for," Mychal said, and tilted the hilt of the Sword forward until it flashed in the sunlight. Loran's eyes locked on it, and the red and blue still visible under the cloth. When he looked up at Mychal again he smiled, eyes narrowed, unreadable.

"Yes, you did," he said, and motioned for them all to come inside the pavilion. "Let's talk."

# APPENDIX I. ROYAL HOUSEHOLDS OF THE CONTINENT, 500 AL

### HOUSE HALWOOD, QUEENSHEARTH

Deronn Halwood, 11, King of the Hartlands

Katheryn Payne, 77, Queen Grandmother

Reval Wright, 45, Lord Regent of the Hartlands and Lord of Surpoint, his uncle

### HOUSE HALWOOD, LORDLESS ISLES

Mychal Halwood, 17, Rightful King of the Hartlands

Jullia Halwood, 13, Princess, his sister

Luke Payne, 18, King's Councillor, his cousin

Gerron Payne, 64, Lord of Brookbridge and King's Councillor, his great-uncle

Graham Riley, 18, King's Councillor

Loran Bennett, 30, King's Councillor and Heir to the Riverlands

Darya Vance, 29, King's Councillor and Loran's wife

## HOUSE HOLLIS, HOLLISPORT

Daniel Hollis, 45, King of the Horn of Morra

Marida Dillon Hollis, 38, Queen Consort and Princess of Eirosia

Mason Hollis, 13, Crown Prince of the Horn

Samira Hollis, 16, Princess of the Horn (New Astoria)

Sanya Hollis, 52, Princess of the Horn and Lady of the Riverlands, King's sister (Riverlands)

Lyam Bennett, 51, Knight of the Horn and Sanya's husband (Riverlands)

Brandon Wythe, 41, Chief Armorer

Brother Andrian, 43, High Priest of Hollisport

## HOUSE THORNE, CASPAR'S DALE

Bastian Thorne, 60, King of Thorncliffe

Edris Thorne, 21, Crown Prince of Thorncliffe (in exile), his son

Charles Thorne, 58, Lord of Norport and Prince of Thorncliffe, his brother (Norport)

Malya Warren Thorne, 53, Lady of Norport and wife of Charles

Jonn Thorne, 36, Lord Marshal of the Holy Army, his nephew (Astor Post)

Brother Spencer, 56, High Priest of Thorncliffe and King's Councillor

Tristan Warren, 44, Lord of New Astoria and King's Councillor

Nora Warren, 19, Lady of Thorncliffe, betrothed to Prince Edris

## HOLY COURT OF THE GODHEAD, NEW ASTORIA

Riyan Duane, 22, Godhead of the Duality

Samira Hollis, 16, Princess of the Horn, his bride

Jacob Denastor, 55, Knight of the Valley and Chief Mage-Catcher

Various High Priests of the Duality

## HOUSE DILLON, ILLON'S FAST

Silas Dillon, 39, King of Eirosia

Alexander Neill, 29, King's Councillor and Knight of Eirosia, Castellan of Illon's Fast

Edris Thorne, 21, King's Councillor and Prince of Thorncliffe in exile

Elliot Carroll, 67, King's Councillor, High Mage, and Lord of Carroll's Pass

Various surviving Knights and Lords of Eirosia

# APPENDIX II.
# HOLY BOOK OF
# THE DUALITY

## BOOK 1: MOTHER MORRA

From the Shadow at the Beginning of Time came the first Being, a woman, luminous and white with a shift of blue about her form. And she walked the Earth when it was nothing but a ball of fire, and her cool steps turned the fire to stone. But she was cold and lonely and longed for a partner. Before long, she began to try to cast her light outside of herself, and fashioned a ball of Earth from pieces of the cooled fire upon which she wandered. She cast it into the sky and its luminous form glowed dimly with the light from far-off stars, but it was not enough. Restless, she waited. And she was Morra, Mother of the Moon and Goddess of Water.

## BOOK 2: FATHER ASTOR

Shortly after the beginning of time, the Second Being came from the Shadow, a man, bright and burning with passion and fire. And the man came down to the Earth, cooled from the steps of the Mother, and his steps brought balance to the now frigid land. He saw Morra from afar and thought her so beautiful that he cast a ball of his own light into the sky to better look upon her. And his light illuminated her orb and she rejoiced in the warmth the two lights brought the Earth. And so the man became Astor, Father of the Sun and God of Fire, and took Morra as his wife.

## BOOK 3: DEN MORRA

Morra and Astor wandered together, alone, but soon grew lonely and sad at the barren world before them. And so Mother Morra draped the train of her blue gown about the Earth. These trains became the rivers and oceans, which obeyed the rise and set of her Moon. And Astor's Sun, which had been made only bright enough for the two of them, grew until it could warm and bring life to all of his wife's creations. So the first life in the world swam in the rivers, and they were called Den Morra, the Children of the Mother. And for a time, satisfied, the Father and Mother rested, as the life in the waters grew and grew.

## BOOK 4: THE HARVEST

When Astor and Morra grew restless once more, they longed for a child of their own. And so one night, they retired to a flowering tree that had grown from their water and light, and they laid together. And Astor's seed gave life to a prince inside Morra's womb. While the Mother was with child, Astor wandered the Earth, breathing his light into the ground that had been soaked in the water of Morra's rivers. And life came out of the oceans and spread throughout the Earth. And some time later, Morra brought forth Tol, the first man. And they together, with the clay wetted by Morra's waters and baked in Astor's light, created a people for Tol to rule. And Tol's children forever were the kings of men. And Astor and Morra and their child finally found a hearth at Cor Hara, the City of Spring.


## BOOK 5: EIROS'S CHILL

Soon, man grew the life the Father and Mother had created to such a great amount that there was no longer plenty for all. And at this time, Eiros ascended from the Core of the Earth, broke His word, and attacked Cor Hara. Eiros spread his Chill across the Earth, and for the first time Tol's people knew Death. They cried for help from Father Astor, and he traveled to the Core of the Earth to duel with Eiros. The army he brought with him, he blessed with his own magic, as much as man could withstand, and these men's children became the Mages. But none of these were Tol's children, for that would be too great a burden for one man. Astor's duel with Eiros shook the foundations of the Earth, but he emerged victorious and his Sun melted the Chill at last. And every winter thereafter they duelled again.


## BOOK 6: THE THREE PRINCES

One day, three brothers in Tol's line were called to the Mother and Father. The three princes, called Caspar, Amon, and Faris, were bade approach the Holy Thrones. Astor commanded them to travel across the Mother's widest sea to spread the Holy Kingdom across all the Earth. They were told never to return until they had died, but their children would one day see Cor Hara living. When the new kingdoms of Man were worthy in their eyes, the Father and Mother would welcome the Last King and his people home again. And so the Brothers set out in holy purpose, and only the dead looked on Cor Hara from that day onward.

# APPENDIX III.


## STEWARDS' NOTES: THE HISTORY, CULTURE, AND GENEALOGY OF THE CONTINENT AT THE TURN OF THE QUINTENNIAL AND THE WAR FOR THE TRIAD

### (ACCORDING TO THE PRIESTHOOD)

### *The Landing of the Three Princes*

Not much is known about the land that the founding peoples of the Triad hailed from, but if the devotees to the Duality are to be believed, they are direct descendants of Tol, the son of Morra and Astor and the first King of Man. And Cor Hara, the legendary city of souls, is their original sailing point. What is known is that the three brothers landed at Cor Altol in the Lordless Isles, at 0 AL (After Landing), of course. At landing, Caspar was 27, Amon was 24, and Faris was 21. They sent scouts to the mainland, and found what is now the Triad to be habitable, but the land to the East snowy and harsh.

### *Founding of Thorncliffe*

The brothers and their people abandoned Cor Altol and sailed to Astor Post. From there they went north, through the Holy

Mountains until Caspar, the eldest, claimed his seat at Caspar's Dale and built the Keep there. Caspar and his wife, Malla, held court there, and Thorncliffe was officially founded in 2 AL. Also this year, Faris met Queen Valyha and took her as his wife.

## Founding of Farisia

When Amon was gone, Faris set out with some of their people to find his own kingdom, with Caspar's blessing. He peopled the lands south of the foothills of the Mountains, and called them Farisia. Valyha gave birth to their heir, Orran, in 5 AL. The next year, Faris found his seat in what is now Queenshearth.

## The Bastard Hart

In 10 AL, Faris travelled to a friend's wedding and there met a maiden so fair that he lost his honor. Some months later the woman came to Queenshearth, with child, and Valyha was heartbroken. Faris sent the maiden to Brookbridge, where he promised to provide for the child, and she gave birth soon to Faris's bastard son Hart.

## Casting Out Amon

The Brothers and their people worshiped Morra and Astor, and feared Eiros, the spirit of Death from the Core of the Earth. But Amon was enticed by the dark power of Eiros and began to worship him and study fire magic. When Caspar discovered this, he cast Amon out of Thorncliffe, in 19 AL. They sent him, and those who remained loyal to him, to the cold land east of the mountains, now called Eirosia, so he could live in his master's Chill. Amon swore revenge.

## Daemons

Amon's study of dark magic had grown over his years of exile, and the king of barren Eirosia soon devised a race of evil from the core of the Earth with the help of his council of fire-element mages. These beings were fire-casters and larger and stronger than humans, and he called them Daemons. He sent them to the borders of his lands, commanding them to infiltrate his brothers' courts and seek his vengeance, in 55 AL.

## Faris and the Skytower

Faris in his old age grew restless and sought greater glory, and in the early 50s AL he set out to build the tallest tower on the continent, allegedly, to reach the lands of the Gods once more. Queen Valyha and Prince Orran remained at his old keep, and Faris travelled north into what is now the Horn of Morra to build his tribute.

## The Deaths of Caspar and Faris

In 63 AL, Caspar passed peacefully back to his home, Cor Hara, and sent Thorncliffe into a succession crisis. Amon saw the opportunity in this and, on the night of High Winter, an assassin acting on Amon's orders slaughtered old King Faris in his bed. Prince Orran, too old for war, called on his younger brother Hart to avenge their father. In 64 AL, Amon died at Hart's hand, and Farisian armies drove the Daemons back over the mountains.

## Hart and Orran

Orran felt obligated to finish his father's final project, and held court at Skytower from then on. He gave the first keep, now called Queenshearth for Queen Valyha's lonely vigil, to Hart and his children as thanks for his bravery. Hart's sons founded House Halwood, who served Orran's sons, the Hollis kings, for generations as the lords of Queenshearth.

## Farisian Civil War

The sons of Orran's and Hart's lines started to see friction over the years. This escalated to war in the time of King Haddon Hollis and Lord Artur Halwood, in 164 AL when Artur stole Haddon's wife Harra away from him. The Civil War lasted two years, and the children of Hart ultimately won their independence. The Hartlands, with Queenshearth as their capital, became its own independent kingdom, and Orran's line kept the Horn of Morra, with their seat at Skytower.

## Illon and Aria

In 223 AL, the grandsons of Haddon, James and Illon, parted ways. Illon traveled to Eirosia, being void of superstition and hoping to unify the fractious land into his own kingdom. He married Aria, the descendant of Amon himself, and together they united the land. House Dillon, their children, ruled there, and James's children continued to rule in the Horn.

## The Fall of Eirosia

In 485 AL, the long-dormant Daemon cities in the North of Eirosia descended on the human lands and the people fled. King Silas Dillon conscripted many Mages to fight, but mundane Eirosians flooded into Thorncliffe and the Horn. The Siege of Illon's Fast ended in 487 AL. Silas was taken captive and his High Mage and husband, Perin, and son Ari were killed.

*The Godhead*

The Priesthood of the Duality had been gaining moral authority in the Triad for some time, but the Fall of Eirosia turned the people fully towards the Faith. They declared that Eirosia had fallen as divine retribution for their permissive culture. Eirosian refugees were either deported to Cor Altol or back to Eirosia, or sent to work in the mines of the Holy Mountains. In 487, King Bastian Thorne empowered the Holy Army, and the heretics were slowly pushed south. In 489, Queen Mina and Prince Mychal of the Hartlands were executed for heresy (*note: potentially inaccurate*) and the Forges at Surpoint surrendered. This signaled complete control of the Triad for the young Godhead, Riyan Duane of Thorncliffe.

# Acknowledgments

There are so many people who played a part in bringing this book into the world, so this list is just the beginning.

Thank you firstly to all the amazing contributors to the Kickstarter that got *The Heretic Prince* published, as well as everyone who has ever followed my author page on Tiktok or shared a video to help promote this book. This would never have happened without you!

Thank you also to the people at Damonza for designing the book cover, especially Claire! The process was so much easier than I had worried it would be and the creativity and professionalism from the whole team made it such a great experience.

The amazing artists at Canva and Vistaprint were an invaluable resource creating promotional material and merch. The map was hand-drawn and converted to digital formatting via Apple.

Thank you to everyone at IngramSpark and Amazon and everyone else who played a part in the formatting and release!

Thank you to my family for being some of my first and most supportive readers, ever since I first started writing but especially throughout the journey this book has gone on since 2016!

My amazing husband Oliver has been my first reader, biggest fan, editor, and the biggest believer in this project from day one and I cannot begin to thank him enough for all of his help and for his faith in me. He deserves more credit than an acknowledgments page could ever give him.

And to all of you, who've read this story, thank you.

# Sneak Preview: The Renegade King, Book 2 of The Heretic Prince Series

### *Prologue*

The sword swung heavy down on the old man's neck, and Jonn Thorne thanked the gods he had long since stopped flinching when the heads rolled onto the stone. He moved on, severing the next man's head from his body without even stopping to wipe the blade, and the next, and the next. Eleven in all today, all the leaders of a village that had harbored a messenger from Mychal Halwood to his traitorous sister. The borderlands of the Horn of Morra were full of the heretic's sympathizers, but it wouldn't remain that way while Thorne was still breathing.

"Clear away the crowds, and put the heads on spikes on the road to Queenshearth," he told his men, and with one last savored glance at the hatred on the villagers' faces, the Lord Marshal descended the steps of the scaffold and returned to his tent in the Army's encampment.

They'd been at Red Ford for weeks now, regrouping with forces that had been sent to deal with the siege at Surpoint. Wright's bastard wasn't any closer to falling to their forces than he'd been weeks ago, but he wasn't a Holy Army priority anymore. There was plenty of steel to be squeezed out of the work camps in the mountains. The little boy playing king could keep his Surpoint Forges.

Mychal Halwood. The traitor left an especially bitter taste in Jonn Thorne's mouth ever since he put together that the boy that had squired for Reinhold was the young king opposing him now. He'd been so close, just within his grasp, for so long and he'd been absolutely none the wiser. He couldn't have known, he told himself. There'd been nothing remarkable about the boy. But then... there was always something, an unsettling feeling, a look in the boy's eyes. Some part of him had known all this time.

And then of course, there was the matter of having already killed him. The Lord Marshal remembered it like it was yesterday, swinging his sword down on Mina Wright's neck and her son's just after, the entire rest of the Halwood family looking on in stunned silence. Thus always to traitors; he hadn't felt any remorse. And he'd been part of the raiding party during the Sack of Hartshold Keep that had pulled the little prince out of his bed. He had no idea how that conniving queen had switched out her son for some peasant boy, but it was clear that she had. One last way Queen Mina had defied them. The thought made him want to scream.

Despite his conviction, he had begun to feel afraid for his soul again, as he always did after executions, and so he walked over to the wall of the tent where the glass imprint of his Declaration altar hung and began to pray. To ask the Father for a clear head and right judgment, and the Mother for forgiveness of sins committed in their name...

"Your gods have already abandoned you, Lord Marshal," a booming, laughing voice said from behind him. "But mine is still walking among us."

Thorne whirled around, drawing his sword almost all the way out of his sheath before a thin, ash-gray hand stopped it at the hilt. He fought this tall, smirking Daemon for control of the blade until the creature let it drop, turning away, as he staggered back and almost knocked the glass web to the ground.

"You're him," he managed to say. "The Daemon King."

"In the flesh," the creature said, turning back to bow with yet another smile. "Avery Dearril. So good to make your acquaintance. If you'd be so kind as to sheath your weapon, I only came for a civilized conversation. One commander to another."

Still shaken, Thorne could do nothing but take his hand off his sword and ask, "What do you want?"

"I want the same thing you do," Dearril said. "To see Mychal Halwood's head on a spike. And Silas Dillon's, of course. That won't be a problem, I trust?"

Thorne felt himself wavering from his initial urge to kill Dearril as soon as the opportunity arose, but he still asked, "And why would you come to me? We're your enemies, same as them."

"You needn't be," Dearril said.

"His Holiness the Godhead is–"

"A figurehead at best, Thorne, don't play games with me," the Daemon King snapped. "We know you're the real power in the Priesthood's plan." Dearril started to back away from him, back toward the tent's opening, and said, "I'll come back to discuss further. But take this one piece of information, as a gesture of good faith."

Thorne swallowed hard. "What?"

"Mychal Halwood," he said, eyes gleaming. "You were right. You did kill him. This one's not who he says he is."

## 1: *Mychal*

Mychal was still struggling to keep the full weight of the sword from bearing down on his neck when he hit the ground hard and the breath flew out of his lungs. He gasped for air as he did his best to keep his weapon raised in defense over his face, and felt his chest constrict even more once the cloth binding his chest down went taut under his shirt. After another terrifying moment, luckily, something finally gave and air returned to him, just in time for him to find the strength to throw the other blade back and scramble to his feet.

"Took you long enough!" Loran Bennett shouted, with a kind of battle-frenzied air that Mychal didn't find comforting. Before he could respond, the knight was swinging at him again, and with each parry he felt himself wearing down in the face of the other man's strength.

"Come on, Halwood, fight back!" he shouted, and though it was a risk, Mychal found an opening to back away and swing hard down at Loran's shoulder. But the knight was already blocking his attack by the time he reached him. "Fight better than that," Loran added, with a smirk, and Mychal rushed forward to aim another hit at his opponent. Instead, he found his sword knocked away easily and Bennett's blade at his throat. Again.

The man met his eyes for a second, then pulled back and sheathed his dulled sword at his belt. "You were a little better than yesterday, but your tells are still clear as day to any trained fighter."

"Thanks a lot," Mychal muttered, hands on his knees as the blood pounding in his head ebbed away and he began to feel the blow to his chest again.

Loran came over and clapped a hand on his shoulder, which very much didn't help his recovery, but he didn't complain. "It's true,

Mychal. You've got to stop hesitating. Every time you attack you wind up. It leaves you open and it means you lead with your body, not your sword."

"I know," he said. He remembered James Reinhold, the knight he'd squired for back in the Holy Army, telling him the same thing. "It's always been a problem for me."

"The sword's not the problem, then?" He shook his head, staring down at the woven hilt of the Sword of Faris. Ever since he'd arrived and started training with Loran, Mychal had started using it, and its size was doing him no favors. But he knew that wasn't it. "Alright. We'll work on it. But," he said, and waited for Mychal to look him in the eyes, "remember. When you draw your sword, you need to be ready to kill. You can't be afraid of what happens when the blade comes down."

He nodded, trying to swallow the lump in his throat, and when Loran backed away he sheathed the sword, more than glad to be done with the session.

"Are you done, then?" His sister Jullia, watching from the top of the stone steps leading down to the beach below them, bounded up the last stretch of rocks to be level with him and his teacher. "I think Edris wants to see you before they go."

"Let's go, then," Mychal said, and started down to the shore with her and Loran following behind.

The sunsets in the Lordless Isles seemed more beautiful than any-where else in the world, but Mychal still remembered feeling that way about the view of the horizon from the towers at Queenshearth. He would give anything to be back in his father's castle, but it was closed to him now, and to most of the world if the reports were to be believed. His brother Deronn was the only member of the Halwood family left at their seat in the Hartlands, ruling as more of a prisoner than a king, and his regency was hardly any better off. As Mychal descended from the stone ledge overlooking the shore, with

Eirosian ships anchored in the grotto filling with refugees returning home and soldiers bound for Illon's Fast, he felt unaccountably
restless for the home he hadn't seen in years.

Cor Altol was unlike any city in the Triad he'd ever been to,
if only because no one here seemed to know or care that he was a
king. No one, that is, except for Loran Bennett. He hosted Mychal's
council now, in a manor house on the western coast of the central
island, and at times when the crown he aspired to was brought up,
Loran glanced rather nervously at Mychal. He knew the feeling. It
had only been a little more than a month since he'd taken the Sword
of Faris from the caves at Surpoint, and only two weeks since he'd
set foot on dry land in this strange new place, but he felt the difference in the way people saw him instantly, as soon as he'd claimed a
throne greater than the one he'd been born to.

Not that *he'd* been born to any throne, of course. The empty
potion vials in his pockets made him all too aware of that, and he
was more than a little paranoid that any day now the effects would
begin to wane and someone would notice that he wasn't, in fact, the
twin they thought he was. Edris had told him not to worry about
that, but he still did. There were almost 8,000 men here with him
now, most of them solely because they believed he was the Mychal
Halwood the Priesthood had condemned to death. And he knew
that most of them would leave if they found out which Halwood
child he really was.

Jullia quickened her pace to walk at his side, and after a quick
glance to make sure Loran was far enough away, asked, "Are you alright? You looked like you couldn't breathe for a moment there."

"I'm fine," he sighed, though in truth the air was still coming in
hard and thin.

"I can take a look at it later, make sure you didn't bruise your
ribs or something," she offered, but he waved her off. She added,
"You really shouldn't bind while you're sparring."

"I need to the most when I'm sparring," he muttered. "Loran will see."

Jullia sighed and nodded. "I'm just– trying to keep you alive, you know." Her tone was light, but Mychal knew she did spend a lot of time worrying about him. It made him feel terrible, to know she was worrying about Deronn too, and advising him on top of all that. His sister was far too old for fourteen.

The two walked in peace for a while, but he could feel her watching him as he let his mind wander. After a moment, he asked gently, "Was there anything else?"

His sister huffed and said, "You've been brooding too much. I'm not going to go away just so you can do it some more."

Mychal laughed a little and said, "I'm fine, Jule. Really."

"Well, good, then." He could tell she didn't believe him. Jullia stayed quiet a moment before she asked, "Is it about Samira?"

He stared down at his feet again, and muttered, "No. Not specifically."

Samira. He'd never imagined coming this far without her. This whole ludicrous plan had been her idea anyway. He never would have been mad enough to think that anyone would call him king on his own, but she'd believed in him first, and others had followed. That night at her Declaration, he'd promised to protect her, but she hadn't let him; instead she'd gone to marry the Godhead despite the magic that could get her killed, all in the name of whatever rebellion they were all fighting in now. Aiming for the Farisian crown over the Hartlands had been her idea too. She never failed to think bigger and bolder than he ever could, that's why he needed her. But he didn't know if he'd ever see her again now.

"She really did want to come with us, Mychal," Jullia said quietly. "You know she had good reasons for what she did."

"I know," he said, breathing deeply to stop the conversation from weighing too much on him. The Council on the Isles, four of the most formidable and frustrating men and women he'd ever met, had been clear that Samira had gone to New Astoria under the aid of their Resistance allies, and with a mission to kill her intended husband, no less. He couldn't imagine his old friend as an assassin, but he supposed that war was changing everyone. He tried not to think about it too much. That was her battle now, and he had his.

He, Jullia and Loran wove their way down a path through the thick brush clinging to sandy rocks all the way down to the beaches of the central island that hosted the capital city. In the near horizon, Mychal could see the shore of the western island, and beyond that, the ocean opening seemingly endlessly in all directions. From personal experience he knew that some hundred miles north, Eirosia lay waiting.

When his boots touched the sand, the people standing in the looming shadows of the *Queen Aria* and the rest of the Eirosian fleet turned to meet them, including Loran's wife Darya and Mychal's friends that were sailing any moment now. Their host disappeared into the crowd once they'd reached the shore, speaking to a few highborn Eirosians intently. Almost all of the close to ten thousand Eirosian refugees and mage-soldiers had already boarded the ships, but Edris Thorne and a few others met them in the middle of the beach. Xander Neill was one of them, the knight of Eirosia who'd led them to victory at his king's castle just months before. It didn't strike Mychal as odd that Neill had waited for them-- he and Edris never left each other's sides these days.

"Good of you to come," Edris said, embracing him in an enthusiastic, brotherly way that he was still getting used to. Those parts of manhood were still new and ill-fitting, like a shoe that he hadn't broken in yet. The Thorncliffe prince relented almost as quickly, knowing this, and bowed to Jullia with a grateful smile. "I expect it'll be a long time before I see either of you again."

"Thank you, Edris," he said, and he hoped that all he meant by that would be clear to the man, though he couldn't say hardly any of it here. The prince had made mistakes, that was true, and the Islanders they'd met here seemed to know it better than most, but without Edris, Mychal wouldn't be standing there, and he knew he wouldn't forget that. "Good luck."

Edris smiled and bowed, more confident than Mychal was used to seeing him, before Loran returned, followed by two others, a woman about his age walking with the Eirosian Lord Carroll they'd met in the Norport mines. The woman was outfitted in the armor and heraldry of a royal soldier, displaying the whiteflower of House Dillon on her chest.

"Well, Sir Xander, you said you wanted to meet the commander of the refugee forces before you set off. She'll be on the flagship with you, if that's alright," Loran said. Mychal blinked and grinned at Jullia. *She* was the commander?

Neill straightened to his full height immediately when he saw the commander and Lord Carroll and bowed his head to them. "Good to see you again, Lord Carroll. And your name, my lady?"

"Suppose I do look different enough you wouldn't recognize me," the woman said, smirking. "Though I think you'll find I've done alright for myself, Xander."

Neill stared at her for a moment, blinking, before his eyes flashed with recognition. "Kira!" he exclaimed. "Gods! The last time I saw you you were... what, thirteen?"

"I know," she said, grinning now. "You weren't much older. You finally look like a proper knight."

"This is Commander Kira Henry," Loran said, and with an awkward cough he added, "For those who don't know." He turned back to her and gestured to Mychal. "This is him," he said quietly, and she inclined her head toward him, solemn.

"I'm Kira Henry," the woman said. "Commander of the Ariadenn, the female warriors of Eirosia."

"It's an honor to meet you," Mychal said, and meant it more than she could know. He couldn't believe he was meeting a real living Ariadenn. He used to be obsessed with the tales of their battles, at the Academy.

"Commander. How did you manage that?" Xander exclaimed, still grinning at her with an easy happiness Mychal hadn't seen much in him.

"There weren't many of us left," she said quietly, and he seemed to sober at that. Kira bowed dutifully to Mychal, before Loran looked over to his wife standing several paces away and nodded after a moment of intense eye contact.

"There'll be storms going round the northeast," she told the Eirosians. "And they'll only get worse throughout the day." Mychal frowned slightly, understanding the pause now. She'd said the same to her husband first, in his thoughts. The mind mage was still a little unsettling to him, even after two weeks sharing the manor with her.

"Then with Your Majesty's permission, we'll take our leave," Neill said, turning to Mychal.

"Of course, Sir Alexander," he said, bowing politely. "Thank you for everything."

"King Silas told us to leave you thirty mages to go with your Drowningmen wherever you go next," Neill told him. "He'll come soon himself to spend some of the winter here."

"We'll be waiting for him," Mychal said. "Thank him for me."

"Your Majesty," Neill said, nodding, and bowed low before Edris and the Eirosians climbed up the gangway onto the *Queen Aria*. Mychal watched the ships sail out of the harbor, keenly aware that with them went his pretense of a navy, and his most immediate way off the Isles. The specter of Jonn Thorne and his Holy Army forces was starting to loom larger than before.

"Mychal," Jullia said, breaking him out of his quickly worsening anxiety. When he turned to look, she smirked again. "Are you alright? You've been like this all day."

"I'm fine," he said. "Just... thinking about our options, is all."

"That reminds me," Loran said. "We've got a war council. We should get back to the Hall." The Vance family manor, or the West Hall, had been their host for two weeks now and this would be the fourth war council, which the Isles Council still refused to attend. With a resigned glance in Jullia's direction, Mychal nodded and followed Loran as he led the way back. Darya and the children fell in step behind them as they passed, and the coastline soon gave way to the thicket of trees and then the westernmost streets of Cor Altol.

The roads were bustling with people already, even at just before nine in the morning, with oil lamps hanging on wires from poles on the sides of the road, ready to be lit at nightfall to fill the city with lights. Mychal had never seen anything like it, except in the wealthiest parts of Hollisport. Ancient cobbled streets led them down zigzagging patterns far into the heart of Cor Altol. They passed taverns, row houses, and all manner of shops and gardens and people, until their trek finally led them to the door of the well-kept West Hall. The land the Vance family owned was vast, but it stretched out of the city behind the street they approached from; the rest of Broad Street flowed directly up to its doorstep on all sides. No gates or guards separated the Vances' home from the rest of the inhabitants of the island.

"This one will be different," Loran assured him once he'd seen the boredom on Mychal's face. "There's someone I want you to meet. She just got back from the North Island."

Admittedly intrigued now, Mychal walked inside the limestone mansion with a little more life in his step. It still struck him when he entered West Hall that it would be hard to tell the Vance family was important on the Isles from the inside. There was no receiving hall, no servants to be seen, no family crest prominently displayed upon entry. Instead they were already in a sitting room, a rather grand and elegant one but a sitting room nonetheless. The signs of longevity were mostly in the wall hangings, large tapestries with Old Language runes decorating their borders and depictions of moments in history woven into the fabric. When he'd first come in the night they arrived, the old patriarch Cyrus Vance had seen him looking and said, "These have been in our family for centuries. It's the Brothers setting sail for the Triad." He remembered thinking it was an appropriate decoration, now that he was claiming to be something akin to one of the Brothers themselves.

That day, however, Cyrus Vance wasn't waiting for them in the doorway, but Luke Payne was, his best friend from his time in the Holy Army. Luke was dressed in much more finery than he'd been wearing since they'd arrived, silk tights and a tunic with an embroidered doublet, his house's wolf crest displayed prominently at his chest. Mychal felt a little underdressed in his linen shirt and gambeson, with his sword-and-fire chain the only symbol of his rank. The two embraced quickly, and Luke said, "Thorne's gone, then?"

"Yes," Mychal said with a smirk. "You can breathe easier."

"I didn't mean it like that," he muttered, but shrugged and moved on, asking, "Has Loran told you who's here?"

"No, why does everyone know everything before me?" Mychal asked, whirling around to look back at the knight. "Honestly. Who's here?"

"Your Majesty?" A woman's voice appeared behind him, and he turned back to find a young woman standing in the doorway to the great hall, dressed simply in the Triad style and definitely Farisian by blood. She carried herself with an unmistakable nobility that Mychal had only guessed at before she said, "It's an honor to meet you. I'm Maeve Allyn."

Mychal, startled, glanced back at Jullia, who seemed just as shocked. When he turned back to Maeve, he only managed to say, "My lady, I thought your family had been..."

"It's just me now," she said, with a rueful smile. "I'm all that's left of the fifth Great House of the Hartlands."

At a loss for what to say, Mychal bowed to her in turn and could only follow as this woman led them all into the council, like a ghost from before the Godhead's time. He'd heard about the razing of the Allyns' lands and castle ever since he could remember. They were the first to stand against the Priesthood, and the first to suffer the consequences. Now, Maeve was here, very much alive, and watching him intently as he moved to sit at the long oak table, the idle conversations between the others seated there dying out as they entered. Darya sent Haddon and Celia, her and Loran's young children, off with a nurse and sat down at her husband's right, and when their guests had fallen silent, Loran gestured to Mychal to take the lead. At the head of the table, staring down the war map spread out before him, he cleared his throat and prayed to the gods his voice wouldn't break again as he spoke.

"Thank you all for coming again. How are the armies on the Western Island?"

"The camps have settled down somewhat," Lord Payne, Luke's father and an incomparable grouch, said as he surveyed the changes to the map. "Your boys seem to have adjusted to sharing the camp with my men. They know it isn't all drinking and songs."

"Right," Mychal said. "I trust the training's also coming along, Lord Gerron?"

"They'll learn to fight properly when we're finished with them," he said, nodding. "What about you, Your Majesty? Can you hold your own against that one yet?" he asked with a jerk of his head toward Loran. Luke went red, like he always did whenever his father spoke for too long, but Mychal had learned to expect it from the man they called the Old Dog.

"He's brilliant," Loran said, loud and pointed. "Not to speak for you, Your Majesty, but your only handicap is you were raised without a master-at-arms. You'll catch up in no time at all if our sessions so far are any judge." Mychal appreciated the defense, but he wasn't sure he would characterize the sword training he'd done with Loran quite the same way. He still felt years behind any other boy his age and this was no time to be a poor fighter.

"Well it won't matter if we can't get to the Triad anyway," Graham, the other squire from the Army days, said from the other end of the table, and Mychal was grateful for the change of topic.

"He's right," he said. "Will the Council see me yet?"

At that moment, the doors to the West Hall slammed open and nearly everyone at the table jumped. It was then that Mychal noticed that Cyrus Vance still hadn't arrived yet, until now. When the older man entered, his face looked pallid and shocked, more grim than he'd ever seen the dignified old Councilman.

"Your Majesty," he said, and crossed the room to place a letter directly in Mychal's hands. "This came for you."

All the energy felt as if it had fled the room the moment Cyrus walked through the door, leaving only a dreadful silence as Mychal slowly opened it.


*TO THE COURT OF MYCHAL HALWOOD*


> *Your insolence and heresy will not be tolerated long, but let this be a warning to you that if your renegade forces enter King Deronn's lands I will be forced to consider him a co-conspirator. The Hartlands are closed to all who stand with you, by order of His Holiness the Godhead.*
>
> *Jonn Thorne*

Mychal tried not to let his anger get the best of him as he set the letter down in front of him and said, "So he's threatening Deronn now."

"I imagine the siege at Surpoint is making the Lord Marshal nervous you intend to use it as an entry point into the Triad," Lord Penn said.

"So Castor's still holding it? That's something at least," he muttered.

"This is justification for battle, Your Majesty," Lord Geronn barked. "The Lord Marshal wants to settle his record. Couldn't kill the first Halwood prince and now he wants to try his luck on the second one."

"That's quite enough, my lord," Mychal snapped, seeing the obvious distress the Old Dog's joke was causing Jullia. Payne, to his credit, bowed his head to her and went silent. When the moment had passed, he asked, "So what do I do if I can't go home?"

Jullia and Luke exchanged a look then, obvious to Mychal sitting right next to them. With a confused look from him, his sister said, "Well... he said the Hartlands. You should go to the Horn, at least, that's what we think."

"King Daniel would at least let you petition him," Luke said. "His wife's Eirosian. If you decide to go after the Daemons, that's even better."

Mychal nodded slowly at his friend, then looked up at Loran. "What do you think? He's your uncle."

Loran's brow furrowed and he stared at the map for a while, and the ten small panther medallions that stood for 1,000 each of the Hornish king's men. "I think we should try it."

"As soon as we have a way off these islands," Mychal muttered. "Our navy left with Neill this morning. And even with a ship, it would be insane to sail right into a harbor somewhere under Holy

Army control." Turning to Vance, he asked, "Anything new from the Council on that front?"

"We've had two meetings since you've arrived," Cyrus Vance said from Loran's left side near Graham. "They've talked *about* you at length, Your Majesty, but I don't know if they'll ever let you in the doors again." Mychal had been expecting that, but he was still irritated; when he'd arrived, they'd called an emergency council, but once they'd found out about his paltry forces and his almost complete lack of a plan, they'd given him a 'season's shelter' of six months and refused to speak with him further about the war.

"I understand they don't want to get involved," he said, trying to keep his tone respectful, "but really, they *are* involved already, with this business with Samira--"

"Samira Hollis?" Maeve asked, the first time she'd spoken since they sat down. "The Godwife?"

"She's not the Godwife yet," Mychal said, a little more short than he'd meant to be, and by way of apology he softened his voice and said, "She's working with the Triad Resistance."

"Really with the Council's connections through the Priesthood," Darya told her. "Samira's a mage. When the time is right, the goal is for her to kill the Godhead."

The whole council was quiet then; all of them save Maeve had heard this before, but it was still a topic heavy with all it could mean. Finally the Lady Allyn shook her head and said, "Gods. That's your cousin, isn't it, Loran?"

He nodded. "My magic must not be on my father's side after all. The royal family of the Horn of Morra has magic in their blood, so let's not worry too much about what the Priesthood's Holy Book says, eh?"

Luke and his father were both grinning rather wickedly at that, but Mychal saw it was making others, like the quiet and excitable

Lord Penn, nervous, so he changed the subject again. "So what do you suggest we do now? Right now. I want to start moving forward."

It was quiet for a moment before Cyrus said, "I'll keep trying to convince the Council. But otherwise, it seems to me that if you wait long enough, there are things already in motion that would make everything much easier for you, Your Majesty."

"He's right," Lord Gerron said. "You should wait till that girl kills Duane for you. The Army will scatter."

"Thorncliffe will only get bolder after that," Mychal said, not thrilled with the idea of Edris's father coming after them with religious zeal.

"At least you'll have just the one enemy," Loran said. "I agree. We should start with the Daemons. Which means staying here and waiting for King Silas, at least at first. And then we'll start thinking about the Horn."

"That'll be more than a month," Mychal said, frowning.

"All the better," Loran said. "You can build your strength in the meantime. As soon as you land in the Triad there'll be battles to fight. This way, you'll be ready."

Mychal let his head drop a little, down to stare at the map below him. "Fine. Thank you," he said quietly. "May Morra bless our efforts." No one there seemed to recognize the Holy Army axiom, save for Luke and Graham and neither were bold enough to finish the response alone, so the room remained quiet after that. As he stared sullenly at the table, he felt the screeching of chairs and low voices that meant the council was adjourned. When he next looked up, Maeve Allyn was at his right side, following his gaze to where he hadn't even known it had been resting on Queenshearth.

"I'm sorry about your brother," she said, and he nodded, trying to seem grateful. "So the council won't see you?"

"No," he sighed. "They don't seem to like me very much."

"They wouldn't," she said, smiling. "Although Cyrus Vance of course supports you, and that's not nothing. And I think Rabia Dain would too."

"The woman with the headscarf? She seemed more open than the others to the idea," he said. Maeve nodded.

"You should get closer to her. She's from the western island, where your armies are staying."

"I'll try to speak to her soon. Thank you," he said. Maeve smiled and bowed slightly as she stepped away from the table.

"I'll be going now, Your Majesty. If it please you," she said, and turned toward the door.

Mychal remembered a little late the manners required of him now and asked, "Would you like an escort, Lady Allyn? I can send one of my men to walk with you."

She smiled again and said, "Thank you, Your Majesty, but if it won't be you walking with me I'll decline." She left the Hall then, and Jullia came up on his other side as Darya followed her to close the doors behind her.

"That was a bit forward," Jullia said, looking pretty amused, and Mychal frowned.

"No, she didn't mean it like that," he said.

"Sure," Jullia said, with significant doubt in her tone, but Mychal wasn't paying attention anymore; he'd just seen Darya come back into the room and he remembered what he'd meant to ask her.

"I'll see you later, Jule," he said, and when she'd gone Mychal gathered his courage and pulled the woman aside.

"Lady Darya," Mychal began, as casually as he could, and she stood, waiting, while he asked, "I've been wondering... if your magic was practical, like your sister's?" Farrah Vance's potions had run dry, and if he couldn't find another mage-- he didn't even want to think about it.

She looked startled and shook her head. "No, I'm afraid not. I'm largely focused on mental magic. I was trained in potions and all that, but I was never very good, and if it's precision you want…"

"That's alright," he said, but he was sure she could tell he was disappointed. "If you know anyone who could help me, there's a potion I need, very badly, as soon as possible."

"I'll do my best to help, Your Majesty," Darya said, nodding, and he thanked her as they both ascended the steps to the chambers upstairs. He watched her go after he'd stopped at the door to his room, hoping she wouldn't mention it to her husband. He could feel the circle of people who knew something was odd about him widening and he didn't like it at all. Whoever Darya found, he hoped they could keep a secret.

Mychal was the only one left awake in the house when he heard the taps on the outside of his wall. He had sat up in bed, squinting to see in the black night when the stone came sailing through his window and landed with a hard rap against the floor. He leapt up and rushed to the window, only to see a small figure tearing away down the high street. Just a messenger then, probably only a child. Warily, he stepped back, found the stone and picked it up. With some difficulty, he fumbled for the wick and lit a candle on his bedside. Just as he'd thought, there was a note attached, in a scrawling hand, addressed TO THE KING.

*I know who you are. Come to the west island on the high moon.*

Mychal felt his blood go cold. Whoever it was, they couldn't *know*, how could they? He couldn't really listen to them… could he? Even as he said it, though, he knew that he would. He didn't have much of a choice. If there was any chance at all, he had to try to stop it before they told anyone else.

He slept uneasily that night, feeling his difference more sharply in this strange place, and dreaming of Samira.

# THE RENEGADE KING

## THEO J. MALLOY

### FALL 2024

# About the Author

Theo J. Malloy (he/they) is a transmasculine queer author from Cleveland, Ohio. He has loved fantasy worlds for as long as he can remember and has always dreamed of being able to one day write stories in that genre they could see themself in. They attended Cleveland State University and New York University and now teach theater in addition to writing. Theo and his husband Oliver live in Cleveland with two cats, a corgi, and far too many books.